Prologue

Well, hello, Dear Diary, any future are again.

This episode in my life ought to interest you.

There's no doubt I was right in the middle of some historic events.

You might think I was riding pretty high at this point, and feeling serenely confident, after saving humanity from extinction or enslavement as a result of having arrived on the interstellar stage.

And, it's true, I was pretty happy at having achieved that. Not going to pretend otherwise. Not going to indulge in false modesty. I'd devoted my entire life to achieving that extremely ambitious goal, and despite bumps on the way, I actually managed to carry it off.

I was happy about that.

And not a little relieved, too.

But history didn't stop at that point.

I'd saved the human race. They'd made me an admiral. And I had no idea what came next.

I didn't really care about the promotion.

I'd never planned to become an admiral for the sake of being an admiral. I've never wanted to 'be' anything. I only wanted to give humanity the best possible chance of surviving our reaching the stars, and the Darwinian struggle I was sure existed there.

In a theoretical sort of way, I'd understood that the alternative to the end of humanity was that life would continue. Only, I hadn't really planned, let alone prepared for it.

Also, it was hard not feeling I'd done enough for one lifetime. My goals, for the first time in my life, were unclear.

Skills and knowledge wise, I was something of a fish out of water. I was plain tired, too.

I was completely lost.

This is the story of how I found my way again.

KATIE KINCAID ADMIRAL

Andrew van Aardvark

Katie Kincaid: Admiral

Author: Andrew van Aardvark

Editor: Margaret Ball

Copyright © 2023 NapoleonSims Publishing

https://www.napoleonsims.com/publishing

Cover Image:

Spaceship image: 35219943 @ Abidal | Dreamstime.com
Katie figure based on LaFemme from Poser 12 | Posersoftware.com
Space ship interior: 127380755 @ SDecoret | Dreamstime.com
Galaxy - Illustration 210228619 / Space @ Ievgenii Tryfonov | Dreamstime.com

All rights reserved.

Paperback ISBN: 979-8-86981-328-2

Hardcover ISBN: 979-8-86981-352-7

Table of Contents

Prologue	
Square Pegs	1
Need to Know	13
Assembling	25
Pre-game Scrum	47
Contemplating the Future	63
Gathering Intelligence	81
Casting the Die	105
Meeting Engagement	127
Counting the Cost	151
Further Adjustments	159
Only This Far	173
Unto the Breach	189
What Now?	203
The Enemy Votes	215
Or On Your Shield	225
To the Bone	237
And Called It Peace	249
Appendix A:	261
Appendix B:	271
Appendix C:	277

Square Pegs

One moment Katie was upright and trying to act dignified, as an admiral should, the next she'd face planted and was lying on the deck with a heavy body on top of her.

The sounds of gunfire and the sizzle of plasma bolts punctuated the sounds of shouting and constant screams.

"Stop squirming, ma'am." It was Sergeant Bloggins. Bloggins was one of her bodyguards. The one currently lying on top of her trying to keep her from getting killed.

"Yes, Bloggins," Katie replied. It was annoying. They were lying on the steps of SFHQ and she had a meeting there, and she was going to be late for it because of this interruption, but the man was just doing his job.

"Good, ma'am," Bloggins said. He sounded distracted. Doubtless trying to look around while still covering her. Doubtless, no happier than she was to be lying down while the action went on all around them.

Keeping her alive was other people's job. All she could do was wait and try not to make it any harder for them. Katie wasn't used to having free time. Not since she'd been promoted. Seemed everyone wanted facetime with her. Her aide scheduled her down to the minute. She might as well chill out and take the time to reflect.

Truth was she'd accomplished her life's work, and between that and having faced death repeatedly in the process, she just couldn't get that worked up worrying about her personal survival. Severe injury was a bigger concern, but modern medicine was pretty darned good.

So far, being an admiral had meant interviews, public appearances, and writing the odd appreciation paper.

It'd quickly gotten old.

Katie had been looking forward to the coming meeting. Rumors were rife that ships were being assembled for an expedition up the galactic arm. She was hoping she'd get command of that expedition, whatever its purpose.

It wasn't likely there'd be any more fighting. She'd pretty much crushed all local opposition. Still, a command was a command, and being back on ship away from politicians and the public they served was enticing in its own right.

Katie noticed the screaming had stopped. Replaced by whimpering. She wondered at how inured to the pain of others she'd become. It wasn't anything to be proud of. "Safe now?" she asked.

"Patience, ma'am, not long now," Bloggins answered. A short time passed.

"You can let her up, Bloggins," a voice came. It was colonel - no, brigadier general now - von Luck. One of the people she was supposed to be meeting. Trust a marine to move towards danger.

Bloggins rolled off of her.

Von Luck offered her a hand.

Katie taking it, found her feet, and looked around. The area had been cordoned off. A wall of marine backs surrounded her. A disheveled figure was being bundled into a police utility vehicle. A whimpering woman on a stretcher, a civilian employee of the Space Force most likely, was being loaded into an ambulance somewhat more gently.

Was it too much to hope it was the would-be assassin that had injured that woman and not return fire from the marines?

Did it matter? Katie felt the need to apologize to the woman. To comfort her if she could.

But von Luck took her elbow. He shook his head. Bloggins did the same. She looked his way. "Best get you to safety," the marine sergeant said. Katie allowed herself a sigh.

She let von Luck guide her into the grandiose monstrosity of a building that was SFHQ.

Well, maybe she wouldn't be too late for her meeting.

* * *

Rrolff Sweets-Swiper was enjoying his garden.

It was a lovely late, spring day in the northern hemisphere of New Big Trees. The sunshine was bright and warming, but not harsh. A slight, occasional breeze kept the quiet from being oppressive. The only sounds were the odd buzz of an insect or half-hearted call of a flying creature. Light dappled shade and scattered bright-colored flowers pleased the eye.

The flowers also provided pollen for hive insects to produce nectar from. Generations of Sweets-Swipers had cultivated both those flowers and those insects. The resulting nectar was famous throughout the Empire.

Lord Earl Rrolff Sweets-Swiper, Second Paw of the Emperor, Commander of the Third Imperial Battle Fleet, was as proud of that as of any of his titles or his command.

And he took great pride in being an aristocrat of the Grrumm Empire and the fact that, as was also traditional in his family, he'd earned his command.

Sadly, that fact was about to take him away from both his hobby and his gardens. The need for a punitive expedition against barbarians had been triggered.

Tradition as codified in the *Book of Barbarians* was clear on that. The Imperial orders he expected any day now were a mere formality.

Delay was also unacceptable. Both Rrolff and the Expeditionary Fleet he'd be assuming command of had a great deal of preparation to do before they could depart.

Rrolff was diligent and conscientious, and the Third Fleet was in excellent condition. He could only hope the same was true of the Expeditionary Fleet. In any case, he could do nothing yet. Not before his formal orders arrived. He could in good conscience visit this favorite corner of his estates one last time before his duties consumed him.

They wouldn't last less than a whole season, almost certainly several. He would have to spend those seasons in the sterile confines of a space ship where seasons were a mere measured passing of time.

Rrolff knew he was privileged. Privileged just because of the duties he was about to assume. He felt regret, not resentment. A certain satisfaction, too. It'd been generations since a punitive operation had been mounted and some argued that despite the guidelines tradition provided, the frontier had been allowed to grow too wide and too wild.

Rrolff's father had held command before him but had never seen action. His grandfather had, but only as a junior officer. Rrolff would be the first of his family in three generations to perform the duties that justified his family owning vast estates on the planetary surface of New Big Trees and their resulting great wealth. It pleased him to be able to thus justify their position. It was a sign that all was right and proper in the universe. How could that be anything but satisfying?

And he had to admit there was a certain excitement around the prospect of being among the first of his race to see new stars and visit new planets. He'd only had time to skim and randomly dip into his briefing papers, but he had spotted a report on the products of the target planet. Apparently, they too had hive insects that produced a form of nectar the natives consumed. He looked forward to investigating that, once the planet had been brought under control.

He did not expect that to be a difficult task.

Technically, but quite clearly, the offending barbarians had conquered another specie's home planet. One of the traditional criteria for a punitive expedition had been unambiguously triggered. It was also quite clear that it'd been a fluke. Lucky or unlucky depending on how you looked at it. The barbarians in question possessed neither great military nor economic strength. They'd cleverly bought sufficient technology to compete on the local interstellar stage, but it was obvious that their actual native technological level was rather low. They'd reached the stars before they were ready to. Heavens above, they were still mostly concentrated on the surface of their home planet. They hadn't even really occupied space in their home system, let alone reached and properly colonized others. And more amazingly, within the small footprint they occupied, they weren't yet truly unified. According to the reports he'd read, their multiple factions - which didn't all possess the same language, writing system, or religion - had allied in the face of external threats but weren't yet truly integrated.

Rrolff almost felt sorry for the poor barbarians. He almost wished he had the power to call this punitive expedition off. But the constraints of tradition, and the words of the "*Book of Barbarians*", were clear and unambiguous. They left no room for interpretation. The expedition must go forward. Any hint of empire building among barbarians must be crushed.

Rrolff growled a sigh.

He returned to tending his plants. It improved his mood.

"Gardener! Gardener!"

Rrolff looked up to see several individuals approaching. Two older ones, male and female, with snouts starting to silver, a young male just approaching adulthood, and a young female. It'd been the young male who'd been yelling. It was probably a family of tourists who'd wandered off from their tour group, and out of the public parts of the gardens. The gardens were a huge maze, and it wasn't hard to get lost.

"Yes, how can I help?" Rrolff asked.

The older male came up. "Can you give us directions back to the main path?"

"Certainly," Rrolff replied amiably and proceeded to do so.

"Thank you. Thank you," the older male said.

"No problem. My pleasure."

Apparently encouraged by Rrolff's friendly demeanor, the young male spoke up. "These gardens are huge. They're amazing. You must really like working here."

Pleased, Rrolff rubbed his nose with a paw. "They are amazing, aren't they? And yes, I do."

The previously shy older female had a question too. She fidgeted and shuffled her feet, and then it burst out. "Do you ever see the Lord Earl? What's he like?"

Rrolff rubbed his nose again. This was amusing. "Yes, I see the grand Lord all the time," he replied, not adding it was in his mirror during his morning toiletries.

"Is he nice?"

"Well, he's mostly polite. Regular folks really on a personal level."

The young male snorted. He obviously had his doubts about this.

The young female, though, was transfixed. "You ever talk to him?"

"Now and again," Rrolff answered. "It kind of goes with my job."

"Wow!"

The family's parents were now looking a little embarrassed. "I guess we should be on our way," the older male said.

"Thank you, again."

"Again, my pleasure. Have a pleasant day."

The family waved as they trotted off in the direction Rrolff had given them.

He watched them go.

It was keeping families like that safe, and perhaps somewhat blissfully ignorant, that justified both the existence of the military and of the aristocracy that led it.

Too bad they didn't always recognize that, but virtue is its own reward.

* * *

The Assassin was somewhat disappointed. The attack on his target had failed.

The Assassin - he'd used so many names that for practical purposes he had none - hadn't been responsible for the attack on Admiral Kincaid. He'd have been paid all the same if it'd succeeded. His contract specified only that he'd be paid so much if she died within the next four MaTok, roughly a couple of the human months. It did not require he be responsible for that death.

As much as the Assassin liked a challenge, it would have been easy money. The Assassin liked playing games where the odds heavily favored him and enjoyed seeing his calculations work out.

His profession being what it was, he didn't seek recognition.

Still, he had his pride, and he wasn't sure what to think of this latest job. He was outside of his comfort zone. Normally, he worked in or at least close to civilized space.

He knew the species there and how to work with them. Looking about the concourse of this human station from his seat in a "cafe patio" he saw individuals that were overwhelmingly human. The Snouts weren't uncommon, and he'd seen the odd Limer, Swimmer, and Varkoid "Big One". He'd even seen one of the Scaly Ones. But mostly he'd seen humans.

Fortunately, the humans seemed to be divided against each other and easily bribed or extorted, so there was that. Very disorganized, though he supposed that was to be expected with their huge push off-planet. All the same, he anticipated it presenting many openings for him. Ones he could sneak through to reach his target.

He could have wished his client hadn't waited so long to procure his services. Kincaid would have been an easy target at any of the many victory celebrations she'd attended. Rather premature victory celebrations in the Assassin's mind. He did have to admit they'd dodged a bullet, as they liked to say, but not expecting more incoming fire was silly of them.

The Assassin sipped his heavily sweetened coffee. He rather liked the human beverage. He wasn't fond of weakness of any sort, but as mildly addictive substances went, it was quite pleasant. No, it presented difficulties that Kincaid was normally present only in military settings now, but given the porous and ad hoc nature of the humans' security, the Assassin had no doubt he could overcome them.

It'd take patience and skill, but the Assassin had both in plenty.

He'd never failed a mission before. He didn't expect to this time either.

* * *

Lieutenant (Senior Grade) Tanya Wootton chewed on a lip.

She was tired. She wasn't thinking clearly. She knew she should be getting more sleep.

Only she was now the head of the Space Forces' Intelligence station here on Far Seat Trade Hub and utterly convinced of the extreme importance of the work she was doing. Work that was overwhelming her.

She'd risen early a couple of days ago and had been constantly busy ever since. Morning reports. Morning meetings. Out and around gathering rumors and background. Another set of reports. An evening hob-nobbing with various alien lowlifes, gaining trust and information both. Late hours reading yet more reports and writing several of her own. More morning reports and more morning meetings. More eavesdropping. Afternoon reports that suggested that something serious was brewing, and it needed following up immediately. Another evening and most of the early morning milking various contacts for some confirmation of those rumors.

It'd taken too long, and she had too many irons in the fire. Her head was full of cotton wool. She was about to fall over.

Only what she'd discovered needed to be reported and without delay.

The "civilized" powers further up the galactic arm were stirring. They were about to act and that was not good news for humanity and the Space Force tasked with protecting it.

She sighed, looked around the dim and crowded little closet that was her office, and took a deep breath. She needed to clear her mind, try to summarize the situation, and figure out what she needed to tell her bosses back in the Solar System. And how, of course. She had to convey the gravity of the situation without sounding like she was panicking or losing her mind.

To her surprise, she found herself wishing that Kincaid was here, or at least that she could be sure it was Kincaid who'd be reading her report and deciding what to do about it.

Tanya hadn't much liked Kincaid. She hadn't been nearly as impressed with the woman as everyone else seemed to be.

True, Kincaid was smart, and even well educated in technical matters. She knew a lot of history, although in an old-fashioned way, lacking in explanatory theory. Kincaid had also been right about the dangers achieving FTL had posed and made a number of good decisions in dealing with the resulting crisis. Tanya couldn't deny any of that.

But she had also thought Kincaid was a narrow-minded, cocksure, loose cannon, who'd had only that one big idea. Tanya had been of the mind that Kincaid had shot her bolt. To be fair, she had the sense dealing with the woman that she'd recognized this herself.

Only now Tanya, having been promoted very quickly from green Ensign to Senior Lieutenant and having been given a job that could easily have been assigned to an officer a couple of grades above her, was feeling crushed by the responsibility she'd been given.

She was feeling a lot more sympathy for how Kincaid must have felt. A lot more respect for how Kincaid had handled it, too.

Most of all, Lieutenant Tanya Wootton was coming to appreciate how Kincaid had accepted that responsibility and made the necessary decisions when it'd have been easier to have dodged them or have left them to someone else.

And she understood she needed to do the same herself. So, she'd reported on the basic geopolitical background in the local part of the galaxy repeatedly, but knowing how busy senior officers were, she didn't dare assume they'd actually read and retained the content of those reports. She sighed. She'd best recap it.

Humanity lay beyond the frontier as it was viewed by the more advanced races further up the local galactic arm. As annoying as it was, they considered themselves "civilized" and humanity and the other locally based species "barbarians". Tanya had spent long hours acting out of character, getting various alien individuals to relax around her and speak their minds openly. They might be too polite to say so in a formal setting, but that was definitely the way the Galactics thought.

More to the point, the Galactics, as represented by the powers on the edge of "civilized" space, didn't consider the barbarians as much of a threat, but they were also determined they didn't become one either. The Galactics had multiple civilizations old beyond easy human comprehension. They'd been in space for millennia, and although reasonable enough as individuals and in most circumstances even in groups, they dealt with perceived threats ruthlessly.

Humanity had found the Trade Union to be a powerful and difficult to deal with entity. Compared to the frontier powers, they were nothing, but a loosely organized group of merchants interested only in profit, peaceful and not really interested in acquiring power or the associated responsibilities.

The frontier powers further up-arm were three in number, the Karook, the Grrumm, and the Craah. They competed, but avoided violent clashes with each other.

The Karook were amphibians who liked warm, wet worlds, and seemed to think like ambush predators. They were also great philosophers, according to Tanya's sources.

The Grrumm were large, heavily furred, forest dwellers. Their agriculture seemed more like that of the pre-Columbian Amazon than the open field cereal cultivation practiced by most human civilizations. They seemed a bit pompous and slow. They were, if this made any sense, apex omnivores. They didn't fear much. They were devastatingly dangerous if provoked.

The Craah were some kind of bird people. They favored forests but more forested mountains and uplands than plains. They had a reputation for being curious and technically innovative, but more as individuals than as a society. They'd flock together against outsiders, but absent any threat they abhorred subordination to others.

The Karook and Craah were not of immediate concern. All of Tanya's sources concurred in this. Humanity's chunk of space wasn't in their zones of influence. No, it was the Grrumm that were responsible for containing the barbarians in humanity's part of the universe. And, unfortunately, if what had been hinted at by various alien individuals was true, Kincaid's fleet had crossed some sort of red line when it forced the Lizards to surrender by threatening their home world.

The Grrumm, according to what Tanya had been told, did not feel it necessary to explain themselves to lesser races, and they didn't act frequently or quickly, but when they thought it necessary, they acted with irresistible force. Threats to galactic peace and their own predominance weren't accepted.

They would accept surrender, and they weren't prone to genocide. They didn't accept the existence of independent, sovereign, barbarian powers. According to Tanya's sources, that was probably what humanity looked like to them.

According to those sources and others, there were military stirrings up-arm in Grrumm space, the so-called Grrumm Empire, that indicated a punitive expedition might be forming.

The local Galactics were abuzz with speculations about how this might be best handled. How losses could be avoided and profits made.

Tanya was desperate to alert her superiors to the threat. If nothing else, something had to be done to determine if it was real and what form it might take.

She gave up trying to figure out how to best word her report.

She just wrote down what she thought, hit the send button, and went to bed.

Exhausted, she had no trouble falling asleep despite her worries.

She'd done what she could.

Need to Know

As her marine bodyguards and Brigadier von Luck bundled her through the long corridors of SFHQ, Katie noticed multiple small knots of officers, enlisted, and civilian employees all gossiping about the attack that had just been made upon her. They'd look up at her and her party with wide, curious eyes and quickly look away. She wondered that none of them seemed to have anything that needed doing, and at just how many of them there were.

Maybe she wasn't in the best of moods.

This huge new SFHQ building had been built while she was away defeating the Lizards. She wasn't that familiar with it. Furthermore, it'd been built on Earth's surface, just outside of Bristol in England. It was a fast train trip away from both the Government offices in London and the Cornwall spaceport, and she supposed it'd been faster and cheaper to build it here than in space, say as an extension to Goddard Station.

Still, Katie had her doubts about building the HQ on the surface, not in space and about just how large it was.

Not her concern, though. Nothing she could do about it. She ought to get her head in the game and try to get in a better mood for the coming meeting. She had little doubt it was about what her next mission would be. If she wanted to have the best chance of influencing the goals of that mission and getting the most possible resources for achieving it, she needed to be at her most persuasive and diplomatic.

Charging into the meeting with a chip on her shoulder was not a good idea.

Finally, they reached the conference room she was destined for. A large wooden table dominated the center. Almost a dozen people surrounded it. She knew them all, though she'd not seen some for a long time, and not all of them well enough to consider them friends.

Admiral Yuri Tretyak, her boss, and a friend, rose to greet her. "Katie, glad to see you're not hurt. You feeling okay?"

"Fine. Thank you. It was all over before I knew what was happening."

"Great. I'm sorry that happened." Tretyak paused, looking concerned and at a loss for words.

"What the Admiral is having trouble saying is that as long as you're on Earth, in the Solar System, really, you're going to be a target for all sorts of crazies. You're a political lighting rod in stormy times."

Katie looked at the man speaking. It was Pierre "Pete" Radison, now a commodore. He'd been a close political ally and friend of her grandmother's. He was ostensibly a political ally of Katie's too, but Katie hated politics and found Radison altogether too coldly calculating.

"And you've got a plan, right?" she asked.

"Of course," Radison replied, visibly amused, "but mainly I'm here to help Admiral Tretyak brief you. There are events you need to be brought up to date on."

"Brief the rest of us, too," another man, Commodore John Smith, interjected. "But first, I want to know if you're okay working with me. Neither Pete nor Yuri have said so, but I'm sure most of us are here as candidates for positions in a new command of yours."

Katie nodded. It'd been a long time since she'd seen Smith and he'd outranked her then. Both Radison and Smith had been on the review board she'd gone in front of at the end of her Basic Officer's Training Course back when she was still a cadet at the Academy. They could have ended her career then and there before it'd even really begun. Katie shuddered. Katie's life would have unfolded very differently. No false modesty, but the world would have been a very different place. Probably one without much room for the human race. "I don't see any problem working with you, Commodore. I trust you don't either or you wouldn't be here."

Smith quirked a smile. "No. I look forward to it. Admiral, I'm not buttering you up when I tell you that voting to let you pass that course was, without doubt, the best decision I've ever made."

Katie blinked. "Thank you."

"Glad to see you're getting along so well," Tretyak commented dryly. He looked around the room. "As you are all doubtless aware, we've been building ships faster than we can train officers to command them. Each of you is here because I believe you're the best suited person that can be found for a vital slot. All other considerations have been secondary, but an ability to work well under Admiral Kincaid's command is necessary."

"Sounds dire, but I'm glad for the second chance," a young commander at the far end of the table said.

"Timothy McLeod," Katie said. "Haven't seen you since the *Sand Piper*. I'm sorry about how that worked out."

McLeod grinned ruefully. "Not as sorry as I was, ma'am. But that was my fault and that of the rest of the crew. No offense, ma'am, but you were just a kid caught in the wrong place at the wrong time."

Katie nodded. The *Sand Piper*'s crew had been sucked into a smuggling scheme that Katie had discovered. If the Space Force had remained a peace time organization, it'd have wrecked their careers permanently. Some resentment on McLeod's part wouldn't have been surprising. But she couldn't detect any. Like Smith, McLeod had a reputation as being both competent and easy to work with. "Well, water under the bridge. Looking forward to working with you again."

Katie looked around the room as she sat down. In addition to the two admirals and Brigadier von Luck, there were five commodores, three commanders, and one lowly lieutenant commander. "I'm looking forward to working with all of you, but I have to say that whenever Lieutenant Commander Hood is around, I know there is trouble in the offing."

She got chuckles for that. Hood just ducked his head.

"Pot, meet kettle," her old friend Susan commented. Commodore Susan Fritzsen, who was pretty prone to finding trouble herself.

Katie smiled. "Admiral, what have you got for us?"

"Straight to the point," Tretyak answered. "Well, I won't beat around the bush, either. We're considering a major expedition up the galactic arm. We don't know nearly enough about what's up-arm from Far Seat Trade Hub. We're also hearing from all our alien friends that we've created a local power vacuum that needs to be filled."

Katie looked at Hood.

Hood grimaced. "The Admiral, if anything, understates the problem. We just don't have the people available or the means to go out and find out what's actually happening. Tanya Wootton is doing her best at Far Seat. Young as she is, she's the least green and most experienced operative we have. But she's severely overworked. We don't have many people who know the background, who speak the languages, or who have the contacts. In a few years, we might have an organization built up, but right now we're all but blind. Worse, although none of the aliens seem hostile anymore, not even the Lizards, most of them don't seem to have any faith we're going to be around very long. They're not betting on us. I, for one, would really like to know why. It looks like showing the flag and poking around in force is the only way we're likely to find out."

Dead silence greeted this. Commander Henry Vane broke it. "There's a closer to home reason for having Admiral Kincaid taking a fleet up-arm. Commodore Radison touched on it. She's a political problem as long as she's here. Everybody is afraid she might lead a coup. She's also personally vulnerable, so love her or hate her, you might be happy to see her somewhere else other than the Solar System."

Radison chuckled. It was a dry sound. "That was the elephant in the room."

Katie sighed. She didn't feel any need to put a false front on for the people in this room. "I'm one of the people who wouldn't mind me leaving the Solar System and its politics behind. Also, the assassination attempts and other messages from random weirdos. They're annoying. But as Lieutenant Commander Hood knows, the Galactics have politics too, and they're as murkily tricky as anything we have." She paused and looked around. "Sadly, I suspect humanity can't be safe on its own. We're going to need allies so we can't ignore those Galactic politics. I'm not one to be modest, but I'm no diplomat either. I might not be the best person for this job."

Tretyak snorted. "You think there's someone who could do it better?"

Radison answered for Katie, "She knows very well there isn't. She just doesn't like that."

"Thank you, Commodore, for telling everyone what I think," Katie said.

"It's true. No point beating around the bush because the fact makes you uncomfortable."

Tretyak coughed. "In any event," he said, "it's my opinion and that of SFHQ that a major expedition up-arm for the purposes of reconnaissance and showing the flag is necessary. Admiral Kincaid is the obvious choice to command it." He glanced at Katie meaningfully. "In fact, if we don't give her command, both the public and parliament will have questions. Understood?"

"Politics," Susan Fritzsen commented with disgust.

Heads around the table nodded in agreement.

"We're all getting to the point where it's part of our jobs now," Amy Sarkis said. She was another old friend of Katie's and also a commodore now.

"Commodore Sarkis isn't wrong," Henry Vane added.

"Unless one of you can come up with a good reason why not," Tretyak said, "we're going ahead with this. You all have full briefing documents in front of you and we're going to give you all a couple of days to digest them. But besides a lot of background detail, useful but not germane to this decision, what it amounts to is that the Solar System seems secure right now, but we have no idea what's waiting out there. So we intend to send all our best ships, both first and second generation new tech, out there under Admiral Kincaid's command. You people, barring issues, will be her key subordinates."

Tretyak paused and surveyed the room.

Katie took the chance to ask a question. "You already have an idea where you're going to slot everyone in?"

Tretyak nodded. "Yes, pending your approval. Commodore Hoffman will be your Chief of Staff. The fleet's major subdivisions will be a set of four task forces. Commodores Sarkis, Smith, Wong, and Fritzsen will each command one. We believe that will allow you maximum flexibility. They'll each be based on a pair of carriers, but there'll also be a Support Group we're proposing Commander Vane command. Your flag will be the *Bonaventure* under Commander McLeod. It, along with its escorts, will form a Command Group commanded by Commodore Haralson. Brigadier von Luck will be the overall commander of your attached marines. Lieutenant Commander Hood will head your intelligence section. Sound good?"

"Off hand, yes."

Commodore Radison spoke up. "One thing I don't think the briefing documents have emphasized enough is that all of you will need to keep your eyes open for information about any technological advantages various alien groups might have. We're pretty sure that in addition to the standard package everyone has, they all try to hold out secret advantages. Ones they guard carefully. It's frustrating we don't have more solid detail, but the general consensus among the Galactics seems to be that the further you go up-arm, the higher the technological level."

For practical purposes, the meeting was over at that point. There were some questions that Tretyak or Radison answered briefly and a bit of small talk, and then they retired with their homework.

They'd do their due diligence, but Katie had little doubt they were going to go ahead with this.

It was a shot in the dark, but one they needed to take.

* * *

Lieutenant Commander Robert "Rob" Hood yawned and

leaned back in his desk chair. He looked around the mostly unlit quarters he'd been assigned in SFHQ. It was also his office. Technically he was on call twenty-four seven, and he was certainly working long hours, burning the midnight oil as he was tonight, or this morning maybe, more days than not.

He had been an intelligence operative and sometime analyst for most of his adult life and had in truth seen more than his share of murder and other skullduggery.

He'd first met Katie Kincaid, then a very young lieutenant, on such a mission. He'd helped keep her alive. He often wondered what would have happened if he hadn't. Certainly the relationship between them, distant and passing at first, but later growing closer as he became something of a confidant of hers, had resulted in his playing a role in some very historic events.

Had kept him from having much of a life of his own, too. He figured it was a fair trade. There are times and places in which people can live their own lives undisturbed by events in the wider universe. This wasn't one of them.

He snorted.

For all the drama and consequence the job involved, it also involved an amazing amount of tedious drudgery trying to find and piece facts together. Then more boring paperwork figuring out how to accurately report those facts, and maybe draw some useful conclusions from them, for the benefit of the people who'd make decisions based on them.

Rob was pretty sure some reports never got read and all the effort that went into them was wasted. It was depressing, hence the little pep talk he was giving himself.

If he was honest with himself, this wasn't likely to happen with his current effort. Kincaid might be action oriented and busy, but she was also conscientious. She trusted Rob to not waste her time, too. Moreover, his current news, based on the latest reports from Tanya Wootton at Far Seat Trade Hub, bordered on alarming.

Tanya herself seemed to be on the edge of panic, and Rob thought it was more than simple overwork and a sense of being overwhelmed, that was informing her mood.

Lieutenant Tanya Wootton wasn't in his experience given

to emotional overreaction. If anything, she was too coldly distant at times from the implications of her studies. She was reporting the possibility of an expedition to local space by a power up-arm as mere rumors, but it was clear she took those rumors very seriously. That she was alarmed by what they might mean.

Rob's task was to convey some of her urgency without being seen as exaggerating.

Simply making it clear that there were thousands of years of records of such expeditions and that in all of them the "barbarians" got crushed, should suffice to wake up anyone paying attention.

He'd keep it clean and shuffle as much distracting detail as possible into appendices. Ought to work.

One thing was for sure, he hoped Tanya was overreacting at least some.

Otherwise, it didn't look good.

* * *

Imperial Guard Hrrwa Thorn-Paw, Sixth Claw of the Emperor, Commander of the Second Frontier Patrol Fleet, supposed he ought to be happy to be back in civilized space.

Only he must have been out on or past the frontier too long. He'd been granted a short leave to visit family he'd not seen for many seasons. He was in civilian garb, and that felt odd. It felt odd, too, to be sitting in a civilian station's terminal waiting to go down to the planetary surface of New Big Trees. His family were all station dwellers or spacers, but his trip back was apparently an excuse for everyone to have a vacation at a resort down on the planet.

The terminal was strangely lacking in non-Grrumm individuals, too. Out on the frontier, even in places that belonged to the Empire, actual Grrumm individuals were a minority if a large one. Even the ships of the Frontier Fleets, unlike those of the Empire's main forces, were manned by a mixture of Grrumm and client races. Though most of the crews and almost all the officers were Grrumm.

Still, the lack of non-Grrumm was jarring to his current sensibilities. Almost as jarring as a pervasive feeling of soft complacency that seemed to pervade the place. There was little hurry, and no edginess, here.

There wasn't constant death and conflict on the frontier, but the possibility was always there. People kept an eye out for it. Most of them went armed. And they were serious and didn't like to waste time. Generally, people made a good living out beyond the reach of the gates. Some even struck it rich, but there was always the chance of falling through the cracks.

Nobody around Hrrwa on this station seemed concerned about falling through a crack if they didn't hustle.

He rubbed his snout with a paw. He'd changed to find his old home so strange. He wasn't looking forward to retirement. Was there any place that was truly home anymore?

Well, he wasn't retired yet. He still had his duties, even if he wasn't looking forward to his next assignment.

Apparently, the local dignitaries were about to get off of their butts and go do something about the latest set of upstart barbarians. Barbarians a good four Trading Hubs out past the last gated system. That system, Damp, well named after a local planet that was heaven for moss and fungus but not for any sensible Grrumm, was only two gate transits from New Big Trees. The frontier hadn't moved for many generations. Hrrwa Thorn-Paw was no historical scholar, but he wondered at that.

In any case, since no one who was aristocratic enough to command a regular Imperial fleet was likely to know much about either fighting or the frontier, Sixth Thorn-Paw was going to be their adviser. Joy.

He ought to try to enjoy his vacation with his family.

It might be a while before he had much to be happy about when it was done.

It was always tricky dealing with aristocrats.

Damned aliens were less trouble.

* * *

Dim lights and dark wood. Again. Although it'd been a long time. Katie had last been here just before shipping out to Mars and that mess on the *Humber*.

Here being an ancient Irish pub in the quaintest imaginable little Irish village. One conveniently not too far from the West Eire Spaceport.

Katie's goal here was two-fold. She wanted to say goodbye

to friends and family before most probably departing on a long expedition she mightn't return from, and she wanted to get a better feel for her proposed command cadre. This was, in fact, in part, one of those infamous team-building exercises.

It was a night out for a few drinks, being severely overburdened with ulterior purposes.

Katie wasn't a people person.

She had some friends from the Academy, and she had some idea of how to command a Space Force ship or fleet. That was it.

This place had positive associations for many of the people present. It was a place where groups of Space Force officers liked to hold get-togethers, to greet new arrivals, see off people leaving, celebrate birthdays, and otherwise generally mark significant events. Many romances had begun here, and many friendships cemented.

For Katie, it was the place she'd broken up with her last proper boyfriend. She hadn't had a relationship of any depth or length since. Her career had had to make do. Also, it was the place she'd departed a happy ship she'd felt comfortable on, for a very unhappy one where some of the crew had attempted to kill her.

Katie was no coward, but it's not pleasant having people trying to kill you.

"Not going to start crying into your beer, I hope," Amy Sarkis said, sitting down on one side of her. Thor Haralson sat down on the other side, and Susan Fritzsen across from her.

Katie huffed. "No. Just thinking. It's been a long time since the last time I was here. A lot has happened."

Amy nodded. "And not all of it good. Got that."

"Too much to ask you to relax, I guess," Thor said.

Katie sighed. "I wish this was only a night out to relax, but it's partly work, too. Not everyone coming is an old friend, and I need to get to know them a little better if I can." She shook her head. "You know, Thor, I'm just not all that great with people or politics, but this business of being an admiral seems like it's mostly people management and politics. I'm not really sure I'm cut out for high command. Leading a fleet into battle, sure. Organizing fleets and telling them where to go, not so much."

"Our Katie's getting cold feet?" Susan said. "Wow, that's a new one. Getting cautious in our old age, are we?"

Katie tried to frown at Susan. It was pointless. There was no intimidating Susan. Katie wasn't one to back down herself. "Everybody has their limits. It could be I've reached mine. It'd be irresponsible not to recognize that."

Susan laughed in Katie's face. An unusual reaction for a woman who was normally grimly sphinx like. "Sure, you're indulging yourself in an emotional funk out of a sense of responsibility. Tell me another one, Katie. Nope, you've spent your whole life executing a master plan. You had it all worked out, except for the odd awkward detail. You've never been uncertain about your goals before. But you didn't think this far, did you? Now you're having to make your way without being sure where you're going, just like the rest of us. Welcome to the real world, Miss Kincaid."

"You're not helping, Miss Fritzsen."

"Sure I am. You're already so pissed at me you've forgotten to be all maudlin."

Katie took a sip of her Kronenbourg and looked around at her friends. She sighed. "You're annoying, but right."

"Of course I am."

"And modest as always, too," Amy interjected. "Look, Katie, sure you're out of your comfort zone and have some new skill sets to perfect, but you're up to it. I don't know if anyone is completely irreplaceable, but I'm sure there's no one else with either your reputation or ability to lead a space fleet. And able to deal with aliens, too. A lot of people have a lot of trouble with that."

Katie snorted softly. "Heck, half the time I think the Galactics make more sense than humans."

Thor chuckled. "Maybe you should think of humans as just another sort of alien."

All of a sudden, Katie didn't feel so bad. She might feel tired and out of her depth, but she was only human herself, wasn't she? Maybe she should cut herself at least as much slack as she would someone working for her. She expected them to pace themselves. To do their best, but not delude themselves into trying to be superhuman. Superhumans belonged in escapist fiction. They didn't exist elsewhere. "Thanks, guys. Thanks for being good friends."

"No problem. You're buying, right?" Thor answered.

Katie laughed. "Sure." She looked around. Others were starting to filter in. "But I'm going to have to go and mix."

Which she did. Partly for personal reasons, and partly for reasons of the job.

It wasn't entirely true that she hadn't thought about the future past this point. She had, but not in detail, because she hadn't really quite thought she'd get so far, and because she didn't want to. She didn't want to because increasingly it looked like charting humanity's future would mean politics and shady compromises. It didn't appeal to her. But surely she could handle an evening out with people who were either friends or wanted to be? Time to be nice with people.

It didn't turn out to be that hard. The evening flew by.

A good time was had by all.

Later, as she was leaving, Katie felt satisfaction at a job well done.

Maybe she could learn this politics stuff.

She'd do her best anyhow.

Assembling

"Hrrumphh! Hrrumphh! Hrrumphh!" the crew of the *Celestial Dominance* roared out the traditional greeting for an arriving fleet commander. Second Paw of the Emperor Rrolff Sweets-Swiper accepted it with apparent impassivity, but in his chest his heart warmed with pride and excitement. No decent civilized being looked forward to the deployment of violence, but nevertheless Rrolff couldn't help feeling proud that he would be the first Sweets-Swiper in generations to serve the Empire in this fashion. He was indeed fortunate to have been born when he was.

The performance of great deeds required living in trying times.

The flight deck of his flagship was immense and filled with crew and space soldiers arrayed in neat, glittering, formal lines. It was an impressive spectacle.

A long, empty aisle through the ranks stretched out before him and a small party led by the ship's captain was marching along it towards where Rrolff waited patiently. There was no hurrying ceremony, and this was the only chance many of those he commanded would get to see him. There could be no short-changing them.

In time, the medal-bedecked ship's captain, Commander Rrolf Stout-Belly, reached a point just in front of Rrolff and bellowed out his greeting. "The *Celestial Dominance* and her crew at your command, Second Paw!"

The crew punctuated that with a loud "Hurrrah!" before subsiding.

Rrolff and the captain bowed to each other. The captain then spoke, gesturing to a skinny, grim individual next to him with the insignia of a Claw. There were only two-twelves of Claws in the Empire, and this was the Sixth, the well-named Thorn-Paw. Rrolff knew him well by reputation despite having never met him in person. The captain's words were no surprise. "Paw of the Emperor, allow me to introduce Sixth Claw Thorn-Paw who has spent long years on the frontier. The Emperor, in his wisdom, recommends him as an adviser on the lay of the land in that benighted region."

"I welcome the esteemed Claw's service," Rrolff answered, gesturing Thorn-Paw to take a place at his side.

Together they proceeded across the flight deck between the ranks of arrayed servicemen before entering the passageways of the ship proper.

Having paraded half the length of the ship they entered Rrolff's new quarters, where he turned to his aide. "You have the *'Book of Barbarians'*? Please, hand it over."

Rrolff took the thick volume bound with actual animal skin and opened it on his reading podium. It fell open to a passage first written many thousands of seasons before, and annotated by earlier Paws every few generations. "*Never on the border, let alone past it, is it safe to relax or take anything for granted. Remain alert always. Triumph is sure over barbarians, but the cost and whether that triumph will be yours or a successor's is not.*"

Rrolff grunted. The last bit of commentary on the passage was from seven generations before and by a distant ancestor on his mother's side. It was not reassuring. "*This is wisdom incarnate. It is wasted on the unwary and inexperienced, but heed it as best you can. You must try to dissect reality out in the dark as a dedicated botanist dissects a small creature, trying to learn how it works."*

Rrolff looked up at the aide. "You may leave. I wish to be alone with the Claw. We have much to discuss that deserves privacy."

The aide left.

Rrolff glanced at the patiently waiting Claw. "You're familiar with the book, Claw Thorn-Paw?"

"Only from my student days," Thorn-Paw answered. "Copies of that book are closely controlled."

"Yes, we wouldn't want one to fall into the wrong hands. What did you think of it?"

Thorn-Paw paused, then grimaced. "It is ancient wisdom."

"It is holding fast to our traditions that has kept us from declining into decadence and feckless ignorance, as so many races do," Rrolff answered.

"It is fine as far as it goes. In a general way, little has changed since we first ventured out into the stars and claimed many new worlds for ourselves."

Rrolff snorted. "So you accept we might have something to learn from our ancestors?"

"Of course," Thorn-Paw said, "but although the rapid changes each species experiences shortly before reaching the stars seem to largely cease once they do so, all the same, each of them seems to bring something new to the galactic community. We must be wary of that."

"So you accept the barbarians as members of the larger community?"

"As children starting to become adults, rambunctious, and rash in their new power and dangerous because of that."

"Indeed, so you accept the need for this punitive expedition?"

"It is past due. We've let matters drift on the frontier too long. Never should have two barbarian powers been allowed to come to blows as has happened. The transgression was egregious, but those that committed it were probably ignorant of the lines they crossed."

"Hardly seems fair to punish them for it, then?"

"But we must. Life is not fair. Order must be restored."

Rrolff tilted his head in affirmation. "Just so.

***

Shadowguide sipped his drink slowly in one of the many fine drinking establishments on Far Seat Trade Hub station he'd become comfortable, and well known, in.

He was watching the young human female, Lieutenant Tanya Wootton, by name, trying to spy. She was getting better at it, although from a rather low level. He smiled to himself. He wasn't improving his own spycraft here. In fact, he was guilty of two cardinal sins for a spy. He was setting down roots here on Far Seat. He was becoming sentimentally attached to the place and its people. Sentimental attachments hindered both analytical objectivity and operational flexibility. It was important to avoid them. One ought to strive to maintain a cool detachment. And, second, he was becoming comfortable. Comfortable and a little too well known. One wanted to be well known enough to avoid sticking out as an outsider and to be, if possible, trusted, but no more. Being comfortable led to complacency and a lack of alertness. Things that could lead to a spy's demise.

A spy's only defense was to remain undetected, unsuspected if possible.

A spy must remain alert to being detected, and ready to flee or hide at a moment's notice.

And Shadowguide was getting sloppy.

Maybe he'd been doing this too long. Maybe he was becoming old and complacent, just like the Grrumm were, as it happened.

If they'd been alert to events out here around Far Seat he'd never have had to intervene in the struggle between the humans and the Scaly Ones. And now they were finally deciding to act. Like the humans had earlier, they in their desperation were overreacting.

For an individual who worked for an organization dedicated to maintaining a rough sort of order at a higher level in the frontier regions, it was all rather frustrating. On the other hand, it hardly mattered who prevailed in the coming conflict. The Grrumm were a known factor and if they extended their influence out further, that was fine. The humans were new, but oddly - partly because of having come to space too early in their development - open to compromise and different ways of thinking. They might be able to build a stable alliance and defeat the Empire. That would be fine, too. Shadowguide's masters wanted order. They didn't much care who maintained it.

Ideally, observing would be all Shadowguide would need to do during this latest round of the Great Game.

Observing while slowly sipping fine liquor.

Maybe philosophizing some.

***

Katie and her proposed command staff were back in SFHQ, in the same conference room as before.

She looked around and the mood she sensed was one of grim determination.

Both Tretyak and Radison seemed uncharacteristically anxious. Well they might. What they were proposing was a huge commitment of the Space Force's resources based on vague, uncertain facts and conjecture. There'd been gaping holes in the briefs they'd provided. They were asking a lot of Katie and her people. And although they might be providing a lot of ships, they hadn't given a lot of direction, or even clues about what the expedition would encounter. This was really an expedition to boldly go where no human had before to see what was there. They couldn't be sure of the buy-in they needed from everyone.

At least now, Katie felt confident that her proposed command team were all on the same page, and were all people she could work with. Work well with, really. Given the standing start the Space Force had had, it was a minor miracle they'd been blessed with so many capable officers. Katie knew her history. Usually, militaries facing battle for the first time in a long time suffered multiple egregious command failures. Sometimes they never got their acts together.

Katie wondered how the Space Force had managed to dodge that bullet. Maybe being a space-going police force had required a higher level of performance than being in a garrison of some sort. Maybe the Academy had actually done its job. She didn't know. Maybe when this was all over, she could retire and study the matter. Write books about it that her fame would help sell. Be nice if it was good for something. Right now, she still had a job to do.

She looked at Tretyak.

"The floor is yours, Admiral," he said.

"Thank you, Admiral." She looked around at her prospective reports. "You've all read the briefing papers? Had time to digest them?"

Mostly, that just elicited short nods. Susan all but grinned at her, though. Thor Haralson gave a "Yes." And Wong, a full out, "Yes, Admiral." Hood granted her a thin crooked smile. Knew too much, that one. What was it with her friends?

"Good," Katie said. "Then we're all on the same page, but let me summarize."

She took a breath.

She looked to Tretyak, then glanced Radison's way. "With all due respect, Admiral, Commodore Radison, the 'facts' in the briefing docs were mostly hearsay and conjecture. We know what various alien groups have been willing to tell us. It's a lot of data, but once you get done wading through it, you realize there are huge gaps in it. That it's not at all clear how much of it can be trusted, and it's even less clear what it means. Anybody have anything to add?"

Commodore Smith coughed. "Yes, reading between the lines," he drawled, "none of that's accidental."

Katie gave him a hard look.

Smith shrugged. "Knowledge is power."

"I believe the commodore has a valid point," Hood interjected.

"Might I remind you, Admiral," Radison said, dryly as always, "that we paid with land and political concessions for most of that information. The Galactics have never pretended that they give away useful information for free."

Katie gave a deep sigh. She didn't feel inclined to hide her exasperation. "And what exactly did we manage to purchase with chunks of our home planet?"

Admiral Tretyak answered her. "For one, the tech that gave you a fleet capable of achieving victory. Also, your efforts against both the pirates and the Lizards bought us a lot of useful information. In addition to a lot of detail that our intelligence services will be able to piece together better as they grow and become more skilled, we have a solid take on the geopolitical situation in our local arm of the galaxy."

"That there are several trade hubs between us and what the Galactics consider 'civilized space' where they rely mostly on star gates for interstellar travel. That doesn't seem like much."

"Reading between the lines, it's a lot more than it seems," Hood answered for Tretyak. "Lieutenant Wootton wrote a paper on it."

"I would remember if that'd been in the briefing," Katie replied.

Radison and Tretyak looked at each other. "We thought it rather speculative in nature," Tretyak said. "We didn't want to prejudice your judgment."

Katie looked at Hood. "Spill."

Hood looked resigned. "I'll do my best. Not only was her paper speculative, it was written using jargon and concepts that render it, umm, not very accessible to anyone not specialized in the academic field of cliodynamics."

"I've met Wootton. Summarize in plain language."

Hood grimaced. "Well, she starts off claiming her thesis is general for Imperial Oeconomia Barbarian relations, but mostly it's an extended model of the Roman Empire's relationship with the barbarians on the other side of the Rhine and Danube." He looked at Katie.

"Go on," she answered the implied question.

"Long story short, she says that although trends internal to the Roman Empire weakened it, and that there were climate and epidemiological stresses, that the main thing that caused it to fall was the relative rise in power of the barbarians across the frontier. Basically, she claims the Romans should have preempted the rise of the Germans mostly by conquering their homelands as they developed economically. She goes on to claim, based on the data from several millennia of Galactic history, that this is exactly what the 'civilized' powers up the galactic arm have done. That as soon as the barbarians across their frontier reach a certain level of economic development or cohesion that they invade, conquer, and integrate them into their empires."

"And she thinks we're now on the menu?"

Hood nodded. "Exactly."

"And when is dinner?"

"Soon, she thinks. In her latest report, she suggests our forcing the Lizards to surrender by attacking them in their home system was some sort of trigger."

Katie refrained from pointing out they hadn't had much choice. It was beside the point. "Thank you," she said. She looked around the room. No one looked happy. "So, I figure that means we have to do this. We've got to go up-arm and see what's really happening. We can hope Lieutenant Wootton's analysis is wrong or at least too alarmist, but hope is not a strategy. Is everybody on board? Does anybody have anything they'd like to add?"

Head shakes were most of the response she got to her question.

Tretyak, having waited, finally spoke up. "That tracks with the analysis Pete and I, and the rest of SFHQ did. We believe this reconnaissance in force is necessary. Try not to provoke an unnecessary fight, try to collect allies, but if you have to fight, you're authorized to do so. We have the necessary orders to assemble the fleet cut. All we need is your okay and we'll send them out. Far Seat is your first stop, obviously. After that you'll have to improvise, but we expect you'll likely want to visit each of the Trade Hubs further up-arm until you reach the first gated system. Maybe take the odd detour to make friends. So is it a go?"

"It's a go," Katie confirmed.

"Okay, I want to consult with you, Pete, and Hood before you issue your final orders. I've penciled a meeting in for a couple of days from now. I believe we're done here for now."

"Concur."

So, the meeting was over. Katie was one of the last to leave, but before she could finish leaving, Commodore Radison stopped her.

"I have something for you," he said.

Katie raised an eyebrow. Radison was an ally, but she'd always had a hard time completely trusting him.

"It's a set of letters from your grandmother," Radison said, handing her a data chip. "She always thought you'd make admiral, and she had things she wanted to tell you, but you weren't ready to hear them before she passed. Or so she told me. I haven't read them myself. But she was dying and thinking of you, and she made these and asked me to pass them on to you when I thought the time was appropriate. I think this is that time."

Katie gazed at the little data chip. She almost teared up. She'd only known her grandmother a few short years, and they'd not always seen eye to eye, but Katie thought Katrinia Schlossberg had understood her in a way nobody else ever had. Thinking about it, she missed the woman. Painfully. And Katie could certainly use all the advice and moral support possible. "Thank you," she said.

Radison nodded. "Just do your best. That'll be thanks enough."

"I will," Katie answered.

* * *

The Assassin did have a cover to maintain, to which end he was selling "alien" trinkets in the main concourse of Goddard Station. He was somewhat stunned that he'd been allowed to set foot on the military station. But here he was, selling trinkets and subverting the odd human individual.

Amazing what people would say to the apparently sympathetic ear of a total stranger here.

The humans had had it soft for far too long. They weren't ready for the big time.

They were adapting, it was true, with amazing speed and thoroughness. Their leadership obviously recognized the precarious situation their species was in. Something the leaders of many species before them had failed to realize. Still, moving their entire species off of their home planet and building a competitive space fleet at the same time was a big ask. It immensely disrupted the lives of many individuals. Also, despite the best efforts of their military and security apparatus, the wider civilian culture, or cultures - the humans were anything but homogeneous - was incredibly prone to the promiscuous sharing of information.

All of which worked to the Assassin's advantage.

True, he was working against a time limit. Worse, he had only limited access to a moving target.

Still, the presence of many disaffected individuals, along with a lack of security consciousness, and a general hectic lack of organization all worked to his advantage. He'd managed to organize several attacks on Kincaid from within the human community.

And if those failed, he'd still have his chances at Far Seat Trade Hub. It was obvious the human fleet forming up would need to go there. Once there, Kincaid would need to participate in many diplomatic activities, some of which were bound to leave her exposed.

Galactics were more tight-lipped and security conscious than the humans, but the Assassin had long experience with pushing the necessary buttons.

"Exotic goods from the far edges of the known galaxy," he shouted. Keep it up and he'd get some bites and make some sales. It was the same with the death business. Follow enough leads and you'd make a sale.

Not really the most efficient way to work, but he was under a deadline.

The reward was substantial. He might be able to retire.

And, with so many chances to collect, he liked his odds.

* * *

Rob Hood rubbed his eyes. He knew he needed to get more sleep. But he'd been stung by Kincaid's obvious unhappiness with the intelligence he'd been able to provide. Besides, Tanya Wootton's increasingly frequent missives from Far Seat tended to arrive at odd hours. And he never wanted to wait to read them.

He wasn't sure if that increasing frequency was due to an increased sense of urgency on her part, or because she was afraid each report might be her last and wanted to pass on the most recent information as soon as it arrived.

Neither possibility was encouraging. Tanya might be a formerly head-in-the-clouds academic, but she was not a nerve case. She did not lack for courage. She'd shown herself to have a surprising degree of moral fortitude. Hood had the definite impression she was being more aggressive and less cautious than was safe in her information gathering.

She was reaching out to contact dangerous individuals who had no moral compunctions about taking advantage of someone if they saw a profit in it. Individuals who'd not hesitate to kill in order to preserve their secrets.

Hood had always suspected a dark underside to the affable outer face of Galactic society and Tanya's investigations were confirming it.

He was rather impressed by her work. He'd not have expected it of her. On the other hand, he was also very worried. He was going to make a point of sending her a message to the effect that she was a valuable asset to human intelligence and she ought to be careful about risking herself. Telling her to be careful for her own sake wouldn't do, but putting it that way might work.

He sighed.

He was working alone in his little office-cum-sleeping cabin. He missed the days when the two of them had shared a somewhat larger hole in the wall. As frustrating as she'd been at times, she'd been company, and affirmation that someone else believed in their work.

Kincaid, Tretyak, Radison and others claimed to value intelligence work, but at times he thought they failed to properly appreciate it. They wanted a clear picture when all that was on offer was a set of juxtaposed puzzle pieces.

Even when you did give them an overall picture, like Tanya's work had provided, they didn't seem to see it clearly.

Rob Hood figured it was clear enough in outline. The so-called civilized Galactics up-arm didn't like to let the barbarian problem get out of hand. Barbarians that got uppity or just looked like they could be a problem got hammered down. Sooner or later. Looked a lot like sooner right now. Now what was complicated about that?

Not much.

Now what they were supposed to do about it?

That was a bit more problematic.

***

The whole place had a weird, artificial, chemical smell to the air. Which amazed Katie, who'd grown up on a spaceship.

What were they doing that they couldn't make the canned air smell fresher? She didn't know how many stories deep they were, but up there somewhere they had a whole planet's atmosphere to draw on. You'd have thought they could have made it work. And the lighting wasn't much better: hard, harsh, and too blue.

The place was an above-top secret subterranean lab complex. It was real. She had Admiral Tretyak and Radison along to testify to that, but it felt like a movie set. Katie turned to Hood, who was tagging along behind her. "You believe this place?"

Hood gave her an amused grin. "Yep. You combine cheapness and an indifference to aesthetics or simple decent working conditions and this is what you get. There were places like this on Mars."

Commodore Radison turned around with an annoyed look on his face. "We take excellent care of our workers," he asserted.

"By treating them like lab rats," Katie retorted.

"Bet they can't leave their cages either," Hood added. Hood had clawed his way out of the Martian tunnels. He was no fan of trapping people in sub-standard living conditions.

Radison looked as angry as Katie had ever seen him. "I have to take that from the Admiral," he said.

"I'm not in your chain of command," Hood said, cutting him off.

"You're in mine. Both of you," Tretyak interjected. "Stop it. This is not why we're here. Pete, take a hint. Kidnap a living conditions expert and put them to work here. Let me know how it works out. Understood?"

"Yes, sir," Radison answered. Katie wasn't sure she'd ever heard those words from him before.

Tretyak looked at Katie and Hood. "Yes, sir," they replied.

Tretyak nodded. "Good. Now, as much as I like to take good care of my people, this place isn't a resort, and we're not tourists. We're here for a reason. Pete's managed a few things worth seeing and we have things to discuss. Things I don't want being overheard."

"And this place is as secure as any place ever gets," Hood said.

"Precisely. We've given Katie a job. One it's going to take a magician to succeed at."

Katie managed a lop-sided smile. "Glad you see that, sir." "I do, and this is where we fill your hat with rabbits to pull out."

"Sounds good."

"I hope so. Pete?"

"Yes, we've been working towards goals much more important than mere creature comfort."

Neither Katie nor Hood rose to the bait.

Radison's face twitched. He continued. "We've built on the FTL tech supplied by our tentacled friends and Admiral Kincaid's unknown benefactor. We didn't do the experiments here, of course, but it is where we processed the data from them. We believe that with re-programming, our current FTL drives will be capable of medium length in-system Faster Than Light hops. It could be decisive in some battles, I'd think."

"You believe?"

Radison sighed. "Yes, I believe. We've done some short hops well away from any gravity wells, but time and security concerns have prevented doing as many experiments as we'd have liked. I think you yourself in your after-action reports emphasized the very sensitive nature of our having this technology. I think you said it could attract the adverse attention of powerful players and be more trouble than it was worth."

Katie nodded slowly. "That's true. I guess this is one rabbit we want to keep in the hat unless we absolutely need it."

Radison pursed his lips. "There's another possible problem. I'm not sure your engineering staff in the field will be able to properly implement the necessary modifications. My scientists managed to do them on a small scale. It should work theoretically, but I don't know of any technology that ever got transferred from the lab to the field without teething problems."

Katie bit a lip. "I can't think of an example either. So this a last ditch expedient that probably won't work perfectly."

"But it could make a decisive difference under the right circumstances," Hood volunteered.

"It could," Katie allowed. "So I'm glad to have it. What else?"

"A grab bag of electronic warfare improvements," Radison answered. "Turns out the Lizards had a number of projects on the back burner and turned up the heat after their initial engagements with you. Didn't get anywhere really with them before you finished the war, but the Chief-Queen was surprisingly quick to share it all with us. Some of the other Galactics, particularly Snout friends of your Tee-Nah, have also shared interesting data on ship and weapons signatures with us. Should help with your situational awareness on the battlefield and buff your weapons capability moderately too. Again, there are security issues, but once you're past Far Seat, I'd suggest promulgating the necessary software updates to your fleet under some sort of cover story."

Hood snorted.

His superiors turned to him. He looked uncharacteristically abashed. "Sorry, I like some of these guys, but they're all looking out for number one. You could be finishing up a cup of tea with the Chief-Queen and suddenly notice you've bled out from the dagger she slipped between your ribs."

"Very colorfully put," Tretyak commented.

"Yes, sir, but to get to the point, if these folks slipped us useful info, it's because they expect they'll profit by it in the future."

"I'll worry about the long term once we've solved our immediate problems," Katie said. "Right now, I'm glad for every edge I can get."

"Yes, ma'am."

"Anyhow," Tretyak said, "Pete'll pass Hood the necessary info and you the keys to access it. We've got some less technical rabbits for you, too."

As he spoke, he stopped before a door and looked at Radison, who gave him a small nod. Entering the room after him Katie saw both the usual wooden conference table. She'd have sworn that, unusually, this particular table was cheap veneer. Also, very unusually, the opposite wall consisted entirely of transparent windows that gave them a view of a cavernous space full of complicated machinery and equipment.

Katie figured she was pretty tech savvy, but she didn't recognize most of it. It looked like a cross between a physics lab and a high-end manufacturing facility. The presence of multi-spectral scanners and large multi-material 3D printers gave that impression. Katie looked Radison's way. He was smirking. She ignored that. "Fancy," she said.

Radison, looking out at the view, smiled. "I'm proud of what we've achieved here."

Tretyak looked amused.

Hood staring out the windows gave the impression of someone cramming just before an exam. Like he was trying to memorize every detail of what they were looking at.

"It's all ultra-top secret, compartment keyword '*Ring Saga*,'" Radison said. "Consider yourselves read in. You'll have to pretend you never saw any of this."

"Of course," Hood replied. Katie simply nodded.

Tretyak gestured to them to sit. Once they'd done so, he got right to it. "I've been following Lieutenant Wootton's work, and your analysis of it, Lieutenant Commander Hood, I haven't commented on it much because I think you've both been doing a fine job. Please, feel free to tell her that the next time you see her in person." He turned to Katie. "So, although the briefings we've given you and your command staff earlier are technically accurate when hedging on what we know, I definitely have a scenario in mind I think is the most likely."

Katie nodded. "They didn't hedge that much. Wootton and Hood here, think we're going to meet a Galactic punitive expedition launched by these Grrumm folks and that if we face them alone, they'll wipe the floor with us. That just maybe with the right allies and if we're clever we might be able to avoid that fate." She looked Tretyak in the eyes. "You agree. That right?"

"That's right."

Katie looked over at Hood. "Anything to add?"

"No, you've pretty well summed it up."

Tretyak continued. "Even if all of Pete's little surprises

work out, I don't think it'll make enough difference. We're going to need allies. Allies willing to fight with us. Even then, I recommend you avoid a head on fight with these new Galactics until you have their measure. Apparently, they've been successfully suppressing barbarian threats for thousands of years. You have to believe they've got a few surprises of their own up their sleeves."

"But we don't know what?" Katie asked.

"We've tried," Hood said. "We're still trying."

"Afraid you're going to have to figure that out, Katie," Tretyak added. "You'll have Hood, of course, and Wootton if you want, but basically we've done what we can here. That's one of your main tasks despite not being explicitly in your formal orders. Your other main task is finding those allies we're going to need. Our various alien friends here in the Solar System and at Far Seat have given us a few leads there."

Katie couldn't help frowning. "But nothing solid on either front, and you want me to avoid direct conflict until I've resolved both issues."

"Final decision is yours, but yes," Tretyak replied. "For what it's worth, both the Chief-Queen and the various Snout chieftains seem eager to do what they can to help. They seem extremely averse to having a 'civilized' power exert control over our local bit of the galaxy. Given a choice, they've made it abundantly clear they'd prefer our dominance to that of a power from up-arm. Exactly what their support is worth in the end, I don't know, but we have arranged meetings for you with them. We expect if those go well, you'll get nibbles from other factions."

"Okay, that's something," Katie allowed. "Anything else?"

"Yes, we've succeeded in bribing several important Trade Union officials. They were only willing to deal with me directly, but I'll pass on contact details via Hood through the normal secure channels. They can't openly support us. The Trade Union is supposed to be apolitical and neutral. On the other hand, they've enjoyed their freedom from serious supervision the last several decades too. They're willing to do the odd 'favor' as long as it's plausibly deniable. They can pass on information now and again too. In fact, they've already done so. One tidbit that'll interest you is that someone has contracted with high-powered assassins to eliminate you. You should feel flattered. You also need to pay full attention to von Luck and your security detail. Understood?"

"Yes, sir," Katie replied. "That it?"

"For me. I think Pete deserves a chance to show off all his goodies in detail."

"I'll be happy to deal with honest technical questions and not all this mushy political maneuvering."

Hood just nodded.

Katie did enjoy Radison's briefing. When it came to technology, he was a genius. An enthusiastic genius working with other technical nerds on some very interesting tech. They had some neat gadgets.

Katie almost felt guilty taking a vacation from more political matters.

Winning space battles was hard enough without all the diplomatic stuff to consider.

But she had a job to do, and she was going to damn well do it.

* * *

Tanya was experiencing a distinctly itchy feeling between her shoulder blades. Her independent merchant contact, someone by definition not in good odor with the Trade Union that de facto ruled on Far Seat, had picked the place for their meeting. A seedy dive in the less pleasant, and less safe, part of the station.

She didn't have so many good contacts that she could afford to be fussy about such things, but she was worried. There was a certain sleazy Swimmer without obvious means of support who spent all of his time hanging out in the market or various establishments like this one. Dark places, not overly clean where the light was good enough to see, and utterly lacking in ambiance.

Strangely enough, if you knew what you were buying you could get good liquor here. But it was definitely buyer beware. You wanted to poison yourself, that wasn't the barkeeper's problem. And the barkeeper being a Varkoid, there was no arguing with him.

Multiple sources had said it was a place where deals got done.

All good enough if rather excessively shady, but there was that damned sleazy Swimmer holding the bar up. Tanya was sure he'd been watching her. He was turning up at too many of the same places she was frequenting.

She was feeling distinctly vulnerable. This wasn't a good area for a single, slight female at the best of times. With the game that was afoot, and with the stakes involved, she felt a lot like incipient roadkill. Or maybe one of those helpless females in the classic videos tied to the tracks as a freight train barreled towards them.

She was scared.

Strangely, not mainly for herself. That was just sprinkles on the cake.

She'd become convinced weeks ago that disaster was looming over the whole galactic sector and humanity in particular. She'd sent report after report back to Earth trying to convince them of that and that they needed to do something. Only she wasn't sure she was getting through to them. All they'd done was answer her with perfunctory thanks and requests for more data.

It wasn't clear they were taking her warnings seriously let alone doing anything about them.

She sipped the extraordinarily expensive Scotch she'd bought. The barkeeper might be lackadaisical about everything else but he did expect his customers to buy drinks. It burned pleasantly slipping down her throat. She had heard rumors, from various alien contacts - her superiors back on Earth hadn't seen fit to let her know - that a large fleet under Kincaid was about to leave Earth for Far Seat and points beyond. She hoped that was true.

Finally, a Swimmer less sleazy than her shadow, but rather twitchy, slipped into the seat across from her. "They're coming," he greeted her.

"You're sure? When?"

"Certain. They'll depart in a MaTok or two. I'd bet my ship on that. When they get here is less certain. Not less than a hand and some MaToks, but it could take them several times that."

Tanya did the mental arithmetic. Two to four weeks before departure. At least a couple of months before they reached Far Seat, likely more.

The Swimmer in the meantime explained. "They'll stop at each Trade Hub on the way and get their supplies and the politics settled before continuing. The Furry Ones do nothing in a hurry. They're easy to dodge, but impossible to stop."

"That's defeatist."

"Realistic. They're slow, but not stupid. They're inexorable. They've been doing this since before your people had agriculture let alone science and industry. They know what they're doing."

"But you made the arrangements I asked you to?"

"I did. Perhaps all we can do is harass and delay them, but that is worthwhile. It will allow us time to withdraw to the unknown space beyond your home world and eke out a living there."

Tanya nodded. "Good," she said. She'd not got formal permission for it, but she was trying to set up a campaign of harassing the "Furball" communications. It was a long way, longer than they were used to, back to the star gates of the so-called "civilized" galaxy. If their access to local supplies was denied and their communications interrupted maybe they'd be forced to retreat. Maybe Tanya could convince Kincaid to fight something like the Russian campaigns of 1812 or 1941. She hoped like hell that the aggressive Space Force commander, now an Admiral, didn't try to meet the Grrumm in a head-to-head battle. She didn't think that'd end well.

"You don't agree?" the patiently waiting merchant captain asked.

Tanya was too tired to be anything but honest. "It's like investing." She knew the Galactics favored business metaphors. "There are no sure things."

"Truly," the Swimmer merchant agreed. "Only fools believe otherwise."

"But you bet the odds if you can."

"Sad they are not favorable."

"True, but my people's history has examples of the clever

turning arrogance against itself and evening those odds. You match risk against reward. Continued freedom is a valuable reward."

The Swimmer dipped his head in affirmation. "True, but unfortunately the Furry Ones have a history of doubling down until they win."

"No purse is infinitely deep," Tanya quoted an aphorism she'd frequently heard on Far Seat.

"True."

"My people have a story of a battle, the Teutoburger Wald it was called, in which the forces of an arrogant empire used to victory overreached and stumbled into a trap far beyond their borders in terrain that did not favor them and were annihilated. They never conquered that territory or the people that lived there."

"An inspiring tale," the Swimmer merchant said politely.

"One we can learn from, I hope," Tanya replied.

* * *

This was getting old. Katie was once again lying under the weight of a large marine bodyguard. She was distantly aware of the fact her shoulder hurt like hell. Apparently this would-be assassin had managed to hit her. With a slug thrower she suspected. They were on Goddard Station. No plasma guns here.

This incident had begun with the boom-crack of several slug thrower shots, before the sound of shouting and screaming overlaid with that of needler fire had started up. Needlers, which fired small hyper velocity rounds, were comparatively easy on the outside walls of stations and ships. Much less chance of that ever so inconvenient explosive decompression to worry about.

And once again it was making her late for an important meeting. The final O-Group before her command staff dispersed to their ships, and they all sailed off into the wild blue yonder. Which at this point was looking like it might be safer than Earth and its environs.

For a second Katie felt a flash of anger. This wasn't much thanks for saving humanity from extinction or at best something close to it. She quashed that. Turbulent times and unclear ones too, it wasn't surprising people got angry and lashed out. Just unfortunate, and very, very annoying. She shouldn't add to the problem.

At least this time she was being a good little admiral and not squirming.

She waited patiently until Bloggins let her up. Von Luck had arrived by that time and was taking charge. That was his job, not hers. Her job right now was enduring the now not-so-distant pain of the wound to her shoulder as a paramedic treated it. He sprayed it with something cool that didn't sting too much.

"Just a few seconds for the anesthetic to take hold and it won't hurt so much, ma'am," the paramedic said. He had a corporal's chevrons and a name tag that said "Thompson".

"Thanks, Thompson," Katie answered.

"You were very lucky, ma'am. It was a slow slug and not so big. The body armor of your uniform took most of its energy and it didn't hit anything important. No bones or arteries. Very lucky, ma'am," Thompson said as he finished up. He'd bandaged and bound the wound and stuck her arm in a sling. The left one fortunately. She could still work without too much trouble.

Thompson checked his work and ended by saying, "Take it easy on it, ma'am."

He then left her alone with Senior Sergeant Bloggins and Brigadier von Luck who seemed done with yelling at everyone.

"Very lucky," Bloggins said.

"I agree with Bloggins," von Luck added. Katie sighed.

"Listen, Katie," von Luck said, "you've got to take this more seriously. The last one who got through was a whacko who'd lost his job, then his family because of all the economic disruption. He blamed you for it all and thought he had to stop you from taking over and leading us into a new Dark Ages. Not too many like him, but still a non-zero number. Only this attempt was more professional. The trigger puller was being blackmailed, but the people pulling his strings were professionals. Could have been a human faction, or one of our galactic neighbors, we don't know yet. But you've got multiple groups gunning for you, and you have to take that seriously."

Katie studied von Luck. It might have intimidated someone else, but not von Luck. Still, maybe he'd pay attention to what she was going to say. She took a breath. "I do take it seriously, but it's not my job to worry about it. It's yours, and Bloggins, and my other guards' job. I'll co-operate as best I can, but I can't really do much about the fact people want to kill me. And," she said stabbing his chest with her forefinger, "I will not let it interfere with me doing my job. My job being to find out what's going on out there in the wider galaxy, make friends, turn them into allies, try to avoid conflict, but if it comes to a fight, win that fight. It is not my job to worry about politics back here on Earth, and it is not my job to worry about my own personal safety. Those are the concerns of the politicians, and of you and your people. Not mine. I've got enough on my plate. Understood?"

For a few long moments von Luck just stared at her jaw clenched.

She stared right back.

"Understood," he finally said, "but, please, do try to co-operate as much as possible. You'll not achieve much if you're dead or comatose in a hospital bed. You understand?"

"Yes. Let's get on with it," Katie said stomping off the way she'd been going in the first place.

She had a fleet to get on its way.

Pre-game Scrum

Katie looked around at her command staff assembled for their initial Orders Group. Probably the last O-group they'd all attend in person until Far Seat Trade Hub. She made a point of making eye contact with each of them.
"Our goal is to convince everyone in this section of the galaxy that we'd make good friends. Powerful friends, that are going to be around a long time."
She flashed a wolf smile.
"We need friends. Lots of good friends. But we have to convince them they need us more."
She looked around to see how that was being taken. She had everyone's rapt attention. But although Amy, Haralson, McLeod, and others seemed pleased by the idea of thinking of this as mainly a diplomatic mission, others weren't. Susan Fritzsen, for instance, was frowning. Katie wondered if this was because she wanted a good fight, or because she thought conflict was inevitable. Probably both. Others seemed non-committal. Smith seemed almost amused.
"We need friends, because as much as we want to avoid conflict - that'd be nice - we can't count on it. And it's not likely

we'll be able to prevail in the absence of real help."

"Understood?"

Nods and murmurs of agreement.

"Good. I imagine you all understand that it's a bit of a chicken and egg problem, too. In summary, the Grrumm Empire is the local representative of the current powers that be in the Galaxy. Nobody is going to be willing to challenge the powers that be, if they don't think that challenge can succeed. But if they're not willing to take a chance on us, such a challenge will probably fail."

Katie took a breath and looked around. "You'll find a lot more detail and nuance in your briefing notes, but that's what it boils down to."

Amy put up a hand. What the heck did she think this was? A kindergarten?

"Yes, Commodore Sarkis. You have a question?" "Admiral," Amy, Katie's old friend, was being very formal, "why do we need to challenge the powers-that-be, as you put it, at all?"

"Good question. It's not that we want to. It's that we do so by just existing. We can't help it. I'm afraid that our success in forcing the Lizards to surrender didn't help. I'm sorry if that got lost amongst all the other details in your briefings."

Hood caught Katie's eye. "Lieutenant Commander Hood, you have something to add?"

"Yes. Reports from Lieutenant Wootton on Far Seat bear that out. Some of her sources explicitly stated that our forcing another species' home planet to surrender was crossing a red line. They also made it clear that we were bound to catch the attention of the Grrumm Empire at some point. They said it's been Grrumm policy for thousands of years to suppress potential barbarian threats. Possible threats. You don't have to actually be aggressive towards them. You just have to have the potential to be a danger. If they think you might be potentially dangerous, they act preemptively before you become a real problem. It's worked well for them for a very long time."

"That answer your question, Amy?" Katie asked.

"Thoroughly. Thank you, ma'am."

"Good. Anyhow, as Lieutenant Commander Hood said,

they've been doing this for thousands of years. Successfully. With that track record, nobody is going to be eager to bet against them."

That was greeted with the glumness it deserved. Katie didn't want to discourage her people, but she had to make the problem they faced clear.

"They move with overwhelming force on any planets or major stations a potential threat possesses. They force their surrender, and dismantle any state or organization that might oppose them. They often resort to direct governance. For what it's worth, they don't usually resort to genocide, and aren't considered particularly exploitive or harsh occupiers."

"That's nice," von Luck commented.

"Sounds like we're particularly vulnerable with so much of our population and industry still on Earth," Susan Fritzsen observed.

Katie nodded. "Exactly. We either need to keep them from reaching the Solar System, or figure out how to conduct the fight without it."

"Which I imagine means we need the Support Group to be able to sustain the fleet for a prolonged period," said Commander Henry Vane. He commanded that Support Group.

"That's right, Commander Vane," Katie replied. "You're not going to be able to rely on supply lines to Earth. You're going to have to plan for the contingency of cutting loose from the Solar System as a supply base."

"Damn," Haralson commented. He was far from the most senior officer here, but the study of military history and strategic theory was a hobby of his. He knew darned well what Katie was proposing was easier said than done. "So, we need allies willing to supply us when we've got our backs to the wall, and it looks like the Grrumm are winning."

Katie smiled. "Exactly. It's not like air, water, food, fuel, and munitions will manufacture themselves from empty space, is it? So, yes, we need to butter up as many aliens as possible and make some solid deals." She looked around. "Ideally, it won't come to that. Ideally, we'll proceed without problems to the nearest world with a gate. We'll make contact with the so-called 'civilized' Galactics and the Grrumm in particular. And we will all agree to peaceful co-existence."

Somebody snorted. Katie didn't see who, but she suspected Susan Fritzsen.

Katie answered the unspoken observation. "And yes, that's a tall, contradictory order. We should be so lucky. But, it is what we're aiming at. Fact is, folks, is that we're in unexplored territory. It's true the Grrumm have preemptively taken care of threats in the past. In the past they've expanded their empire whenever the frontier areas have reached a high enough economic level. But it's been hundreds of years since the last time they did so. Also, from everything we've been told, they always had both numbers and organization on their side. We have reason to hope we may roughly equal their numbers and organization. We don't know how they'll perform without numerical superiority against a well-organized foe."

"Technological level?" Commodore Smith asked.

Katie sighed. "From what we can tell from open sources, we're roughly equal. We both have the standard galactic tech package. We bought that with bits of Earth, but it was worth it. The Grrumm might have some hole cards, wouldn't be surprising, but we haven't any actual evidence of it."

"We're sure we have equal numbers?" Commodore Wong asked.

"No. We're not sure. Current reliable reports are sparse and incomplete. If they follow precedent they'll send a dozen heavy ships along with escorts. There will be twice as many escorts as heavy ships. The escorts are comparable to our light cruisers. Their heavy ships are bigger than anything we have. Call them
battle ships. They have a form of jump drive much like ours. They have a frontier patrol made up of smaller ships like our corvettes and destroyers. They don't send those on punitive expeditions. Within 'civilized' space, they don't use ships with interstellar drives at all. There's a gate system operated by a third species that links civilized systems. That species is neutral. They're called something like '*The Spiders*', many legged web spinners. They don't allow military or armed ships to use their gates. Systems interior to civilized space don't allow access by ships with interstellar drives. They're too dangerous. It's not worth it if you don't need them."

Susan, Commodore Fritzsen, spoke up. "That was all in the briefings. Although it's not as if even interplanetary drives aren't horrendously dangerous."

"I thought it was worth repeating," Katie replied. "Civilized systems aren't keen on allowing barbarians or semi-barbarians into their systems. In fact, our sources suggest that space drives of all sorts are heavily regulated throughout civilized space. That was glossed over in your briefings because it's not germane to our mission. At most, we hope to reach the edge of so-called civilized space and then negotiate a modus vivendi. What is of interest is that it means the Grrumm maintain a whole fleet of ships whose only purpose is to conduct these punitive missions. We suspect it has a static composition. A few heavy ships with escorts, like I said."

"That seems rather hand-wavy," Wong said. Wong's reputation was that he was very by the book. On the other hand, he was the only one of her subordinates who'd ever held independent command of a fleet and he'd proved competent in the role.

Katie smiled at Wong. "Busted," she said. "It seems that way because it is. Unfortunately, it's not going to be possible to prepare a detailed worked out set of orders for the campaign. We know what forces we have and the general goals I've started setting out, but we don't know a great deal beyond that. We don't know a lot about the Grrumm or their military forces beyond what I've already given you. As I've tried to imply, we're not even sure of their precise goals and whether we'll actually have to fight them. It seems likely, but I'm hoping we won't. We're pretty sure that they don't have a technological edge. Our sources are clear that the fleet currently forming up
doesn't outnumber us. Unfortunately it's also clear that their empire does have greater resources available. Worse, that we can't get to most of their multiple systems, but they can get to our single system. So even if we were to win initially, we'd still be facing a prolonged fight we couldn't win if they wanted to persist."

Wong blinked and looked blank. After a long second or two, he took a deep breath. "Should we just surrender and accept their terms, then? You've said they're not genocidal."

Katie grinned. It wasn't a happy expression. At best, a grimly amused one. "I'm glad to say that decision is above our pay grades. Our political masters have charged us with a mission to find out what we're facing, and if there is a fleet moving on the Solar System, to do our best to stop it."

She looked around the room. She was glad to see a set of serious, but determined, expressions. "I, for one, approve of that decision."

Susan snorted. "I assume they asked your opinion." "Yes, but I wasn't in the room when they cut our orders. No matter what various news presenters or other fruitcakes say, I'm just one well-known Space Force officer. I don't tell the government what to do. They figure that out between them based on their own sense of what's right and what their constituents want."

Wong nodded slowly, if not happily. "I assume you do have some direction to add."

Katie gave him a genuine smile. Wong was thinking for himself, but seemed determined to work as part of the team. She couldn't ask for more. "Yes, we will make our way to 'Damp', the closest gated system, via a series of Trade Hubs. While doing so we're going to contact and try to make friends with as many of the various groups of Galactics as we can. My primary order is that you're not to try to intimidate them or make demands. We want willing friends."

Susan Fritzsen spoke up. "Even one of our Task Forces is going to seem a little intimidating. And, you know, no matter how sympathetic some of these folks might be, they're awfully pragmatic. If they don't think we're going to be in the game much longer, they're not going to bet anything on us."

"True. It's a bit of a conundrum. We're going to have to seem strong, but not threatening or intimidating. You all have my utmost sympathy." Katie grinned in a way that was anything but sympathetic. "Because not only am I going to get to play diplomat, but so are you."

"You're splitting us up?" Amy asked.

"Yes, we're tasked with getting up-arm as quickly as possible and reporting on the situation, while also making as many friends as we can. We will travel separately for most of the campaign. We will move within supporting range of each other. The outlying forces will never be more than two or three jumps from the central force. We will come together at the Trade Hubs for consultation and re-supplying. Also, when and if the tactical situation calls for it. Right now, that means in the last system before the Damp one. We'll also do so if it looks like we're about to meet the Grrumm expedition. Clear?"

Katie looked each of her people in the eyes, getting a nod or verbal affirmation from each of them before continuing. "Good. I wish I could add more to that general plan."

"But you can't," Susan interjected.

"We've all read the briefing documents," Thor Haralson said, looking around. It was clear they all had. They were professionals, after all, even if those documents were full of detail not directly germane to their mission. "But I believe it'd be useful if you tell us what you think about the various groups of Galactics we're likely to encounter."

Katie looked at Hood and suppressed the urge to delegate this part of the orders group. She found herself in the unexpected position of wishing Wootton was here. She had Hood, but nobody else had the experience Hood, Wootton, and she herself had in dealing with Galactics. Amy, Wong, and Susan had some informal unofficial exposure during stop overs at Far Seat Trade Hub and that was it. "Yes, I was planning to do that," she said. "Particularly because I'm afraid I won't be able to spare you Hood or even any humans fluent in Galactic languages. You're going to have to hire translators. Alien individuals who can act as native guides in effect. It will be a problem, but it's critical."

She looked around. Her commanders weren't happy. They did seem to accept that these were the cards they'd been dealt.

"So, try to find native guides," Katie continued. "Now, about who the natives are, where they live, and how to approach them. First thing is that you're not going to find many, if any, inhabited planets. Surface dwellers are targets. All the Galactics try to keep surface operations small, expendable, and hidden. It's much the same with large stations. The big exception is the Trade Hubs. It's not good business to mess with the Trade Union. If some group gets out of hand, they'll hire mercenaries or dragoon some other group that needs their favor to take care of them."

"Some group like us," Haralson said.

"Yep, or the Lizards," Katie agreed. "The Trade Union doesn't like to pay for what it can get free.

"Bloody greedy profiteers," Susan said.

"That's one way of looking at it," Katie allowed. "Most of the Galactics seem pragmatic and commercial-minded to various degrees in their own ways.

"One species we haven't had much contact with are the Meerow. The Galactics nickname them 'Roamers'. You can think of them as space cat gypsies. We expect to encounter them in systems further away from the Trade Hubs. Closer to the so-called 'civilized' gated systems. The Trade Union is not fond of them and the feeling is mutual. They don't have a space navy. They're at best semi-organized in small groups. They do have high end FTL drives and many contacts with small scattered groups. Groups interested in staying hidden from the Grrumm, Trade Union, and anybody else that could be a threat. Which includes us, the Lizards, and the various Snout bands."

"Ouch, hurts to be lumped in with the same pirates who attacked the Solar System when they thought they could get away with it," Susan said.

Katie grimaced. "The 'Snouts' do tend to be very opportunistic," she allowed. "They aren't monolithic. They're not unified. They're not, in general, vicious."

"They won't kill you for the sake of killing you, just to get what you have," Susan said. Susan's feeling about threats was that they should be eliminated as completely as possible as fast as possible. Treating the Snouts as allies didn't sit well with her.

"They prefer profitable trade, it's less risky, and certain individual Snouts have thrown their lot in with us and are proving very useful," Katie said. "Exactly because they're entrepreneurial. We'd be silly not to take further advantage of that."

"We expect to get translators from among them. We also expect some lightly armed ships to supplement our scout forces. What we mainly hope for from the Snouts and the Meerow is information and a little help with logistics."

"Logistics?" Amy asked. She had a professional interest in them, having started out in supply.

"Food in moderate quantities. Water and air if needed. A limited number of spare parts for standard Galactic tech, and small batches of standard Galactic munitions. Point defense ammo, anti-missile missiles, and things like that. Our sources are secondhand and hearsay, so the details aren't clear. They seem to sell just about anything in small quantities. They sound like roving interstellar convenience stores."

"So high prices," Amy said.

"But maybe exactly what you need when and where you need it," Katie replied. She grimaced. "This is Top Secret and not to leave this room, but we've got a substantial portion of the Earth's gold reserves on board the *Bonaventure*. I will dole it out as needed. I will have to answer to the politicians in the end for what we spend, so don't go nuts with Dad's credit card. Please?"

That got chuckles.

"Imagine we don't want the Trade Union hearing we're flush," Wong suggested.

Katie sighed. "We certainly don't. They're likely among the best friends we can make. They don't want the Grrumm Empire expanding out here, but they'll take us for as much as they can."

"Not a nice galaxy, is it?" Smith said.

"No, it's not," Katie agreed. "From what we've seen of them, and going by the chronicles of prior Grrumm expeditions, the Trade Union will try to maintain a nominal neutrality."

"That's pleasantly surprising," Thor Haralson observed, "but you've put in a few qualifiers too, haven't you?"

"I have," Katie answered. "Generally, they've tended to tilt towards supporting the supposedly civilized power. I imagine because that's where they get the products they sell. Gated space is also where most of their individual members hope to retire to. On the other hand, their customers are the supposedly less civilized species. They'll sell just about anything to whoever turns up on their doorstep with something to trade. Gold, minerals, rare artifacts, and spices, etc., they'll take it all. Bottom line, the Trade Union as one player will try to avoid annoying both ourselves and the Grrumm too much."

"Very practical of them," Smith observed.

"Indeed," Katie agreed. "And in turn, both we and the Grrumm don't want to annoy them too much, either. We're both going to be a long way from our own supply bases for a long time. The Trade Union controls most high-volume trade beyond the frontier. If they start finding it hard to supply a fleet, that fleet is going to have to head home in short order."

"We need the Trade Union for most of our supplies and the Grrumm do, too?" Wong asked incredulously.

"Hard to believe, isn't it? But that's the case. For most entities, large scale interstellar trade of staples simply isn't profitable. The Trade Union makes it work by providing links between areas where resources are depleted and they aren't. They trade between low-tech areas and higher-tech ones. They trade high-tech gear for raw resources. They're classic middlemen. We suspect they don't directly profit from the trade of staples, but rather they use them as a way to control their customers."

"It's a good deal if you want to continue to breathe, eat, and drink," Susan observed caustically.

"With planets being so vulnerable, and all closed systems having limitations, it's a service someone has to offer," Katie replied.

"And profit mightily off of," an unrepentant Susan answered.

"Be that as it may," Katie continued, "we want to stay on the Trade Union's good side."

"Understood," Susan conceded.

"The other thing it's important to realize about the Trade Union, is that it's a loose organization. It's composed not just of different individuals, but different species."

"And we can use that?" Amy asked.

"We can," Katie confirmed. "Oddly enough, sentient beings, whatever they look like, and where ever they originate, seem to like to have their cake and eat it to."

"Aliens all eat cake?" Timothy McLeod, Commander McLeod, her flag captain, finally contributed something to the discussion.

Katie smiled. "Or their version of it. Social organizations are even more universal. The practical constraints tend to produce predictable results. If anyone doubts that, they can find a paper modeling various galactic entities in the appendices to the briefing documents. Lieutenant Wootton wrote it. It's heavily mathematical."

Someone groaned.

Katie couldn't help thinking it was a rather young group of senior officers. "Commander McLeod did ask. Long story short, the members of the Trade Union have common interests. Only those interests don't always precisely align. The Trade Union makes lemonade out of this lemon by using it to play both sides of any potential conflict. It's never the Trade Union's fault if associates or certain members make under-the-table deals with someone's opponents. The Trade Union hedges its bets, and it always has members discreetly in good odor with whoever wins."

"Nice. And let me guess, in this part of the galactic woods that usually turns out to be the Grrumm Empire," Susan commented.

"Correct," Katie answered. "But that's beside the point. As it happens, the Trade Union only operates on the frontier. It acts as an intermediary between what you might call the developed galaxy with gates and the less developed part of the galaxy without gates. When that developmental differential disappears, in particular once the gate system is extended to an area, they have to move on."

Amy perked up at this. "That makes sense. Trade Hubs aren't going to work in a gated system that FTL ships aren't allowed to visit. Wow, that's got to hurt."

Katie nodded. "Exactly. The station owners and workers have to abandon their stations. The owners of FTL ships have to move further out into undeveloped space. Costly and risky. It might be inevitable, but they like to put it off as long as possible."

"Whereas others have claims on resources and places which

become much more valuable once they're in civilized space," Haralson said.

"We're less clear on that," Hood answered, "but we think that's so. Plus there's a social dimension. Being a bigwig in a civilized place counts for more. But extending the gate system is costly. The Spiders seem even more predatory than your average Galactic, and require security guarantees. Usually it's the Grrumm Empire and the other galactic frontier powers that provide those guarantees."

Katie coughed. "Which is all very interesting, but we have more immediate concerns."

Katie checked that everyone got her point. They needed to get down to brass tacks. "The key point is that this means divisions in the Trade Union ranks that we'll be able to take advantage of.

"These economic interest groups break out along species lines too. For instance, the Limers, or Climbers, are mostly station builders, owners, or operators. They're conservative and not inclined to sticking their necks out. They've got no interest in seeing the Grrumm Empire or the gate system extended to the systems their stations are in. Keep that in mind. Even if one of them isn't willing to help us, they'll not likely want to aid the Grrumm either."

"Also, most of the small-time traders, ship owners, ship captains, and crews of FTL capable ships working out of the Trade Hubs are Swish, a.k.a. Swimmers."

"A slippery lot," Amy commented.

"Yes, although they're less blatantly opportunistic than the Snouts," Katie said.

"Who isn't?" Susan snarked.

"Indeed, but like the Snouts, they can be expected to supply both information and some logistical help. Keep in mind they'll want to keep that help low-profile. They won't want either the Trade Union or the Grrumm to catch them at it, but they will provide help."

"For a profit," Susan added.

"Of course, that's business," Katie said patiently. "Respect that. Be polite. All the evidence is that Swimmers play the long game, and that those that don't respect them tend to have mysteriously bad luck."

"Bad luck?" Susan snorted. "I can respect that."

"Good. Now the Ras-Kas."

"They seem like intelligent prairie dogs to us," Hood said. "The most common Galactic nickname is 'Grass Lovers'."

Katie nodded. "Another major group in the Trade Union, they're less traders than they're merchants and industrialists. Their main interest is in building up and expanding their settlements. Well-hidden settlements, generally, out here. They favor becoming part of civilized space as soon as possible."

"Don't trust them," Susan translated.

"That's right," Katie confirmed. "Nothing personal and all that, but their interests and ours tend to diverge. Although if we seem to offer security, they might be interested in that. Also, when it comes to munitions, ship parts, and other manufactures, they're the main source outside of civilized space. We want to keep our channels as open to them as we can."

Katie looked around. "You see how complicated this can get?"

"Anyhow, the remaining big specie you see in the Trade Union are the Varkoids. They're big ant-eater like creatures. Their Galactic nickname 'Big Ones'. They're small to medium business people. They're not sneaky, opportunistic, or untrustworthy. In fact, they're almost pathologically honest and trustworthy. Very transactional, but you get exactly what you pay for at the agreed price. Doesn't matter if it's a beer or a shipload of FTL drive parts from up-arm. If they have any bias at all, it's towards whoever provides a secure, predictable business environment. Otherwise, it's cash on the barrelhead for whatever and whoever, no questions asked."

"Sound like decent people," Susan mused.

"Talking about decent, likable people," Katie replied, "there's one group we haven't had a lot of contact with but every one that has enthuses about. They're the 'Sambur'. 'Rock Weasels', 'Diggers', or 'Borrowers' in Galactic slang. They're asteroid miners. They don't own a lot of FTL capable ships. They do have mining stations in most Frontier systems with any mineral wealth. They provide most of the minerals in the Frontier area, both for local use and as a major trade good that goes up-arm. They're not organized much above the mining colony or station level. They make a point of getting along with everyone as well as they can."

"Information and some minerals?" Haralson asked.

"That's right," Katie replied.

"My head is starting to hurt," Commodore Wolf Hoffman said. He was Katie's new Chief of Staff. Wolf had been a year ahead of Katie at the Academy. So although he wasn't an old friend, and Katie hadn't worked with him closely before, she did have a good sense of what sort of person he was. She didn't expect any problems from him. Katie figured he was trying to signal to her that she needed to wrap this evolution up sooner than later.

"And I haven't even mentioned the Star Rats, the Lizards, the Squids, or the independent Grrumm yet," Katie responded.

"Ouch," Hoffman said with a smile.

"Okay, to sum up then. The Star Rats, Galactic nickname 'Builders', are organized system by system. Those in the Solar System are allies of a sort. The rest are going to tend to be coldly neutral. They might trade air, water, food, and some minerals.

"Next the Lizards, the Galactics have nicknamed them the 'Scaly Ones'. They are insanely aggressive genocidal murder lizards. They are probably, now that we've defeated them, our best friends. Only we gutted their navy and confined them to their own systems. They don't want to be part of anyone's empire either, but they prefer us to the Grrumm and having to be civilized. They'll help us as much as they can.

"The Squids, 'Tentacles' to most Galactics, are a bit of a mystery. One group of them up-arm is considered one of the Elder Races. The ones we know here are some sort of religious offshoot, sort of like our Mormons. They don't want to lose the ocean depths on Earth we sold them, but otherwise their politics are a mystery. They're insanely intelligent and possess very high tech. Given that and their Elder Race cousins, nobody seems inclined to rattle their cage. Best we don't either."

Taking a deep breath, Katie looked around. "And that, friends, is all. You've got plenty to study. Your orders are to follow roughly the routes in your briefings. You may divert when it seems profitable, and if it doesn't take you too far away from the other Task Forces. You're to make all the friends you can. Be ready to fight if necessary. Got that?"

Nods and the odd "Yes, ma'am," greeted that. "Dismissed."

Contemplating the Future

Katie was alone in her cabin on the *Bonaventure*. It was a suite, really. It had not just a sleeping pod, but a small private office, a little living room with several chairs and a coffee table, and a small kitchenette. She didn't necessarily have to impose on her steward when she wanted a hot beverage or snack at some odd hour.

She'd come here immediately following the O-group on Goddard Station, but with the meeting going over time, the length of the trip out to where the *Bonnie* and her escorts were moored, and all the ceremony of a ship and fleet welcoming its admiral, it was now well into the evening.

Katie was tired, but there were still a few more chores to do before she could get some sleep.

Assuming command of a fleet didn't involve just ceremony, there was a degree of inevitable electronic "*paperwork*" involved. Additionally, Katie wanted to do something of a mental post-mortem on the O-group.

Until she'd tried presenting it all succinctly and clearly to her assembled subordinates, she'd not truly comprehended just how complicated a situation they were going into. It'd seemed simple: go up-arm, see what's there, and try to make as many friends as possible. Deal with any obvious threats. There. Simple. No, not really. And she needed to consider that fact.

She also needed to consider just how each of the officers reporting to her had reacted to her briefing. She couldn't hope to micromanage them even if she'd wanted to. More often than not, the different task forces weren't even going to be in the same star system. She needed to know how to point the task force commanders in the right direction, and how they'd react in various possible scenarios.

So, there was that.

And, finally, and certainly not least to Katie, there was this data chip that Radison had given her. Which apparently contained some messages from her grandmother. The grandmother Katie hadn't been there for when she was dying. Katie still felt guilty about that. She wasn't going to ignore her grandmother's last words.

With that thought, Katie got up from where she'd been resting and made herself a thick, creamy hot chocolate in a large mug. An Earth habit her spacer soul had taken time to get used to. It brought back memories of the snow-bound chalets she'd stayed in while participating in biathlons as a cadet. She'd been a bit of an ugly duckling at the Academy. She'd been awkward and driven, and she'd never thought that one day she'd be thinking back to those days with nostalgia.

Well, surprise, she was.

Sitting down, she dealt with first things first. She looked over reports on the largest fleet humanity had ever assembled, one several times the size of the last one she'd commanded, and she signed off on multiple assertions that it was intact, properly prepared, and generally ready to go. Like she could know for sure, but she didn't spot anything that seemed off. She smirked to herself. She really hoped the bureaucrats at SFHQ didn't mind too much if she got the odd ding or scrape on their shiny new ships. It was entirely possible taking on the galaxy might involve mixing it up a little.

She did her due diligence, but she didn't waste a second more on it than necessary.

Now her officers. What sort of people were they, and what

could she expect from them? Well, Susan had certainly been champing at the bit. If there was any fighting to do, Susan Fritzsen was certainly up to it. Katie didn't have to worry about that. Only as much as it pained her, Katie wasn't certain her old friend was going to prove to be much of a diplomat. She was going to have to keep an eye on that.

Amy, on the other hand she could count on to be diplomatic. Amy was good with people of whatever culture or species. As a former Scout Group leader, she could be counted on to handle the scouting and exploration parts of her job better than average, too. With Amy having experience in both logistics and engineering, Katie could count on Amy's Task Force being well supplied and in good shape. The only uncertainty with Amy was how well she could handle larger ships in a standalone fight. Katie would try to coach her in tactics. Amy was a quick learner and solid. It should work out.

Wong and Smith, she didn't know as well as Fritzsen and Sarkis.

Wong had proven competent in fleet command under battle conditions. It was a relief, that. On the other hand, he was very by the book and Katie didn't really expect he'd prove much more than competent. Diplomatically, she expected a similar performance. Katie didn't expect he'd make many missteps, but she also didn't expect he'd show much imagination. She'd have to occasionally look over his shoulder to see he wasn't missing opportunities. Also to be certain he was meeting expectations.

Smith was the subordinate she had the least experience with. He wasn't a friend. He'd been too senior to her for much of her career for that, and he'd been busy in training command during her last expedition. You'd think he was the one of them she'd be most concerned about.

Only she wasn't. Smith was old school Space Force, but he had a sterling reputation for laid back competence. He got results, but somehow his subordinates all loved him. His bosses had sometimes felt he lacked a certain gravitas, but they never complained about a lack of results.

He was new to fleet command, and you never knew how someone would hold up under independent command until they actually had it, but Katie didn't really doubt he'd do well. She'd keep an eye open for the possibility she was wrong all the same.

As for Vane, Haralson, McLeod, von Luck, and Hoffman, they were all competent professionals and good people, and most of all none of them were likely to be out in the deep dark having to make critical decisions far away from her oversight.

So, some caveats and some things to look out for, but it looked like she had a good command team she could depend on.

She sighed. It was nice to think so. She took a large sip of her cocoa.

Now Radison's little gift.

What had possessed her grandmother to prepare such a thing?

Well, only one way to find out.

Having checked the data chip was safe, Katie placed it into her main console and played it.

An image of her bedridden grandmother appeared. "Katie, if you're seeing this, then you've survived both physically and politically to reach high command. In fact, I suspect Pete has delayed rather too long to give these missives to you. Pete is very smart, and good at political calculations. Unfortunately, he lacks gut instincts when it comes to politics and people generally. He also tends to be better at pursuing goals than setting them."

Katie, despite nobody being present to see it, nodded automatically. She couldn't argue with her grandmother's assessment.

"So, my first piece of advice to you; you're going to have to make up his lack in those qualities. I can see you making faces, granddaughter, suck it up. I have no doubt you don't like it, but I also have no doubt you're a political player now, and Pete is a valuable ally. You're going to need all the allies you can get. A second piece of advice."

Katie sighed and paused the recording. She'd loved her grandmother, but, good heavens, even dead, she was trying to control events. Still, these were the woman's dying words. Katie wasn't going to ignore them. She gave herself a few moments to feel sad and tired, and restarted the recording.

"Damn. There I go again. Sorry, Katie. I wish I had the time to do this again and get it right. I love your mother and messed it up with her. I love you too, and we're far more alike. You made an old woman's heart glad, and not just because I had hopes you'd continue my legacy, but also just for yourself. Your enthusiasm and determination to do what's right, your optimism and conviction that a single person can make a real difference, all brightened my days. Thank you. Thank you and congratulations. I don't know what's going to happen out around Ganymede, and I don't know for sure how Pete's special research project has worked out, but I suspect success in both cases. I'm convinced you will have had a major hand in ensuring that success. Also, that you're not giving yourself enough credit. So, congratulations."

Katie wiped an unaccountably wet eye dry.

"And, like the misogynistic bastards like to say, *'the reward for a job well done in this man's Space Force is a harder job'.* Har! And, dear, not more of the same. I can't know the details, but from my own experience and from a careful reading of history, I think I can offer some useful advice." Here her grandmother chuckled. The chuckle turned into a hacking cough.

Katie would have been concerned if she hadn't already known how that had turned out.

"Presumptuous of me, I know," her grandmother continued. She didn't sound all that contrite. "But if I'm right, given the paucity of up-and-coming talent in the Space Force, and the demands probably being made on it, you're still pretty young." Her grandmother sighed. "I like to think experience has some value even if it ends up with you being old, tired, and then dying. I can't know the details of what you're facing, so it's going to seem like a collection of platitudes. No sane person can handle too many of those at one time, so I've broken my advice up into sections titled with various questions you might be asking yourself."

Katie paused the replay and checked to see that this was the case. It was. There was a table of contents. It had entries like; *"What to do when there are no good options"*, and *"Who can you trust?*". Marvelous. Katie resumed playing her grandmother's words.

Her grandmother wheezed. "I'm not so good with sugar, but maybe small doses will help the medicine go down. Even if you choose to disregard my advice, I hope it helps you think, and that maybe it'll be some solace that others have faced problems like yours before."

Katie nodded. It wasn't exactly a comforting thought, but reassuring maybe?

"I'm sure you're busy, but a couple of more thoughts before ending up this episode of *'Letters from Grandma'*." The old lady smirked.

Katie smiled. She'd only occasionally seen this mischievous side of her grandmother.

Her grandmother coughed some more. "You were a superb, if troublesome, junior officer. Too much ambition and thinking for yourself, it makes trouble for your superiors. Junior officers are supposed to solve problems for their bosses. Not create them. Now you've got independent command and you're discovering you sometimes have to figure out what to do, not just how to do it. Also, a lot more people management. I hope you're better at massaging people's egos than I was." She sighed.

Katie heaved a sigh herself. She'd like to think she'd learned a bit more about how to manage people, and lead them too, but it'd not come easily, that was for sure.

"Anyhow, if you're viewing this, it's because in Pete's judgment you're now in high command." She giggled. That was startling. "Politics! A whole different game again. A different set of decisions to make and ones of much more consequence."

Katie grimaced. Wasn't that true?

Her grandmother's image smiled at her. The old lady's eyes glinted in her sadly worn face. "But your choices are more constrained. You never believed me before when I tried to tell you that our ability to influence events as individuals is quite limited. But it's true, isn't it? Your choices are more consequential now, but also more limited. I'd bet my left lung, which I assure you I can't spare, it's so. And, although consequences aren't clear, at times it will seem none of your choices are good ones. Sometimes you're just looking for the least bad choice."

Katie nodded. She wasn't sure about only bad choices, but the bit about murky consequences seemed right.

Her grandmother frowned. "Even worse, sometimes you'll have to choose between two good but mutually exclusive options. Sometimes, you'll have to unfairly gore somebody's ox. Don't automatically favor current friends or placate possible enemies. Calculate. Talk to Pete or someone like him. Friends will forgive you up to a point. Some people will never be grateful. It's tough. Accept that and do your best. People will always be buttering you up. Don't let it go to your head."

Katie thought of all the victory celebrations she'd attended and after that the flattering invitations to give talks to august bodies. A lot of people had been very effusive in praising her. She didn't think it'd gone to her head, but she wasn't entirely sure.

Her grandmother frowned. "I know you hate the word, but you need to play attention to cliodynamics. There is no perfect scientific model of history. There's no mathematical formula for predicting the future." She heaved a deep sigh and gave a short cough. "I used to think so. Not literally, I was never that naïve. Social structures show patterns over time though, and I thought it only sensible to take advantage of that. I still think that. Only I underestimated the impact of unpredictable outside events."

Katie bit a lip. It wasn't hard to imagine what her grandmother meant.

Her grandmother snorted. "The Star Rats turning up out of the blue completely upturned the plans my friends and I had." She stared hard at something outside of camera range for a second. "It did shake us all out of a complacent stagnation and progressively worse centralization of power in incompetent hands, though. The way things were going, we were expecting the outbreak of a civil war between Earth on one hand, and Mars and the Belt on the other. Sooner, and with a less prepared Space Force, than has actually happened. That would have been catastrophic. The Star Rats turning up refocused Earth's politicians on space, and the Space Force in particular.

Unfortunate that it may lead us to reach for the stars before we're ready. I can't go into detail on that. I can't know what's happened and I'm going to have to talk around the possibilities." She frowned. "Awkward that, sorry. My point is that you have to allow for surprises, but that undisturbed social structures have certain patterns it behooves you to pay attention to. Enough said. Love you. Hope this helps." She smiled. "You go get them, girl."

Katie smiled in return. "You bet, grandma."

* * *

At least the *Celestial Dominance* had reached Damp orbit. Rrolff surveyed the cloud-wreathed planet from his observation deck.

Only the odd glimpse of blue and occasional sickly green showed through the expanses of white. Almost five claws out of six of the planet's surface was ocean or shallow seas, and what land there was consisted of islands and micro-continents. And that land was scattered in a way that did not impede the place's ocean currents, and was not so placed as to induce the growth of ice anywhere. Of the relatively few mountains, only one set, on a micro-continent situated in the mid-northern latitudes, was so located as to cast a rain shadow.

That rain shadow created the only patch of somewhat dry land on Damp's surface. It was there that its main settlement, Not-So-Damp, was located. A name selected by a survey ship captain lacking gravitas many, many seasons ago. Not that Damp had much in the way of seasons.

Damp was not a place many Grrumm wished to live.

Doubtless one reason it'd not served as a good base for further expansion down-arm.

The place wasn't totally useless. It paid its way most seasons. It exported a surprising variety of medicinal plant products, as well as wood and fish products.

Unfortunately, the planet lacked much in the way of both fossil fuels and minerals. The system's small sparse asteroid belt failed to compensate for the planet's lack of minerals. A decent sized gas giant did provide support for a ship refueling station.

So neither the planet nor the system were a burden to the

Empire, but neither were they a good base for expansion across the frontier. Or great support for an expedition down-arm either, much to Rrolff's chagrin. The bulk of the supplies for his expedition were having to be imported from further into civilized space.

A space soldier stepped onto the observation deck. Thumping his chest in salute, he announced, "Sir! Your guest has arrived."

"Show him in," Rrolff directed.

Rrolff's guest was a sleek Swish, one of the species known vulgarly as "Swimmers". He was a Trade Union merchant recently arrived in-system from down-arm. The Empire's sources reached out less than a hand past the frontier, and the new barbarians, the humans, sometimes called the "Furless Ones", were well over a dozen jumps down-arm. It was Rrolff's hope that politely interrogating the Trade Union member would provide some information about what he was facing. He wanted to wrap this expedition up as tidily as possible.

In addition, it was in accord with the advice provided by the *Book of Barbarians*. The book advised "*seek all sources of information, both the meanest and oddest, as well as the respectable and obvious, and listen carefully. Welcome the strange and surprising as they carry the most information. Listen for the unexpected breaking of a twig in the forest.*"

Very poetic, true, but the meaning was clear despite that. Rrolff intended to take the advice to heart.

The Trade Union merchant entered the room. Small and slender compared to the Grrumm, he was all the same poised and dignified. He halted a short distance from Rrolff and, giving an adequate bow, waited for the Lord Earl to speak. He had some manners at least.

Rrolff returned the bow and gestured to a little table with two chairs, one suitable for a Swish and the other for a Grrumm. The table held a tea service. The tea service was several generations old and of the finest porcelain. Anything less might have been taken as a subtle insult. It was always wise to keep one's best foot forward when meeting with a new acquaintance. "Please, Captain Steady Hoarder, sit and enjoy some tea with me."

Once they were seated, and tea poured, and sipped, Rrolff got right to the point. "So, Captain, what news from down-arm? What do you know of these newcomers, the 'Humans' I believe they're called."

"Ah, yes, the 'Furless Ones' some are calling them informally, though it's not quite caught on. Not vicious, and they didn't seem to be much of a threat at first, not like the 'Scaly Ones'." Steady Hoarder paused and stroked his whiskers briefly. He glanced at the porcelain pot and cups arrayed before him. "They do have some excellent versions of tea. We were really hoping the production areas on their home planet might be spared any unfortunate accidents."

"We all enjoy a good hot brew," Rrolff agreed.

Steady Hoarder bobbed his head in amusement. "And those of us in the Trade Union a good profit. We had hoped, too, that the humans would bear the greater part of the cost of containing the Scaly Ones as well as the ever-present Snout pirates. As their dues for being allowed to join the wider galactic community."

"You consider those outside the gated systems as part of the galactic community?"

"The wider community. As children sitting in the children's dining area for dinner. Children do grow up, those that survive, and you must deal with them as adults when they're older. Best not to create unnecessary resentments while they're still young."

"Indeed. How has that gone with these humans?"

"They are like juveniles that have just had a great growth spurt. They're clumsy with being larger and more powerful than they're used to. They stumble about without knowing what they're doing. They create disruption and do damage unintentionally, and not always even realizing what they've done. They do seem amiable and well intentioned. The Trade Union wishes them no harm. The guidance of a senior race might benefit them if they're wise enough to accept it."

"I'm personally sympathetic to that perspective," Rrolff said. "Only it has been reported that they appeared in orbit above the Assherraskillas home world and bombarded its surface, inflicting severe damage and forcing them to unconditionally surrender. Rumor holds they threatened genocide. This is not peaceful defensive behavior. It crosses a clear, long established red line. Are these reports wrong? Are the rumors ill-founded?"

Steady Hoarder fidgeted. Rrolff found that fascinating. Next to the Grrumm themselves, the Swimmers were renowned for being imperturbable even in the worse circumstances. They were notorious for finding the positive aspects of the most inauspicious developments. Steady Hoarder bobbed his head. "True, the bare facts appear disturbing. The real situation is less clear. The humans were not favored to win their contest with the Scaly Ones. I lost considerable funds myself betting against them, but all the same was relieved when they prevailed. They struck sneakily and hard against a vulnerable point in the Scaly One defenses. If the Scaly Ones had been less offensively oriented, that vulnerability would not have existed."

"My emperor has nevertheless already ordered the assembly of a fleet to settle the situation," Rrolff said. "And appointed me to command it. I cannot question his direction based on could-have-beens or how my stomach feels. The Empire decides policy, as it has for millennia, based on cold, hard indisputable facts of a sort not susceptible to interpretation. You understand?"

Steady Hoarder bobbed his head. "Yes, I understand, but I also greatly regret it."

"Do you have solid facts about what the humans are doing? Or even news about what they might do next?"

More fidgets from the Swimmer. Fascinating. "They are assembling a fleet in their home system. It will be several times the size of that which visited the Scaly Ones. Given the speed with which the hairless monkeys seem to work, it has probably already formed up and departed. All agree that it will be led by the same young female that led their last fleet."

"Departed? Departed for where? A young female battle leader? Seriously?"

The Swimmer froze like a herd animal, used to being prey, hearing an alarming sound. This was even more disconcerting than his earlier fidgeting. "They have asked permission to visit

Far Seat Trade Hub." He paused. "They have expressed an interest in visiting the Trade Hubs further up-arm."

Rrolff froze himself at this disturbing news. This was extremely aggressive behavior from a supposedly harmless and peaceful species. It could not go unchallenged, but he did not wish to further alarm the Swimmer merchant. He did not pursue the point. "A young female, you say?"

Steady Hoarder perked up. "Yes, a unique and fascinating individual. The humans seem to have more flexible gender roles than many species, and will give great responsibility to young ones who prove themselves capable. They appear to value energy and endurance over wisdom in their battle leaders. Doubtless a consequence of their having only recently been pre-industrial planet-bound barbarians."

Rrolff refrained from commenting that as far as he was concerned they were still barbarians if unfortunately neither pre-industrial nor planet bound. The turn the conversation needed to take next was already going to be distressing enough to the Trade Union merchant. "So, do they remain acceptable trading partners to the Trade Union, then?"

Steady Hoarder flinched. Visibly suppressing an urge to fidget more, he slowly dipped his head in affirmation. "They have dealt with us honestly and to the profit of all. They've met all the conditions for good relations we've required, including helping suppress true threats to peaceful commerce. The Trade Union cannot in good faith appear to refuse to trade with them because of pressure from a third party. We must appear to be neutral middlemen. Our whole existence depends on profitable meditation between the more civilized parts of the galaxy and the less developed and organized ones. We cannot refuse to trade and we cannot refuse to supply the ships that defend us all. If they should become involved in conflict with another friendly party, we would, of course, decline to give them military support. We'd sell them no ammunition, missiles, or weapons." He bobbed his head in an attempt to signal his friendliness. It was a forced gesture.

Rrolff grunted.

Steady Hoarder flinched again.

Rrolff hated so discomforting the merchant, but the Lord

Earl Sweets-Swiper had a job to do. "You will, I have no doubt, report fully to us on all such contacts and any information you gather in the course of them."

"Discreetly, of course," Steady Hoarder replied.

"Of course," Rrolff allowed. He sipped his tea and observed the uneasy Swimmer. "I think we understand each other now," he said. "I will attempt to consider the Trade Union's problems while carrying out my mission, but I will do my duty. When we're done, you'll prepare a written reprise of all we've discussed and a report on everything you know, have heard about, and surmised regards the humans. I expect to receive it before this time tomorrow. You may finish your tea before leaving."

Steady Hoarder gulped his tea with a haste that wasn't quite dignified, rose, bowed, and departed.

Rrolff was left alone with his thoughts.

So, the Trade Union was determined to be as neutral as possible. That was unfortunate, if not totally unexpected. It most likely meant meeting the human fleet beyond easy reach of both side's supply bases. The Imperial forces would not enjoy any logistical advantage. In fact, the supply situation might slightly favor the humans. Yes, quite unfortunate.

Rrolff grumbled to himself and sipped some more tea, letting that sink in. Attempting to pressure the Trade Union into being more helpful was tempting. Succumbing to that temptation might backfire. And tradition, in that case, would not protect him. The *Book of Barbarians* was clear. "*Keep your friends close. The closer, the more perfidious they be. Above all, keep your enemies, the Barbarians, divided. Do not create new enemies. Deal with them one, isolated group at a time.*"

Great advice, he was sure. Only easier said, or written, than done. He was fully aware the Book had been written by experienced commanders but still couldn't help feeling some annoyance.

So the humans might be a real threat and, worse, an urgent one if they'd already started up-arm. He wanted to settle this issue as far from civilized space as possible, whatever the logistical complications that entailed. So, he needed to act quickly, but only after being fully prepared. No contradiction there. And he needed to act decisively, but cautiously, without offending anyone. Again, no contradictions there.

Rrolff snorted. He didn't know whether to be more amused at himself, or sorry for himself. In any case, it was a tricky matter and he needed to calculate carefully what to do.

The classic military solution at an operational level was to seek out the main barbarian force with his own unified and well supplied main force. That done, he'd issue conditions for peace they couldn't accept. Then all he had to do was defeat them decisively and impose slightly harsher conditions. Conditions that would include the disbanding of any major naval forces and accepting Grrumm "advisers" to, if not outright governors in, every major position of authority among the Barbarians.

If he wished to avoid the Emperor's displeasure, he'd best obtain that decisive victory without offending or depending on factions other than the Grrumm Empire itself.

No big deal. Sure.

He could at least severely prioritize the rapid assembly of an adequate logistical train at Damp. He might offend fellow Grrumm, including fellow aristocrats, in the process, but Rrolff was willing to do that.

For dealing with the Trade Union and the factions on the other side of the frontier, he needed more information. Let's face it, he needed advice, too.

It was urgent he have a long talk with his Frontier Force adviser.

A talk likely to be as uncomfortable as it was necessary.

* * *

Rob Hood chewed on a thumbnail. It was a habit he hadn't indulged since he was a kid. Not since before his parents had died prematurely in an accident that'd destroyed their farm dome on Mars. He'd been at pains to appear to be a confident, mature adult ever since.

And, now, as he contemplated how genuinely important his present work was, the confidence of a lifetime spent in the school of hard knocks was dissolving.

Rob looked around his little cabin lit only by the light of his spreadsheet filled computer screen. He felt quite discombobulated. The close confines didn't bother him. They felt cozy and safe. Rob didn't trust safe, but there were no immediate threats to him here. The idea was preposterous.

No, all the threats were a fever dream of assessments of ancient alien texts, and other alien allusions and whisperings. Of the numbers in those spreadsheets. And, of course, they weren't threats to him personally. They were just threats to the fleet he was a part of, and the human race in general. Nothing personal.

Kincaid had soft-peddled the problem they faced in her initial O-group. She'd emphasized the importance of diplomacy. She'd implicitly oversold the likelihood this would be a purely peaceful expedition. She'd emphasized the need to recruit allies over why they'd likely be needed. She'd outlined the need to move up-arm to see what was there, and underplayed the fact that what they'd probably find was a large fleet moving down-arm with the goal of putting humanity firmly in its place. A fleet they'd have to try to stop as far away from the Solar System as possible.

Rob Hood couldn't fault Kincaid's goal of attempting to resolve the issue peacefully. He just didn't think it was very realistic.

Local galactic history was long and consistent. Whenever a potential threat to the Grrumm Empire rose above the horizon, the Empire assembled a force and went out and hammered that threat down.

Consistently and without fail.

Not a very encouraging record from humanity's point of view.

Worse, for the life of him, Rob could not figure out how the Grrumm had achieved that. If it'd been a matter of pure numbers or a distinct and persistent technological edge, he'd have been happier. Those would have been problems he could have understood, briefed Kincaid on, and maybe proposed solutions for.

The records humanity had purchased with parts of its home planet were extensive and detailed and not very helpful. They recorded the names of Emperors and their dictates, the names of commanders and the missions they'd been assigned, and the various entities they'd fought. They did not record much about either logistics or weapons.

Time after time, the Empire assembled a fleet that crossed the frontier and met opponents roughly equal in numbers and technology and prevailed in a succession of actions. Without fail and apparently without ever taking significant losses. It was a mystery that had Rob tearing his hair out in frustration trying to solve. He was going to have to bring the problem to Kincaid's attention without a ghost of a solution to it to propose. That did not make him happy.

But enough of that. He had some more immediate duties. For purely logistical reasons, it was essential they recruit some allies. It'd also be very nice if they could get some help in actual operations. They could never have too many scouts. It was unlikely they could win in just one big operation, so help with repairs and replenishment in the aftermath of battles could also prove decisive.

And to get allies, they needed to be able to find them, talk to them, and convince them it was in their interest to throw in with the humans.

Kincaid had flagged this as currently the main responsibility of her Task Force commanders.

It was Rob's job to provide them with the information they'd need to carry out those tasks.

A job complicated by the fact that all those potential allies seemed dedicated to flying below the radar. Apparently, they'd been quite successful at doing so. The Swimmers, the Builders, the Grass Lovers, the Roamers, and the Diggers all had long histories, but their numbers and the exact locations of their homes were rarely mentioned. Their exact role in the various campaigns of the Empire was vague. They seemed prone to providing the Empire verbal support, but no substantive aid.

Not that any of them ever seemed averse to making a profit.

But although it went unsaid, they seemed happy to do what they could to slow down the Empire's spread. Life in the civilized Grrumm Empire seemed safe, but reading between the lines, all non-Grrumm were second-class citizens. They were permitted to exist, but not allowed to get ahead.

Rob figured the humans could likely expect as much help from most of them as they could provide short of being obvious. He hoped he was right about that.

In the meantime, he'd smooth the process of procuring that aid, by providing the fleet with as much information on the history and values of each group as he could.

He'd put together some simple phrase books for the various languages. He'd also assemble a handbook on body language and social mores.

He'd add to Kincaid's list of what each group could likely provide, and what they'd value receiving in return.

It was going to be a lot of work. Only some of it could be delegated to various subordinates. He was really missing Wootton.

Still, it was mechanical and kept him busy.

It was a relief from contemplating the bigger, more ineffable issues.

Gathering Intelligence

Despite himself, Thorn-Paw found himself enjoying the *Celestial Dominance's* observation deck. He'd spent most of his career on much smaller ships, and was not only more comfortable on them, but believed them to be more useful for most purposes. Still, larger vessels did have their points, and being able to stand in comfort, alone - imagine that - and view a planet and the space around it was one of them.

Currently, the view was one of the planet Damp, and the bright dots of the fleet orbiting it. It was very unusual to be able to directly see visual evidence of ships in space. The distances were usually just too great. So, Thorn-Paw did feel privileged.

Of course, he'd have been happier if the planet he was looking at hadn't been Damp and if the many ships he was looking at had included more transports and other support ships. It was taking far too long to assemble the fleet's supply train.

Something, multiple somethings really, had changed since the Empire had launched its last punitive expedition across the frontier. Some of those things Thorn-Paw had seen for himself during his long career with the Frontier Fleet. Many of the trends, he was sure, had been present for generations beforehand. None of them were positive for the Empire.

Thorn-Paw had persistently, more out of a sense of duty than anything else, warned of their deleterious effect. He'd been thanked for his opinion and otherwise ignored by his superiors and the intelligence bureaucrats back home. At times Thorn-Paw had had the impression they'd been rather amused by his sense of urgency.

Well, at least when he'd raised them earlier this shift with Lord Earl Sweets-Swiper that worthy had been anything but amused. Politely but distinctly annoyed, but not amused. Sweets-Swiper was a circumspect creature, but as best as Thorn-Paw could discern he didn't feel pointing out problems neither of them could do much to solve right now was very useful. Sweets-Swiper seemed to think it a distraction from his more immediate problem of expeditiously assembling a fleet with sufficient logistical support. This fleet was going to need to plunge much farther across the frontier than any before it. On one level, this expedition was historically unprecedented. Not something designed to make any normal precedent-loving Grrumm happy.

Thorn-Paw found Sweets-Swiper's attitude understandable. He also thought it short sighted.

The broadening of the near-frontier for generations now was one of those trends he'd warned about. The near-frontier was that area of space not served by the gates but in contact with the civilizations that were, and therefore able to access the technologies they possessed. That didn't mean the peoples and various political entities there were necessarily able to acquire any of those technologies for use, let alone gain some ability to manufacture devices incorporating them, most especially FTL capable ships and modern weapons. That all took time and resources, and a degree of size and continuity it was hard to attain beyond the borders of civilized space.

Additionally, one of the Frontier Fleet's purposes was to restrict the flow of technology outward and maintain the technological differential between the Barbarians and civilized peoples.

Thorn-Paw snorted. That was a dam that had long since started to leak. There was still a big lake behind it, but a lot of water had made its way downstream too. The near-frontier was now much broader than the Frontier Fleet's reach. Thorn-Paw couldn't remember the last time an Imperial ship, even a small scout had visited the farthest out Trade Hub, Far Seat. Nicknamed the Butt End of Nowhere, it had nothing there to attract imperial attention and the Frontier Fleet had had enough troubles to attend to further in.

The fact was that previously, species that reached the stars did so with inferior technology and when they came into contact with galactic technology, they didn't get enough time to absorb and adopt it before being overcome by more civilized, earlier comers. Unfortunately, that was no longer so true.

When Sweets-Swiper had asked Thorn-Paw for advice, Thorn-Paw had raised all these issues. He'd been asked to focus on issues within their purview. So, he'd raised the issues that there were many fewer Grrumm merchants and merchantmen working out past the frontier, even in the near beyond, then there'd once been. Whether because the Grrumm had become soft and complacent or because the other races had become harder competition, Thorn-Paw wasn't sure, but the fact had long worried him. Specifically, it'd meant the Frontier Fleet often having to depend on alien manned FTL transports for supply, and now there was a deficit of Grrumm manned vessels to hire. Past expeditions had had no problem hiring loyal merchants to supplement their supply trains. The Empire paid well and reliably. But now there simply were too few such ships to be had.

Sweets-Swiper had allowed this was an issue of immediate concern, but had also asked, rather coyly to Thorn-Paw's mind, what either of them could do about it in a timely fashion.

Thorn-Paw hadn't known what to say in reply to that. His face or body language must have given his feelings away. Sweets-Swiper had sighed and poured Thorn-Paw some more tea, heavily sweetening it with a large dollop of nectar. Nectar Thorn-Paw recognized as being the very expensive product of Sweet-Swiper's own estates. He'd then promised to look into the matter later when the expedition was done, and to raise the matter with the Imperial government. He'd then got right to the point.

Lord Earl Rrolff Sweets-Swiper's main concern was trying to ensure as much supplemental supply from the alien races in the near-frontier as possible. He also wanted to deny his potential opponents as much such supply as possible. He conceded this was a lesser concern because he understood from his reading of history that groups on the frontier also bet on winners. The Empire always won when it exerted itself. So that wasn't a big issue.

Thorn-Paw had agreed this was true, but told Sweets-Swiper many parts of the frontier hadn't seen much of the Empire for generations.

Sweets-Swiper had twitched in displeasure at that, but said nothing.

Thorn-Paw had recommended reaching out to the Ras-Kas, the Grass Lovers, for help and being rather generous in the deals struck. Good will being more precious than any mere metal. Also, of course, to remain on good terms with the Trade Union even if they were a pack of two-faced, treacherous, untrustworthy money-grubbers and short sighted, to boot. He'd recommended deals with Varkoids as they could be depended on to keep the letter of the agreements they made.

He recommended not trusting the Swimmers or the Snouts but not being unduly harsh with them either. Conversations and the odd small bribe might bring in much useful information.

There was not much point in annoying the Diggers, the Builders, or the religiously deviant Tentacles whom they could expect to encounter, but neither could much be expected from them.

None of this had appeared to please the Lord Earl, but he had thanked Thorn-Paw for his advice before allowing him to finish his tea.

It'd been good tea.

But Thorn-Paw wasn't sure that much else had come of the meeting.

Still, Sweets-Swiper was trying. It'd have to do.

It had in the past.

* * *

Katie hadn't wanted a set of big Varkoid mercenary bodyguards. Only, not only had Hood, Wootton, and von Luck insisted they were necessary, but so had friends like Susan and Amy. Traitors. They'd worn her down in the end.

They'd told her straight out she wouldn't be safe on Far Seat Trade Hub's decks. The price on her head was just too high.

The result was that Katie didn't get to see much as she moved through the Trade Hub's bazaar. Disappointing. It was a fascinating place, unlike the backs of her Varkoid guards. The Varkoids were the tallest and the widest of the alien species she'd seen and they weren't transparent.

Also, she didn't see the assassin coming. One moment they were all shuffling along, the next there was an explosion and bodies were flying everywhere. Hood beside her was knocked over. Katie herself would have landed on her butt, if she'd not bounced off the back of the Varkoid behind her. Grabbing him and pulling herself upright, she was just in time to see the assassin lunging at her. He held an oily green dagger in his extended hand. Katie was so close that stepping sidewards brought her inside his reach as his lunge went past her to her right. She deflected his arm with a hard whack to the inside of his wrist. The crazed looking Swimmer was smaller and lighter than she was. A palm strike with her left hand to his face forced him back, and she followed up with a kick to his head fueled by plentiful adrenaline and frustration.

Before the would-be assassin could pick himself up, he was grabbed by her rallying guards.

Then the station authorities arrived.

The ensuing confusion and loud babble went on much longer than the violence that had precipitated it. Katie derived a glimmer of amusement from realizing she was going to be late to yet another important meeting on account of an assassination attempt. It was beginning to resemble a pattern. She idly wondered, while her guards argued with the station authorities, whether someone would accuse her of hating meetings so much, she'd rather risk death than attend one. She snorted.

Hood looked at her with an expression of puzzlement.

"Maybe if all these meetings come with a risk of assassination, I'm going to have to give them up," she deadpanned.

Hood looked annoyed. "This is a critical meeting. Wootton went to a lot of trouble to set it up. Not a lot of the Galactics here on the Trade Hubs even want to talk to us. Nothing personal, mind you, so to speak, just that it's a bad, unsafe bet to be associated with humans right now." He looked around at the chaos surrounding them by way of emphasizing his point. His gaze lingered on a lumpy sheet covering the body of an individual who'd been one of their Varkoid guards and the stoic figure of another guard sitting nearby, injured and in obvious pain despite his attempt not to show it.

"Loosen up, Lieutenant Commander," Katie retorted. "Believe me, I understand how serious this is. And I appreciate both Wootton's efforts and yours. Only nobody can stay too keyed up for too long. You'll wear yourself out." She gave him a smile. They knew each other well enough for that. "I'm hoping you'll last for the long term. Okay?"

Hood nodded. "Sorry, Admiral. I guess it's old age. The worry is getting to me. Given your reputation, our various potential allies want to talk to you personally, but if we lose you, I don't know what we'll do."

"I'm sure you'll manage," Katie said in a distracted manner. The hubbub around them seemed to be quieting down.

"I'm not," Hood answered.

Before he could elaborate, the head of her bodyguard loomed before Katie. Katie almost regretted she'd not kept her marine bodyguards. They were less intimidating. Unfortunately, more offensive to Galactic sensibilities, it seemed. And the heavens above knew they had to be sensitive to Galactic sensibilities. "Yes, Markraatov of Clear Ponds, Force Leader," she said, giving the being his full name and title out of respect. Just "Mark" might work informally, but one of his people had just died defending her and others wounded. Katie figured a little respect was due. "What can I do for you?"

The big being bowed as deeply as the room they had

permitted. "Forgive me, Admiral Katie, but it is we who took your gold and who have failed you. I should be asking what we can do for you."

Katie grinned and then remembered to bob her head in the Galactic equivalent. She'd told Markraatov to just call her "Katie". Apparently, he'd heard her, but not fully understood. "You kept me alive. I am satisfied that you have honored your contract. You have my condolences on your losses." She spent hours of every already crowded day practicing her trade galactic and she could now speak in it like that without too much effort.

"You are too kind, Admiral Katie. It is a price of the trade. In any event, we are now ready to continue on."

And so they carried on, soon reaching the doors of a rather posh restaurant in a less than entirely reputable part of the station. Entering, they were directed to a large backroom. Apparently, the establishment frequently catered to private parties.

Arriving in that backroom, they found two individuals seated around a very large table. Katie noticed the table was mostly metal, with only the thinnest of wood veneers topping it. The utilitarian aesthetic suggested the room was intended for practical down-to-earth business not show. Interesting. Of the two individuals already present, one was Wootton in civvies, and the other was a slender alien in a hooded robe. The alien, probably a Swimmer Katie guessed, gave her the odd feeling he was channeling a Jedi Master. Maybe she was still feeling the after-effects of the assassination attempt.

"This is your contact?" Katie asked Wootton.

"No," Wootton answered Katie in a barely polite tone. "Your guards are going to have to leave."

"No. Your guards are going to have to leave, *Admiral*," Katie replied with patient amusement.

Wootton's lips twitched. Was she trying to suppress a smile? "Your guards are going to have to leave, Admiral," she said. She sighed and looked about. "I'm sorry, but our contact is very skittish. With reason. They won't talk if there are third parties in the room. I told them there'd be me, Shadowguide," she nodded to the be-robed, probable Swimmer, "you, and

Lieutenant Commander Hood here, and that was all. I vouched in detail for everyone of us."

Katie looked at Markraatov on the other side of her from Hood.

"You understand, Admiral Katie, that we cannot take further risks with your safety. If you do not co-operate, our contract will be void."

"Yes, but this meeting is essential," Katie answered.

The big Varkoid stood still for a moment. He looked up and away, staring briefly at an empty corner of the room. He brought his gaze back to Katie. "A compromise, perhaps? You vouch for all the individuals here," he glanced Shadowguide's way, "the spy and this shy contact, too. We check the room for problems and for all its accesses, then we place guards outside each entrance. Is that acceptable?"

"Yes," Katie replied. "Good. It is agreed."

It took a while. Katie seated herself in a Varkoid guard-vetted chair at a place at the table they'd also checked, and inspected the other people present in the room. She was particularly interested in the "Shadowguide" person, but that individual remained calmly inscrutable. Wootton looked tired, but not unhappy. Sort of like a long-distance runner who could see the finish line. Hood was tired too, but seemed edgier. An interesting turnaround.

Finally, the guards finished up and left.

Katie cleared her throat. "Who is Shadowguide? And why is she or he here?"

"Shadowguide is a spy. He has been keeping careful tabs on me," Wootton replied.

Katie blinked. "And you thought it'd be simpler to just have him in the room?"

"Yes, ma'am."

Katie looked at Hood. He shrugged. "Very well. Who's he a spy for?" she said to Wootton.

"Don't know, ma'am. He's been rather vague."

Katie looked Shadowguide's way. "Who are you a spy for?"

Shadowguide chittered softly. Swimmer laughter. "Not for the Empire or any of the Grrumm. For a co-operative, shall we say, of like-minded individuals interested in a frontier region that is as peaceful and orderly as such a region can be."

"The Trade Union then?"

"The Trade Union profits from differences between the gated parts of the galaxy and those that have not yet joined that community. It has an interest in maintaining those differences. It is sometimes heavy-handed and short-sighted in the efforts it makes to sustain what is ultimately unsustainable. Neither I nor my associates approve of this."

"What do you think of us humans?"

"As long as you are not an overly aggressive force for peace and order, we approve of you."

Katie frowned. And who got to decide that? Based on what criteria? She wasn't sure it was worth trying to pursue that. "And hasn't the Grrumm Empire long been the main force for peace and order in this part of the galaxy?"

"For a long time they have been, but the Grrumm have become complacent and content to play in their own gardens. Admirable in its way, but it means they are much less of a force for anything on the frontier and beyond. Far Seat, even Clear Ponds further up-arm, are lucky if they see a single Imperial scout in a generation. They have been left on their own. Grrumm merchants and explorers have all but disappeared. The few individuals that remain feel little connection to the Empire."

"It seems to me you're sitting firmly on the fence. You understand the idiom? Why should we trust you? Why should we let you sit in here?"

"I understand the idiom." That fact as well as the fact they'd been speaking English told Katie that Shadowguide had indeed been studying humanity quite carefully. She wasn't sure how she felt about that. Shadowguide continued, "As I have said, we are quite definitely on the side of peace and good order. The Empire has been a force for that since before your people invented agriculture, but now it is no longer the force it once was. Sometime within the foreseeable future, it will have to cede the role it has filled for so long. If you can show that you're the dominant force in this region now, and that you will ensure both peace and good order, an equitable order, then we are on your side." "Great," Katie said.

"It is indeed an enviable, if challenging, position to be in," Shadowguide replied. He bobbed his head in a gesture Katie had learned to interpret as a smile from Galactics. "I, for one, believe it is a challenge you can rise to. I can provide you with useful information. I am a friend."

Katie kept her face blank. The wording of the slippery Swimmer's statement was familiar. It was possible, if not certain, this creature was sending a message they weren't willing to make explicit. Katie had become quite dependent on, even fond of Hood and Wootton, but damned if spooks and their smoke and mirror games didn't give her headaches. Give her a good clean straight up fight any day. "Apparently you think we can defeat the Grrumm Empire despite this having never been done before. Why? How?"

Shadowguide graced her with a quick head tilt to one side. None of Katie's studies told her what that gesture might mean, but if he'd been human, she'd have thought it a demonstration of amused inspection. And Shadowguide had studied them. "I do not think you can defeat the Empire in its home territories within gated space. I do think you may be able to defeat its expeditionary force and even press them back as far as a gated system. The one called Damp most likely. If they lose that force, they may not care to be bothered replacing it."

Katie nodded. It was good news indeed. She'd feared that the task she faced might be impossible, that Wong's suggestion of just surrendering and getting the best terms they could, might actually be the best idea. It didn't escape her that there was much, however, that the slippery Swimmer spy hadn't said. "Is that necessary? Do we have to fight them? Does it have to be defeat them or be defeated?"

Shadowguide bobbed his head. "You didn't ask me for news of that fleet. You didn't ask whether it was assembling, how big it was, when it is to leave, where it is going and when it might be expected to arrive here." He nodded to Wootton. "As good as Tanya is. I doubt she has answered all those questions, or that you don't want verification of what answers you have."

"Tanya, is it?" Katie said, looking Lieutenant Wootton's

way.

Wootton gave her a shrug and raised hands. "Shadowguide has his ways and likes to act like he's everyone's friend." She paused and bit a lip. "Seems to work for him."

"Great," Katie said, turning back to Shadowguide. "Okay, yes, I'm interested in answers to those questions. I also figure the more limited and specific my questions, the less likely it is you'll evade them. First things first. I'd like to avoid fighting at all. Contrary to what my record might suggest, I figure the best fight is no fight at all."

"A commendable sentiment," Shadowguide replied. "But as I'm sure both Lieutenant Commander Hood and Lieutenant Wootton have told you, it is not the way of the Empire to suffer potential threats once they've become aware of them. The Empire does not negotiate with threats. It suppresses them. If you wish to surrender, they may accept that, but I do not believe you'll find their terms acceptable. They will insist you disarm. And they will insist on a say in how you run your internal affairs. At the very least, they will insist you accept advisers whose advice you will have to take. Worse terms than you granted the Scaly Ones, in fact."

Katie grimaced. "But they will talk."

"Maybe. Having from their point of view been forced to mount an expedition, they may feel it desirable to demonstrate its power. They will probably insist on talking with their fleet in orbit around your Earth."

"That certainly isn't acceptable," Katie said. "My clear orders are to see the threat doesn't get that close."

"Then I believe you will have to fight." "I see."

"My information is a couple of your weeks old, but at last report their expeditionary fleet was assembling around Damp, some nineteen jumps and another three Trade Hubs up-arm. It is the closest planet in a gated system. If all went well for them and they decided to depend on purchasing needed supplies from the Trade Union at the Hubs, they could be leaving that system as we speak. I do not expect their assembling of their supply train will have gone that quickly. It's been a long time since they last did this and their fleet of

FTL capable civilian ships has dwindled. Also, although the Grrumm are cautious, and usually slow, it's best not to depend on it. They are not cowards and can act quickly if provoked. But usually they proceed cautiously and slowly. They will do their best to assemble a supply train adequate to sustain them as far as your home system. Being cautious, they'll attempt to have sufficient supplies to allow retreat all the way back to Damp. If you depart quickly, you may be able to meet them before they even reach Plenitude, the first Trade Hub after Damp. There will be Frontier Fleet units at Plenitude, but all smaller ships that are no threat to you if your scouts are careful."

"Thank you," Katie said. It was more than she'd hoped to get from the secretive spy. "Supplies?"

"If you deal with those you meet fairly, pay well, and are discreet, you will be able to find supplies of fuel, food, water, and standard galactic tech small munitions such as anti-missile missiles, small anti-ship missiles, and decoys. Nothing with a source that can be easily identified. Nothing free or cheap."

Katie nodded. It was pretty much what Hood and Wootton had already told her. Still, good to have it confirmed. "Thank you again. Allies?"

"The Roamers, Snouts, and Swimmers you encounter will all be predisposed to helping as much as they can in their own ways, but none of them can afford to stick their necks out for you. The Snouts are more inclined to taking risks than others, but by the same token you can never be entirely sure with them. If you can make a deal with a Varkoid like the force leader I just saw, they will stick to the terms of that deal religiously. On the other hand, they're very careful about the deals they make."

"Okay," Katie said. "What about the others? These 'Diggers' I've yet to meet, the Ras-Kas, and the Limers who seem to run the stations. What about them?"

"The Diggers try to get along with everyone. Turn up at one of their stations and they'll sell you minerals and what other supplies they have and tell you what they know. But they don't have much in the way of either supplies or information to give.

The Grass Lovers have no particular feelings about other species. For them, there is their clan and there is everyone else, and they're not inclined to discriminating between flavors of everyone else. They do, however, prize raising their clan status and ensuring its members' safety. Being incorporated into the Empire and therefore eventually gated space will be seen as furthering those goals and therefore they will be inclined to aiding the Empire. They won't be inclined to fighting or taking chances on its behalf. Faced with the possibility of outsized profits, they may allow greed to overcome their desire for increased status. This is important because they're the best source of spare ship parts and munitions."

"Tricky," Katie commented.

"Indeed," Shadowguide agreed. "As for the Limers, they won't feel able to defy the Empire. They like order and they have big fixed assets at risk in the form of the Trade Hubs. They're going to try to stay as far out of it as possible. They'll trade for basics. They won't talk or take sides."

"And the Trade Union will try to play both sides," Katie said.

"Of course," Shadowguide confirmed.

Katie turned her attention to Wootton. "Well, that was a useful summary of what you and Hood have been telling me, I think. Good to get it from the horse's mouth."

Shadowguide chittered lightly.

Wootton gave a slight grimace. "Our friend the horse has also stepped on our contact's lines. I do believe he has something to add, though."

Katie smiled. "But you're not entirely sure. So, the fog of war lies heavy on the land. What's new? Bring him in. Maybe he'll help shed light on some things."

Wootton nodded and, flicking it back into active mode, muttered something into her personal comms device. That done, she addressed Katie, "Another Swimmer in robes like Shadowguide's. He'll use the pass phrase '*deep dive*'."

Katie snickered despite herself. More spy stuff, though practical under the circumstances. She'd forgotten the guards outside. Activating her own device, she passed the news on to them.

Minutes later, Wootton's contact slipped into the room. Seeing Shadowguide, he immediately tossed his head and emitted a loud burst of chittering.

The newly arrived Swimmer pulled back his hood. He was sleek even for a Swimmer. Despite a lackadaisical air, he was somehow possessed of more gravitas than most of them. Katie thought she recognized him.

What's more, since Wootton had claimed she'd run Shadowguide's presence past him, Katie felt certain there was some play-acting going on. She decided to go along with it. "You recognize Shadowguide?" she asked.

The new arrival took the time to seat himself. This was interesting. Katie had expected someone more nervous and deferential. "This creature that calls itself Shadowguide is infamous. Useful that your language has two words for '*very well known*,' that denote reputation as well. We Swish pride ourselves on not leaving unnecessary ripples to mark our passage, but Shadowguide is a half-seen reflection on the water. One is never sure one has seen anything, let alone what it might have been."

Katie managed to place where she'd seen this individual. "Captain Swims Up Creek, I thought you were in the Solar System drumming up business. I hear you commissioned Mars Heavy Industry to build you a new ship."

"Yes, indeed. I'm betting heavily on you, Admiral."

"I'm flattered."

"If you knew the odds being offered, you might not be."

Katie forced a smile and bobbed her head. "And yet here you are."

"I find that if you can survive it, keeping a stake intact, that betting against the odds pays off. One win more than compensates for a few losses."

Katie found this rogue amusing. "Let me guess too, that this being no game, you intend to alter those odds somewhat to your favor. Our favor, I mean."

Swims Up Creek stroked his whiskers smugly. "'*Fair*' can make sense when playing games for entertainment. When one is serious, one takes every advantage possible. To use your English idioms, one fixes the dice or stacks the deck. We Swish

Gathering Intelligence

speak of shaving the sticks, picking the leaves, or stirring the water." He glanced Shadowguide's way as he spoke. Katie figured Shadowguide was a past master at deck stacking. "We Swish have somewhat different games than you humans, that involve throwing things upon the water and seeing what patterns emerge."

"So what patterns do you see and what, um, adjustments might you be making?" Katie asked.

Swims Up Creek looked over at Wootton. "May I assume that our esteemed colleague," he glanced Shadowguide's way when he said that, "has already done the fifty-thousand-foot travel guide introduction?"

Katie thought that informative in two ways. Apparently Swimmers did do sarcasm. Also, it seemed Swims Up Creek was indeed personally betting on humanity long term. Why else spend so much time learning English idioms?

Wootton gave her contact a small twisted smile, and an oddly off-kilter head bob. Seemed the Swimmer entrepreneur wasn't the only one working on his communications skills here. "You may, Captain. Shadowguide covered all the main species, their probable attitudes in the event of conflict, and how they might assist us."

Swims Up Creek stroked his whiskers. "Nothing new or surprising then," he said, "but I imagine it'll save us a little time."

Shadowguide replied with a tilt of his head to this. He looked for all the world like a scientist that's spotted a new insect species.

Swims Up Creek pulled a data chip out of the folds of his robe and placed it in the middle of the table. "I have solid information. Names, places, times, and other information. This identifies other individuals and specific groups willing to meet you and provide actual value. We are risking the wrath of the Grrumm to provide you with help."

"For a price," Hood said. Katie appreciated the fact he'd saved her from playing the villain. Wootton, too, for that matter. Katie wasn't sure what sort of relationship she'd built with the aliens in the room, but she'd obviously put some effort into it.

"Of course," Swims Up Creek replied. "Risk requires reward." He looked Wootton's way again.

"Lieutenant Commander Hood is merely trying to make sure everything is clear from a human perspective," Wootton said. "Our past as tribal warriors is not far behind us and our records include those of societies distinctly non-commercial in their outlook. Ones in which ostensibly the cost of supporting allies or in fighting battles was something an honorable individual would not calculate. I assure you that I understand this is not a rational attitude in the modern galaxy. I strongly believe Admiral Kincaid also understands it, and that Hood himself does, too. I think your superior command of our language and culture has lulled the Lieutenant Commander into forgetting he's not dealing with another human being with human cultural baggage." She looked Hood's way as she said this last.

Hood bobbed his head. "Indeed, forgive my forgetfulness, Captain. In many of our cultures, business, and military types were distinct groups with different belief and value systems. Business types would pretend that all business was a matter of win-win co-operation. Military types would pretend some goals were to be achieved at all costs. I forgot that the wider galaxy has long since moved beyond these misconceptions."

"It is hard work to learn so many new things, Lieutenant Commander. Harder yet to forget old ones. I understand," Swims Up Creek replied with a small, dignified dip of his own head.

"So!" Wootton exclaimed brightly. She was obviously trying to get the conversation back on track. "Perhaps Captain Swims Up Creek can summarize the data he's provided before we wrap this up so that we can ask any needed questions?" She looked around the table, her gaze lingering on Katie. "That sound good?"

Captain Swims Up Creek bobbed his head, folded his paws on the table before him, and looked around.

Katie bobbed her head at him.

Swims Up Creek dipped his head back at her and began. "Most of the people out past the frontier of the gated systems aren't eager to fall into the clutches of either the Spiders or the

Furry Ones. A certain amount of safety and predictability is desirable, but not being permanently subject to the dictates of other species. To work hard to have the fruits of one's efforts skimmed off with no say in the matter is something no thinking being likes. A safe, orderly world is good, but on the basis of mutual accommodation, not coercion." He looked around.

"I think we all feel that way," Hood said.

Swims Up Creek acknowledged that with a slight head dip. "But the way we'd like the world to be and the way it is are not necessarily the same." He paused to let that sink in. "The Grrumm Empire has dominated this part of the galaxy since almost before history begins. Most of our records are not terribly reliable so far back. With time, records are lost and memory fades. What is remembered by some is not always shared with others. But we know there have been several potential challengers to the Empire. Ourselves, the Builders, the Snouts, the Diggers, as well as others no longer extant all had home worlds. We all reached the stars, expecting to find endless vistas for exploration and development."

He chittered lightly.

"We were sadly disappointed. We were all crushed by the Empire's expeditionary fleet. Our home worlds were incorporated into their Empire. Those of us who could not live with that were forced out beyond the frontier. The Empire doesn't seek to kill us all or even deny us profit or the opportunity to flourish as individuals or even small groups. It doesn't, however, accept the existence of any group that could pose any threat to it. Humanity, through no fault of its own, appears to be such a group and now the Imperial fleet is coming for you. Except for maybe some of the Grass Lovers, all of us sympathize with you and would like to see you defeat the Grrumm."

Katie bobbed her head in acknowledgment of that. "We appreciate that," she said.

Swims Up Creek nodded in her direction. He was meeting them more than halfway. "But we have little hope you can do so. In my case, I'm gambling on your success, but most will be much more careful. Some of the Snouts and some other

Swimmers are willing to be seen to be openly supporting you. Some will actively help, but try to hide the fact." He gestured at Shadowguide as he said this. "But, most will help some as long as they don't think that help will be detected by the Grrumm or cost them much. Many will try to strike profitable deals. What I have done is identified these various groups, where they are to be found, what they will want, what they can deliver. It is profitable information and necessary if you wish to meet the Imperial fleet close to Damp and far from the Solar System."

"You don't think we can defeat them in one big battle. You think we're going to have to conduct a fighting retreat back to the Solar System," Katie said.

Swims Up Creek nodded. "Yes." He looked at Wootton. "Lieutenant Wootton and I have together gathered all the records of earlier Imperial punitive expeditions. Oddly though there is some mention of some of their light units being damaged there is no record of any of their heavy ships ever being lost. They can't be everywhere, and their offensive power seems to be no greater than that of any other advanced species, but we think they've got some sort of special defensive technology."

Katie glanced Wootton's way.

"Speculation, ma'am, but the evidence is suggestive," Wootton said. "We doubt they're completely invincible. We suspect they have some very good armor with a very good auto-repair capability. Also, the ships might be the next best thing to indestructible, but the crews still need to eat, drink, and breathe. If we can pick off their supply ships and prevent them from reprovisioning then maybe they'll turn back before reaching the Solar System."

Katie looked back at Swims Up Creek. "You think the folks you're in touch with can make that happen?"

"I do, but they're going to need some convincing. The Roamers in particular will want to assess you for themselves. They will want to know that you can win. They'll want some assurance that if you do win, you won't be worse than the Grrumm."

"Why do I get the feeling there are those out there who'd like it if somehow we both managed to lose?" Katie asked.

"I feel confident that's how the leaders of the Trade Union feel," Swims Up Creek replied, "and doubtless others. However, many of us are tired of this old dance. As I said, we'd like to see a more reasonable galaxy based on friendly, mutual accommodation."

"So you'd recommend getting up-arm via the Trade Hubs as expeditiously as possible?"

"Yes, but first you accompanied by at least a part of your fleet should visit Assherraskill. The Scaly Ones might be your best allies."

"Because they entertain greater hopes of escaping domination by us than the Grrumm?"

"Perhaps, but also perhaps they have noticed you don't always favor those belonging to your species over those who don't."

Katie grunted. She certainly didn't want to get into a discussion of humanity's long fractious history of mixing tolerance and intolerance. "Guess it doesn't really matter which, does it? After the peace terms we imposed can they really help us much?"

Swims Up Creek nodded. "They could prove an important secondary base for your fleet to fall back on if you lose your home system. One that might surprise the Grrumm."

Katie had to admit she was rather surprised by the idea, too. She also wasn't pleased their Swimmer contact considered the loss of the Solar System a likely contingency. "That could prove very valuable," she said. "Whom would you prioritize contacting after that?"

"The Roamers. I've seen the little vermin catchers you keep as pets. They somewhat resemble them. In character as well as appearance. Very independent, very clever, and very slick. They operate only in small groups. As far as anyone knows they're nomadic and live and die aboard their ships. There are rumors they have stations and even planetary colonies, but no one has ever seen one. They keep their secrets well. They'll take chances, but they calculate the odds carefully, and execute quickly and precisely. They're the Trade Union's main competition. They trade between gated systems and non-gated ones but they work in the shadows and only deal with those they trust. They won't tell you anything about their other customers, but you can depend on them to keep your secrets too. I've vouched for you Admiral with some of them I know. Please, do not betray my trust."

Katie nodded. "I won't, but what can I expect from them in the way of substantive help? It doesn't sound like they're going to be providing much information."

"Not about trusted customers, but about competitors and non-customers, ones like the Trade Union and the Imperial Grrumm, those they'll keep you well informed about. Cheaply or even for free in the hope any setbacks you deal their competition will rebound to their advantage. The Roamers don't hate, but they consider the gatekeepers, the Spiders, and the Empire to be the enemies of all they hold dear. They value their independence above all and are willing to pay any cost to maintain it. In extremity they will provide almost anything in moderate quantities. Basic supplies and munitions, but even spare ship parts. If they decide you're an ally worth the cost they will enable you to sustain your fleet, even if you lose your home system."

"Let's hope it doesn't come to that," Katie replied. "My people have told me they charge high prices."

"They expect a profit and one suspects their costs are often high," Swims Up Creek said. "Also, they believe friends should be generous and understanding. They tend to charge what they think you can afford. If they don't think they can do good business, they will absent themselves. Treat them well, Admiral, and overall they'll treat you the same."

Katie sucked her teeth. "Okay. Understood. Others?" "I think you know the Snouts, and have come to understand my people to a degree as well. We're not unified, either of us. Some of us are more than willing to bet on you. Some aren't. You will have to deal with us on a case-by-case basis, each ship, and station on its own merits. I've listed some groups and individuals you should consider reaching out to, but, in general, the willing will appear on their own to offer help, and the others will sit on the fence until it's clear who has won."

Katie bobbed her head. "Somewhat disappointing, but I

understand. That it?"

"The broad strokes, yes. There are more details on the data chip."

"Will you be staying in contact?"

"I am heading back towards Earth. I have business there that needs watching. If your campaign brings you back that way and I can help I'll get back in touch."

Katie looked at Wootton who gave her a slight shake of her head.

"Very well." Katie said. "Thank you, Captain Swims Up Creek. I will remember this, but not spread your name around."

"Until we meet again," Swims Up Creek said rising, and then slipping out of the room.

Katie looked around the room. Shadowguide stroked his whiskers. He seemed amused. Hood and Wootton both looked tired and contemplative.

Hood pocketed the data chip Swims Up Creek had provided. "Guess that's it?"

"I think so," Katie answered. "I want you and Wootton to provide me a preliminary report on that chip's contents by this time tomorrow."

"Yes, ma'am," they both replied.

Wootton glanced at Shadowguide who silently bowed and left by the backdoor.

Katie, with Hood and Wootton in tow and surrounded by her Varkoid guards, made her way back to the docks. The trip was uneventful.

Thank heavens for small favors.

Katie had had enough excitement for one day.

***

Shadowguide sipped a fine liquor and surveyed the clientele of one of his favorite dives. He'd been there a while and truthfully there wasn't much to see. Mostly he'd just been losing himself in his own thoughts. In idle speculation, in all truth, although occasionally such apparent wool gathering could yield valuable insights.

Old spies don't retire. Not really. Rather, they tend to fade away. The seldom glimpsed shadow becomes dimmer and less frequently seen until it is not seen at all anymore.

It might be past time for Shadowguide to fade away, but events didn't seem to be co-operating.

Crashing that meeting between Admiral Kincaid and Captain Swims Up Creek hadn't exactly been keeping a low profile.

Shadowguide chittered lightly to himself. Swims Up Creek calling him what the humans would term a slippery character was certainly the pot calling the kettle black. Also as the humans would say. Interesting that cooking over open fires was still so recent for them that it continued to be reflected in their popular sayings. Also interesting that both he and Swims Up Creek had found it worthwhile to spend the time and effort to learn their culture and idioms.

The study of alien cultures was the part of his job that Shadowguide with his scholarly inclinations most enjoyed. So he had his own reasons for taking the trouble. Swims Up Creek was a more practical sort. Shadowguide found his interest in the humans a reassuring validation of Shadowguide's own assessment of the humans' importance.

He swirled his drink thoughtfully. He'd claimed to Kincaid that he thought humanity might be a force for order. That wasn't precisely true. The world was not so simple. The broad sweep of deep history had always been a personal interest of his. A certain grasp of context had been part of his job, but not one of any immediate importance. Not before the appearance of the Scaly Ones and humans. Indeed before their twin breaking in upon the local Galactic scene he'd been more of a cross between a guard at a boring post and a reporter for a large news organization in a small settlement where little ever happened, then an operative of any importance.

He'd resigned himself to being someone that did his little bit, but didn't really matter in the broader scheme of things.

And, now, he found himself giving fateful events serious nudges that might change the course of galactic history in this region for millennia to come.

How odd.

He really wished he knew what he was doing given that it now mattered.

Shadowguide didn't lack confidence. He didn't suffer from false modesty. Nobody out alone in a hostile environment, unable to share the emotional burden of their work with family, friends, or colleagues, could last if they didn't believe in themselves. He believed he was one of the smartest and best-informed individuals in the region. Only he wasn't crazy, he knew he didn't know everything. And, one of his primary weaknesses was in regard to large-scale military operations. It was a widely shared one. There'd been no real such operations on the galactic stage for generations. Shadowguide had no doubt this was one of the strengths of the Grrumm. They had strong military traditions they observed religiously. They benefited from lessons learned by their great-grandfathers. Their traditions had lasted many more generations than even that and they took heed of them.

It was not an area Shadowguide had studied, but he had a sneaky suspicion both the Scaly Ones and humans had their own traditions and more recent ones at that. Kincaid had a toolbox available that might shock the Grrumm. Her conversation with Swims Up Creek suggested as much.

He'd already bet heavily on that supposition.

It looked like some study of the issue might be in order. It'd be interesting.

And, if it looked like he needed to throw more into the pot to keep the game going, maybe it'd be useful.

***

They were on their way. Lieutenant Tanya Wootton was burning the midnight oil again, but somewhere other than her little office on Far Seat Trade Hub. She'd given up her command of the Intelligence Outpost there to her second-in-command. He was a mere junior lieutenant only a year out of graduate school.

It'd hurt. She'd built her little organization there, and it was her baby and giving it away pained her. On the other hand the chance to fill her old post as Hood's intelligence sidekick as the largest fleet humanity had ever assembled went where no human had ever gone before was just too unique an opportunity. Besides it'd been an order.

Also, Bob Barker might be a new lieutenant and a just-hatched xenologist, but he was also a middle-aged man. Mature with some experience of the world. He'd given up a promising law career after Second First Contact to go back to school and learn about aliens. So dedicated as well as smart and competent. Tanya couldn't imagine anyone better for the job of heading the outpost on Far Seat than him. Other than herself, of course.

But she was needed with the fleet and so here she was back in her old cabin on the *Bonaventure* burning the midnight oil once again.

She had managed two days straight of sleep after reporting so there was that. Hood and Kincaid had insisted, and she now realized they'd been right. Another lesson learned.

Tomorrow they'd reach Assherraskill. Tanya wanted to be sure Kincaid was as ready as possible to deal with the leadership there. Tanya was impressed with the size and power of the new human fleet, but she was also well aware the Grrumm were undefeated. Any help they could get from the Lizards was welcome. It might be what tipped the scales in humanity's favor.

Who knew?

Tanya sighed. When she thought about it, she almost wished she'd wasted her youth playing games of chance. It might have been more useful than anything in the thick textbooks she'd chewed her way through.

Nobody had really known much then. It'd been a bunch of theory and speculation applied to damned few actual facts.

Well they were certainly learning a lot now.

Only Tanya wasn't sure they were learning enough, fast enough.

Only thing Tanya was sure of was that if they failed to learn fast enough, it wouldn't be because she didn't try hard enough.

Tanya was determined to give her all.

Casting the Die

You see one Trade Hub, you've seen them all.

Not strictly true, in all fairness, but it did make sense that the Limers, when building the Hubs for the Trade Union, should standardize the design. After all, Trade Hubs were intended to attract visitors from far and wide and making it harder than necessary for those visitors to find their way around and do business wouldn't do.

Still, Katie felt like she'd been on a cheap package tour to the European part of Earth. It's Tuesday, this must be Brussels. No, Brussels is Thursday, Tuesday is Paris. The haste to hit too many places in too little time was real.

So it was no surprise that it was all blurring together. It'd taken Katie and her Command Group not much more than a month to reach the current Trade Hub, Wild Forests by name. It'd been a fast transit. That despite the multiple stops she'd made along the way to meet various individuals. Katie had tried to delegate as many meetings as possible to her Task Force commanders and, in truth, had managed to keep them all busy too. Only everyone wanted to talk to her. It was like she was the only human most of them had ever heard of and were willing to trust.

Said a lot about the structure of politics in the wider galaxy. Not much that was good in Katie's mind. No single individual could hope to have the bandwidth to handle all the major decisions in any organization of any size. But the Galactics mostly seemed to deal with that by extreme decentralization; for the most part they didn't seem to have large-scale organizations. Those they did have seemed to be very static and to do everything by whatever book it was they had. So actually those large organizations didn't have many important non-routine decisions that needed making. And when the need for such decisions came up, they either had a huge meeting of all the players involved or a single top honcho handled it.

As huge meetings have a proclivity to deadlock or at best to take a long time and reach compromises that pleased no one, often enough it was the single top honcho that decided. The Galactics had apparently decided, despite whatever the humans claimed, that Katie was humanity's top honcho. She was the only one most of them wanted to talk to.

So, she'd been very busy.

It'd started with the Lizards. The Lizards and their Chief-Queen, who made Machiavelli seem like a mushy-minded model of sentimental compassion. Her meeting with the Chief-Queen had been in equal parts chilling and pleasing.

Katie had given the diplomatic spiel she'd prepared with the help of Hood and Wootton. She'd blathered on about how much she regretted the earlier misunderstanding and having felt the need to impose such a harsh peace, and how she hoped in the future they could cooperate to their mutual benefit. She'd only hinted at how humanity in temporary need of some help would look favorably on whatever the Lizards could do to provide it.

The Chief-Queen had waved a limb airily and in clear English replied, "Yes, yes, I understand the need in human diplomacy to play nice, but you don't have time to waste. Let me cut to the chase. We will provide every bit of help we're physically able to. We will risk our lives as individuals and our existence as a species to provide all the support, military as well as logistical, as we can."

Katie had been shocked. It'd taken her long seconds to respond. "That's very generous. I understand the terms of our peace deal might complicate things."

"We will build the ships and weapons you need and give them to you. We will allow you to place nuclear charges in all the shipyards and ships to ensure we cannot repurpose them against you. You may need help manning them. It would be foolish of you to trust us to man warships, but you might have to. So we will need to figure out ways of our helping man warships without violating the peace treaty or your having to trust us. I suggest you hire Varkoids and others to help keep us under control. Deadman switched collars on personnel and encrypted keys to weapons and controls might also be helpful. I understand you'll not be able to stay here to supervise, but I expect you can set the ball rolling."

"You have an impressive command of idiom," Katie had replied, stalling for time.

In the end, she'd agreed to all the Lizard leader's suggestions. They were far more than she'd have dared ask for. They probably had some risk associated with them, but by that time Hood and Wootton had managed to convince her they were involved in an existential struggle. A struggle they dared not lose.

The rest of the trip had been a long sequence of meetings with a series of Snout and Swimmer leaders with either a single ship or a small group of them, every one of which had pledged support of some sort. A few had pledged only supplies and information, but most had placed themselves under her command. They added somewhat to her straight-up military strength, and a lot to her long-range scouting capacity. Apparently the Grrumm weren't into scouting a lot, so this was one area in which the humans and their allies would have a distinct advantage.

She'd also made contact with a number of Digger stations who'd contracted to provide minerals both to the Solar System and the various Lizard systems. It'd resolved a number of potential rare mineral bottlenecks that'd been in danger of constraining their industrial production.

She'd sent a long missive back to Tretyak after the last of

those meetings, alerting him to the need for a crash program to build more large warships. She'd made it clear that the Grrumm expeditionary fleet was coming and that the records said it'd never been defeated. She'd said she'd engage that fleet as far from Earth as she could and learn more about it, but that she was not certain she'd be able to stop it. Earth had to prepare for the eventuality of a full out effort much closer to home. An evacuation might even be necessary.

Last but not least, she'd visited Clear Ponds Trade Hub up-arm from Far Seat and managed to get the authorities both station and Trade Union there to promise her full support including munitions and ship repairs. She'd also managed to get tacit agreement that if she had to retreat they'd supply only minimal support to the Grrumm that both munitions and ship facilities would become somehow unavailable. Also that even normal ships supplies would turn out not to be available in the quantities the Imperial fleet would need.

Katie wasn't sure how well that agreement would be honored in the actual event, but still she was glad to have it.

She hoped to get the same sort of agreement from the authorities here at Wild Forest Trade Hub.

She also hoped there wouldn't be yet another assassination attempt here like there had been on Far Seat and Clear Ponds Trade Hub stations. Those were distracting and inconvenient. And if one were to succeed, it'd certainly mess her plans up.

She snickered to herself.

Hood next to her muttered, "We're supposed to be keeping a low profile. Species-specific vocalizations aren't good." They were both swathed in robes that hid not just their identities but their actual species. They were trying to pass unnoticed in the crowd.

Katie bobbed her head. Nods were another human-specific trait. Her Varkoid guard was off in another part of the station's main concourse surrounding a young lieutenant who happened to have the same slight build and red hair that Katie did.

Katie really hoped the young woman didn't fall victim to an assassination attempt aimed at Katie, but she had a vital mission. And like it or not, Katie was more important in achieving that mission than the young lieutenant.

Katie suppressed a sigh. It'd be another sign she was human.

Well, the young lieutenant would be spared making the same threadbare speech to yet another bunch of po-faced aliens.

Who knew that higher command had so much in common with being a cold-calling salesperson?

Rationally, she knew diplomacy was preferable to fighting. And that even if a fight was unavoidable, diplomacy was important to setting the stage for victory.

Only right now she ached for a good fight.

Katie wanted to kill something.

***

The Assassin was beginning to feel concern. Not worry - he was too professional for that - but concern.

Concern for his professional reputation surely, but also that events were spiraling out of control.

He'd lost track of the human leader completely when she'd accompanied her fleet to the Scaly One home world of Assherraskill. The humans were unfamiliar, and he hadn't had prior contacts there, but they'd proven surprisingly easy to infiltrate. It hadn't been hard to find individuals to bribe or otherwise subvert to his ends.

The Scaly Ones had been another world entirely, a completely different kettle of fish, as some of the humans liked to say. The human sayings were as baffling as everything else about them. In any case, the Scaly Ones were not only an unfamiliar group he didn't have prior contacts with, they'd proved impenetrable to infiltration, too. He'd been unable to gather information there, let alone organize any assassination attempts. And it'd meant he'd temporarily lost track of his target. Very frustrating. Problematic, too.

The attacks he'd sponsored on Clear Ponds Trade Hub had been quickly improvised after her appearance there, using resources that were less than ideal. The Varkoid guards Admiral Kincaid had hired had proved sufficiently competent to thwart them.

Worse, it meant the human was able to rejoin her fleet

where he had no way to reach her for almost a MaTok. He was rapidly approaching the deadline for success he'd been given.

Fortunately, it'd become predictable that she'd be going to Wild Forest Trade Hub to try to drum up more allies, or at least tacit support. The details hadn't mattered to the Assassin, just the fact she'd come here and be vulnerable once again.

With sufficient time to plan and contacts that were more trustworthy, he'd been able to mount an attack that had penetrated her Varkoid guards. Penetrated them and severely wounded the individual they were guarding.

Unfortunately, not only was that individual not outright killed, he was now hearing rumors it hadn't been Kincaid herself at all.

His standard backup plan of having people in place in the closest medical facility had also failed. The Varkoids had bundled their charge back to the docks and then the human fleet. Presumably, they had their own medical facilities there. Most targets weren't so fortunate.

Didn't help that it left the Assassin hawking cheap trinkets in the market, listening for rumors about whether his target might have been seen somewhere else alive and unharmed.

Nothing about this contract had gone as planned. So he was concerned. At this point, he was becoming convinced he'd fundamentally misunderstood the problem he faced. That the humans were something unseen in this part of the galaxy during recorded history. In which case, the failure or success of his contract was a lesser concern.

There was some chance he'd already succeeded. Failing that, he expected to get in at least one more shot at the human. And failing that, there was always some chance that the obviously risk prone human leader would get herself killed without his help. It'd all mean a payday and an unblemished reputation for the Assassin.

And perhaps it was more important he survive the upheavals on the horizon. Decamp for safer places. Lie low until the crisis subsided, maybe. Maybe take some advantage of the chaos.

There were always opportunities for the capable and enterprising.

The Assassin was both.

* * *

Katie didn't know for sure if meeting the latest set of Roamers was accidental or deliberate. She had a sneaky feeling she'd never know for sure.

Whatever. It didn't really matter.

The Roamers, Meerow more formally, were cat people. They didn't just look something like large cats, they thought something like them. In particular, they seemed to have an insouciant conviction that the universe was arranged for their benefit. Because that was the way it ought to be.

Katie and the ships of her Command Group had encountered them in a literally no-name small system. That system was roughly half-way between the Wild Forest and Plenitude Trade Hubs, although somewhat off of the most direct route between those places.

They'd purchased charts with information on the system, but that data wasn't always up to date or complete. So Katie, as usual, had sent scouts ahead. They'd found what they'd expected. The system had a single K7 primary. Such systems weren't as small or common as ones with M class primaries, but they were pretty common and significantly smaller than the Sun, which hardly stood out itself. There were three rocky inner planets, an asteroid belt, a gas giant, and a couple of ice planets. Superficially almost a smaller Solar System. But only superficially, none of the planets had horribly eccentric orbits, but neither were those orbits as round as those of the planets in the Solar System. In particular, the smallish gas giant had an orbit fatally off of being perfectly circular. It made the nameless system's asteroid belt much thinner and less stable than that in the Solar System. There weren't so many minerals to be easily found in it. Worse, for any chance of advanced life developing or permanent habitation, the asteroids pushed out of the belt had kept up a sporadic but significant bombardment of the inner planets. One of the inner rocky planets, the second one out, had managed to develop microscopic life and even had an atmosphere fairly rich in oxygen, but being hammered every few million years by a big meteor pretty much ensured that it'd never be home to any large lifeforms.

Given all that, it was no surprise the system was not only uninhabited but infrequently visited. As expected, Katie's scouts had found nobody there.

So when the *Bonaventure* and the rest of the Command Group had popped out into it, they'd been surprised to find a Roamer mother ship orbiting the third planet. A conveniently central location for a small swarm of smaller craft harvesting resources throughout the system.

A rather amazing, and very suspicious, coincidence in Katie's mind. Proceeding slowly in-system, she'd kept her escorts close. Once they were within a few light seconds of that alien mother ship, she sent a guardedly friendly hail.

The response had been much less guarded. "Ah, how fortunate!" a Roamer individual with a cat-person body right out of a popular video game and a face mid-way between that of a Maine Coon and a Raccoon had enthused in the Galactic trade tongue. "We're so glad to have happened upon you here. I think there's much that holds the promise of being mutually beneficial we can discuss. But not remotely, of course. Let's meet and share food, drink, and air, and do business."

Katie wasn't sure she'd have bought a used car from the Roamer spokesman. But she did need to do "business", so she soldiered on.

"I'm agreeable to that," Katie answered. "My fleet will join your main ship in orbit and I'll shuttle over. May I ask who I'm talking to? And speaking of business, there doesn't seem to be much in this system, so I'm surprised to find you here."

"Not much is not nothing. My name translates as *Masked-Eyes*," the Roamer responded after several seconds of delay. "Your proposal is acceptable. I look forward to seeing you in person, but maybe we can get some preliminaries out of the way. The time delay is still high, but I have heard you're in great haste." Masked-Eyes stroked his whiskers, having said this.

Katie had been told this indicated amusement on the part of a Roamer. "Not in such great haste that I can't spare a little time to talk to potential allies, or even friendly neutrals with whom good business might be done."

After a long pause, the very relaxed Masked-Eyes

responded. "Ah, yes, indeed. I do believe we have interests in common and we have information I think you'll find useful. No charge. Friends can do each other favors, yes?"

Katie perked up at that. "Yes, indeed," she echoed the Roamer spokesman, "I think we do. What information?"

Another pause and Masked-Eyes bobbed his head. A Galactic smile. Yep, this guy was a salesman. "Nothing either of us would like broadcast to the universe, I think."

"If we can't talk about anything substantive, perhaps we should take a break and resume this conversation once I'm on your ship," Katie suggested. She knew von Luck wouldn't be happy about the risk involved with her visiting the Meerow mother ship. This could be another assassination attempt, or maybe these Meerow would just find taking her hostage profitable. Still, you need to extend trust to get trust and she badly needed all the allies who trusted her she could get. It was her decision, and she thought the risk justified. Clearly too, if it wasn't just a ploy to get her on their ship, the Roamers had important intelligence for her.

Masked-Eyes graced her with both more head bobs and more whisker stroking. "Oh no, I've been very much looking forward to speaking with the great human Admiral Katie Kincaid. Please, indulge me. I want to learn all about you and your people."

Katie forced a smile, then remembered to give a quick head bob. For a fleeting, strangely fey moment she found herself wishing she had whiskers she could stroke. "I'm very flattered, Masked Eyes," she answered. "But a little surprised, too. I had been told that the Meerow neither offer much information about themselves or expect it of their trading partners. That you very much specialize in extreme discretion and respecting the privacy of your clients. Have I been ill-informed?"

More whisker strokes. At least she didn't seem to be boring her Roamer counterpart. She very much suspected Masked-Eyes was no random ship's deck officer or captain. She'd been told the Meerow were organized mainly in clans, each with one or more mother ships. She'd heard their clans co-operated freely and easily with each other, but only as the need arose. Exactly what that meant hadn't been clear. In any event, she suspected Masked-Eyes was at least a clan head, and that maybe he was speaking for more than one clan. That he'd sought her out and that a deal was in the offing if she played her cards right.

"Perhaps not wrongly informed, but not completely informed," Masked-Eyes said.

"How so?"

"That is how we often conduct business, it is true." The whisker stroking had stopped. Masked-Eyes was serious now. "Often for good reason beings do not want to risk extending trust more than is absolutely necessary. We Meerow respect that. However, sometimes one wishes for something more than simple, reliable business transactions. Sometimes one wishes for allies or even friends, whom one helps without expecting immediate recompense, and on whom, in turn, one can call on in need, and expect help from without having to pay immediately. Outsiders, whom one treats somewhat like clan members. And to that end, one must seek to know them as one knows one's own clan."

Katie blinked. That'd been quite the little speech. She decided to take it at face value. "I'm not sure where to begin. You want me to talk about myself?"

"At the beginning? Where you are from and what experiences you had as a cub, and how you achieved the responsibility you now have. I myself am young for a Clan head, but not unusually so. I am more than a quarter through the lifespan typical of my people. We live about a third longer than your people do. The former Clan Head is still with us, but resigned to make way for me. As a cub, I was always accidentally getting into trouble because of being energetic and very curious. I learned to charm my way out of serious punishment." Masked-Eyes cocked his head here. "Mostly. As a young adult, I earned a reputation for coming up with novel solutions to unexpected problems. When the former Clan head divined that we were moving into uncertain times, he decided they would suit my talents."

Katie was more certain than ever that meeting the Roamers and Masked-Eyes here was no coincidence. Also, that playing along was a good idea. "My family owned a small non-FTL survey ship," she answered Masked-Eyes in common. "My mother had me on an asteroid colony, but I grew up on that ship and was granted significant responsibility from an early age. I was better at technical things than dealing with people. My education meant time on the asteroid station I was born at and there were other people my age there. I had some friends, but not many, and was something of an outsider. Back on ship I had a lot of time alone except for my parents. I had a lot of time to think and dream. I wanted to make a difference, not just live my life on one little ship. I believed that the time would come when we figured out FTL. Because of a Builder colony that arrived in our system via slow travel, departing before we had space travel but arriving afterwards, I knew we'd find others out here, some of whom would not be friendly. I wanted to be in place to help with that problem and shaped my whole life towards that end."

Masked-Eyes whisker's twitched. "Amazing. So, your success hasn't been an accident, but you weren't born to your position, either."

Katie waggled a hand. "I've had more than my share of luck. Also, my grandmother, though I didn't know it until after I arrived at our Academy, was important within the Space Force and that helped in many ways."

Masked-Eyes bobbed his head and asked for an explanation of exactly what the Academy and the Space Force were. He then reciprocated by explaining how the Meerow handled the education of the young, and also how they organized themselves for conflict. It was fascinating. They detoured into the family relationships between people, and what Katie's grandmother's Vermont had been like. Life on a planetary surface was an exotic thing for the Meerow.

It went on like that.

Katie completely lost track of time.

She was surprised when the time came to shuttle over to the Meerow mother ship.

She hardly noticed her surroundings or the guards around her as she made her way to the shuttle bay and during the trip over. She had so much surprising to think about. She'd not been inclined to trust Masked-Eyes at first, and logically she still shouldn't. But the Roamer clan head hadn't been bragging about his charm. She didn't have much doubt he could sell ice to Eskimos, and make them into thankful lifelong friends in the process. If Hood, who was in his position at her side, had told her that an alien belonging to a completely different species, and a very different culture, could get so far inside her head, she wouldn't have believed him. She looked Hood's way as they docked with the Roamer mother ship.

He managed a twisted smile. "Overwhelming charm," he said. "You've got to wonder why the slick bastard wants to put so much effort into it."

Katie suppressed an urge to come to the defense of her new friend. It'd just make Hood's point. "Not really. The Roamers don't build fleets and get into toe-to-toe slugfests. They also don't like being forced to follow other people's rules. They want us to do the hard fighting."

Hood nodded. "Yep, that sounds right."

"I might like the guy, but I'm not stupid."

"No, ma'am. Never thought so."

"Anyhow, it wasn't like we weren't going to fight if the Grrumm wanted to expand their Empire."

Hood sighed. "So we should be glad for all the help we can get."

"But damned if I'm not going to try to get all I can," Katie said. The docking clamps clunked to, and seconds later, the shuttle's air lock hissed open.

She led her party on to the deck of the Meerow mother ship. A ship whose name she'd failed to get, she now realized. Which was odd. She was going to have to be very careful not to be beguiled by Masked-Eyes.

That individual was waiting for her. "Welcome aboard, Admiral. I'm afraid my people aren't much on ceremony. So no whistles, or honor guard, or anything, but if you follow me I have refreshments in pleasant surroundings available. No reason we shouldn't be comfortable as we talk."

"Sounds good, Clan Head Masked-Eyes. Can I ask first what the name of this lovely vessel is?"

"*Mother Bright-Eyes* is the ship's name, although our naming conventions aren't exactly like yours. She is the main mother ship of our clan, the Bright-Eyes clan. We usually just call her our mother ship. Our other large ships we call her daughters."

Katie looked around as she followed the Roamer, who continued to regale her with his clan's history. The Roamer ship felt more like a cruise ship than one of the Space Force's large warships. The corridors were large and pleasant. They were painted in subdued but subtly varied colors. All the various corners were rounded. The lighting was bright, but not harsh. Greenery and what she had to think were objects of art graced the odd niche. The ship looked used, but well and lovingly maintained to Katie.

The space Masked-Eyes led them to wouldn't have been out of place in a vacation resort back on Earth. Wood, potted plants, artfully arranged furniture and lighting. There was an area cleared for them, with refreshments laid out on what looked like an immense coffee table surrounded by low couches.

Masked-Eyes waved them forward. "Sit, please. Tea?"

"Earth tea?"

"Most certainly. The universe has already been improved by your species because of it."

"That's good," Katie responded absently as she sat herself down. Her guards didn't seem comfortable, but she waved them down too. She didn't think the Roamers were hostile, and even if they were, there wasn't much to be done for it. She'd brought the guards along mostly as other sets of eyes and to placate von Luck. The marine could be rather rigid at times.

The tea proved to be oolong and although there was a scattering of pastes, meats, and berries wrapped in leaves, Katie didn't see any of the cheese you would have seen in a human spread. The Roamers secured meat somehow, but they didn't seem to have anything like dairy.

She asked about that, and that set off a long conversation that a fascinated Hood joined.

Finally, Katie offered to send over some milk and cream for Masked-Eyes to try. "We put it in some types of tea," she said. "I hope you'll like it." She really hoped she wasn't placing too much weight on the Roamer likeness to Terran cats. She also realized that as interesting and pleasant as this all was, it wasn't why she was here. "I wish I had more time to explore these issues, only I'm due to rendezvous with the rest of my fleet in the Plenitude system soon. You had news you didn't wish to broadcast to possible listeners?"

"Ah, yes, and although it has been a few too short of your hours, it is news that will probably spur you to greater haste. The Imperial Expeditionary Fleet is due to leave Damp to move down-arm in less than a Ma-Tok. In one of your weeks."

"You're certain about this and the precise timing."

"I am certain. The Grrumm are nothing if not straightforward and predictable. They like their routines and doing things as they have always been done."

"Then I will need to leave soon," Katie said. "I don't think you'll be surprised to learn that I intend to meet that fleet as far away from Earth as I can."

"And fight them?"

"I'd rather not, but I expect so."

"Then some friendly advice, Katie. I think you can win this campaign, but not in one big battle in which you trade blow for blow. Neither will pouncing on them from ambush work. The Grrumm give as much as they take, but they've always been able to shrug off blows that would end any other combatant. We've long sought to learn the secrets of why their ships are so tough, but have had little success. You will need to dance around them and take swipes until they tire and give up or risk perishing. Perhaps if you survive long enough, you'll be able to divine the source of their toughness."

Katie nodded. "That sounds plausible, but to see what they have, I'll need to force them to engage. I will try not to commit or let myself get cut off. Is that all?"

"For now. A lifetime would not suffice for all I'd like to discuss, but we have covered what was immediately necessary."

Katie bobbed her head. "I do wish I could stay longer."

"But, you can't. Until we meet again, Katie."

* * *

Rrolff was not normally impatient. Nor did he normally rush into anything unprepared. He prided himself on both of these traits.

So, it was with disappointment that he watched his fleet form up for departure from Damp orbit. It was a disappointment he was careful not to show to his staff and the bridge watch as he watched the symbols on his tactical display crawl into place. The display was a huge screen that took up the entire forward wall of the bridge. To the not fully informed, it doubtless looked very impressive.

He did have all the warships he should. That much was reassuring. It'd been a tense wait for the last of his battleships. Several generations and many seasons in storage with only skeleton crews to maintain them, and there'd been problems getting them ready. Problems that had caused delays.

But in the end, all the ships of the Expeditionary fleet had arrived. Albeit some with smaller crews and in a worse state of readiness than would have been ideal.

"Too few supply ships," Thorn-Paw next to him commented. There it was. Thorn-Paw was not one of the ill-informed. Unfortunately, he wasn't very discreet either.

Rrolff decided to overlook the adverse effect his adviser's comment might have on morale. It was Thorn-Paw's role to bring issues to his commander's attention that he might otherwise miss or neglect. Rrolff did not wish to discourage the Frontier Fleet leader from playing his vital role. Rrolff had already heard much from Thorn-Paw about the state of affairs beyond the Frontier that he hadn't liked. He fully expected to hear much more in that vein. "I'm aware," he replied patiently. It wasn't like this was the first time they'd discussed this.

"Those living beyond the Frontier are a varied lot, as well as scattered, but very few of them are eager to see us extend our rule. Not many will risk open defiance, but we can't depend on them for much in the way of supplies. Not even the Trade Union can be trusted to sincerely support the fleet. They will have plausible excuses. They will claim they greatly regret they cannot easily find what we need in adequate quantity. In particular, we have little hope of finding either munitions or spare parts for our ships. Those will have to come from our stocks, or be sent for from the Empire. Our supply lines will be vulnerable to strangely aggressive pirate attacks. We must be careful not to overextend ourselves. It would have been wise to have built a bigger supply train."

"Perhaps, but tradition does not agree with your assessment. The *Book of Barbarians* is clear. '*Do not rush or skimp on your preparations, but do not delay excessively either. A half season is long enough to assemble the fleet and all it needs. There is no need to be rash. Barbarians are rarely well organized or able to sustain large alliances. Do not throw away the advantages of our organization and patience. But, do not delay action trying to be perfectly prepared either. The time will never come when you're perfectly prepared. Listen to the wisdom of the ages. A half season is long enough,*' it says. Our ancestors have invariably succeeded following that advice."

"And it would have been politically difficult to have ignored it. The Emperor, for one, would not have been pleased. I understand. Still, I'm not sure all is as it was in the time of our ancestors. I would be remiss not to point out possible problems."

"Indeed, and I appreciate your efforts," Rrolff replied. It was true. For all of Thorn-Paw's reputation for being difficult, Rrolff had found him rigorously professional. He refused to smooth over problems. He did not invent them to be difficult. "Your colleagues in the Frontier Fleet have reported rumors that the humans have a large fleet about to arrive at Plenitude Trade Hub. The rumors say it composes most of the warships they have. Rumor says they intend to come all the way to this system."

"I greatly regret that the Frontier Fleet cannot offer more than rumor," Thorn-Paw said. The sentiment seemed genuine. He stared grimly at the tactical screen as he spoke.

"As do I," Rrolff said, "but it is not your fault or that of the Frontier Fleet. We neglected it for generations, allowing it to grow weaker while its responsibilities increased. I know how few Grrumm volunteer to serve in it and how you must make do with those from other species who lack conviction. We tend to sloth, we Grrumm, I fear. But we are tough, as are our ships. Now that we've woken from our slumber, those who've forgotten it will be reminded. Those who were unaware of it will learn. Our battleships may be old, and it's a scandal how they were maintained. I'll be raising that with the Emperor, but in a head-on fight they will win and these impertinent humans seem determined to meet us head-on. It will be a learning experience for them. If they are at all rational, they will take their lesson to heart and surrender. If so, the rest of our expedition will be a parade and all and sundry will rush to curry favor with us. Supplies will not be a problem."

Thorn-Paw looked his superior's way and tilted his head in affirmation. "I cannot deny the logic of what you say."

Rrolff rubbed his nose in amusement. "And yet you're still worried. I will keep an eye on the issue. If we fail to defeat the barbarians decisively before Plenitude, I will linger there to remedy our deficiencies. As long as the barbarians cannot defeat us, they cannot win as long as we exercise a modicum of prudence. I assure you, we will."

Again, Thorn-Paw tilted his head in agreement. "It is all I can ask, Lord," he said, seemingly placated.

"It is as it should be."

* * *

Rob was briefing Kincaid in her cabin.

He'd just got back from an excursion to Plenitude Trade Hub. He'd posed as a supply officer trying to supplement the human fleet's rations. One who might not be averse to striking the odd personal deal on the side. He wasn't sure who, if anybody, it'd fooled, but the various denizens of the last Trade Hub before gated space had seemed willing enough to talk.

That was the good news.

What they had to say was the less good news.

"They all said that there's definitely a major fleet assembling at Damp, the first gated system several jumps up-arm from here. It's a once every few hundred years event, and major news. Everyone is talking about it."

"Okay," Kincaid said, bending over to drink some tea from the service laid out between them. "It's good to have that clarified. Back on Earth, even on Far Seat it was all just rumors. I know you must be frustrated at how hard it's been to get actionable intelligence, but this is real progress. It justifies the government having sent us out here. So look on the bright side."

Rob gave a weak little smile. "If you say so, ma'am."

Kincaid snorted. "Ma'am, is it?"

"Yes, ma'am. You're being very optimistic. Also all the serious commentators, and there's lots of them because this is the news of the century, agree that the Empire won't settle for anything less than our complete surrender. It's a political necessity for them that their expedition shows significant results. Results commensurate to the unusual effort they've made."

"Great. I'll include that in a special dispatch back to Earth. I do have plenipotentiary powers, but I'm not going to surrender. Any more bad news?"

Rob grimaced. "Everyone agrees their main expeditionary fleet has never been defeated. It's not clear that it's ever taken any serious losses. Its past history is shadowed in secrecy and obfuscation. Still, everybody I talked to agreed on that."

Kincaid sighed. "Okay, any good news?"

"Well, we've a count of their large warships from sympathizers. They don't seem to have any real security at all. Rather cocksure of them, but the main takeaway is that their fleet isn't any larger than our combined one. In fact, it seems somewhat smaller even counting what we're sure are secondary warships and fleet train vessels."

"That's odd."

"It is and we're going to have to revisit the historical accounts to see what sort of numerical odds they've faced in the past."

"But I'm guessing you're pretty sure they've consistently won despite being outnumbered."

"Yes, so they've got some sort of secret advantage, but at least we're not outnumbered. Also, I'm pretty sure they don't have a general advantage in technological level over us. The way the small and medium-sized ships of their so-called Frontier Fleet have fallen back only fighting a few accidental skirmishes strongly suggests that."

"So, if we can figure what the secret advantage their larger ships have is, then we can hope to figure out how to counter it, and probably pull off a victory?"

Rob took a sip of his tea and paused before answering. "Yes, ma'am. Only two things, ma'am. First, they've still got more worlds and vastly more resources than we do."

"All in gated space. We don't have to go there and defeat them. We only have to keep them from crossing the frontier and defeating us."

"That's true. But the second thing; if we're going to beat them we do have to figure out what their secret is."

Kincaid nodded. "And, you think that means engaging them in a serious fight. A fight we're not likely to win."

"Exactly ma,am." Rob grimaced. "I'm glad you're the one having to decide on that."

Kincaid chewed a lip. "Somebody has to."

"Yes, ma'am."

* * *

Katie wondered if it ever got easier.

On an intellectual level she knew she was being silly, and likely self-indulgent. She also knew she was making a decision that at the very best could result in many of the people under her command dying. It was unlikely many of them would be merely injured or maimed. Between the basic nature of combat in space and the miracles of modern medicine there wouldn't be many wounded. What there were could be restored to full function with minimal trauma.

That was something positive.

On the flip side, a lost battle could mean the end of humanity's future as an independent species. They might be able to survive as isolated individuals and small groups but that'd be about it.

So once again the future of humankind rested on Katie's shoulders. Well, she'd asked for it.

Self-examination wasn't mere self-indulgence under the circumstances. She was bearing a heavy burden, and it was reasonable to think about how well she was handling it and how that was influencing her decision making.

She had to decide whether to step back from confrontation with the oncoming Grrumm expeditionary fleet or whether to meet it head on. Neither option thrilled her. She never liked to back down from threats and it'd only be delaying things anyhow. On the other hand, Hood and others had been clear, the Grrumm weren't likely to accept anything but outright surrender, and nobody had ever beaten them in battle.

Katie already knew which way she was leaning. She was just reviewing her decision before issuing her final orders.

She looked around her Flag Command Center. As usual, Hood stood at her right shoulder. They weren't in combat. There was no need for them to be in their combat pods. Her staff went about their tasks quietly. More quietly than usual. Everybody was waiting in anticipation for the orders she was about to give.

They were going to have to wait just a little bit longer. Katie surveyed the symbols on the huge tactical display screen that took up the whole wall opposite her. They showed Plenitude Trade Hub as well as the primary and planets of the system. They showed her entire fleet too. A single symbol not far from that for the Trade Hub station. A blow-up box detailed the fleet's order of battle. Four large Task Forces, each of them with at least one carrier and several cruisers, plus dozens of destroyers and smaller ships. Each with a dedicated Scout Group. Smaller but still formidable were Katie's Command Group, based on the *Bonaventure*, and Henry Vane's Support Group.

The rest of the system showed dozens of scouts. They belonged to both the human Scout Groups and allied alien forces, mostly Snout and Swimmer. Some scouts were in other nearby systems. They provided Katie with eyes. They blinded the Imperial commander by pushing his scouts away.

Katie believed she had both better operational intelligence and a larger number of hulls. From what her scouts and friendly Galactics had told her she at least matched the Imperial fleet in large capital ships and had several times the number of smaller ones.

That much was encouraging.

Only none of it guaranteed her ships could go toe to toe with the Imperial battleships and win.

Her display also showed jump points and prospective fleet tracks. Two different tracks, one green and one blue, led to different jump points. One jump point led back down-arm to

Wild Forest Trade Hub, the other was the start of the path to Damp and gated space. She needed to choose which one to take.

"Thoughts?" she asked Hood.

"You haven't got much choice really," Hood replied. "It's not that you're letting your natural aggression get the better of you. We need to find out what we're facing. The sooner and farther from Earth the better. It's risky and I suspect it'll cost us, but it needs to be done."

"Thank you, Lieutenant Commander," Katie answered. She needed to be formal here, where they could be overheard.

She took a deep breath. "Commodore Hoffman," she addressed her Chief of Staff in a loud clear voice, "dispatch order set alpha to the fleet."

She paused.

"Comms, message to the fleet. Prepare to move up-arm immediately. Folks, this is it. We're going to visit so-called civilized space. If they're really all that civilized they'll talk to us. I'm afraid our intelligence indicates that's not likely. If it does come to a fight, I have every faith you will all do your duty. Their fleet is not larger than ours. I refuse to believe it's any better. Kincaid, out."

Mere minutes later the data started pouring in. They were moving up-arm. On time and in proper formation it appeared. Harder things to obtain than might be obvious, but Katie's fleet was composed of well-trained professionals. Katie permitted herself a degree of pride.

"We're on our way," Hood commented somewhat unnecessarily.

"Yep."

Meeting Engagement

Katie stepped through the door to her Flag Command Center and paused.

The room was busy and brimming with anticipation. Almost everyone was closed up to their station and in their combat pods, although few of them were fully closed yet. An exception was Lieutenant Commander Hood, who was standing at parade rest, his hands folded behind him, calmly surveying what was going on. He was waiting for her. Technically, he didn't have a duty station here and was only present at her explicit request to provide timely intelligence. In fact, he provided an emotional crutch for Katie, as well as a second opinion she trusted. Facts she hoped weren't too obvious, though push come to shove, it was more important to her to make correct decisions than it was to seem infallible and strong beyond the need for assistance of any sort.

"Attention all hands. Jump emergence in five minutes. All hands to combat stations," blared over the *Bonaventure's* Public Address system. For the Flag Command Center's staff, this meant being closed up in their combat pods.

It was Standard Operating Procedure, SOP, as close to

liturgy and ritual as the supposedly secular Space Force got.

There was no reason to believe they'd be emerging into a combat situation. They'd checked the system they were emerging into before jumping. The scouts had reported it clear and any ships that entered from elsewhere than where the human fleet had jumped from would be emerging multiple light hours away. Practically speaking, they'd not have the time to reach a point where they could ambush Katie's ships on emergence.

Moreover, clouds of FTL capable scouts and three of her four Task Forces should have emerged before her. More than enough to have cleared the jump point if there'd been anyone there.

Still, it was SOP to be in one's combat pods on jump emergence into a potentially hostile system. Better safe than sorry. And sticking to SOP both made everyone feel better and acted to prevent sloppiness.

Katie marched up beside Hood trying to project responsible gravitas as she did so. Sometimes she felt so-called leadership at the high command level was more about acting than it was about anything real. "Anything you want to say before we snuggle into our pods?" she asked him.

He shook his head. "We've beaten the issues to death, given the information we have. We have a plan. A rather simple plan until we have more information, which means finding the enemy and engaging them. Then maybe I'll have more to say, but it won't be anything I'll mind saying over the command net."

Which was the point of her question. Everything said on the command net was recorded. By tradition, *sotto voce* remarks directly between individuals weren't. "We are going to try to talk with them first, remember?"

"Yes, and I hope it works, but it's a pretty forlorn hope."

"Have to try, though. Okay, let's strap in."

"Right."

It didn't take them long. Every Space Force member was drilled on entering their combat pods until they could do it in seconds under any circumstances. While half asleep, injured, or drunk, as the case might be. It could mean their lives and the Space Force didn't intend to lose anyone's life because of their being inadequately trained.

So, the upshot of that was they got to wait a couple of minutes for emergence. Katie was almost glad when the gut wrenching, mind whirling sensation of emergence hit her. Finally, things were happening.

Sensors reported first on the full watch channel so everybody could hear. "Jump Point locality clear, ma'am. Task Forces One, Two, and Three spread out a light-second ahead of us towards the primary. Enemy force in close formation past the primary near jump point on route up-arm."

Comms came next. "Task Forces and scouts dumping tactical data to us, ma'am."

"Thank you, Sensors, Comms," Katie replied. She watched the tactical display update to reflect the situation.

The system they were now in was pretty nondescript. It had an M3 red dwarf primary, a half dozen uninteresting planets, and no resources of note. It was extremely small. Less than twenty light-minutes across.

It would be impossible for the two fleets to avoid each other. It would also be possible for them to talk with minimal lag.

A single unmanned emergency rescue and repair station belonging to the Trade Union on one of the orbiting rocky ice balls was the sole sometime habitation present. The only value the place had was its location halfway on the direct route between Plenitude Trade Hub and Damp, where gated space began.

At some other time, they might have found a civilian trading ship or two in transit, but not now. The civilians were giving both the human, and the Grrumm fleets a wide berth. There was no profit in wandering through a war zone.

"Ops, what do we have on the composition of the enemy fleet?" Katie asked on the full watch channel.

"Some small ships, all of which we've identified as being Frontier Fleet. They're not going to serve in the line of battle. They're scattered to the sides and rear. They're probably serving as listening posts and couriers. The main fleet consists of exactly twelve very large ships we're calling battleships, and exactly twenty-four smaller ships we're calling light cruisers. They're in groups of six. The battleships are almost as large as our carriers by volume, but don't have the large landing and launch bays you'd expect to see on a carrier. Their lines are very clean. Same with the light cruisers. They're actually a little smaller than our cruisers, but significantly bigger than our destroyers. We outnumber them, ma'am, but I suspect we don't have anything that can go toe-to-toe one-on-one with one of those battleships within effective missile range, let alone beam range. Currently, they're slowly proceeding on a line directly towards us and past the primary to the north."

Katie nodded despite the fact that nobody could presently see her. "Thank you, Ops. Issue orders to the fleet to prepare for a torpedo bomber strike as soon as we're in range. All Task Forces are to close on the opposing fleet at quarter speed. We can relax combat stations to quick standby pending further developments."

She barely heard the operations officer's reply of "Yes, ma'am," before climbing out of her pod. After all these years, she still found the things claustrophobic when she was not distracted by being busy. She preferred to spend her time waiting standing beside her pod, not in it.

Standing there watching the various symbols on the tactical display crawl along like paint drying, she was joined by Hood. "I believe I'll wait until Amy's Task Force and the Support Group arrive, before hailing them," she said to him.

"Marginal chance it'll make a greater impression, but sadly, nothing we know indicates they're likely to back down."

"We still have to try." "Of course, ma'am."

Katie knew patience was a virtue. It just wasn't one she enjoyed exercising. It wasn't really that long before Amy's rearguard Task Force Four emerged, barely more than ten minutes.

Wasn't much longer before her sensor officer reported, "Ma'am, Support Group has emerged."

"Thank you, Sensors," Katie acknowledged. "Comms, orders to Task Force Four. Close to remote station at rear of main force. Orders to Support Group. Take close station at rear of Command Group. Kincaid out."

A couple of minutes passed. "Ma'am," Comms reported, "Task Force Four and Support Group both acknowledge their orders."

Watching the big tactical display, Katie could tell they were already moving to execute them. Those orders had, in fact, been redundant. This was all going to plan so far, and Amy and Henry Vane and all their ship's captains all knew the plan. Still, Katie was a belt and suspenders sort of girl. Though in truth modern trousers didn't need either to stay up and Katie had needed to search the net for what the phrase meant back when she was a young nerd girl and had had the time for such diversions. Along with *"in for a penny, in for a pound,"* it was one of her favorite sayings.

Well, time to bite the bullet. Diplomacy wasn't Katie's forte. "Comms, hail the Grrumm fleet, please."

It didn't take long to establish the connection, and the Grrumm didn't palm her off on a junior officer.

A Grrumm, a big bear-like creature wearing a kilt, an odd little hat, and a gaudily decorated sash appeared on screen. They looked all for the world like a chunky, dangerous Yogi bear dressed up for a Shriner's parade. While at the Academy, Katie had spent many summers in America learning the local culture of her forefathers. "Greetings, I am Lord Earl Rrolff Sweets-Swiper, Second Paw of the Emperor, Commander of the Third Imperial Battle Fleet, currently commanding the First Imperial Expeditionary Fleet. To whom am I speaking?" he asked in Galactic Trade Language.

Katie replied in the same language. "I am Admiral Katherine Kincaid of the Terran Space Force, currently commanding an exploration fleet to investigate what's up-arm from us. We hope to establish peaceful relations with gated space. Including with the Grrumm Empire, of course."

Earl Sweets-Swiper gave a slight dip of his head to that. "You've brought a large number of armed ships along on your peaceful expedition," he noted, deadpan.

"In addition to pirates, we were warned that our appearance on the Galactic stage mightn't be accepted peacefully."

That earned a more emphatic head dip from the Grrumm admiral. "The Grrumm Empire does not accept threats. It deals with them preemptively. If you've heard that, you also have likely heard we deal fairly with all. Surrender and you and your crews will be well treated, as will your race generally."

"It is not our intention to pose any threat to the Grrumm Empire or any other race or state. We want to peacefully co-exist."

"From what we've heard, you specifically, and your race generally, have made a poor start on those intentions. We hear you took the orbitals of another race's home world and gave them a choice of extinction or humiliating total surrender. That doesn't seem peaceful. Regardless, whatever your personal intentions or those of the rest of your current leadership, the Empire has long experience of barbarian races. They're unstable and prone to being greedy. We do not allow them to become sufficiently powerful for those traits to be problematic. Again, surrender and you'll be well treated."

"And if we do not? I don't have the authority to surrender my whole fleet, let alone my race. What are you threatening if we don't surrender?"

"The Grrumm, and the Empire in particular, don't threaten. I warn and promise you that you must surrender or be destroyed. I regret the necessity, but surrender or be destroyed. I trust that's clear enough."

"Yes, clear. Surrender or be destroyed. Not reasonable, though. We'll see if you can make good on your threat. I hope not too many lives are lost before you decide to reconsider."

"I also hope not too many lives are lost, before you reconsider. Lord Earl Sweets-Swiper out."

And with that the Grrumm broke the connection.

A grim silence reigned in Katie's Flag Command Center.

Katie wondered if she should directly address that mood. She decided to be mildly indirect. "So, Lieutenant Commander Hood, the predictions you made in your briefings appear to have been accurate. Congratulations."

"Thank you, ma'am. I'd rather have been wrong." Katie gave a slight nod. "Of course, but it's not like we didn't plan for the eventuality you weren't."

Hood dipped his head a little. "Yes, ma'am."

Katie smiled. Not with humor. "Comms!" she declaimed.

"Yes, ma'am," the Communications Officer answered.

"Broadcast message for the fleet. We are proceeding with Plan Alpha. Repeat. Plan Alpha is a go."

Plan Alpha was for a full-out, direct attack with three of her four task forces. Only Amy's rearguard Fourth Task Force and the Command and Support groups would hang back.

In an ideal world, Katie would have been more circumspect in dealing with a dangerous foe whose technologies and fighting capacity she was uncertain of. All the intelligence she had, however, suggested that the heavy Grrumm ships were impervious to minor attacks at range. That was the only way to explain the lack of any mention of lost or damaged ships on their part. So, Katie wasn't going to mess around. She was going to get in close with her heavy units and hit as hard as she could with almost her entire force, and then see what happened. She didn't doubt it was going to cost her. Cost her ships and crew. But she had to learn what it took to inflict damage on the Grrumm capital ships.

The Grrumm didn't seem any more inclined to mess about than Katie. Their fleet picked up velocity directly towards the oncoming human fleet. The swarming human and allied scouts kept the Empire's light ships from their Frontier Fleet from closing, but they dared not challenge the main fleet which moved forward inexorably.

If nothing changed, the two fleets would collide head on at a point almost due north of the system's primary. But, of course, the fighting began earlier. After a little more than a long tense hour of waiting, the two fleets were approaching the maximum effective range of human missiles. It was a matter of some minor relief to Katie that the Grrumm didn't start salvoing missiles before the humans. It wasn't that she hadn't believed Hood's and Wootton's conclusion that the Grrumm missiles were comparable to the ones that Katie's fleet had. Probably they were exactly the same. Both of them being standard Galactic models. But intelligence assessments can be wrong. Discovering that the Grrumm had missiles more effective at long range would have been unpleasant.

"Ma'am, the Task Force leaders report they're ready to launch the initial attack," the Comms officer reported.

"Acknowledge that, and tell them we're still going with Plan Alpha," Katie responded.

Short minutes later, the sensor officer reported what they could all see on the tactical display, "Ma'am, Task Forces One, Two, and Three have all launched full missile salvos. They're following them with a full strike by their torpedo bombers escorted by all their fighters not on defensive combat air patrol."

"Thank you, Sensors," Katie answered. It was all according to plan. She was maintaining a minimal defensive force and some reserves, but the plan was for one big strike, not a drawn-out trading of blows.

She just didn't know enough about her opposition to get fancy. She should have a better idea of what she was facing soon. She sincerely hoped the cost of acquiring that knowledge was not too high. She did wonder why they weren't replying with a missile salvo of their own. Were they really that confident?

"There's no such thing as being invulnerable," Hood next to her volunteered.

Katie nodded. Taking the opposite side to that point of view and being a devil's advocate wouldn't be good for morale. All the same, she couldn't help thinking that even if the Grrumm capital ships weren't invulnerable, that wasn't the same as knowing their vulnerabilities and being able to take advantage of them.

"I trust all that fancy electronic gear and the annoying specialists operating it we stuffed our scouts with are going to pay off, then."

"It should, ma'am." Hood paused and looked pensive. "It may take some time to fully analyze it and put it to use, I'm afraid."

"I understand."

"And I don't like it either."

"But there's a reason we're doing this as far away from Earth as possible."

"Indeed, ma'am."

Katie gave a little smile. Their little recital of what they both already knew was a sign of nerves. An attempt to reassure themselves they hadn't missed anything. She'd had a little time to catch up on her historical reading during the transits out here. Apparently, it was a historical constant of high command that one of the hardest parts of it was waiting for the consequences of decisions already made to work themselves out. And looking confident while doing so. She'd read that Napoleon liked to nap after issuing his orders for a battle, but before the action started. Maybe he was able to do that because he'd been the Emperor as well as the commanding general. Somehow Katie didn't feel lying down on her Flag Command Center's deck and taking a nap would go over well.

"Something amusing, ma'am?" Hood asked.

"Just an odd thought," Katie answered. "Maybe I'll explain over a drink sometime when this is all over. Not the time for it now."

Hood just nodded.

It was a short while later, a little under twenty minutes, that her missiles and bombers began to close in on maximum beam weapon range. Just before they reached it, it'd be only a few more minutes, they would start to jink. Undertake rapid short evasive maneuvers, in the formal jargon. Jinking used propellant and increased time to target, but boring straight in made one a sitting duck for enemy counter-fire.

Turned out the enemy had a surprise up their sleeves.

Her sensor officer yelled, "Ma'am! Enemy beams have destroyed multiple fighters and bombers." She gulped audibly. "Forty-two fighters destroyed outright. Twenty-one bombers destroyed outright. Six fighters damaged. Two bombers damaged. It looks like they fired six extremely powerful beams from each of their battleships. Our attack wave has begun evasive maneuvers."

Katie kept her face impassive. "Thank you, Sensors. What about their cruisers?" She was shocked at how calm she managed to sound.

"They're holding fire, ma'am."

Hood, who'd been fiddling with the console in his pod, looked up. "A small, silver lining. A quick preliminary assessment suggests it isn't a more advanced beam technology. Rather, they've just built and deployed bigger, significantly more powerful regular beam weapons than most weapons designers think makes sense. They probably don't use power very efficiently and if I'm right, they're going to have a long cycle time. It'll grow longer as they heat up. Their longer effective range for doing damage if they hit something doesn't make sense for most targeting scenarios. Given reasonable EW and evasive maneuvers, they shouldn't get a much greater effective range because of difficulty in hitting their targets."

Katie hoped she was managing to keep her unhappiness off her face. If she'd just thought to order evasive maneuvers a few minutes earlier, hundreds of her people would still be alive. She wouldn't have lost almost a third of her fighters and bombers. It wasn't useful to dwell on that, let alone say anything about it. "Thank you, Lieutenant Commander Hood," she said, "that'll be useful to know in the future." Briefly she considered aborting the strike, but nothing had really changed and their main goal here was testing the defenses of the Grrumm battleships. They hadn't done that yet. It would be a few more minutes.

They all waited in quiet anticipation for those few minutes. It was interesting and rather strange that the Grrumm hadn't engaged in any specific anti-missile defense yet. A few of the human missiles had been caught by the beams that had decimated her bombers and their escorts, but that was it. Everyone was dreading the next beam salvo and praying it took at least as long to come as Hood had suggested.

Finally it came.

"Ma'am," her sensor officer announced. "A second beam attack by the battleships." She paused before continuing. "Seventeen fighters lost. Three damaged. Eleven bombers lost. Four damaged."

"Thank you, Sensors," Katie answered calmly. She didn't feel that calm. Half her strength in strike craft and fighters was gone. Gone in the first attack before they'd even launched their torpedoes. It wasn't great. The small craft were much easier to replace than larger FTL capable ships and they'd planned for possibly heavy losses. Replacements were already on the way from Earth. Not enough, however, they hadn't planned on losses this high. Also didn't change the fact that people she was responsible for were dying.

She didn't have long to indulge in angst.

"Ma'am," Sensors announced again, "Enemy battleships and cruisers have launched a large number of small missiles. They look like anti-missile missiles. The enemy cruisers are also engaging with medium beam weapons. We're down to ninety per cent of our original missile count."

Katie nodded. "Thank you, Sensors." Ninety per cent wasn't bad. A single missile hit was likely to cripple a cruiser. At least any human, Lizard, or Galactic cruiser they'd seen so far. A direct missile hit ought to hurt, possibly even cripple, a battleship sized vessel. Katie certainly wouldn't want to see one of her carriers get hit. Multiple missile hits ought to manage at least a soft kill on any size of ship. Which was why nobody other than the Grrumm had built such large ships. Past a certain point, you didn't get any more capability. You were just a larger target. The Grrumm obviously had some secret sauce. Katie was on tenterhooks waiting to learn just how tough the Grrumm ships were. Right now, each of them was going to get hit by dozens of missiles even before the torpedoes were launched. Katie didn't care how tough those ships were, she couldn't believe anything could survive that sort of firestorm undamaged.

Her main question was just how many of her missiles and torpedoes would get through.

Her operations officer partly answered that question a few minutes later. "Ma'am, their anti-missile missiles appear to be standard Galactic models." He paused and grunted. "Good news of a sort. They don't seem to be very efficient at using them. They've fired only a moderate amount per ship, and they don't seem well co-ordinated at a fleet level. Actually, it's almost as if there is no fleet co-ordination and each ship is launching them in the direction of perceived threats without much ongoing direction of any sort. They don't seem to have much in the way of EW or decoys either. The light cruisers do seem to be trying to protect the battleships. They're maneuvering to impose themselves between them and our strike wave."

"Thank you, Ops," Katie responded. It was, in fact, very good news if rather preliminary. Not only did it look like many of her missiles and torpedoes were going to get through, but apparently that fact was of some concern to the enemy. So far, so good. Katie's forces had already paid a heavy price, but maybe it hadn't been in vain.

Bare seconds later her sensor officer spoke up. "Ma'am, we have torpedo launches. Looks like they're mostly launching at maximum effective range and that some have diverted to secondary targets. The closer light cruisers it looks like. The data could be clearer. It's a right mess."

The data became less clear, more scrambled as the Grrumm light cruisers and human attack wave closed in on each other. The Grrumm might have limited Electronic Warfare assets in play, but the humans were scrambling as much of the EMF spectrum as they could. Exploding missiles, torpedoes, and small craft added to the noise. The participants in the attack wave were quite understandably prioritizing survival over reporting back to their superiors. The action was quick and turbulent and the information reaching the *Bonaventure* time-lagged. It was not entirely clear exactly what was happening.

But despite that, it looked like the operations officer had called it correctly. It was looking to Katie like far more of her missiles and torpedoes were going to get through than she'd dared hoped in her wildest dreams. If those had been human ships she was facing, she'd have been looking to wipe them out completely. She was expecting the Grrumm vessels to be tougher, but was beginning to feel genuinely hopeful that victory was in hand.

The entire watch in the Command Center was feeling it. A hopeful excitement was building despite everyone's effort to remain professional.

They weren't all entirely successful. Katie's Operations Officer, LCMD Thomas "Tommy" Kooperman — a brilliant mathematician somewhat better with figures than people, emitted a puzzled, not entirely happy sounding grunt.

"What is it, Ops?" Katie asked.

"Sorry, ma'am," Kooperman answered, "not really anything

we can do anything about." He paused. "Not even sure we should, but looks like we've got multiple torpedo bomber strikes going in on their leading light cruiser. Potentially rather wasteful on our part, but also it's rather ragged station-keeping on the Grrumm part. They're not sticking together in a proper formation. It's almost like they haven't really trained together much."

"And that offends your perfectionist little heart, does it, Tommy?"

Kooperman chuckled. "Yes, it does, ma'am. I know you can't expect the real world to go as cleanly and predictably as a simulation, but that's all the more reason to control what you can. These are errors that could have been avoided."

Katie smiled and nodded. She was happy Kooperman hadn't taken her jab the wrong way. She was also happy that people were paying attention and drawing lessons from the way the battle was developing. This was a serious large-scale battle. It was the largest the Space Force had ever fought. The stakes were high. The losses were already worse than any other battle, except for Ganymede. Despite all that, in strategic context, it was essentially a large-scale reconnaissance in force.

They just didn't know enough about what they were facing.

Katie decided it wouldn't hurt to say so. By way of emphasis. "That observation about their training was valuable. We don't know exactly what we're facing here. We could have guessed that with such large gaps between their expeditions across their frontier they might be out of practice, but we couldn't have been sure. Also, we've got absolutely no record of anyone taking out even one of their light cruisers. They're probably pretty tough. So there's that. And even if it does turn out multiple torpedo strikes are overkill, it'll still be a big moral victory. It'll help with all the diplomacy we've been doing. That's important."

"Yes, ma'am. I can see all that," Kooperman said.

Hood beside her, glanced Katie's way. She gave him a slight nod.

"We're going to analyze the hell out of this battle," Hood said. "And when we're done, you can be sure we're going to have training plan suggestions to make."

"Glad to hear it," the Ops officer responded to Hood. "Better get back to the current battle. Sorry for the distraction, ma'am," he said to Katie. "Looks like it'll be just a few minutes before our first missiles hit. One hundred and eighty-three point seven seconds. Take that with a grain of salt. The first torpedoes will follow closely. Surprising how many of them seem to be getting through. We'll know soon how effective they are."

"That's okay. Glad you're on top of it. Thank you, Ops," Katie answered. Fact was there wasn't much they could really do. At some point, Katie might have to decide to break it off, but that point wouldn't come until the two main fleets had engaged. She had to know if her capital ships could go toe to toe with the Grrumm ones. She had to know how tough the Grrumm battleships were. She desperately needed to know what vulnerabilities they might have. So they were committed until she had answers to those questions.

And in less than three minutes, because the Grrumm ships made no attempt at evasive maneuvers whatsoever, those answers started to roll in.

"Ma'am," Sensors reported, "we have missile hits on the leading light cruiser. Multiple missile hits, five, no six of them. Very bright flashes. Anomalous, that. Outside of the parameters of our damage assessment software." The sensor officer paused for a second. Katie looked over at her. She seemed puzzled.

"Preliminary assessment?" Katie asked.

"I don't think they're secondary explosions. Ah, yes ma'am, looks like total energy and spectrum match what you'd expect if all the explosive and kinetic power from our missiles was being reflected back. Reflected back perfectly. No evidence of actual damage. No lasting change to hulls apparent. No apparent debris. No apparent outgassing either." The sensor officer, LTSG Miki Kawasaki by name, bit her bottom lip and was seemingly seized by indecision.

"Your best guess is fine, Sensors," Katie said.

"Looks like a perfectly reflective force field or armor of some sort, ma'am," Kawasaki replied. "Can't be sure, as not all the energy is getting reflected in our direction, but I don't think the missiles are doing any damage at all."

Katie nodded with ostentatious calm. She wanted to give orders. She would have liked to tell the forward elements of her attack strike to concentrate on a single battleship now and to break off completely once they'd delivered that attack. She knew better. Her people knew their jobs and the mission as well as she did. In the middle of a battle that they were closer to her, she was getting data that was less complete and more delayed than that they had. There'd be a further slight but real delay before any orders she gave reached them. There was a real risk of such orders being untimely. Out of date and unhelpful. So Katie kept her peace and waited on developments.

It was only a couple of minutes before Kawasaki, the sensor officer, spoke again. "Ma'am, it looks like they're concentrating on one of the battleships. In addition to that light cruiser."

Katie allowed herself a slight smile. "Thank you, Sensors."

"Yes, ma'am. Ma'am, we're getting multiple missile hits and several torpedoes. Five. No, just lost one. Four torpedoes. They've hit, ma'am. Wow! Excuse me. A big light show. Ma'am! We have debris and outgassing from the leading light cruiser. At a guesstimate, what was reflected was two to three torpedoes worth of energy, but at least a torpedo's energy got through to her." Kawasaki looked up at Katie and grinned. "They're not invulnerable, ma'am."

Katie responded with another smile. "Thank you, Sensors. Very good news." She looked over at Hood.

He gave a non-committal little nod.

Katie knew he knew what she was thinking. She wondered if their increasing closeness might become a problem. But mostly she wondered just how tough the battleships were going to be. It was great the Grrumm didn't seem to be invulnerable, but more than two torpedoes delivered almost simultaneously in order to damage a light cruiser was insane. And she had no doubt the battleships would be tougher. It just wasn't yet clear by how much. Also wasn't yet clear how much this valuable intelligence was going to cost them. They had some more waiting to do.

"Ma'am," the sensor officer added a short while later, "it

looks like that light cruiser has lost way. It's not accelerating or maneuvering any longer. But it got power and weapons back after a short outage, and its life support appears to be mostly intact."

"More damage to one of these guys than we have any record of," Katie replied. "They've got to be feeling the pain."

"Yes, ma'am."

Unfortunately the Grrumm weren't alone in feeling the pain. Nothing as shocking as that first salvo that decimated the attack wave happened again, but the losses rolled in steadily. The Grrumm were concentrating on the missiles and whittling them down. Katie wasn't sure why. It was clear single missile hits had effectively no impact. None that was perceptible at least. Was there some sort of cap to the total amount of energy the Grrumm super-defense technology could deal with? It'd be nice if there was. Only even though most of the torpedo bombers had launched their weapons and were jinking for home, accompanied by their escorts, their already catastrophic losses were mounting. There was going to be no second bomber strike. Not before those lost spacecraft and their crews were replaced.

Katie just wanted to get it over with now. A clash of the main fleets was unavoidable, but if the Grrumm were hurt enough to break it off, it might be a very brief clash. Katie might be able to get the bulk of her larger ships away safely and figure out how to win some future battle.

"Getting our first torpedo hits on the battleships, ma'am," Sensors announced.

"So far no discernible damage," the Ops officer added, "but there haven't been more than one or two hits per ship yet."

All their wargames and planning had assumed even a single torpedo hit on the largest ship had a good chance of being crippling and that multiple hits spelled a ship's doom. Well, guess not if they were Grrumm ships. At least the Grrumm didn't seem very good at stopping missiles or even the slower and less maneuverable torpedoes. Although it was disconcerting that they didn't seem to feel the need.

"Multiple torpedo hits on the main battleship target, alpha," Sensors reported.

"Analyzing reflected energy signatures," the Ops officer announced.

"That's key, Tommy. Keep up the good work," Katie answered.

The picture was anything but clear. The vicinity of the enemy battleships was a maelstrom of energetic radiation. Katie really hoped the observing scouts were getting an eyeful. They needed that data. There had to be some counter to the Grrumm technology.

The storm subsided. For a while, at least. All dozen of the enemy battleships emerged from it. Several of the light cruisers lagged. Katie doubted they were all damaged and none of them had been outright destroyed.

"Ops, damage assessment on those battleships?" she asked. "No obvious damage, ma'am. From the radiation curves, it looks like the light cruisers can deal with the energy of about two and a half torpedoes and the battleships with half again as much. A little less than the equivalent of four torpedo hits close together."

Nobody actually groaned, or audibly sighed at this news, but you could have cut the gloomy silence that greeted it with a knife.

Kooperman, the ops officer, went on. "It appears to be some sort of shield technology that actively uses energy. It restores itself quickly, but we saw weapons fire stopping for short periods after a series of hits. Especially with the light cruisers, but with the battleships too. They must have some passive armor too, because I'm sure some energy got through. We probably did some damage to the passive armor even if it's not apparent from this distance."

"Good news," Katie said cheerfully. She hoped she wasn't exaggerating it too much. "Time to maximum effective beam range between fleets?"

"Six minutes and twenty seconds."

"Thank you, Ops." Katie was careful to keep her disappointment out of her voice. If the enemy shields restored themselves as quickly as they appeared to, then that delay between the attack strike going home and her leading three Task Forces engaging was going to give the enemy all the time they needed to recover. Unfortunate and they'd have to do better in the future. She looked over at Hood.

"We don't know yet how well those hypothetical shields handle beam weapons," he said correctly interpreting her gesture. "But if they're as effective against them as they were against our torpedoes than we're going to be hard put to overwhelm them while also maneuvering to avoid their overpowered beams. That's assuming their targeting continues to be awful, their cycle times slow, and that they divert power from their weapons to defense. It's a very preliminary estimate, but I think we'd need somewhere between three and ten times their numbers in large hulls to beat them. Even being generous and counting the destroyers at worth, say, a third of a battleship we've got at best little more than one-to-one odds."

"We can't avoid at least a brief engagement," Katie answered. "And if they're determined, it's not clear we'll be able to break contact at all."

Hood sighed. "True, ma'am. And we're not sure of any of this and we desperately need more data."

"Ma'am," Sensors reported, "Grrumm fleet is decelerating. They seem to be attempting to approximate our fleet's velocity."

"They seem to be aiming to hold us at a range just under their maximum beam range," Ops reported.

"And just out of ours," Katie replied. "Makes sense. Thanks, Sensors. Ops."

"Well, at least, all the bombers and fighters are back on the carriers," Hood commented.

"That is something," Katie agreed.

Pot shots at distance tended not to be terribly effective. After twenty minutes of watching the two fleets trade attacks at around maximum range to no obvious effect Katie began to become impatient. The Grrumm were managing to keep the humans from closing to a distance near enough that the shorter-ranged human weapons could do significant damage to the Imperial ships. They seemed to have succeeded in taking their crippled light cruiser under tow. It was slowly but surely being pulled out of the danger zone. Several of its fellows provided an escort, preventing the lighter human ships from dashing in and finishing it off. Katie didn't think this was going to end well for the human fleet. Eventually the Imperial fleet would whittle it down. "Ops, your assessment, please," she ordered.

"At range they've got the advantage, ma'am. We can't really hurt them, but they can whittle us down with the odd solid hit. Our beams joule for joule seem as effective as the torpedoes and if we could get in close and concentrate them on single targets, I think we could take them down. We'd take losses though. We're already taking damage and our main fleet doesn't have the Delta Vee to close with them."

"Thank you, Ops," Katie said. She looked at Hood.

"We've got to break off somehow," he said grimly. "We don't have the numbers to do this."

Katie nodded. "Comms, orders for Task Forces One, Two, and Three. Disengage. Contingency Plan Yellow. Break off and make for down-arm exit at flank speed. Orders for Task Force Four. Contingency Plan Black. You are to go to maximum velocity and close to point blank range to the enemy fleet's battleships. You are to time your maximum velocity intercept to coincide with an all-craft strike. You will push this attack home at all costs. Kincaid out."

Katie's communications officer repeated that all back to her breathlessly and then transmitted it.

Katie waited impassively. She'd just condemned thousands of men and women, including one of her best friends, to almost certain death. All in the hopes that she could delay the enemy fleet long enough to get her main force away mostly intact. It was an ugly gamble. An ugly trade-off at best.

"Ma'am. All Task Forces have acknowledged their orders," Comms soon reported.

"Good," Katie answered. "Order the Support Group to retreat to Plenitude system immediately. The Command Group will cover the retreat of Task Forces One, Two, and Three. Inform the spy ships it's time to break off. Order all scouts to screen the maneuvers of the main forces as well as possible but be prepared to exit the system."

So the orders were given. All that remained was to wait and see how they worked out.

It was the better part of an hour before anything other than the velocity of Amy's Task Force changed. The main part of the fleet attempted to break off, but between their need to conduct evasive maneuvers to avoid giving the Grrumm good targeting solutions, and the fact they'd started with velocities towards their enemy they were unable to do so. So far it didn't seem they'd come close to taxing the Imperial fleet's propulsion systems. The Grrumm were easily maintaining exactly the range they wanted to. A range that distinctly favored them and disadvantaged the human fleet.

But with Amy's Task Force Four having built up a high velocity towards the Imperials that was about to change. If the Grrumm wanted to maintain their favored range from her, they were going to need to back off. Deciding to do so would mean allowing Katie's other Task Forces to break away.

That was what Katie was waiting to see. What all of them were waiting to see.

"Ma'am," the Sensors officer declaimed. "The Grrumm heavy units are decelerating. Their range to the main force is opening. That to Task Force Four is still greater but closing quickly."

An almost imperceptible sigh of relief ran through the Command Center.

Katie ignored it. She took a deep breath. "Thank you, Sensors," she said. She hoped their relief wasn't premature.

Given a heads-up Katie could see the exact magnitudes and directions for herself. Checking she found that the main tactical display, her Heads-Up Display (HUD) and the console in her combat pod all agreed. The enemy forces were all moving in formation, albeit a rather ragged one, and they were all decelerating away from her forces. The projections were clear. Her main force consisting of Task Forces One, Two, and Three was going to successfully break contact. She was going to get away with most of her fleet intact.

Good.

The question now was how much more the butcher's bill was going to be.

The projections were unforgiving. In the extreme case of the Grrumm accelerating away at their probable maximum acceleration and Amy's ships also decelerating as much as they could, Amy's ships were going to reach point blank range from the Grrumm and still retain significant velocity. The Grrumm were only retreating slowly. Amy was continuing to follow her orders to close as quickly as possible.

Katie's best guess was that the Grrumm didn't want to take the chance of having to deal with all four of her Task Forces at once, and also that they wanted to have the highest possible relative velocity to Amy's force at the point of closest approach. They were trying to minimize their own possible losses.

That suited Katie fine. She too wanted Amy and her people to be in harm's way for as short a time as possible.

Unfortunately for the Grrumm and humans both there was no way to avoid a massacre now. Maybe mutual but probably heavily in the Imperial favor. Apparently not a prospect that reassured the Grrumm commander. One thing they were learning here was that the Grrumm were very averse to casualties.

Katie dearly wished she had that luxury.

Along with her staff she watched as Amy's group bore in through the maximum effective missile range and then through maximum effective beam range.

During that interval Amy launched her full complement of fighters and bombers. They didn't burn away to try to weaken the enemy force. They took station bare minutes ahead of the ships that'd launched them. Amy was keeping her forces concentrated in a dense fist. Even her destroyers and cruisers were spread out less than usual.

She was holding fire.

The Grrumm started firing off both missiles and beams as the human ships came in range. Amy's ships answered those with an adequate response from anti-missile missiles and beams both. Between that response and the weak and ineffectual quality of the Grrumm efforts her losses were relatively light.

Relatively.

Kawasaki the sensor officer listed off the losses of fighters and bombers as numbers. She named the larger ships lost.

"Ma'am, we've lost another destroyer, the *Scythia*. It's in pieces. Big pieces. Might be some survivors."

"Let's hope, Sensors. Thank you," Katie responded.

She got to say similar things every few minutes for almost forty minutes. It became almost automatic, but she felt sick each time.

Finally the groups were almost colliding. And Task Force Four's remaining bombers dropped their loads at point blank range.

"Ma'am, torpedoes away," the sensor officer announced. She then audibly swallowed. "Ma'am, the bombers, they don't seem to be turning away."

"Where are their carriers?" Katie asked. She knew well enough but didn't want to say it bluntly.

"Right behind the Task Force's cruisers." Kawasaki looked up with shock on her face. "They're too close, ma'am. I don't see how they're going to survive this."

Hood bit the bullet. "They aren't. They know it and those bomber crews do too. This is a kamikaze run, Lieutenant."

Kawasaki blanched white.

Katie spoke into the silence. "Thank you, Lieutenant Commander Hood. Thank you, Sensors. Now let's concentrate on our jobs and see that our comrades' sacrifice isn't in vain. We can indulge our grief later."

"Yes, ma'am," Kawasaki answered. She was an automaton for the rest of the battle.

She reported loss after loss in a toneless voice.

"Multiple torpedo hits on Battleship Gamma," she reported at one point, "Estimate at least six. Battleship Gamma has lost way. It appears heavily damaged." Muted little cheers greeted that, but Kawasaki's tone changed not one whit.

It didn't change when she reported the loss of the *Glory*, Amy's flagship, either.

Katie felt like she'd been kicked in the stomach. She'd hoped Amy would survive somehow. But her sensor officer's words, "She was hit by one of those heavy beams. Not much more than dust left," stripped Katie of any hope. She almost reprimanded Kawasaki for it, but realized it'd be hypocritical.

"Ma'am, the *Endeavor* has rammed Battleship Epsilon. Not much left of either of them but debris," the Sensors officer reported at one point. She might have let slip a hint of glee. It was a significant success if at a cost that left no one inclined to cheer.

Katie wanted to say so somehow. She wanted to cheer up her shocked and gloomy staff. She couldn't find it in her. She settled for an automatic, "Thank you, Sensors."

By silent agreement everyone else was quiet.

And so it went.

It was by the clock a rather short battle although subjectively it seemed to go on forever.

In the end, a half dozen badly damaged destroyers, and a single battered cruiser englobed in a cloud of wreckage and debris exited the scene of the two fleet's collision.

"Comms!" Katie said. "Message for survivors of Task Force Four. You've done all that could be expected and more. Stand down and surrender."

She hoped the Grrumm would be in the mood to accept those surrenders. She looked over at Hood who gave a small nod of reassurance.

Thinking about it coldly, it could have been worse. They might be able to win this with what they had learned here.

But when the *Bonaventure* finally jumped for the next system down the arm towards Plenitude, the last of Katie's fleet to do so except for the survivors they were leaving behind, Katie had a hard time feeling good about it.

"You're all relieved. Good work. I know you're all tired and hurting. You're on stand down for the next twenty-four hours. Try to get some rest," Katie ordered.

She looked over at Hood. She was feeling completely wrung out, but she felt she needed to review what had happened while events were fresh in her mind. Waiting for the memories to scar over was not a viable strategy. "Not you," she said. "My cabin. We need to review this now."

Hood grimaced. "Yes, ma'am."

"I'm sorry," Katie said. "Believe me."

Counting the Cost

Katie felt ashamed of her momentary weakness. Embarrassed too. Not emotions she was accustomed to. She tried to hide her feelings as she led Hood into her cabin.

She didn't venture any words as she poured two drinks and handed one to Hood.

It was a fine Scotch. One of the many bottles gifted to her during her victory tour of Earth after forcing the Lizard surrender. She'd carefully cataloged all those gifts. Declared them, and passed as many as she could onto museums and other public collections. Most of the remaining ones were stored at her grandmother's estate that she'd inherited. Maybe she'd get to retire there some day. Seemed a remote prospect right now.

But in any case, she'd kept a few fine liquors, and they'd been mostly gathering dust here in her cabin. She couldn't think of a better time to break out a bottle.

She sipped her drink and looked at Hood. He looked right back, visibly tired but not bowed.

Katie didn't feel so good herself. "Here's to Amy and all those with her. Here's to absent friends," she said. The words were a hallowed tradition and easy to find, and they did help a fraction.

"Here's to absent friends," Hood echoed.

The booze was a smooth burn down her throat. That was nice. There was a lot that wasn't. Katie's job was to deal with it. Only she felt too tired to think. Too disturbed to sleep. She was supposed to be stronger than this. "Well, Rob, they're not invulnerable," she said. "But they are tough. We paid heavily to find that out. I don't want to do that again."

Hood nodded. "It's easier when you're not the one responsible. I don't envy you that. But, yes, they're not invulnerable and, yes, that doesn't mean beating them is a sure thing. But I think if we can stay the course we can figure out a way clear to victory. Doesn't mean it'll be easy."

Katie snorted. "Okay, anything besides platitudes?" "We're not up for another fight any time soon. We all need to rest and recuperate."

Katie turned and slumped into her chair. She waved at Hood to do the same. "Can't argue with that," she said. "Figure there's any chance the Grrumm will give up and go home, or at least, not continue to push down-arm?"

Hood shook his head. "I suppose it's not impossible, but I don't think so. They're obviously casualty-averse, but I don't think so. I think they're going to push all the way to Earth if we let them."

Katie grimaced. "Don't see how we can stop them right now." She paused. "They do seem weak in their lighter ships and they do seem determined to stick together. We should be able to harass them and minimize their resupply. Not sure what good that'll do if they're determined, though. I don't see how we can stop them." She bit an offending thumbnail. "Rob, I'm not sure I can do this."

"You have to."

"After that disaster, I wouldn't blame the politicians back home if they decided to replace me."

"They won't. There's nobody to replace you with."

Katie laughed. Harshly. "Nobody is irreplaceable."

Hood fidgeted and took a deep breath. "Practically speaking, Katie, you are. You aren't just a military technician.

You are and the finest we have too, I think. But you aren't just a highly professional military technician. You're a symbol. An inspiration not just to the men and women of the Space Force but all of humanity. They look to you as an example. They believe we can win when the odds seem poor because of you. They give a little bit more when it's needed because they think that's what you'd do." He took another breath and looked at her hard. "They make the last ultimate sacrifice if need be because they trust you'll make it worthwhile. You can't give up. It'd be betraying us all."

Katie wanted to laugh at the man, but he seemed dead serious. "Well, okay, you convinced me. I'll give it my best. But right now, Lieutenant Commander, I need some sleep." She gave Hood a slight, twisted smile. "So, drink up and get out."

"Yes, ma'am."

* * *

The Grrumm, especially their aristocracy, were notorious for their complacent, easy-going natures. They were known to be slow to anger. They prided themselves on it. But they were equally notorious for their insensate, irrational rage once they were angered.

Rrolff was close to tipping over into rage. His belly burned. His eyes itched. His vision was narrow and red-tinged. He felt as if his head was about to burst. He desperately wanted to slash something into shreds. Anything or anyone, everything, in fact. He wanted to rip existence apart.

He resisted that urge with everything he had.

Acts performed in the midst of mind-blinding rage were considered the results of temporary insanity. Legally, they'd not be prosecuted. Socially, they'd not be condemned. The victims of rage were treated with kindness. But they'd be watched for the rest of their lives for recurrences, and they'd not be trusted with important responsibilities. If they'd had some before succumbing to their illness, they'd be divested of them and shuffled off somewhere they could do less harm.

Rrolff had no intention of being shuffled off into being an ineffectual placeholder. He had a humiliation to avenge.

Never before had a ship of the Expeditionary Fleet been lost. He'd lost three, two of them battleships. Others were damaged beyond being immediately useful. In fact, half of his battleships and a third of his cruisers had sustained some damage, though it was minor in many cases. It was, in any case, humiliating.

A cough interrupted his thoughts. Apparently Thorn-Paw had decided it was safe to attempt to speak to him. They were in Rrolff's office attached to his day quarters. There were no other witnesses to Rrolff's embarrassing loss of self-possession.

"This is a day that will live in infamy, and I'm the one who'll be blamed," Rrolff growled.

"Perhaps. Not fairly. This was a setback that was generations of complacency and neglect in making."

"That fails to reassure me," Rrolff returned, though in all honesty he was somewhat mollified by the observation. One, he rather sadly thought, that had some truth to it. He'd have liked to think better of the Empire, his peers, and his predecessors.

"These humans are outliers too," Thorn-Paw replied. "It is a contradiction to see such aggressiveness combined with the capacity to co-operate in creating such a large and capable fleet. That they whetted themselves on the Scaly Ones before us was another fluke of ill fortune."

Rrolff grumbled and growled. "Ha! That'll impress the Emperor. *Sire, it was just neglect on the part of you and earlier emperors, plus a lot of bad luck. Not my fault at all, sire!*"

"It is our lot to serve. You can't always expect life to be fair."

"That's true. In the best of worlds, we'd retreat back to Damp or even the ship-building systems beyond it and there we'd re-build the fleet as needed. We'd properly prepare ourselves, our personnel, and our ships. Make certain of having enough of both ships and the crew to man them. Then, that done, we'd return and deal with these human barbarians properly and without further undue loss."

"But this is not the best of worlds."

Rrolff snorted. "Indeed. I'm not concerned that it would seem like weakness to the Trade Union and others of the lesser races, but the butt lickers at court would see me disgraced and removed from command. They'd then debate and scheme over what to do next endlessly. Nobody would be eager to step forward and risk my fate. Who knows how many seasons or even generations it'd be before some actual action was taken?"

"And in the meantime, the humans would grow even stronger."

"Just so. For me and the Empire both, the best way is forward. Once I've crushed these upstart barbarians, whatever the cost, I will have the influence necessary to bring about the improvements we both know are necessary."

"And so we persevere." "Duty requires it."

* * *

Rob knew he was tired. He'd been awake long enough and under enough stress that he had to be. And he was pretty sure that the large shot of Scotch Kincaid had made him take hadn't helped.

Also, his bones did ache, and his wits did seem slow. Despite that, he didn't really feel tired. He'd felt much more so several hours ago. He must be too numb to feel as tired as he really was. So having let himself back into his little cabin, he didn't immediately crawl into his sleeping pod, or strip off his uniform and have a shower. He sat down at his little pull-out desk and tried to think while waiting for his fatigue to catch up with him.

Kincaid was probably right. It was probably a good idea to assess what had just gone down before a degree of recovery rubbed the edges off of his raw impressions.

Unlike Kincaid, he hadn't lost any close friends along with the rearguard Task Force. He'd always liked Amy Sarkis, but what with her outranking him, and being significantly younger, and of the opposite sex, they'd been friendly but never become genuinely close. He'd lost acquaintances and valued colleagues along with the Task Force, but nobody really close.

Sitting and thinking about it, he had to admit he had no close friends. His life had followed a path that had made that difficult.

He knew what loss and grief were. He had felt those when

his parents had died. It'd catapulted him from a comfortable, upper middle-class existence to the Darwinian struggle of the Martian tunnels. In a way, that struggle had precluded dealing with the loss. He'd loved his parents, but he'd not had the luxury of properly mourning them. He wondered what that'd done to him as a person.

Sure hadn't helped that his way out of that predicament had been becoming a spy. True friendship wasn't a luxury afforded spies. True friendship requires honesty and trust and spies can't afford either. The current rolling crisis had put paid to his hopes of retiring and having a normal life.

He'd been promoted out of the social milieu he was comfortable in and kept incredibly busy. Kincaid and Wootton were likely the closest things to friends he had, and they were both in his chain of command and, in truth, too good for him. Maybe if one or both had been male, a closer camaraderie would have been possible.

Rob didn't really know. He felt like a heel, even thinking about it when others had just lost so much.

But so much death did get you thinking about life. Some day he'd have to indulge that urge. Right now, he still had a job to do. Kincaid needed advice from an intelligence officer who was fully engaged.

Rob didn't think the situation was hopeless, but it was certainly desperate. He needed to get his ducks in a row and help Kincaid do the same.

That the Grrumm ships weren't invulnerable and could be destroyed was great news. What it had cost wasn't.

Letting aside the moral issues and the human tragedy of it, humanity might not be able to pay that cost. It might not be possible to build and man enough ships to do the job.

Quite simply, the Grrumm had lost less than twenty per cent of their fleet. They might be able to repair some of those losses.

The humans had lost almost a quarter of their strength doing kamikaze runs to damage that much of the Imperial fleet. They might not be able to replicate that feat. If they could, cold math said that the two fleets could just about annihilate each other, leaving one side, maybe, with a surviving remnant. Hard to say which side exactly.

If Rob hadn't been so tired, he might have been inclined to puke in the corner at the thought. As it was, he was only dully appalled at the prospect.

Letting aside the moral and human horror of the idea, and assuming it was the humans who 'won', there remained issues. If the Space Force was reduced to a rump who'd defend the Solar System from the many armed opportunists inhabiting Frontier space? What was to prevent the Grrumm from building and sending yet another fleet from their far greater resources?

Rob supposed it was possible to hope that the obviously casualty-averse Grrumm would throw in the towel before things got that bad. Only hope was no strategy. They had to do better than they had in the battle just past.

One thing was for sure: they needed to message Earth and tell them to stop producing missiles, fighters, and the smaller warships. The big Grrumm battleships had proven able to one shot the Space Force's corvettes and frigates. The destroyers had only been a bit more survivable.

It was interesting that they'd in fact spent the fire power to do so. Rob doubted it'd been the smaller ship's weapons they'd been afraid of, though the possibility had to be analyzed. Perhaps there was a directional or range component in how their shields worked. Maybe they were vulnerable to beam attacks from multiple directions or too close. He rather doubted it. He suspected it was the fear of kamikaze attacks that had prompted the Grrumm behavior.

Which was interesting.

Perhaps some sort of equivalent of the fireships of the pre-space surface sailing ship navies of Earth was what was needed?

He didn't know.

For the time being, the best idea seemed to be giving ground while harassing them. Rebuilding the human fleet until it was strong enough to have a good chance of winning a stand up battle. Hoping the Grrumm would get tired of the game and go home before it came to that.

Sort of like the Russian 1812 campaign against Napoleon.

Rob sighed.

And like the Russians had to fight Borodino before conceding Moscow to the French in that campaign, the humans would have to fight a battle before they allowed the Grrumm to reach the Solar System. Ready or not, it'd be politically impossible to do otherwise.

Rob felt like maybe he could get the sleep he needed now. It was grim, true, but maybe not impossible.

He'd been able to wrap his mind around the enormity of it. Sort of.

Further Adjustments

Thorn-Paw moved through the large ship bay. The *Celestial Dominance* was an immense ship and its ship bay was correspondingly huge. He moved between piles of wreckage and near wreckage and small groups of survivors, both Grrumm and barbarian. Occasionally, he stopped to inspect a piece of wreckage, observe a group, or talk to them.

He had a barbarian, a Swimmer, in tow. That Swimmer, Twitch Snout by name, knew the humans' main language. Amazingly, the human barbarians had multiple languages. They were that primitive and unevolved. Socially, at least. Technically, and in their command of warcraft, they seemed proficient enough.

He stopped by one bedraggled group of them. They all struggled to their feet and, facing him, gave respectable bows. So they were quick on the uptake and willing to learn how to be civilized. Reasonable sentient beings on an individual basis. That much was promising.

"Ask if they've been fed, watered, and had their injured cared for," he told Twitch-Snout. Some mutual chatter affirmed that they had been. Thorn-Paw both bobbed his head and nodded it in reply. He'd learned that nodding was the human method of signaling approval.

It was always good to understand one's enemies. That was what both the *Book of Barbarians* and Thorn-Paw's own experience said.

He moved on. His goal here was to make sure that the clean-up operation after the battle went well, but also to do an initial assessment of the results. The task fell to him as the Lord Earl Sweets-Swiper was resting. Thorn-Paw, who ached with fatigue himself, would get to rest after he was finished here and had briefed the Lord Earl.

A Lord Earl, who was hopefully calmer as well as more rested than he'd been in the battle's immediate aftermath.

Thorn-Paw could easily understand his superior's frustration.

Sweets-Swiper had proceeded exactly as tradition required and taken unprecedented losses as a result. Faced with the unexpected, he'd reacted in a manner Thorn-Paw found admirable. The Lord Earl wasn't just another empty title. He'd kept his calm and prioritized the defense of his ships from suicidal ramming attacks by the enemy's smaller ships.

Doubtless, some of the butt lickers back at court would criticize him for not continuing on to engage the enemy main force. Perhaps he could have defeated the entire enemy fleet if he'd done so. Perhaps. But it would surely have cost both sides heavily.

True as that was, it was not something anyone back in civilized space would be interested in hearing. And so they were committed to a desperate campaign with ships and crews that had proved inadequately prepared.

The Lord Earl may have been angry, but his decision to continue on once they'd cleaned up after this first battle was the logical one. It'd do no good for Thorn-Paw to advise differently.

"Sixth! Sixth Claw Thorn-Paw!" someone called. Thorn-Paw looked to find one of his old captains from the Frontier Fleet calling out to him. He was one of a group of such captains. Most of them known to Thorn-Paw. "What can I do for you, Talon Clear-Sight?" he replied, walking over to them.

"Do you know if we're going further? I heard a rumor we were being ordered back to the Frontier," Clear-Sight said.

Thorn-Paw looked about at inquiring faces. "The lighter ships of the Frontier Fleet are being sent back to Damp and other points on the Frontier," he replied. "The barbarians have nothing to match the big ships of the Expeditionary Fleet. They will continue on until the barbarians submit."

"It rankles to retreat from barbarians," one captain growled.

"Our damaged capital ships will need escorts and the barbarian small ships vastly outnumber ours. It is no disgrace to face reality," Thorn-Paw answered. "And someone needs to defend the Frontier from opportunists."

"It's a sad day for all that, Sixth," Clear-Sight said.

"It is," Thorn-Paw admitted, looking around at his colleagues, "but we all know it's been coming for a long while. The Frontier has been neglected too long. When the Emperor hears of this, he will now doubtless act."

"Hurrah! Long live the Emperor," came the general response.

"Do you think we will have to annihilate their home planets before they surrender?" Clear-Sight asked.

"They only have one home planet and one home system according to our reports," Thorn-Paw said. "I've been talking to their survivors. They seem like a sensible species. It's not unreasonable to expect they'll see it's hopeless for them and surrender before the losses in sentient beings on both sides rise too high."

"Good, good. Thank you, Sixth," Clear-Sight said. "Thank you, for taking time from your duties to speak to us."

The other captains bobbed their heads in agreement.

Thorn-Paw responded in kind and moved on.

* * *

Yet another bug-out. This one from Clear Ponds Trade Hub and its system. Katie was sick of bug-outs.

She was equally tired of explaining the necessity of them. Seeing nothing but the backs of her Varkoid bodyguards every time she left the safety of the *Bonaventure* was also tiresome. That despite the fact they'd saved her life several times.

In fact, some sort of attack had occurred on every one of the Trade Hubs she'd been forced to abandon after assuring the local dignitaries, especially the Trade Union officials, that the retreat was temporary and she and humanity would both be back.

There'd been two attacks at Plenitude. One semi-professional by an apparently well-known local thug. A Climber, somewhat unusually. The other had been an amateurish attempt by a small group of Snout spacers. They'd been drunk when they heard about the easy money to be made in some bar and had given it a try. All but one of them were dead now. Her guards had kept one alive, if damaged, to answer questions. Mark, her head guard, had been rather disgusted by what they'd learned. He was a professional and the spur-of-the-moment amateurishness of it had offended his professional pride.

Katie sighed. Mark's pride had been less offended by the attempts at Wild Forest than Clear Ponds Trade Hubs. The assassin at Wild Forest had actually managed to wing her. Without the combination of light body armor and overhead cover from a decoy drone scrambling targeting solutions, doubtless Katie would be dead as contracted for.

Katie's death would have seriously offended Mark's pride, but Katie wondered if it mightn't have been restful. She was seriously sick of fighting, losing battles, retreating, and making excuses to neutrals and allies alike about it.

"Heads up, Admiral Katie," Mark at her side said.

"Problem?" she asked.

"None detected, but allowing yourself to be distracted while in hostile territory is unwise."

Katie nodded, then remembered to bob her head. "True. I'll be more alert."

She took a deep breath. For the remainder of the trip back to their shuttle craft, she focused on her immediate surroundings. Although all she could see was the back of her Varkoid guards, she could feel a tension in the air. Her guards were not relaxed. The sounds of the station around them seemed different. Maybe it was Katie's imagination, but they seemed quieter, lower but less settled, more on edge than they'd been on her previous trips here. Nobody was happy or certain what was going to happen. Welcome to the club.

Once they were back on the shuttle craft, she could finally relax. Relax, somewhat at least, and think about the overall situation. Staying alive might be part of her job, but thinking about the strategic situation was why she was paid the big bucks.

She snorted at the hoary old joke. Mark gave her an inquisitive head tilt.

"Just a mildly funny stray thought," she told him. "Not worth explaining."

"Yes, Admiral Katie."

If they survived this, Katie was definitely going to reward the Varkoids with a bonus. They, and Markraatov in particular, were models of professional tact. It made her job much easier. It was unfair to characterize their ongoing interactions with the Grrumm Imperial fleet as a set of losing battles. In truth, Katie had confronted them with her fleet in each system between here and the last real battle. She'd forced them to deploy and to proceed cautiously, and she'd prevented them from receiving outside supplies. She'd been able to keep transports from reaching them. By the time they'd reached the Trade Hubs along their route, Plenitude, Wild Forest, and Clear Ponds in turn, they'd been stripped of all surplus supplies of any military utility. So there was that. Only she'd dared not actually face the Grrumm capital ships in toe-to-toe battle. They'd pressed forward inexorably, and she'd retreated just as inexorably. It grated.

Katie had gained her position and reputation by aggressively taking the battle to the enemy. She'd led from the front and that had seemed to inspire others to follow her. She'd been comfortable with that, despite the risks. But now the circumstances called for something different. It was a Fabian strategy of avoiding her foe, hoping they'd weaken or make a mistake given enough time. It required sending others forward to take the risks while she remained carefully protected in the rear.

She hated it. She knew she had to suck it up.

There was no clear evidence the Grrumm were weakening.

They appeared quite self-sufficient. For all that, Katie was certain that no isolated force could survive indefinitely without resupply or repair. Unfortunately, the Grrumm wouldn't have to. Katie and her fleet were running out of space to retreat to. Far Seat was the last Trade Hub left after Clear Ponds. Once it was gone, the Solar System and Earth were next. Katie would have to give real battle before then. Militarily, she wasn't certain it was the best idea.

Politically, it was necessary.

Most of Katie's fleet was still intact and had been refurbished and resupplied. It was also now better configured to meet the Grrumm. Hood had had a whole series of recommendations on how to achieve that, and Katie, with the full support of the government, had adopted most of them. The corvettes and frigates that had been too far along to abandon building had been converted to a new-fangled kind of "fireship". Highly automated, armored, packed with explosive devices, and given skeleton crews with skiffs to allow quick escape, they were essentially big kamikaze ships minus the need for suicide.

It was too much to hope they'd all get through, but if even a few did, it'd make a big difference. A couple of new cruisers had strengthened her fleet. A half dozen more had been building, but were being converted into large heavily armored versions of the fireships. Sad fact was they could build new ships more quickly than they could train crews to man them.

Given time, Katie was sure she could beat this existing Grrumm fleet. Too bad her time was running out, and she didn't know how many fleets the Grrumm could send.

There was no chance she could reach the Imperial shipyards in gated space, so there was nothing she could do about the possibility of the Grrumm building new fleets. So no point worrying about it.

She could try to make the best possible use of the limited time she had.

Even if, sadly, a large part of that amounted to keeping everyone else, human, and allies, working as hard as possible.

She'd do her duty.

***

Shadowguide watched the scrum of Varkoid bodyguards work their way through the crowds of Far Seat's bazaar. He had no doubt Admiral Kincaid was embedded in that knot of bodies. He also didn't doubt she was fuming in impatience at the indignity of being so coddled and stifled both.

Shadowguide had developed a clear picture of Kincaid's character. His surreptitious interrogations of Lieutenant Wootton had helped flesh out and confirm the details of that picture, but it was one already clear from open, public sources.

Kincaid was talented and determined, not complicated.

But, very, very, effective all the same.

Shadowguide was convinced part of that was because the humans were still very close to their barbarian roots. Until very recently, mere tens of tens of their home planet's rotations around its primary, they'd been divided into competing, often warring, factions. So they retained a memory of how to conduct warfare effectively. Kincaid had benefited from the close study of those that had gone before her. Her cognitive toolkit for conducting war exceeded that of any other galactic space going species, even the Scaly Ones. The Scaly Ones were aggressive and logical in pursuing that aggression but they did not have the human history of what the humans called 'peer-to-peer' conflict.

The Grrumm, like the other middle powers, had established themselves in what was practically pre-history. There had been records made, but over time they were eroded and their meaning increasingly obscured. It had literally been all but unthinkable that their supremacy could be challenged, let alone overturned.

Well, times were changing.

It was still not clear to Shadowguide who would win the current conflict. The Grrumm seemed unstoppable, but the humans weren't quitting. The humans, Kincaid herself in fact, had produced surprise after surprise. They seemed confident they could produce yet another. No one was willing to bet they couldn't.

In a way, it didn't matter.

Not to anyone, not Grrumm or human.

Whoever won would have been shaken out of their complacency. They'd be looking both to ensure their own strength and good relations with all the other actors.

Whoever won would be more engaged and more thoughtful than the Grrumm had been for many generations.

A new order was coming to the galaxy. Like it or not.

* * *

Katie was in a foul mood as they approached Far Seat docks where she'd board her shuttle and abandon the place to its fate. She most certainly did not like that. Strategically the right thing to do, it didn't sit well with her at all.

"Stop! Stop! Only humans allowed on these docks," came a loud imperious command from in front of her.

Her Varkoid bodyguards stopped, then parted to allow her to see what was going on.

A ground force captain was standing in front of her guard leader, Markraatov, barring the way to the docks where her shuttle waited.

Katie stepped forward. "What's the problem here?" she asked.

Without turning, the captain began, "No aliens allowed on these docks."

"By whose orders?"

Sneering, the captain turned and began, "Need to know." His voice trailed off as he took in Katie's rank and realized who she must be.

Katie smiled. She knew it wasn't a nice smile. The captain turned pale. The soldiers around him all shrank back a little.

"Captain." She looked at his name tag. "Wilkins, I'm not going to ask why you're here. Or why you're offending the people we've worked so hard to be friendly with, but you are not going to get in the way of me and my fleet doing our job. Make way for me and my guards."

"Yes, ma'am," Captain Wilkins choked out. "Move."

Wilkins and his soldiers moved. Katie and her Varkoids marched out onto the docks.

It was a scene of chaos. The docks were full of ground force troops and what looked like civilian refugees. human civilian refugees. It was a puzzle to Katie why they'd be here just before the Grrumm fleet was due to arrive. Her best guess was that some authority back on Earth had decided it was a good idea to evacuate some of her population via Far Seat using Galactic shipping, but hadn't felt it necessary to run the idea past her.

Annoying and somewhat problematic, as obviously, they were getting in the way of the marines and Space Force members also sprinkled about the docks trying to get back to their ships.

Once she was back on the *Bonaventure* and had the resources of her staff and command center available, she'd have to look into it. Not that she could allow it to be her top priority, however disturbing the situation was.

Right now, she needed to get to her shuttle.

She hadn't made it far before another situation caught her attention.

A child crying. A civvie shouting. A private with an assault rifle shouting back at him. And a distressed ground force sub-lieutenant off to one side dithering. A skinny Lizard was also present. How he had arrived there on the "Humans Only" dock, Katie didn't know. There was a dog barking excitedly just to add to the fun. A dog? On a Galactic space station? Wonders will never cease.

Not really in Katie's wheelhouse, but she wasn't going to just ignore the mess, either.

She stepped up. "What's going on here?" she demanded of the flustered young private.

The private, "Jackson" was stitched on his name tag, turned an angry face to her. Taking her appearance in, he apparently failed to process it. He looked stunned and uncertain as to what to do. Finally, he blurted out, "Evacuees are not allowed pets under any circumstances. The sergeant said so."

Katie smiled gently. "'*The sergeant said so, ma'am*' or '*admiral, ma'am*' might be more appropriate, Private."

Still confused, Private Jackson blustered, "Orders, ma'am."

"We're not evacuees," the civilian man put in.

"You can't prove that," Jackson retorted.

Katie didn't sigh. She remained calm. "Just a second," she commanded. "Everybody hold your horses." She peered over at the sub-lieutenant and stepping up to him, ostentatiously leaned over, and read his name tag. It read "Mountford." "Do you mind if I sort this out, Sub-lieutenant Mountford?" she asked.

"No, ma'am," the flustered Mountford answered.

"Good!" Katie turned towards the civilian man, who now had a crying little girl clinging to one leg. "Who are you? And what are you if you aren't an evacuee?"

"I'm John Robinson, a merchant," the man answered. He turned to the skinny Lizard, who looked familiar to Katie. "This is my partner, 'Seller of Earth Trinkets'. We have a cargo of various novelties we're going to sell on Assherraskill. They love gadgets and toys there. We paid our own passage here on a Swish ship, *Profitable Ventures*, and have hired a Snout one, *Opportunity*, for the trip out to Assherraskill. Our cargo is loaded. We were just escorting my family to the *Opportunity*."

Katie looked at the skinny Lizard who she was now sure she recognized. The Lizards changed names when they changed social roles and she was damned sure that this individual had not been called "Seller of Earth Trinkets" before the Lizard War. She was also extremely skeptical that was all he was now. But be that as it may, it wasn't currently of concern to her. It was a problem for after the Grrumm had been dealt with. Currently, the Lizards were allies. "So, Seller of Earth Trinkets," she said, "you can confirm this?" She spoke English. It was not an oversight.

The skinny Lizard looked back blandly. His teeth clattered, and he gave a final flick of his tongue. The closest thing the Lizards had to amused laughter. "I can, most esteemed Admiral Kincaid," he answered in perfect English. "John is my business partner. We have a profitable trade in small amusing manufactures. He traveled here at our cost and not with the help of any human government. Similarly, our travel on to Assherraskill will not divert any of the resources of your authorities."

Katie nodded. She turned to the sub-lieutenant who probably, along with his private, was not in her chain of command. Annoying and irregular, but she didn't intend to make it into a problem here and now. "Lieutenant," she said, giving him something of a promotion, "are you willing to accept my judgment on this?"

"Yes, ma'am," Sub-lieutenant Mountfort replied with unseemly relief.

Katie looked at the private. "And, Private Jackson, I assume you're willing to accept your commanding officer's decision even if the sergeant isn't here?"

Private Jackson blushed an unhealthy shade of red. "Yes, ma'am. Of course, ma'am," he managed shouldering his weapon.

Katie looked around, smiling. Nobody seemed reassured by that expression.

But the tearful little girl, at least, wasn't intimidated. "Admiral, ma'am, you won't let them take Rory, will you? He's a good boy. We've done nothing wrong."

Katie, looking at the little girl, frowned and sighed. "I'm not so sure. Even sloppy people aren't welcome on spaceships, you know. He'll have to be very well behaved. You'll have to keep a very careful eye on him. You can't have animals making messes and shedding hair on a spaceship."

The little girl knew an opening when she saw one. Her face brightened. "Oh yes, ma'am, he's very well behaved and I watch him very carefully. I brush his hair all the time. He was real good on the ship coming here."

Katie looked up at the little girl's father. "I'm pretty sure you broke some rule or another. Dogs in space aren't a good idea, but you're already here, and going to a planet, so I'll not have Rory confiscated. I will require you to pay a fine of one gold to the lieutenant, so that justice is served."

Robinson blinked and then realized this was a get out of jail card. "Yes, Admiral," he answered. Fumbling in a purse, he fetched out a bright yellow coin that he handed to the still bewildered sub-lieutenant.

Holding the coin up, Sub-lieutenant Mountfort asked, "What am I supposed to do with this?"

"Pass it up the chain of command, or save everyone trouble and forget all about this and use it to buy your platoon drinks,"

Katie snapped impatiently.

The sub-lieutenant looked at her contemplatively. Perhaps he'd learned something today. "Yes, ma'am, I think I'll do that. Thank you, ma'am."

"All in a day's work," Katie replied. She looked down to see the little girl patting Rory's head. "Can I pet him too?" she asked, crouching down to eye level with the little girl.

"Sure."

And so Katie got to pet a dog. Best part of the day so far. Too bad she was in a hurry.

Katie stood. "Okay, Markraatov, we have places to be."

"Yes, Admiral Katie."

* * *

Tanya Wootton looked across a small coffee table at her boss, Rob Hood. She'd had something of a crush on him at one point. It'd dismayed her since she'd considered him a semi-educated plebe and not at all a suitable match. Not someone she could easily introduce to her family.

For better or worse, it'd never been possible to act on those inappropriate feelings.

She'd managed to mostly get over the crush. Time will heal most afflictions. She'd also revised her opinions of the man. Whatever his background, he was as knowledgeable about galactic societies and politics as any human alive. Tanya wasn't modest, she thought much the same of herself. Hood might have different strengths, but overall he matched her understanding of their mutual area of study.

She had learned to respect him and his opinions.

"A penny for your thoughts," he said.

She smiled. When hell froze over. "I'm happy we managed to evacuate Far Seat without problems. I'm thankful for how accommodating you and the rest of the fleet's intelligence group have been of my old crew."

Hood looked amused. Ass. "You're welcome."

Tanya doubled down and dimpled him another smile. "I missed our little tête-a-têtes when I was on Far Seat."

Hood returned her smile. "So did I. There's not many of us who have a good background understanding of the Galactics. More every day, but still damned few. Gets lonely, doesn't it?"

Tanya blinked. She decided to accept it as innocent politeness. "It does," she agreed. "But you didn't call me in to talk about old times, did you?"

"No. Did you have a chance to talk to our Far Seat folks? Did they have anything interesting to say?"

"They've scooped up a ton of data they've not yet started to digest. I've arranged to make sure it gets shared on our group's net. There's a lot of balls in the air. Not just a bunch of different species, but multiple factions within each. You know all this. Makes it hard to be certain of much, but I'd say there's nothing to change the basic picture we've already developed."

"It's been a while. I want to do my due diligence. Before we tie this up, give me a quick one-paragraph summary of that. It's a useful exercise. Gets you out of the weeds. It'll also make sure we're on the same page, so to speak."

Tanya rolled her eyes. "Sure, as you know, Bob..." Hood snorted and shook his head. "It's Rob, Tanya, Rob. This is serious."

Tanya sighed. "And if we take it with all the seriousness it deserves, we'll go crazy. You taught me this."

"Okay, but do as I ask, then go get at least a few hours sleep. I think we're both too fried to do good work right now."

"I think to everyone's surprise that we're going to win this."

Hood looked skeptical, but nodded.

Tanya continued, "But it's not certain. We'll probably win, but at a high cost. How much is to be determined and will depend on exactly how we handle it and on things we really don't know, and don't have any way of knowing, about the Grrumm. Won't recap those. Also, the odds are we won't be able to prevent them from reaching Earth."

Hood looked grim, but not surprised at that.

Tanya gave him a little smile. People tended to believe what they wanted to and to reject bad news. She was happy she wasn't getting static from him on the point. "But we won't surrender. The Grrumm won't commit genocide or devastate the planet. They'll find their position there unsustainable because they've no independent merchant fleet to supply them, and all the rest of the Galactics on this side of the Frontier with gated space are basically siding with us."

"You're sure of that?"

"As sure as it's possible to be."

"So I guess that sums it up," Hood said.

"Not quite," Tanya retorted tartly. This was the least pleasant part of the whole situation in her mind. "After the Grrumm bail, assuming they do, it's all up in the air. The crisis is inevitable. What results from it is anyone's guess. The butterfly effect will be present in full force. Small decisions will have outsized consequences and I've no idea what we should advise Kincaid to do."

Hood looked blank. "Well, keeping Earth intact and independent, at the least cost possible, seems like a good start. Whatever the final outcome, we can keep that in mind."

"Pains me to say it, but concentrating on seeing off the Grrumm in the short term and not counting our chickens before they hatch might be advisable."

Hood nodded. "Kincaid seems to think she'll have to fight the Grrumm before they reach Earth. That politically, she has no choice."

Tanya frowned. She understood the logic, but it wasn't the smart thing to do. It was also above her pay grade and likely something no one could change. "In that case, she should put up the best fight she can, but try to preserve the fleet as intact as possible. Put that above any delusional hopes of stopping the Grrumm if they're determined to continue on."

"I'll rephrase that, but will pass on the message," Hood said dryly.

Tanya looked at her hands. These sorts of messy political considerations made her feel dirty. "We want to win. To survive and be independent, but we can't hope for total victory. We're going to have to live with the other Galactics and the Grrumm in whatever world comes out of this. It'd be best if we don't burn any bridges we don't have to. We don't want to inflict any more pain or suffering than is absolutely necessary."

Hood looked bleak. "Easier said than done, but I'll emphasize that point, too."

"Thank you."

"I think that covers it. Agreed?" "Yeah."

Only This Far

The contract on Kincaid had expired. The Assassin was, of course, not happy that he had failed to collect the award offered. He'd spent valuable time and resources on the matter. Worse, it'd not help his reputation.

Still, as the Assassin made his way through a near deserted Far Seat station, he couldn't help think his failure was for the better. He'd been sloppy, taking on a job in a region he wasn't familiar with against a target he also wasn't familiar with. It was a sharp reminder to him to better research future jobs before taking them on.

A reputation for effectiveness was important for a successful professional assassin. But so was remaining in the shadows and living to enjoy one's ill-gotten gains. Only amateur fanatics didn't care about surviving their attacks. And although very few individuals targeted for assassination were completely unimportant, it was essential they not be too important.

Killing someone too important made one notorious. Being notorious wasn't compatible with the discretion clients prized. Also, killing key military or political figures led to manhunts by governments. Individuals simply don't have the resources that governments can bring to bear. Being hunted by governments is, at best, distracting.

And, so although the Assassin was somewhat disappointed by his failure, he also believed it was for the better. Now his task was to disappear before reappearing somewhere in more civilized space as someone else.

He'd deliberately waited for the lull at Far Seat between the human departure and the Grrumm arrival, just so there'd be fewer people present to note his departure.

He'd be making that departure under the cover of being a fleeing forger. He did, in fact, regularly act as such. It brought in a regular side income, although it was nowhere as lucrative as the assassination business.

The Assassin in his forger identity had, in fact, forged the current identity of his ride out. The ship currently going by the name of *Main Chance* was a fast medium sized transport with a diverse crew of smugglers. They supplied and fenced for pirates too, but the Assassin wasn't supposed to know that. In any event, they were desirous of doing future business with him, so he felt he could trust them.

They were interested in their own gain, not offending against authority for its own sake. Amusingly enough, both the cargo they'd brought to Far Seat and that they'd be departing with had both been completely legal.

The humans mightn't be overly pleased with the cargo of Grrumm culinary luxuries, teas, and nectars they'd brought to Far Seat, but it wouldn't keep more than a few hundred Grrumm spacers alive longer than a couple of days. It didn't really signify. As much as the Grrumm loved their food and drink and might be tired of Navy rations, it wouldn't help their morale that much, either.

The human honey and teas they were taking away from Far Seat would sell well in civilized space as exotic novelties, but neither the humans nor the Grrumm would have the slightest objection to them.

It was all win-win good business.

As the Assassin approached the docks, he couldn't help thinking it was a funny old world.

And he'd be happy to be back in civilized space, helping solve family grudges.

In a terminal sort of way.

* * *

"I understand your objections, but there's no choice. It's a political necessity," Admiral Tretyak was saying.

Katie had poured them both large portions of Scotch upon arrival in her day cabin. Now she indulged in a big sip. It wasn't because she hated all the ceremony attendant on a visiting admiral's arrival either.

Truth was, that although the ceremony on the *Bonaventure*'s flight deck had been duly impressive and traditional, it hadn't been all that bad. It'd gone quickly and without a hitch. Although operations had been continuous, they hadn't been intense. The pomp and circumstance hadn't interfered with the running of the ship or fleet in any significant way.

No the problem was that Katie knew damn well that Tretyak hadn't come to visit her and the fleet several jumps from Earth to whisper sweet nothings in her ear.

Her forebodings had proven all too accurate. She sighed. There was no need to put on a face for Tretyak, who was an old friend and had known her since she was a girl. Seemed like ages ago. Wasn't really. She was very young for an admiral. Still, even as a girl, she'd known the path she'd set out for herself was going to involve an increasing degree of politics. She'd hoped to avoid making purely political decisions while still in the military. She'd hoped she could complete a successful military career, save Earth and humanity, and then retire before allowing herself to be coaxed out of that retirement to help deal with the problems consequent on peace. Turned out she'd been dreaming in technicolor.

But being young and overly optimistic were no excuses for being immature or irresponsible. She looked at Tretyak over her drink. "Okay. Understand that there will be no more playing at politics if we can't pull this off militarily. Also that I'm far from feeling as optimistic as you all seem to be. But go ahead: explain that necessity to me."

Tretyak nodded. "Thank you," he said. "I do understand

how hard this is for you and the risk it poses, but it really is a political necessity. You have to at least try to stop the Grrumm before they reach Earth."

"Doing so might cost us victory in the end."

"Not doing so might cost us it sooner," Tretyak retorted. Without real heat, but emphatically. "Earth is going full out to support the fleet and to evacuate as much of the population and our industry as we can. People are working around the clock frantically. But morale is fragile. They're doing that because the government has sold them something of a bill of goods."

"Great. What do they think is going on?"

"Well, they think Admiral Kincaid is a towering military genius that can overcome seemingly impossible odds for one."

Katie felt a headache coming on. She wasn't entirely innocent here. She certainly hadn't tried to dissuade anyone from having a high opinion of her abilities. She'd wanted people to listen to her and give her free rein to act on her own. Well, it'd worked, and it seemed maybe she'd outsmarted herself. "Surely Cunningham isn't part of the '*Kincaid-is-great*' chorus."

Tretyak chuckled. "You'd be surprised. The opposition is talking you up to the heavens. Cunningham, in particular, is more Catholic than the Pope. He's beating the drum that whatever failings you might have had as a peacetime junior officer in the Space Force, that as a military commander in wartime, you're without par. He's gone so far as to imply you ought to have my job and that the government isn't supporting you sufficiently."

"Ouch. What's his game?"

"You know what happened to Churchill after the Second World War, right?"

"Yeah, the British figured that a great wartime Prime Minister wasn't what they wanted in peacetime."

"Exactly. Cunningham is smart enough to bend with the wind. He figures he'll get his chance. Also, I suspect he believes the more he builds up your image now, the harder it'll be for you to live up to it later. The greater your fall from grace will be."

"He's worrying about the peace when there's a good chance we'll lose the war? You and the government are letting him?"

"In the short term, we need the support he's providing. Like you've suggested, we need to survive the short term or there'll be no long term to fret about."

"Fair ball. Hoisted on my own petard."

"Quite the day for cliches. I guess they get to be cliches for a reason." Tretyak shook his head ruefully. "So, yes, it leaves us with you having an inflated reputation that has the public believing you can accomplish miracles. Our propaganda has also talked up the new fireships and how we've restored your fleet to an even greater strength than it had at the Battle Past Plenitude. We've also been pushing the idea that all sorts of other species have been lending us valuable aid. We've convinced the public that the Grrumm are alone and isolated and that it just remains for you to chop off their lifeline back to gated space and that'll finish them off."

"Good heavens, I wish that were true. And whatever happened to Op Sec?"

"It is an exaggerated and partial picture, true. In keeping morale up, we may have made the general population a bit too optimistic. It's a problem now. If you retreat now without a fight, it'll be like a bucket of cold water in people's faces. It'll demoralize them completely."

"Just peachy. Op Sec?"

"Not our top concern right now. As far as we can tell, the Grrumm just barge in, indifferent to what their opposition might be doing. They're a lot more into overwhelming invincible force than spying and trying to be clever."

Katie sighed and drank more Scotch. Maybe she should watch that, but it seemed more an evening for getting bad news than being sharp witted. "It does seem to have worked for them. And truthfully, it seems as long as you give them what they want, which is mainly not to be a threat, they're easy enough to get along with."

Tretyak winced. "Yes, about that. That's another problem."

"That the Grrumm Empire treats its subjects rather gently is a problem?"

"Yes, when you've made them out to be bogeymen who

have to be defeated at all costs, it could be."

Katie felt a sudden flash of anger. She hated lies. She really hated being implicated in someone else's lies and being forced to go along with them. She stared at Tretyak balefully.

Tretyak raised his hands in a gesture of defensive placation. "Not my fault. It's not the job of the military to directly contradict their political masters. And to be fair, nobody has been putting out false rumors of their being baby eaters or anything like that. Just a matter of emphasis regarding the known facts. If they get to Earth orbit, they could end life on the planet or impose a harsh occupation, with no mention of the fact they've no record of doing so."

Katie snorted. "So if I can't keep them from occupying the Solar System, not only does my reputation for military competence suffer, but we all look like liars. People forcing the little guys to fight against the odds solely to preserve our own power."

"It won't help morale. It might look to a lot of people like they're being expected to sacrifice a lot for no real purpose. If the Grrumm can get even a large minority of people on Earth to co-operate, they might be able to sustain themselves there indefinitely. Our whole strategy will be invalidated. Some factions have already given up on holding on to the Solar System and are organizing an exodus to unexplored space down-arm hoping to start again elsewhere."

"And that's what might happen to me and my fleet if morale on Earth takes too great a hit."

"Exactly. So you've got to try to stop the Empire before it gets there. If you can't, you've got to at least make it look like we can beat them if we just keep trying."

"Okay," Katie conceded, "I believe you. It's a political necessity. We're going to have to turn and fight before reaching the Solar System."

Tretyak looked relieved. He took a swig of his drink. Katie found that alarming. "What? Surely you didn't think I'd disobey direct orders?"

"I didn't think it was likely, Katie, but recently I've had a lot of unpleasant surprises."

Katie nodded. Mostly, she dealt with whatever came up and

didn't worry about whether it met her expectations or not. Predicting the future, at least in detail, was a mug's game. Though it was one she often wished she'd been worse at. "Any good news?" she asked brightly.

"Actually, yes, that all-out effort we've managed to get has produced significantly more hulls. They would have been fully manned ships if with very green, quickly trained crews."

"It's close to murder sending inadequately trained crews into battle."

Tretyak sighed. "Yes, so on your advice we're hastily converting them to fireships."

Katie grimaced. "I wish I didn't have to use kamikaze ships against the big Grrumm ships. It's very wasteful."

"But you don't always get what you want." "No kidding."

***

"It's simple math," Tanya Wootton asserted. "Surely you can see that?"

Rob Hood, her nominal superior - though she often seemed to forget that - did, in fact, see that. "Yes, but I also know our mathematical model contains assumptions. Ones we can't be one hundred percent sure of. What's more, it's our job to find the best way forward for our boss. Kincaid needs us to find a path to victory. Telling her it's an unpredictable toss-up that could go either way and the only certain thing is that both sides are going to take heavy losses does not cut the mustard. Do you understand?"

Lieutenant Tanya Wootton looked around the little room that doubled as their private office. During off-hours, a mythical thing Rob had stopped believing in, it was his sleeping quarters. "Not cutting the mustard doesn't make it any less real," she said. She sighed and looked at him sympathetically. "We've been beating our heads against this for days. We're not getting anywhere. Surely there are better things we could be doing."

Rob, who'd been spending too much time alone in close quarters with the young woman, couldn't help agreeing. Also, the fact he was letting himself think such things suggested that he was overly tired, and they were getting too comfortable with each other. There, that was a safe thought. "You're right," he said, "we could both use some rest. Maybe after a good sleep it'll look different."

Wootton snorted. "Anything is possible."

"So!" Rob replied, attempting to sound bright and optimistic, "Let's summarize the problem one more time and then sleep on it. Sound good?"

"Okay. First, our assumptions. One, we can't fight at range where they're unlikely to hurt us much because we can't hurt them at all from long range."

"That's a solid assumption, unfortunately."

Wootton nodded. "Two, if we close to short range and slug it out, we lose, too. At least given our relative numbers, the relative weakness of our beam weapons and the relative strength of that shield technology they have. We concentrate our fire carefully, both target and time wise, and maybe we damage a ship or two. In the meantime, they single shot most of our ships. Best case, they get two or three hits on one of our cruisers and they're out of action. Even with the most optimistic assumptions, we lose and we lose badly."

"Well, nailing that down was useful."

"I'm sure Kincaid will think so."

"Surprisingly enough, I think she'll understand. She won't be happy, but she'll understand. She's not unreasonable."

"She's got a soft spot for you, but anyway, it leaves high speed passes, attempting to do severe damage in a short period and then automatically passing out of the range of harm as our only viable tactic."

"For some value of '*viable*'."

"Yes, that's the core of the problem." "Because?"

"Because, although if our kamikaze ships came in with high delta vee against stationary targets, they could hit each one of them reliably and destroy them all."

"But not only are the enemy ships not stationary targets, they'll deliberately maneuver to avoid being hit."

"And our ships, in turn, will maneuver to hit them despite that."

"Which introduces multiple sources of interacting

feedback."

"Brings to mind ear-piercing loud squeals."

"Indeed. The whole thing goes chaotic."

"And even small changes in assumptions and initial conditions result in vastly different outcomes."

Tanya smiled. Rob could have been insulted that she thought so little of his understanding of the math, but he rather liked her smile. "Just so," she said, "though in truth, most of the thousands of runs we've done show high losses on both sides. That's pretty, let's not say constant, maybe probable would be a better word."

"I don't think that's going to reassure Kincaid any."

"I don't think any of us like it, but it is what it is. I seem to remember some boss of mine harping on the need to face up to reality."

"Grim bastard." "Very."

"That's it, I think."

Wootton looked bleak and sighed. "I agree."

"Okay. Good night, Tanya."

* * *

"Somebody ought to be stripped of their titles and possessions and exiled for this," Thorn-Paw growled.

The non-noble leader of weapons technicians they'd been questioning twitched and stared wide-eyed at him. Rrolff, Lord Earl Sweets-Swiper commander of the Expeditionary Fleet to be formal, could see that poor individual wanted to do nothing more than turn and bolt from the room. He hardly blamed the poor male. It seemed Thorn-Paw had spent too long in the Frontier Fleet, living among the barbarians. The next thing you knew, he'd be suggesting the death penalty for officials that failed in their duties. "It is indeed very unfortunate and aggravating that those in charge of maintaining the Expeditionary Fleet's weapons during its long hiatus failed so severely," Rrolff allowed. "But we should commend Technical Paw Leader Careful-Crafter for his devotion to duty. Better we should have learned of the problem now rather then later in
battle."

Thorn-Paw still looked angry, but relented. He looked at

the quailing non-noble leader. "Thank you, Careful-Crafter. It is some relief that there remain those that know their duty."

Rrolff tilted his head at Careful-Crafter. "Yes, thank you, Technical Paw Leader. You may leave now."

Careful-Crafter thumped his chest in salute. He turned and all but ran for the exit from Rrolff's day cabin.

Rrolff waited until he was gone. "It did indeed take courage to bring us that horror story," he said to Thorn-Paw.

Thorn-Paw tilted his head in agreement. "True. It did, and sadly, one cannot assume such courage." He snorted. "We should encourage it when we find it. I should have contained my anger. But it is hard to tell what is worst about this: the problem it presents us, or the rot it reveals in the Empire."

"I'm not so sure the scent of it is so obvious," Rrolff replied. "I didn't know our large energy crystal conduits weren't made in some factory on one of the home planets. I simply assumed without actually thinking about it much that they were. Did you know?"

Thorn-Paw grimaced. "I did not." He wrinkled his snout yet more. "I don't think I thought about it even that much. If they're not heavily used, they last a generation or more with little degradation. In storage, they apparently last many generations without any. If I thought about it at all, I guess I thought supply would magically produce them whenever needed."

"I have talked to city and station dwellers who seem to think their meals appear in the back of the food shop by some sort of magic. I imagine most would deny it if questioned."

Thorn-Paw rubbed his nose in amusement. "Truly, we are mere mortals, not gods who know all."

"The Expeditionary Fleet's maintainers, who knows how many generations ago, chose poorly, it must be admitted," Rrolff said. "When it became impossible to get replacement conduits they should have reported that. For some reason they decided it was better not to create a fuss. They pretended all was routine and well instead. One must wonder why."

Thorn-Paw gave a tired grunt. "They failed in their duty abysmally. If they couldn't do the planned maintenance properly, they should have reported that, and accepted the consequences." He looked bleak, snout still, little black eyes peering at nothing present. "But the real failure lies elsewhere, I think."

Rrolff gave a head tilt and grunt of his own. Not a hearty, decisive grunt, he feared, something more between a whimper and a grumble. If he were to show such poor control at court, they'd eat him alive. He did truly hate court. It was worse than a hive of irate stinging insects on a hot, muggy day for irritation. Still, he feared that if he spent much longer out here in the dark, he'd end up as much a barbarian as Thorn-Paw. "Nobles who wallow in their privilege, but dodge their duties. Ones who deflect responsibility elsewhere. You can be candid with me, Sixth."

Thorn-Paw rubbed his nose again. "Indeed, Paw of the Emperor, you have proven a pleasant surprise. Not all with inherited titles are worse than useless wastes of air."

Rrolff snorted. "Thank you, so kind of you to say so."

"But you can't deny if it were true of all, we'd not be trapped up this tree with the slaughter-cats circling below."

Rrolff rubbed his nose. Thorn-Paw had spent too much time in space among the uncultured. "The cats can climb. Maybe fanged direwolves."

"It has been paw upon paw of generations since our ancestors had to worry about predators if alone in the woods, hasn't it?"

"Yes, we've grown dim-witted, slow, and complacent, and now we may have to pay the price."

"Believe me, I have always respected our forebears, but it was some among those who've climbed the last and tallest tree who failed. Now we're having to deal with it."

"Each generation leaves the next a legacy. I do think we Grrumm have been better than most in preserving what our revered ancestors and parents have left us."

"We do value tradition."

"We do, but now it is our lot to deal with something new."

"Without conduits, not just our beams, but our shields will fail. The tree we cower in will shatter under our weight, leaving us prey to the packs of scavengers below us."

"A traditional way of looking at it. Unduly alarmist too. The conduits haven't failed. The loss in efficiency due to deterioration is still minimal. If not overused, they'll not deteriorate much more, let alone fail completely."

"We can't be entirely sure of how bad they are without ripping everything apart and checking each and every one of them. The maintenance records have been falsified. We can't trust them."

Thorn-Paw gave a low, quiet growl. He was actually foaming at the mouth some. Not much, just a little. "I have always detested those who aren't honest with those they lead. Only I find myself thinking that it'd destroy morale to do that. Worse, we're on campaign. Though our enemy has been shy recently, we know they can strike if they wish. Even doing it in shifts, do we dare take a large part of our fleet off line to do yard type work in space in the face of the enemy? What can we do about the problem other than define it a little more clearly? Do so and make its consequences worse in the process."

Rrolff was startled. "You advise keeping this secret and ignoring it?"

"It twists my stomach, but yes, we'd best not let this news get out. If our opponents learn of it, they will exploit it as sure as the sun rises and sets over the forests of home. Ignore it, no. But we must act in a manner that makes sense for other reasons lest the enemy scents our weakness."

"And how do you propose we perform this magical trick?"

"We show great restraint, acting as is proper for civilized people encountering benighted barbarians who might not be completely lost to reason."

"Really?"

"In truth. We proceed inexorably to the orbits of their home planet, but we do not fire upon their ships except when they pose a clear and immediate threat. Only when they are sufficiently close in and potentially able to overwhelm our shields, do we retaliate in a proportionate manner."

"All the while proclaiming resistance is futile, but that we don't wish to do any unnecessary harm."

"Politics is not my strength, Lord Earl, but that may help."

"It may. I'll have to contemplate the matter. Details aside, I think the path you suggest is a wise one."

Thorn-paw rubbed his nose. "Yes, my lord, I think we'll tame these barbarians yet."

* * *

High above the plane in which 61 Cygni A and 61 Cygni B orbited each other with a period of centuries, Katie's fleet waited. And, in the main conference room on its flagship, the *Bonaventure*, the top officers of that fleet were assembled for a final orders group before the final showdown before the Solar System.

They weren't here because 61 Cygni was a good final stepping stone to Earth. It wasn't. At a little over eleven light-years from the Solar System, it was a longish jump. Also, a not overly stable or safe one. Binary systems make an awkward target for an FTL jump. The gravity field of such systems is inherently more complicated than that of ones with only a single primary.

Katie also didn't like the fact that the large separation of its stars meant the Grrumm fleet had a choice of possible emergence points. If there'd been a single easily predicted point for emergence from jump it would have made her stand here easier. Between them, the vastness of space and the shields of the Grrumm ships made laying obstacles and mines in the path of the enemy fleet rather ineffective. Also, it would have been better if they could have concentrated on a single jump exit and not split their resources between two.

A single possible jump exit would have also allowed her to position her fleet so as to surprise and attack the Grrumm very shortly after emergence. As it was, they were bound to see her coming and to be as prepared as possible. It was far less than ideal.

Katie had worked hard to hide her unhappiness from her officers throughout the current meeting. She'd tried to appear confident and sublimely certain of success.

So far it appeared she'd been successful. It baffled her that nobody brought up any objections to their battle plan. It had glaring flaws in her mind. She'd have been delighted if someone could have found more. She was sure there were ones she'd missed, and she'd have welcomed the chance to maybe, just maybe, fix them. But so far, no one seemed to have any significant objections or criticisms. Damned few questions, even.

She'd give them one more chance. "So," she declaimed crisply, "that's the plan. Any questions? Observations even?"

She looked out at her officers. Susan Fritzsen was looking maddeningly sphinx-like, but Katie could detect a sense of eager anticipation underneath the impassive exterior. Didn't her old friend know this could get her killed just as their last big battle had killed Amy and many of those under her?

Smith looked amused. He always looked amused. Wong had the air of an over eager student, determined to impress his teacher. Most of the others, Vane, von Luck, Haralson, and the rest, just looked businesslike and eager to get the meeting over with and back to their duties. No hint of any questions from any of them.

Well, fine. Katie narrowed her eyes and looked around with a predatory grin. It was an act, but acting inspirational was part of the job. "Great. Twelve hours, give or take. Back to your posts. Do your final checks, but I want every one of you and your main shifts to have had a good eight hours rest when the engagement begins. Dismissed!"

She pivoted on her heel and marched out of the room, addressing Hood and Wootton as she did so. "You two, follow me."

She led her little parade to her cabin, trying to project grim confidence the whole way. She only relaxed once her cabin door had closed behind them. She flopped down into her arm chair. "Sit," Katie told her intelligence officers with a wave.

Hood and Wootton glanced at each other. They knew her well enough to realize she wasn't in a great mood. "Yes, ma'am," they chorused quietly.

Katie smiled. It was an uncommon degree of agreement. She was sure the two were attracted to each other, although she was almost equally certain they hadn't acted on it. They did argue, although generally politely, all the time. Katie figured it made them an effective team. Groupthink in intelligence was undesirable. "I don't have to act all confident and infallible with you two. I want a summary of our situation and I want to hear what you think might go wrong. I want to hear your worst fears. Keep it short. We do need to get our rest, but be honest and complete. I'm going to sleep on what you tell me and keep it in mind during the coming battle. That way when and if I need to make a quick decision, maybe there's a chance it'll be quicker and maybe the right one even."

Wootton looked at Hood.

Hood sighed, sitting down. He waited for Wootton to do the same, which she did after a slight pause. They weren't comfortable. It meant they did have reservations, ones they didn't want to express. Hood took a deep breath. "That's just it, Katie. I assume this is off the record?"

"Yep. No open mics here."

"Yes, ma'am. Fact is, the plan is the best I can think of, given the fact we have to give battle here." He paused.

"But?"

"But it's an all-or-nothing single throw of the dice. We're committing ourselves to a single very high velocity pass right at them and there's really not much you or any officer higher than a ship's captain can do after we start. Theoretically, there might be a short window mid-approach where you could get some information that would allow you to abort the run while it'd still help, but practically speaking, there's not much chance of that."

"And our relative velocity will be so great after that there'll just be no time to make useful decisions."

"Our event horizon will overrun the receipt of timely data. There'll be no time for even a short decision loop. Things are simply going to be happening too fast." He sucked his teeth and attempted a smile. "Good thing is it'll be quick. Whatever happens, it'll be all over very quickly."

"Worst case?"

"We're all just floating debris. Every ship destroyed and no survivors and we do no to minimal damage to the Grrumm."

"That's very unlikely, yes?"

"Yes, but not completely impossible. Most likely outcome is we take a big chunk, several cruisers and two or three battleships, out of their fleet while taking significant but acceptable losses ourselves."

Katie grimaced. "Acceptable losses?"

"Yes, a fleet that is still large enough after its losses to do what we need it to do strategically. Namely to force the Grrumm to keep their own fleet concentrated and not spread out. Spread out and actually enforcing their rule over the local area. Spread out securing the supplies they need to remain in our neighborhood."

Wootton fidgeted.

"Speak up," Katie ordered.

"Admiral, it's like we told you. We're not certain of our facts, and the model is chaotic. It's mathematically impossible to be sure of what's going to happen."

"So, we pays our money and takes our chances then?"

Wootton looked at Hood.

"Carnival games," he answered.

"Oh, well, at least we don't think this game is rigged," Wootton said.

"Great," Katie commented. "Off with you. Get your sleep. It'll be over one way or the other by this time tomorrow."

"Yes, ma'am."

Unto the Breach

Déjà vu all over again. Once again, they were in Katie's Flag Command Center on the *Bonaventure* waiting for a battle to begin, with no way of knowing who'd win or who'd survive to see the next day. They weren't yet in their combat pods. There'd be plenty of time to get into them. The fleet was hours away from the two possible emergence points for the Grrumm Imperial Fleet.

Katie looked over at Hood, who as usual was standing beside her.

He was squinting at the time displayed in an upper corner of the big tactical display filling the wall opposite them. "It shouldn't be long now," he said.

Katie grunted. She figured he was right about that much. She wasn't sure if his and Wootton's opinion that this was a gamble and she'd not be able to do much to influence the coming battle once they'd committed was correct. It seemed to her that they were assuming that the Grrumm wouldn't do anything unexpected. That nothing would happen that she might have to adjust to. In Katie's experience, and from her reading about the experience of commanders that had gone before her, you could expect the unexpected. That, in fact, the measure of a great commander was taking advantage of it rather than being flummoxed by it. "Soon," she replied. "Should be interesting."

Hood's lips twitched. "Very." They fell quiet and waited.

"Ma'am," Sensors spoke up, "we have a close-by jump emergence. It has to be a mini-jump."

"Probably one of our scouts," Tommy Kooperman, Lieutenant Commander Kooperman - her operations officer - put in.

Katie chuckled. An affectation that was more useful than words just now. "Let's not jump to conclusions, Ops, but you're probably right."

Mini-jumps within a system rather than between systems were uncertain and dangerous, but given the size of the Cygni 61 system at almost a hundred light-hours, they were practically unavoidable. They'd trained hard in how to use them. It was the only way to stay ahead of the light speed event horizon.

And that was a necessity. Katie didn't dare disperse her force to cover both Cygni 61 A and B, but she also couldn't afford to let the Grrumm fleet by. If she had to wait days to even hear of the Grrumm arrival and then spend more days trying to close with them, the odds were they'd sail right on past her forces and reach Earth without even engaging her.

It hadn't been an easy choice deciding to meet the enemy in 61 Cygni.

"Ma'am," Comms announced, "it's one of our scouts. They report the Grrumm fleet has arrived at 61 Cygni B at the jump point from up-arm. It looks like all of them in a very tight formation. They're squirting the telemetry over now."

Katie watched as the new data was painted on the tactical display. It looked much as they'd expected. The Grrumm formation did seem extremely tight. Even tighter than it had been before. "Ops," she asked,"see anything unexpected?"

Kooperman took a few seconds to respond. "No, ma'am. Somewhat tighter formation than before. Same basic disk-like formation with the big guys as the bulls-eye. Nothing that merits reconsidering our plans as far as I can see."

"Thank you, Ops," Katie acknowledged. She looked to her side. "Hood?"

"Nothing here, ma'am."

"Very well. Comms, general broadcast to the fleet. We will proceed with plan Beta-One. Immediately. Kincaid out."

It was mere seconds before they started to feel the thrum of the *Bonaventure*'s engines through their feet and in their bones.

"All hands to combat stations," sounded over the ship's loudspeakers.

Katie and Hood complied, swinging into their combat pods and closing the lids of their lifesaving coffins. A brief period of darkness was followed by Katie's HUD filling her vision. A quick series of comm checks and all quieted down again. Once again, they simply had to wait on events.

The whole fleet micro-jumped. The entry was nauseating, the exit just minutes later was horrifying. Katie emptied her stomach into her pod's built-in barf bag. It didn't smell any better than it felt. But the bag auto-sealed and the ventilation worked hard to clear the odor. She'd had the sense to eat a good sized but very bland meal earlier so a quick rinse and spit mostly cleansed her palette. Space travel was so romantic.

"Ops, report," Katie barked. Unnecessarily, the microphone in her pod was too sensitive, if anything, but it made her feel better.

"Everybody made it intact, ma'am. No collisions. No jump failures. Formations are pretty good. Better than I'd have expected. No reports of any significant damage."

"Thank you, Ops. Sensors?"

"Grrumm Fleet at two light-hours, ma'am. Tight standard formation. Unchanged. No scouts. Proceeding at cruising speed for the Earth jump point. No evidence they've seen us yet."

Katie nodded, despite knowing nobody could see it. "Thank you, Sensors." It was exactly what they could see on the tactical display. Nothing had changed substantially from what the scout ship had reported. Her fleet continued to accelerate towards where the enemy would be in several hours. They'd reach a relative velocity that was no more than a small fraction of light speed by the time they met them, but that was still much faster than a speeding bullet or an old-fashioned hypersonic missile. They'd have immense kinetic energy built up, and the window of engagement would be very short. Mere minutes.

She stared at the tactical display. The Grrumm were in a very tight formation. And proceeding on a predictable course without attempting any evasive maneuvers. They were also eschewing any attempts at Electronic Warfare (EW). They had only the one, admittedly very good, trick of being all but invulnerable. She made a decision.

"Comms, general broadcast to the fleet. Tighten up all formations to one half standard separation. We're going to hit them hard with everything we have. Kincaid out."

"Message broadcast. All units have acknowledged," Comms reported shortly.

"Relaxed combat stations for the next ninety minutes," announced the loudspeaker system. That made sense. It'd be almost two hours before the Grrumm even noticed Katie's fleet, given they didn't have any scouts out. Katie climbed out of her pod gratefully.

"Commodore Huffman," she addressed her Chief of Staff, "Please have the watch take brief refreshment breaks in shifts during the next hour. No sense wearing ourselves out waiting."

"Yes, ma'am," Huffman answered. Katie took a break herself and restored her digestion with some juice and a sandwich and then used the restroom. Returning to the command center, she made sure Hood took a break too. Huffman handled the rest of the watch. He was a very competent staff officer. He deserved a command of his own in truth, but Katie had needed someone she trusted as her Chief of Staff.

In any event, in less than an hour, she and Hood were back to standing watching the tactical display. Waiting and watching as the symbols representing thousands of intelligent beings and the embodied wealth of whole planetary systems crawled towards each other and fate.

It was not Katie's favorite activity. But it was her job to be ready in the event something happened she could do something about, and to be a reassuring symbol even if it didn't.

It was most of another hour before Sensors reported.

"Ma'am, the Grrumm are changing course," she announced. "They're coming around to a vector directly towards us."

"Looks like a meeting engagement, ma'am," Ops commented. "They're not spreading out. They're going to meet us head on."

"A good old-fashioned joust, Ops," Katie said, trying to sound unconcerned while not sacrificing gravitas.

She looked over at Hood. His lips gave a thin twitch. He wasn't amused. Katie didn't blame him. Some of the scenarios they'd run had had a concentrated human fleet jabbing through a more spread-out Grrumm one. In those scenarios, Grrumm losses had never amounted to more than a few ships, but the human fleet usually survived largely intact too. The scenarios in which the two concentrated fleets met head on had mostly come out differently. Sometimes the Grrumm were even annihilated completely. But Katie's fleet always took staggering losses in excess of fifty per cent. Sometimes one hundred percent. Those scenarios were rare, thankfully. The Pyrrhic victories unfortunately weren't. Win or lose, this was going to hurt.

Katie wanted to remind Hood that they had to close to extreme short range or any losses they took would be in vain. Only it wasn't the time or place.

"Ma'am, the Grrumm fleet is increasing velocity," Sensors announced.

"They're at what we think is their maximum safe acceleration," Ops elaborated.

"Thank you, Sensors, Ops," Katie acknowledged. She'd watched old videos from the dawn of the Space Age in which irresponsible young people had indulged in insane games, life-threatening games with old-fashioned land automobiles. She'd had a hard time identifying with them, but this felt a lot like one of their games of "*Chicken*". Well, live and learn. Looked like the Grrumm were ready to rumble. They were doubling down on their bet. Katie thought they were making a mistake. They weren't used to foes they couldn't take out with a single blow. The number of hulls they had was already small for how far they were from their bases and the space they were hoping to dominate. Even if Katie and her entire fleet met its end here, if the Grrumm were to lose too many ships, they wouldn't be able to hold on in hostile space so far from support. She wondered if the Grrumm had some concept equivalent to Pyrrhic victory and who was Rome and who was Pyrrhus here.

She collected herself, trying not to be too obvious about it, and reached a decision. They'd had long discussions about whether it was better to try to maximize the total energy delivered to the enemy over the course of the battle or to try to spike it and maximize its concentration in time. No conclusion had been reached. They simply didn't know enough about the Grrumm shield technology and how to best strain it. Katie had the feeling that concentration in time was the way to go. She decided to follow that gut feeling. "Comms, general broadcast to the fleet. Adopt fire plan variation Beta-One-C. Repeat plan is Beta-One-C. Hold all fire until at most effective range. Deploy EW missiles, spacecraft, and torpedoes, but do not close in advance of the main fleet action. We are going for maximum temporal fire concentration at the time of closest approach. Kincaid out."

So not only was she asking her people to suicidally close head on with the enemy, she was asking them not to fire until at point blank range. She knew they'd do it, and she was proud of them for that. She doubted anyone would ever understand how much she regretted asking it of them.

"Orders acknowledged, ma'am," Comms announced.

"Thank you, Comms." It wouldn't be long now. Not with both fleets accelerating towards each other.

Still, space was big and the effective range of even light speed weapons relatively short. It was well over an hour before they went to full combat readiness and locked themselves into their combat pods.

Once in those pods, the excruciating wait continued.

The Grrumm didn't seem to believe in missiles or fighting at range. They were close-in brawlers. Well, Katie planned to give them what they wanted, good and hard. Finally, Ops announced it.

"Crossing into maximum Grrumm heavy beam range." And it started. The inertial compensators couldn't handle the full force of the sudden jinks the *Bonaventure* was making. Katie could feel them through the padding of her pod. The only way the humans had of defeating the Grrumm heavy beams was to stay out of their way.

Tommy, the Ops officer, cursed. Not professional.

"Ma'am!" Sensors exclaimed in a tone too close to panicked shock in Katie's mind.

"Yes, Miki. What is it?" Katie asked with studied, patient calm. Looking at the tactical display, she realized what it was before her sensors officer answered.

"Ma'am, the *Terrible* is gone."

"Yes, I see, Sensors. We knew this wasn't going to be a picnic. Do you need to be relieved?"

Sensors, Lieutenant Miki Kawasaki, gulped audibly. "No, ma'am. Just surprised. It is rather early, isn't it?"

Katie suppressed an urge to give a heavy sigh. Kawasaki was correct; it was early. It was pure bad luck the *Terrible*, CV-006, Larry Wong's flagship, had failed to dodge so far out. Still, she couldn't let panic set in. "It's within the parameters set by the simulations we ran." Which was true if disingenuous. "Unless the tactical display falls behind, it's best you don't announce further losses unless I ask for them."

That fell into a glum silence. Better that than panic.

Katie did have one more task. "Comms, verify that command of Task Force One has transferred to Commander Jarvis on the *Powerful*."

"Yes, ma'am. Do you want further command changes verified?"

"Just for the Task Forces and Groups," Katie announced blandly, as if this was normal.

"Yes, ma'am."

Katie watched the smaller ships being picked off on her HUD's tactical display. Real people who'd trusted her on every one of them. They were dying at an ever-increasing rate.

"Ma'am, Task Force One is under Commander Jarvis's

command."

"Thank you, Comms." Katie couldn't help sounding distracted as she watched her display fill with red. Red numbers, red names, and red symbols all condensing horrible losses into something at least intellectually digestible.

"Ma'am, the *Powerful* has been hit. She's severely damaged. We've lost contact with Commander Jarvis. Commander Campbell on the *Enterprise* is taking command of Task Force One." Sensors spoke in an even, carefully controlled voice. Good for her. Good heavens, Katie hoped Miki survived this. She was so young.

Katie hadn't seen much of Cara Campbell recently. Since Katie had been terribly young herself. Cara had had something of a stick up her backside when Katie was a junior officer. Hopefully, it made for a stiff spine now. She'd certainly need it.

"Also, *Leviathan, Ark Royal,* and *Warrior* are gone or wrecked. Ma'am, command structure in Task Force Two seems to have broken down."

"Confirm that, ma'am," Comms said.

Katie didn't allow herself to dwell on the fact that another old friend, Colleen McGinnis, her old Academy roommate, was likely gone along with the *Leviathan*.

"Thank you, Sensors and Comms. Not to worry. As long as our ships know enough to engage with the closest enemy, they won't go far wrong."

"Yes, ma'am," Comms answered politely. It was surreal under the circumstances.

Katie tried hard to figure out what was happening. It seemed like the Grrumm were prioritizing the largest human ships; their carriers. Only although the carriers were also command ships, their offensive component, their torpedo bombers had already been launched. As depressing as it was seeing friends dying in wholesale lots, this was a major error on the Grrumm part.

"Ops," Katie called, "check the status of our fireships."

"Ma'am, they're all still intact."

And as he said that, they crossed the invisible area in space that was on average their closest approach to the enemy. Indeed, the two fleets were actually interpenetrating. It was a miracle of fatally perverse navigation. And finally Katie's fleet began to fire back.

It felt good even before Sensors started rattling off enemy losses for a change. "Ma'am, an enemy cruiser has exploded. Another has ceased acceleration. Two more cruisers are heavily damaged."

Katie could tell she was still losing ships, but it was good to hear the enemy was finally paying a price for it.

"Ma'am!" Katie could tell Sensors was carefully restraining glee. "A Grrumm battleship has broken in two. Fireship got it."

And at that point, the *Bonaventure* gave a sharp jerk. The lighting flickered. There was a distant thump and Katie saw that her pod was operating on emergency power.

Her HUD froze.

The normal background hum of the ship suddenly decreased.

"Report!" Katie commanded, praying the command net was still up.

Comms reported first. "Ma'am, external comms are offline. We've been hit."

"Confirm that, ma'am," Sensors reported. "I've no external links. No useful local ones either. I still have a connection to some sensors, but most seem to be offline."

Comms spoke again. "Ma'am, Captain McLeod reports that the *Bonnie* has lost power, but is still largely intact. He has crews working to get power back up. He says we're past the Grrumm fleet now and that they don't seem to be firing on us. We'll be out of range in a few minutes." Comms seemed relieved by the last tidbit.

Katie took a deep breath. So that was it, was it? She was out of the battle and still alive. That was something.

Only she didn't know what had happened.

She wouldn't until the power came back on. If it came back on. Maybe they were adrift in space, unrescuable on an unrepairable ship, already all dead, only didn't know it yet.

She didn't know if they'd won, lost, or managed a draw. Somehow it seemed like that ought to be important.

***

Live and learn. Katie was learning what heartache felt like.

Hopelessness slathered with grief, too. She was a regular smorgasbord of negative emotion.

She'd been too busy and too numb to feel much earlier. Only now that she was off duty and back in her cabin was it beginning to hit her.

It'd been a distant relief when the *Bonaventure*'s power had come back on and she and her watch staff had been able to exit their combat pods and take stock of the battle's aftermath.

She'd already known it'd be bad. Of the eight carriers she'd started the battle with, only the *Bonaventure* and the *Triumph* had survived, and they were both badly damaged. Dozens of torpedo bombers had been scuttled for the lack of flight decks to return to. At least most of their crews had been saved. It was personally some small relief that Susan Fritzsen had also survived. Neither of her other two Task Force Commanders, Larry Wong and John Smith, had. Neither had Henry Vane, commanding the Support Group.

A third of her cruisers were also simply gone, along with much of the rest of her senior officer cadre. Another third of the cruisers, half of those remaining, were so damaged that it wasn't possible to tell if they'd ever fight again. They certainly wouldn't if she couldn't find repair yards for them. Somewhere besides in the Solar System.

Because although they'd managed to outright destroy several Grrumm cruisers and at least one of their battleships, and had inflicted significant visible damage on at least a quarter of those remaining, it hadn't been enough to deflect the inexorable Grrumm advance. The Grrumm had turned back towards the Earthward jump point. In a couple of hours, they'd have reached it and be on their way to the Solar System.

They wouldn't find much there. Katie had sent a courier ahead with the bad news of the debacle at 61 Cygni. She'd warned the authorities there to prepare to destroy everything that might be of conceivable use to the alien invaders.

The Grrumm would arrive to find that part of humanity that hadn't been able to flee, air, and food, but no industrial resources to speak of. No factories, no mines, no spare parts for space ships, and certainly no repair yards. The Star Rats, the Builders, and other aliens that humanity now shared the system and their planet with had assured the human government that they'd not lend the Grrumm any support.

Earth and the Solar System would be reduced to an almost pre-industrial state. If the Grrumm felt like it, or the Space Force wasn't able to retake and rebuild the system, there'd be no "*almost*" about it. Humanity's space stations and asteroid bases would need to be evacuated and the human remnants would be reduced to scratching in the dirt on the surfaces of Earth and Mars. The Martians might be facing slow extinction. It was grim.

Militarily, it was scorched earth at its finest. It'd worked for the Russians in 1812 and 1941. Maybe it'd work now.

Katie didn't know. She was tired. The fleet had its orders. They'd make for Assherraskill and hope the Lizards and their other allies were true to their word.

Perhaps if they were, the Grrumm would find themselves out on the end of a long supply line in an unsustainable position. Perhaps they'd realize that and retreat back to gated space. Perhaps they'd decide they'd taken humanity down several pegs and that was enough.

Katie didn't know. She wasn't hopeful, but she didn't know. Given that she had to play her cards out to the bitter end. To do less would be to dishonor the sacrifice of those who'd already died. But damned if Katie didn't just want to find somewhere to hide, curl up, and sleep for several years.

She'd never understood the slobs who couldn't be bothered to wash up and don a clean shipsuit before going to bed.

She did now. Still, she forced herself to strip off her current ripe suit, walk through her shower, and don another.

Crawling into her sleeping pod, she found the energy to hope it'd seem better after some sleep.

Couldn't look a lot worse.

* * *

Rrolff stared at Thorn-Paw back in his quarters. It was tradition that a commander and his adviser review events after every major action a fleet was involved with. They wrote novels about it. Despite that, Rrolff would have preferred to have been alone. He was horrified by the debacle he'd presided over. He'd done his duty, but he had little doubt he'd be blamed for what had happened. He wondered if he'd even be allowed to pass his titles or land on to his eldest.

"It wasn't your fault," Thorn-Paw ventured. "Others elsewhere, some generations dead, failed."

Rrolff growled. It was true. He didn't think he was being self-serving to think so. It also didn't matter. "Should the barbarians surrender now and shower us with flowers, and gifts of nectar, tea, and other fine foods, it would make no difference," he ground out. "Our losses are unforgivable. We've found a place in the Imperial chronicles. We'll be remembered for paws upon paws of generations. They won't be fond memories."

"No, never has the Expeditionary fleet ever taken such losses," Thorn-Paw admitted. "Another battleship lost. A paws-worth of cruisers, too. And one out of three of those that remain have sustained physical damage we've not the means to repair out here in the cursed barbarian dark."

"Many fine Grrumm are dead too."

"And there are always more barbarians, aren't there?"

Rrolff grumbled and rubbed behind an ear. "The conduits? Any word about them?"

"Some failed during the battle. I don't think any others have realized that. We still can't easily do a proper examination of all of them without risking panic amongst the fleet. I can have Careful-Crafter check out a few under the guise of regular maintenance. Such a sample should be indicative of how bad the problem has become."

"Yes, that would be a good idea," Rrolff agreed. "But I don't dare risk another large-scale battle, do I? To do so would be risking the entire fleet, would it not?"

Thorn-Paw looked grim. "I fear so. If war was business, it might make sense to cut our losses and retire to Damp."

"But it is not, and if we were to retreat, the barbarians would smell our blood and perhaps pounce. The *Book of Barbarians* warns explicitly against ever showing them weakness."

"Indeed."

"To do so would destroy a reputation we've spent our whole history building."

"It might."

Rrolff felt anger gnawing at his heart like a worm inside of an old tree. His efforts here would never be recognized, but his duty remained. "We will press on and end this barbarian threat. Now I must rest."

"Yes, Lord Earl," Thorn-Paw thumped his chest in salute and left.

***

Hood had often found the aftermath of a crisis worse than the crisis itself.

During a crisis, one was often too busy to worry, or count minor injuries, or even serious losses. Afterwards you noticed.

As a tunnel rat, enlisted man, spy, and electrical contractor Hood had seen his share of injuries from fights and accidents. Often enough, they were over before you had a chance to fully process what was happening. But then you got to wait in some depressing place for a nurse or doctor to come around and give you the bad news. While waiting without diagnosis or prognosis, you got to reflect on just how bad the news might be, and what you could have done better. And it was close to pointless, because although you wanted to know as soon as possible and you wanted to be there for your people, there wasn't really much material you could do for them.

Hood's cabin wasn't as bleak or as full of other people's suffering as a hospital's waiting room. That was true. Unfortunately, the part about not knowing the diagnosis, let alone the prognosis, was also true. It'd be some time before all the data was in. All the same, it was standard operating procedure to record one's impressions of important actions immediately after standing down, and even before getting more data from elsewhere.

Hood figured it was up in the air whether there'd be a Space Force in the future, or human historians to read his after action report. Still, despair was a sin, wasn't it? The fact you couldn't do everything you like to was no excuse for not doing what you could.

So he recorded what had transpired. And he recorded that although between half and two-thirds of their larger ships had been put out of action, a majority of their smaller ships, destroyers, frigates, corvettes, and scouts were still intact and fully functional. The smaller ships tended to be outright destroyed or unharmed.

Also, the debris from the larger ships that had been trashed was in company with them on a fast ballistic course away from the enemy. They were finding many survivors among the wreckage. That was good.

What wasn't good was that the enemy was obviously making ready to jump to the Solar System.

Kincaid had ordered the fleet to retire on Assherraskill. They were to fight a guerrilla war harassing the Grrumm supply lines from there.

Hood really hoped the Lizards didn't take the opportunity to remove a competitor that had recently humiliated them.

Not that he had any better ideas. Right now, he was just blankly numb. Sleep was the best idea he had.

Might help.

What Now?

Thorn-Paw stood beside the Lord Earl Sweets-Swiper at the rear of the *Celestial Dominance*'s bridge. They were about to emerge from jump into the barbarians' home system.

Thorn-Paw wondered what sort of reception they were going to get. If the humans showed the same ferocity they had in the two previous fleet battles, then the situation might become quite problematic. The secret checks Thorn-Paw and Sweets-Swiper had ordered performed on the state of their energy conduit crystals had been limited, but quite disturbing. Deterioration had developed in all those they'd looked at. Their technician hadn't been able to give precise estimates, but he'd guessed the least damaged one he'd looked at was a third of the way along to final failure. The worst one had looked like it was two-thirds gone. If they had to fight another major battle, they'd find some of the conduits failing. Two such battles would be fatal.

It was to be dearly hoped that the back of the barbarian resistance had been broken. That their will to fight had been beat out of them, or that they had run out of resources to sustain the fight.

Given all this, Thorn-Paw wouldn't have blamed Sweets-Swiper if he was showing signs of nervousness. In fact, the Lord Earl looked as calm and comfortable as someone departing on an afternoon picnic.

Once again, Thorn-Paw found himself surprised at how impressed he was by Sweets-Swiper. He hated to think how things would have gone if they'd appointed one of the usual court fops to command of the Expeditionary Fleet. He decided to provide some moral support.

"They'd be insane to fight in their home system, particularly given that it contains their only truly habitable planet," he said to the Lord Earl.

Sweets-Swiper glanced his way. "Yes, but they are barbarians. It would be a great pity if the place was to be accidentally damaged. I understand it's a first-class planet. Heavy on oceans and a freakishly large moon, but still substantial forests. I would like to visit it and find it unharmed."

Thorn-Paw tilted his head in affirmation. "That they gave battle in the last system suggests they might be accessible to reason."

"Indeed," Sweets-Swiper replied, "it is to be hoped. In any event, in time, no doubt these barbarians will realize that being civilized is not only something they have no choice about, but something desirable. That all we ask is that they pose no threat to others."

"We'll know soon enough." "True."

***

The trip out to Assherraskill had been uneventful. Katie had had plenty of time to think. It hadn't cheered her up. Katie could mess things up. She could get the rest of her friends and her people killed, maybe triggering the extinction of the entire human race as icing on the cake. What she couldn't do was take any decisive positive action. The final destiny of the human race was entirely in the hands of fate.

Fate hadn't been kind so far.

What Now?

Given the faint hope remaining, it'd be unconscionable for Katie to just give up. But the fight had been reduced to the harassment of Grrumm supply lines by small ships and their captains. Currently, there was no need of an admiral to command any fleet actions. Given how the ones to date had turned out, perhaps that was just as well. But Katie hated just waiting for the so-far inexorable Grrumm to get tired of the game and give up and go home.

She did have some small role to play in diplomacy trying to hold the anti-Grrumm coalition together. Keeping some of them at the task of attacking Grrumm transports. Keeping others from supplying or otherwise helping the enemy. But diplomacy was hardly her strong suit. Particularly when it might require outright lying about the ultimate chances of human success and how it was in the best interests of some alien group. Katie didn't believe in lying or candy-coating harsh truths.

"Won't be long now. What sort of reception do you think the Lizards are going to give us?"

Katie looked over at Hood. Jump emergence into the Assherraskill system was due in scant minutes. As usual when something was about to happen, they were in the Flag Command Center together. And as usual they needed to pick their words carefully; to be cognizant of the listening ears of the command center's watch-keepers. Katie couldn't give the honest; *"Damned if I know"*, answer she'd like to. "A very friendly and helpful one," she replied. "They're rational and not vengeful. We're less of a threat to their eventual plans than the Grrumm, particularly now that we've lost the Solar System. Their ideal outcome is that we and the Grrumm cancel each other out. Right now, that means putting the thumb heavily on the scales in our favor."

"Makes sense," Hood said agreeably. "And as long as we can stay in the fight, there's hope."

"Exactly," Katie replied.

"Only, as the famous saying goes, hope is not a strategy," she thought.

* * *

There was an undercurrent of excitement abroad in the bars and dives of Far Seat Trade Hub.

The Grrumm Expeditionary Fleet had been given another drubbing. The humans would doubtless lose their home system and planet as so many had before them, but this part of the galaxy would never be the same again.

Even if the Grrumm fleet didn't retreat back to civilized space after laying waste to the human's industrial base, their writ didn't extend much beyond the beam range of their ships. Those ships that had been reduced in number and shown to be vulnerable.

The glee at this had come as something of a surprise to Shadowguide. He'd been born in and grown up in civilized space. Despite a certain cynicism about the powers-to-be there and despite having been treated as a second-class citizen by the Empire, he didn't hate the Grrumm or resent their rule. It was a role someone had to fill, and they were as reasonable about it as any group of self-interested sentient beings could be expected to be.

But the beings around him in this Varkoid-run bar were celebrating. Climbers, Swimmers, Grass Eaters, it hardly seemed to matter; they were all exorbitantly happy at the Grrumm misfortune. Shadowguide hadn't had to buy a drink all night. Someone, several someones, kept buying rounds for all of them. That was good. Less good were the loud off-key songs people kept belting out.

Win some, lose some.

Shadowguide sipped his drink quietly. He had to admit he was shocked at the degree of resentment towards the Empire. That was a data point worth noting. He'd have to factor it into his analysis.

Sadly, though it was the humans who'd given the Grrumm a bloody nose as they liked to say, they weren't likely to be the beneficiaries of their sacrifices. They'd lost most of their big ships, and were doubtless about to lose their ability to build more. It was likely the Frontier was going to remain in a state of anarchy.

Unless, of course, the Scaly Ones were able to take advantage.

It was enough to drive a self-respecting spy to drink.

* * *

It had to be the weirdest as well as one of the most important meetings Katie had ever been in.

It was just her and the Chief-Queen of the Great People, as the Lizards called themselves. They were in a small, damp cave. Not really small, there was ample room for the two of them and a little raised pond in the middle. Like as not, the place could have accommodated a few more people, but not more than that. It was cozy in a damp, gloomy sort of way. The gloom of the place was broken by two pools of bright light. One came from an apparent hole in the roof of the place and illuminated the little pool in its center, enabling some rather interesting looking greenery there. The second, cast by a full spectrum spotlight on a tall stand, illuminated something truly bizarre in this context. It centered on a pair of chairs and a little table that looked like it could have come from the patio of a cafe in Paris, or an English garden party perhaps. Katie wasn't an expert on either Parisian cafes or English garden parties. Maybe more English garden party because right beside the table was a trolley with a silver tea service on it. She supposed it could have been manufactured by the Lizards themselves, but she suspected the whole shebang had been imported from Earth itself.

It looked to Katie like the Chief-Queen, the ex-Princess, had gone to a great deal of trouble to set the scene for dealing with human big-wigs. Katie guessed she counted as a human big-wig.

"Tea?" asked the Chief-Queen, sitting down on one of the chairs that had evidently been modified for her anatomy. It had no back to impede her tail. Still couldn't be that comfortable.

"I'd be delighted," Katie answered.

The Chief-Queen poured two cups of tea into fine china. Gilt-edged, with blue dragons dancing around the sides. It was soothing, watching the steam rise from the hot liquid. "Milk? Sugar?" the Chief-Queen asked.

"Just milk and a half teaspoon of sugar," Katie answered.

Katie relaxed as she sipped her beverage. It was hard not

to. It was good tea and being served tea didn't seem in the least threatening. Or stressful. Katie could certainly use less stress. So, however contrived the Chief-Queen's little ceremony was, it'd achieved its purpose. The Chief-Queen was one smart, perceptive cookie, and it behooved Katie to remember that. Right now, however, she was being ostentatiously friendly. That was good.

"You like the tea?" the Chief-Queen asked.

"It's very good. Relaxing."

"Excellent. I bought a warehouse full of it. Though in truth, now that the Grrumm are stopping all human ships, and most other Galactics are steering clear of your Solar System, I wonder if I'll be able to replace it. I had hoped to sell it at a good profit, our people like it too. Do you have plenipotentiary powers?"

Katie smiled. "Yes, I automatically received full plenipotentiary powers when the Grrumm fleet entered the Solar System."

"It is not my intention to take advantage of any recent setbacks, but if you were to relax the restrictions on where our FTL ships can trade, we might be able to gather information as well as tea from the Solar System."

"That seems like a win-win proposition. I'll have my legal staff draw up a document for you that we can sign to make it formal."

"Excellent," the Chief-Queen said. "Please, do not worry that I intend to take advantage of the challenges that you currently face. We have no desire to face the Grrumm or the other so-called civilized races alone. I will bend the whole strength of my people to aiding you."

Katie blinked. "We denuded you of defenses. Don't you fear your systems being occupied just as the Solar System has been?"

"It would be feckless not to consider the possibility seriously, but having done so, I find my mind is at ease. Your people have been dealt a severe blow, it is true, but the Grrumm are few and far from home. It is not clear that they will be able to remain in occupation of your Solar System. I do not believe they will dare divide themselves among multiple systems while you lurk, ready to pounce on any isolated weaklings."

"And if they don't seek long-term occupation but simply to destroy our sources of power? It's impossible to defend planets from space."

The Chief-Queen's teeth clattered, making a profoundly disturbing sound. She seemed genuinely amused. "And so you prove you are the barbarians the Grrumm attempt to paint you as."

"You think the Grrumm are too civilized to consider laying habitable planets waste?"

"Yes. My predecessors and yours too might have considered such a plan. I imagine there are still those among both of our peoples who might indulge themselves in such juvenile blood-thirstiness, but I think we both, like the Grrumm, realize there is no gain, only loss to be found in such antics. The wider community will doubtless unite in putting down any that go mad in that manner."

Katie blinked. Obviously, the Chief-Queen had thought long and hard about Galactic politics. Katie had tried to keep up on them, but she suspected the Lizard leader was way ahead of her here. She hoped the Lizard leader was as friendly as she was acting. "I haven't noticed that the wider Galactic community tends to unite much."

Another clattering of teeth. "They wish most of all to be left alone. They recognize, though, that there are always those who because of insanity or greed who will seek to plunder any they see as weaker. Those who will seek to obliterate any who might challenge them. If at all possible, the Galactics will let others deal with such rogue elements, but if needs be, they'll rouse themselves to do what has to be done."

"But no more."

"Indeed. The Grrumm served the wider community by keeping more predatory parties from running amok. And so the wider community, by and large, supported the Grrumm. Having become complacent and weak both, the Grrumm no longer serve. They are, in fact, more of a rogue element themselves. The community sees humans as having the strength and will to replace them."

"Not your people?"

"We have the will, and we were strong, and could be again. We are not, however, a restrained species or society. We are predators used to getting what we want through force. We are rational, we will change with time, and I am attempting to hasten that change, but the Galactics see us for what we are. They find us too harsh, too self-certain, and prone to inflexibility."

Katie sipped her tea. "We've had our share of genocidal maniacs."

The Chief-Queen poured more tea for herself. "And you managed to contain them. A close-run thing if I read your history right. We never experienced a period with multiple competing powers, all of whom had the power to destroy our entire species." Her nostrils flared. "I suspect we'd not be here having this conversation if we had. In any case, you defeated us, costing Galactic bookies a lot in the process. So you are, on the face of it, stronger than us. The bookies are not prone to betting against you again."

Katie was fairly sure she didn't want to discuss just how that had happened. "Well, it's nice not to be alone, but I still don't see how I'm going to defeat the Grrumm fleet."

The Chief-Queen gave a flick of her tongue. "You don't have to. You only have to stay in the fight."

"Could you elaborate?"

"We are as new to the Galactic scene as you are, but I have researched this. I believe the Grrumm lost control of the Frontier a long time ago. Furthermore, I don't think their leadership really cares. They are happy with what they have, and they don't fear anyone taking it from them. The aliens, called Spiders, control the gates in so-called civilized space and restrict large-scale violence there. The Grrumm fleet may be impossible to defeat, but it controls very little directly. You may believe it defeated you, but the rest of the Galaxy sees that it failed to remove you as a threat. As long as you and your fleet remain in existence, the Grrumm must shoulder an unpleasant burden that gains them nothing."

"But if they're determined to bear it, there's still not much I can do. My people will tire and weaken, too."

"You would know better than me, but I think you underestimate yourself. Also, with my people's help and that of others, I don't believe you'll weaken. I think you'll grow stronger as the Grrumm weaken. In time, because of that, or because they make some mistake, you may be able to defeat them directly. I know you've learned how to defeat their supposedly invulnerable ships."

"At great cost," Katie said.

"Indeed, but are their pockets deeper than yours? Did I get that idiom right?"

Katie frowned. "I understand what you mean. Sometimes I think your English is better than mine. To answer your question, I suspect their pockets are deeper. At least, if you consider just the Grrumm and humans alone. Heck, we lost all of our industry along with the Solar System. But with your help and that of the Trade Union, Meerow, and others, maybe not. Also, there's the question of how deep they're willing to dig into those pockets. We live here, they don't. I guess it's possible they might just get tired some day and go home."

"You see, it's not hopeless."

Katie nodded and then remembered to dip her head. "I think you're right."

"Yes, I often am."

* * *

It was a beautiful world. Rrolff found viewing it from the *Celestial Dominance*'s observation deck relaxing. Going by its ocean area, four claws of six of its surface, it might have been as bad as Damp for being wet, indeed if more than a half claw of that surface hadn't been tied up in ice its large continents might have been mostly covered in shallow seas. But it did have large continents. Between how they were situated and the existence of large mountain ranges that accelerated the leaching of greenhouse gases from its atmosphere, much of the water that might have gone into shallow seas was instead ice. The place was colder and drier than was ideal. It actually had large areas of desert. But it also had extensive forests that covered over two claws of six of its land area.

Rrolff's background briefing papers had noted that the barbarian humans had been doing an increasingly good job of taking proper care of those forests since they'd had had their ecological escape that had culminated in their industrialization scant generations before.

It went some way to improving the Grrumm commander's feelings about his barbarian opponents. They had some redeeming qualities. They had, rather insanely in Rrolff's mind, destroyed all of their industry surplus to sustaining their population. They were refusing to supply or otherwise trade with his fleet. Which was more than annoying. On the other hand, they'd not offered any actual resistance to it. They weren't completely insane.

"An attractive planet," Thorn-Paw beside him said, echoing his own thoughts. "Too bad it's already occupied."

"They don't seem averse to trading parts to others for the right price."

Thorn-Paw grunted. No good Grrumm could feel positive about those who'd sell part of their patrimony for their own passing gain. It was theft from future generations.

"It's not just land and trees we pass on to future generations, Hrrwa," Rrolff replied to his adviser's unvoiced reservations. "Without the technology and knowledge they gained that way, they could not have given us the fight they did. They could not have known with certainty that it was a pointless effort."

Thorn-Paw snorted. "They still don't seem to have realized it."

Rrolff rubbed his nose. "They're not admitting it yet. Some of them might hope that having eliminated them as a serious threat, we will decide the job is done and go home."

"And leave them to rebuild. I think not."

"That'll be my decision, but I concur. I think after a little time that cracks will appear. It is uncomfortable here with even the Trade Union not trading and giving us feeble excuses as to why, but sooner or later common sense will prevail, at first with a few individuals acting cautiously, but with ever more after that."

"It is to be hoped."

"But you'll believe it when you see it. You are a grumpy old beast. But clear eyed, I'll admit."

"I don't like that so many of our ships still need repair and that no facilities remain for doing so within a couple of paws of jumps."

"Indeed, but the worst case is that we have to go back to Damp for that, and then come back securing our supply lines as we go."

"They might relieve you of command before that's done."

Rrolff gave a shrug. "My reputation is much diminished. There is little that can be done for it. But I think that volunteers to suffer a similar fate will be few. They'll give me a second chance, I think, until the job is done and they can send me into disreputable retirement."

"It is not the outcome you deserve. It makes we wish we too were barbarians that could credibly threaten these rebels into acting like sensible beings."

"Then we'd be as bad as them." Rrolff gave a soft, thoughtful growl. "And it'd not be practical either, I think. If we were the sort to go about constantly making enemies, I don't think we'd ever stop finding them. The *Book of Barbarians* is emphatic about it. '*You can't beat the barbarians by being a barbarian; those that long for the fruits of being civilized will abandon you. You will become just one lost tribe among many.*'"

"Very poetic."

"It makes sense. Our rule is tolerated by the secondary races because they recognize that it's better than anarchy. We must strive to remove threats, not to become one."

"Makes sense."

"One does not burn down the forest to rid oneself of the biting insects."

Thorn-Paw tilted his head in agreement with the old proverb. "No matter how annoying they are."

"Yes, we must be patient and wait for the barbarians to come to their senses."

The Enemy Votes

Once again, Katie was in her Flag Command Center, although not to fight an honest space battle with a clear enemy this time. She was waiting for the arrival of a more-or-less honest merchant belonging to the Trade Union whom she planned to threaten and wheedle into doing her will. She looked over at Hood, who was here ostensibly as an observer but more as moral support. He looked back and shrugged. They'd discussed everything beforehand. She looked up at her giant forward wall-filling tactical display, which was currently acting as a big view screen. It showed a breath-taking view of the planet Assherraskill below.

    Assherraskill had the usual delicate blue bow of atmosphere stretching the width of the screen, with the dark of space above and the bright planet's surface below. Assherraskill was a dry planet, with not much more than half the water of Earth, and its one main continent was massive with huge expanses of orange and yellow. But there were also vast areas of faint yellowish green, dry grasslands that were the Lizards' home habitat. Some coastlines and mountain ranges had areas tinged a darker green, but they weren't large. It was a magnificent scene. Katie had yet to see a living planet that wasn't spectacular.

It made her wish they'd built the *Bonnie* with an observation deck and that she had tables and chairs like the Chief-Queen, and a tea service like hers too. That'd be nice and there was little doubt that the Lizard leader's props did create a civilized atmosphere conducive to agreement.

Sadly, Katie's approach was going to be a lot less civilized. She'd keep the merchant standing here in the center of her power and not so subtly threaten him.

When that merchant arrived flanked on one side by some of her Varkoid bodyguards and on the other by a pair of marines, she greeted him politely. "Sharp-eye-for-profit, it is good to see you. I trust the trip here was pleasant. I'm afraid I haven't any tea to offer you. Supply chain problems, you understand."

Sharp-eye-for-profit looked at Katie balefully. For some reason, the Climber, who Katie thought of as simply "Sharp", had never warmed to her. She imagined he'd been happy with the status quo and hadn't been pleased to see it changing. Doubtless, he saw Katie as the face of that change.

Sharp gave first a foot shuffle of a shrug and then a little bow. A minimal level of politeness. "Greetings Admiral. I don't believe either of us are fond of babble for its own sake, or empty niceties. I am here so you can see for yourself that I assent to your wishes."

"I appreciate that."

"Good. To be clear, I think you understand I'd have been happy to have never seen you, your people, the Scaly Ones, or even the Grrumm. My life was comfortable and profitable before you started playing your games."

"No game for me or my people. We had no desire to disturb anyone."

"Good intentions and a tenth silver piece will buy you a hot beverage."

"We have a similar saying, but I repeat, we bear you no ill will."

"And yet you threaten our ships with piracy, even destruction, if they dare trade with the Grrumm fleet."

"As we agreed with the Trade Union. It gives you an excuse you can give the Grrumm. What we call plausible deniability."

"It does, but it is odd - isn't it? - how hard it is to tell whether so many people mean what they are saying or something else."

"It is. I assure you it doesn't sit well with me either, but needs must."

Sharp bobbed his head. "We can agree on that much. So know acceding to your wishes is the least unprofitable course I and the Trade Union at Far Seat can follow, and we will do so. I hope this sets your mind at rest and you'll keep your minions leashed."

"I will."

"Good. May I leave?" "You may."

* * *

It was a bar in a station orbiting Assherraskill full of Lizards and humans both. Rob found it rather surreal. Not quite as surreal as what he was doing there. He was sharing a table with a skinny old Lizard currently calling himself Seller of Earth Trinkets. Seller of Earth Trinkets - Rob shortened his name to Seller in the privacy of his own mind - was the Lizard formerly known as the Great Huntmaster. Despite appearances, Rob was pretty sure Seller hadn't really changed his job all that much.

Though he was, in fact, actually selling Earth trinkets, Earth coffee and Earth liquor too. They were currently sharing coffee laced with bourbon that had healthy dollops of cream on top of it. Seller assured Rob that it was extremely popular with humans and Lizards both. He ought to know. Apparently he owned the bar they were in, as well as others scattered about Lizard space. If Rob understood correctly, he'd also started a matchmaker service that was going gangbusters as well. It seemed that the Lizards were new to the business of *"forming small breeding units"* and welcomed any help they could get. Rob had assured Seller the problem wasn't entirely solved on Earth either, but he wasn't sure Seller had completely believed him.

Why Seller had passed on all this information to Rob, he wasn't sure. But he suspected the wily old Lizard had his reasons. Rob was here to learn what he could from him. He figured the Lizards, Seller to be specific, were following the Galactic situation very carefully. Rob wanted to know what they thought.

"Good, isn't it?" Seller asked.

"It is," Rob agreed. "I imagine it isn't getting any easier to get the ingredients, though."

"Not that hard really," Seller replied. "Your admiral has given us permission to trade where we wish. We had a lot of FTL ships for trade between our own planets, and we re-flagged a number of human ships too. Plus, the Swimmers, Snouts, and even the Trade Unionists are all happy to make the run. The Grrumm do the odd search for weapons or military supplies, but they're basically good with it. They're not really interested in interfering with trade. Or even occupying planet surfaces and stations if they don't have to. I believe they expected your authorities to surrender and handle the administrative tasks for them."

"A little naïve. They haven't even threatened Earth, have they?"

"No. I have studied them carefully. It is not their way. They are stubborn and patient, and convinced that given time, you'll see matters their way."

"How patient? How long will they sit in Earth orbit waiting if we keep them blockaded? How long before they start firing on surface targets, or decide to retreat?"

"Impossible to say for sure, but they are stubborn, not stupid. If it is clear that they can't get supplies or repair their ships in your Solar System, they will retire. No ship is so big that it forms a truly closed system. The Grrumm like their comforts, especially their food. They're not going to put up with recycled mush if they don't have to."

"It's food quality, not spare parts or the need to repair their ships that'll decide them? You're sure?"

Seller's teeth clattered in amusement. "I'm sure they'll say it's the latter, but trust me, it's the poor meals that will decide the issue."

"So, we just have to wait and they'll eventually retreat to Damp to lick their wounds. That's it?"

"Yes, probably they'll retreat and probably sooner than you think, but, no, that's not all."

Rob frowned and consoled himself with a sip of his bourbon coffee. It was good. "So, what else?"

"Unless the fleet's current leadership is dismissed, they will retreat to Damp, repair their large ships, gather their smaller ones, and load up transports full of ground troops and marines and repeat the exercise, only this time being sure to secure their supply lines behind them."

"That doesn't sound good. I'm not sure I understand your point about the current leadership."

"The Grrumm are stubborn and you have humiliated the individuals in charge of their Expeditionary Fleet. They will insist on redeeming their honor as best they can. The Grrumm aren't like us. They don't really believe in cutting their losses."

"If they've failed so badly, aren't they likely to be replaced?" "Eventually. The Grrumm are slow to act. And as I've said, they are patient. It is likely their Emperor will let the fleet's current commander seek his revenge."

"Ouch. What if he doesn't? Will a new commander be any different?"

"The Grrumm Imperial bureaucracy is slow and indecisive, even by the standards of bureaucracies in general. The Great People have many fewer scribes than others and we keep them in check, but I've studied how they operate elsewhere. If something happens to the current leadership, it will be many of our years before they're replaced. They're also not likely to risk the fate of their predecessor. The Grrumm haven't been genuinely interested in expanding their Empire for a long time."

Rob took a minute or two to think about that. Assherraskill took only a few weeks longer to circle its primary than Earth did the Sun, so Lizard years and Earth years were pretty close to the same thing. Seller was implying that if they could further humiliate or otherwise force a change in the Grrumm fleet's leadership than the problem they posed would be solved. Given time, Earth could and would rebuild. Especially if none of the other actors took advantage. And the Lizards, the primary candidates for doing so, were proving surprisingly friendly. Was assassination in the cards then? "Are you suggesting it'd be desirable to arrange some sort of accident for the Grrumm fleet commander?"

"No, sadly, that'd be an insult they'd probably feel needed replying to."

"What then?"

"I understand that you won't risk battle while the Grrumm fleet is in your Solar System, but it needs to be defeated. You must force the Grrumm to have to replace both their fleet and their current commander."

"That's easy to say. Hard to do." "Yes, but necessary."

* * *

As soothing as the view of the barbarian planet was, Rrolff was still deeply sad. Restless and unhappy, he rambled around the *Celestial Dominance's* observation deck like he was a lost cub.

He'd made a difficult decision, and doubted he'd live to see his reputation recover from it.

It'd been almost a season of the planet below and his fleet's supply and repair situation had not improved. Given the restraints common decency and his government's instructions imposed upon him, the military logic was clear.

He'd have to retreat to Damp. There, he could affect resupply and repairs both. He'd gather small combatant and scout ships to both screen his main force, and to watch its supply lines. He'd gather transports and fill them not only with supplies, but marines to hold stations, and ground troops to take the surface of the planet below. It'd be expensive and merchants and administrators both would howl to the central government, but it was improbable that the government would act to remove him before he again attacked down-arm, doing the job properly this time.

If nothing else, his report on the crystal conduit problem would cause consternation throughout the upper ranks of the Imperial bureaucracy. They'd cannibalize other ships and installations to give him the replacement crystals he needed. He didn't doubt that. No one would dare risk being seen to fail a fleet engaged in active operations.

Otherwise, and beyond that, the infighting and finger-pointing over who was to blame would be epic. Sadly, it would be some time before officialdom even got to the point of fighting over what to do about the problem.

And again, sadly, that all but ensured he'd be left in place to return here and deal with the human threat in a final if principled way.

Everybody had assumed that once he'd reached orbit around the barbarian's home planet they'd surrender. Having done so, the Empire's practice was to use the existing government structures to impose their will, only making fundamental changes slowly and in digestible pieces.

In the unlikely event the barbarians had failed to be reasonable - they were barbarians after all - Rrolff had been authorized to blockade the planet and to attack military and industrial infrastructure on the surface. After, of course, giving warning so that evacuations to prevent the unnecessary loss of life could take place.

His instructions did not say what to do if the barbarians had already destroyed everything he could legitimately target themselves. It was an inconceivable outcome.

They also did not say what to do if all the multitude of secondary races refused to trade and provide the consumable supplies the fleet needed. And yet they had. Even the Trade Union, which needed Imperial consent to purchase and sell goods within civilized space.

That worried Rrolff deeply. The secondary races, the Trade Union in particular, made excuses and pretended they weren't on the side of the barbarians. Rrolff pretended to believe them. He'd sent that report about the crystals, among others, back to civilized space on Trade Union ships. Failing to deliver his messages would have been an undeniably hostile act on their part. So far, they'd not outright cut his communications. But he didn't expect that restraint extended to not trying to read his mail.

He'd used the best cipher he had to encode the report on the defective crystals. He hoped it was good enough. If the barbarian leader learned of the crystal conduit problem, the

Imperial Fleet was going to be in a world of hurt.

So Rrolff was sad.

Because you can only stay angry for so long.

***

"Why so glum, Katie?" Susan, Commodore Fritzsen, Katie's old friend and commander of her biggest and best Task Force, asked. "You've got what you wanted. They're retreating."

Katie tried to formulate a reply.

They were alone in the *Bonaventure*'s large main conference room, sharing a coffee. Normally, Katie would have met her old friend in her cabin. But as large as that place was by Space Force standards, Katie was finding it claustrophobic these days. She'd been spending long hours locked up in virtual meetings and studying countless reports, not least the ones from Hood and Wootton. She was happy to be anywhere outside of her combined quarters and office. Also, the conference room was immense by spacer standards. Katie didn't suffer from the agoraphobia common to born spacers and she enjoyed the room. It helped her relax.

The multiple reports from various sources that the Grrumm were pulling out of the Solar System, and without doing any further damage to the place, let alone indulging in genocide, weren't helping her relax.

She was glad that they'd been true to their reputation and treated Earth and humanity far more fairly than any human victor would have likely treated a conquered alien species. Better than Katie had treated the Lizards. They'd simply taken up Earth orbit and asked for surrender. When it'd not been forthcoming, they'd shown great restraint. There hadn't been a single strike against Earth's surface and not a single soldier sent to occupy it. They'd put small forces into some space stations, but even in those cases they had left the general population alone.

They'd implied they wouldn't let the humans rebuild anything that might be of military use. They'd reasonably insisted further resistance was futile and wasteful. And that was all.

"Earth calling, Katie!" "What?"

"Why so glum? What's bothering you? We've gotten off incredibly easy. You should be over the moon."

"Tell Amy that," Katie grumped.

"Low blow, but I'll forgive you. Share with Auntie Susan."

"Retreating doesn't mean they won't return," Katie answered. "In fact, according to Hood and Wootton, they'll almost certainly pull all the way back to Damp to regroup and resupply. That done, they'll come back with what they need to properly secure their supply lines, and occupy Earth even if it isn't co-operating."

"And you don't think we can stop them again?"

"They'll be stronger, at least in smaller ships and troops, and we'll be weaker. I don't know if they can replace their losses, but I'm damned sure we can't. It's going to take years to rebuild the needed industry, and that's if we let the Lizards off of their leash."

"Good heavens. You're planning to force another battle, aren't you?"

"From what Hood reports, I don't see much choice." Susan took a deep breath, and all of a sudden seemed much less flippant. "Damn, Katie, I don't like the odds of that working out."

"A big risk likely to get a lot of us killed, and to result in the loss of ships we can't easily replace for many years, yep."

"You're the history freak with a thing for the Great Captains, whatever happened to *'don't interfere with the enemy when they're doing what you want'* and *'build your enemy a golden bridge to retreat across'*."

"According to Hood and Wootton, the Grrumm may be very cautious, but they're very stubborn. They're not quitters. They also aren't used to losing ships, and that's more than a psychological issue. It means they don't build them very often or very fast either. I'm guessing that since they don't do it, they probably can't do it. Not easily or quickly. If we can destroy most of their FTL capable war fleet, at whatever cost, it's likely to be years before they'll be able to come at us again. We need those years."

"At whatever cost." "Exactly."

Or On Your Shield

"Look, Katie," Thor Haralson said with considerable exasperation, "I'm not going to object to the fact that this plan is likely to get us all killed. It's what we signed up for. A chance to make a difference, but big sacrifices, maybe the ultimate one, in return."

Katie raised her eyebrows but otherwise kept a blank expression. Thor was an old friend and formerly her superior, too. But not anymore, and he was close to crossing a line.

Thor, Commodore Thor Haralson, to be precise who was currently commanding the remnants of what had been John Smith's Task Force Two, looked at her, and got the point. He grimaced. "Sorry, ma'am. My point stands. What's at stake here is more than just our careers or lives, it's the fate of our species. I think caution and taking the time to consult with the authorities back on Earth are both in order."

Katie and her immediate subordinates were all gathered together, physically together, in the *Bonaventure*'s main conference room. She needed to get their commitment to her plan, even if they weren't happy about it, and for Katie, that meant being physically face to face.

There were only half the faces there had been at the start. Casualties had been high. Amy, Henry Vane, Larry Wong, and John Smith had all perished in their last two stand-up battles.

It'd meant some reorganization. Only Susan Fritzsen remained in the command she'd started in. Even the nature of that command had changed. Susan's Task Force Three had received all their meager reinforcements. Katie had also disbanded the Support Group and transferred its remaining cruisers and destroyers to Susan's command. She'd given up the Command Group's only cruiser to Susan, too. She'd merged the Support Group's two corvettes and actual support ships into the Command Group. She'd transferred all her remaining corvettes into the Command Group. They were just too fragile to face the enemy directly. She'd transferred Haralson from command of the Command Group to that of what was left of Task Force Two.

So what she was left with was an over-strength Task Force Three under Susan with the *Triumph,* the only carrier she had left besides the *Bonnie*. Also, most of the remaining intact cruisers, and the majority of the damaged ships she'd converted into fireships. The *Triumph* was flying most of the remaining torpedo bombers, the *Bonaventure* most of the remaining scout ships.

Task Forces One and Two were mostly their surviving destroyers and some frigates. Task Force One under Cara Campbell had two cruisers, Task Force Two just the one. They each had one cruiser-sized fireship and three destroyer or merchant sized ones.

Susan's force was going to be Katie's main hammer. Haralson's and Campbell's forces were intended mainly as diversions, albeit ones with a sting they could deliver if ignored.

It wasn't an ideal force structure or plan, but the best Katie and her staff had been able to devise under the circumstances. Thor's complaints had some justification.

Katie studied the faces and the body language of her old friends and sub-ordinate commanders while mentally reviewing all this. It didn't really take long, and it was desirable to appear to be thinking over what Thor had said. Truth was, rather unfortunately, that nothing occurred to her to change her mind. She sighed dramatically. "Thor, I understand what you're saying. And, believe me, I understand I'm taking on a lot of responsibility. Even if from a purely military point of view this works out fantastically better than we have any right to hope for, there are going to be those back on Earth that will say I exceeded my authority. If we survive this, I have no doubt I'll end up in front of a court-martial or a parliamentary committee explaining myself. I'm not looking forward to it. Do you understand?"

Thor frowned and slowly nodded. "Yes, ma'am."

"Good. For what it's worth, I do have the formal authority to make this decision, pending my plenipotentiary powers being rescinded by a free and representative government back on Earth. What's more, we do not have the time to consult with them. If we're to stop the Grrumm fleet before it gets back to Damp and starts to rebuild itself, we have to move now. I believe we have to make the effort to do that. I wish the odds were better, but I'm convinced we must try. I'll recap why again. Okay?"

"Yes, ma'am. A few more minutes to consider such a momentous decision wouldn't be unwise."

"I'm glad you think so," Katie replied dryly to her old mentor. Technically, she still thought he was better at fleet tactics than she was, but that he discounted context and the human factor too much.

"Bottom line is that the Grrumm can rebuild at Damp, but Earth's industry and shipyards are gutted and the situation isn't much better at Assherraskill here. So our relative strengths are as favorable as they're likely to get. Also we think we've got some tactical ideas we haven't completely worked out and involve information I don't want to share while still in an alien system. That said, if the Grrumm were to sue for peace I'd accept. If there was any reason to believe they'll give up once they get back to gated space, I'd say let them go. Only they haven't. And there's no reason to believe they're going to give up. We've been over this. Need I say anything more?"

"No," Thor said. The rest satisfied themselves with nods.

Katie looked around the room. There were only the four of

them. She'd decided to forgo the crutch of having Hood or Wootton present, and the distraction of staffs. She wanted this to be a personal and open discussion. A frank one, if necessary. Thor had certainly provided that. Susan she'd already talked to. That only left one other person.

"Cara," Katie said. "I've discussed this with Susan. She thinks I'm crazy too, but you know Susan, it's all the ride of the Valkyries and Valhalla awaits us with her. Thor has said his piece, but you haven't said much."

Commander Cara Campbell, the junior person in the room and the one least well-known to Katie, pursed her lips. Probably didn't help they hadn't got along all that well when they'd served together on the *Resolute* either. Campbell had always been a stickler for going by the book. Katie had worked hard, but not always by the book. There'd been friction. "I think you're aware that I don't like unusual situations or ambiguity."

"I think I noticed that."

Cara snorted. "Been a lot of both recently. Between that and all the friends we've lost so far, I can't say I'm a happy camper. But," and here she nodded in Thor's direction, "like has been said, we signed up to make a difference. And as much as it pains me, I think your logic is sound. You're our commander and strictly speaking, it's your sole call." She gave a very thin smile. "But given that you're sharing the responsibility to a degree, I have to say we'd be shirking it to use consultation with Earth as an excuse to let the Grrumm escape. I'm not a xeno-psychologist, but I think they'll try again if they can. So our odds may not be great now, but they're not likely to get better, right?"

"That's what Hood and Wootton tell me."

"An odd couple, those two, but they seem to know their stuff. So, like it or not, with all due respect to Commodore Haralson, I think it's our duty to do this. We have got to get ahead of them and stop as many as possible from getting back to gated space. Easier said than done. But our duty to try."

"Thank you, Commander Campbell," Katie said. "Thor?" "I trust you have a plan that holds some chance of success?"

"I think so. I've discussed it with Susan, but you guys were busy reforming your Task Forces and I wanted to firm it up anyhow."

"Just from the way you've divided us up, Susan gets to deliver the main blow. Cara and I will mainly be distractions."

"I do have some tactical ideas I want to discuss with you. Only I want the fleet gone from Assherraskill before discussing them. There are some things we're going to need to check out on the fly."

Thor frowned. "You can trust all of us, and our allies have been remarkably stalwart."

"Thor, just trust me on this. As strange as things have been, they get stranger. There are powers greater than the Grrumm and us both. We'd rather not attract their attention."

"Okay."

"Are you with me?"

"As Commander Campbell reminded us, you're in charge." Thor sighed. "I owe you an apology. You've never been the loose cannon people like to accuse you of being. I ought to know that better than most. It is a horrible risk you're proposing, but I should have realized you thought about it carefully before making the decision you have."

"Thor, I wouldn't have minded if you could have argued me out of it. It's going to cost. Cost in blood and it's a price I'm tired of paying."

"At least humankind isn't likely to go extinct."

"There is that. We only stand to lose our independence and maybe our home planet. I'd rather not."

"Yes, ma'am. You have my full support." "Good."

* * *

Aljanah, a.k.a. Epsilon Cygni, was a giant red-orange star which made it ideal for Katie's purposes. Not perfect: it did have a companion star, but a very distant one. Given her limited time and the route they had to follow to their final destination, it was about as good as she could hope for. It would allow her to check out and practice the tactics that she hoped would allow her to defeat the Grrumm fleet. Maybe even allow a large portion of her people to survive their victory.

That'd certainly be nice.

Katie was feeling a certain blank, numb, overwhelming dread of what was ahead. It wasn't an enervating fear, but it was fear. Katie wasn't used to being afraid. It was an unfamiliar problem for her and she was finding it an awkward one.

The least of her problems was finding a system with a large flattish gravitational field to try her new tactical ideas out in. Aljanah wasn't a perfect solution to that problem, but it was an adequate one. Even working out and then executing the tactics necessary to defeat the enemy wasn't her worst problem.

In outline, the solution to the tactical problem was simple. She had to get most of her fireships in close with the Grrumm fleet without taking excessive losses. Once there, each one-for-one trade of a fireship for a Grrumm ship was a win for the human side. Ideally, she'd find a way to minimize losses among the rest of her fleet while achieving that.

She had ideas on how to do that which she was currently working on.

So far, so good.

Most of all, what was bothering her was the price she was paying to defeat the Grrumm, and increasing doubts about what all the bloody sacrifice was buying.

In a strictly military sense, where one's goal was to beat the enemy and dictate the peace paying whatever price was necessary, it made sense.

But in the end Katie was only human. Although the phrase was inadequate. Katie had met enough aliens to realize they weren't humans in fur suits or even scales, but intelligent sapients living in technologically advanced cultures did seem to have commonalities. Some degree of respect for individuals and their happiness and their lives both seemed to be one of those commonalities. Katie didn't know why, but a lot of people of a variety of species seemed to agree that throwing people's lives away without a very good reason was a very bad thing.

Katie thought so herself.

And yet she'd led many people, many of them good friends, to their deaths. She planned to risk even more of them in the future. And whatever she'd told Thor and others, she wasn't sure it was for an adequate cause.

She might be able to keep the Grrumm from expanding their Empire, but what came after that?

She didn't know. Somehow she doubted it'd be a return to the previous status quo.

Katie sighed and looked around her quarters. Neither the furniture nor the walls had any answers.

There wasn't much for it. She'd win her battle first.

If she did, and she survived, then she'd worry about the consequences.

***

Currently, there were no planets visible from the *Celestial Dominance*'s observation deck. They were outboard bound from Far Seat Trade Hub and even the system's primary was only one brighter-than-usual star among many. Rrolff wasn't alone with his thoughts. Thorn-Paw was present too.

The initial mechanics of their retreat - Rrolff refused to call it "*a strategic regrouping*" in the privacy of his own mind - were completed. Rrolff no longer had the press of his many duties to keep him from thinking about the depressing facts of the matter.

Rrolff fully intended to regroup and return to the human home system and force their subjugation. He didn't doubt he'd succeed. If the humans or their allies had managed to trap his fleet in the human home system, the disaster would have been complete. But they hadn't. He'd exited his forward position cleanly and without opposition. He'd not known what to expect from the Trade Union at Far Seat, but although they'd been unsupportive, they hadn't dared be openly obstructive.

None of this would save him or his family for that matter. Eventually, the carrion birds would overcome their hesitation and bickering between themselves and descend to pick his bones. Never had a Grrumm expedition experienced such a setback as this one had. Someone would have to bear the blame.

That someone would be Rrolff. That he'd done as well as possible given the circumstances counted for nothing. Neither the Imperial bureaucracy nor the Imperial Court would accept the blame they deserved. Rather, they'd place the sole blame on him. Then they'd use his resulting disgrace for their own enrichment. They'd divide his patrimony amongst themselves.

It was outrageous, and it angered Rrolff. He'd do his duty regardless, but it offended his sense of fairness mightily that neither he nor his blameless dependents would gain anything from that. Somewhere in past history, the honorable values of his ancestors had become lost, and it led him to despair.

Not a normal sort of emotion for any Grrumm. It was the nature of his people to accept things as they were and to get on with doing what they could without fuss.

Beside him, Thorn-Paw broke the bleak silence. "We've broken contact. They have few, if any, large ships. Between the crystals we can scrounge at Damp, the ships of the Frontier Fleet, and the troops we can muster, it'll be no problem to return and properly occupy their home system. Morale is not bad."

Rrolff grunted. "Morale isn't bad, but is fragile. They still trust us and they don't know the full story. It bothers me not knowing where the remainder of the enemy fleet is."

"Moreover, you know, no matter how unfair it is, that the hangers on at court will disgrace you, and likely strip you and your family of both titles and estates. Something that would offend any fair-minded Grrumm even if they weren't the target of the injustice themselves."

"You know it'll not be reported like that." "They cannot prevent you from recording your observations in the *Book of Barbarians*. Later generations, as well as those of us in the fleet, will know the truth."

"I suppose that is the best that can be hoped for." "Truly."

***

"You have not only our profound gratitude, esteemed clan heads and captains, but our promise you'll be more than justly compensated for your present sacrifice," Katie declaimed sincerely.

Her fleet had arrived in Rho Cygni to several pleasant surprises. Her and her people's scattered attempts at finding allies among the diverse groups of alien galactics had borne fruit. She'd received good news from the waiting allied ships. The Imperial Frontier Fleet had been driven back from Plenitude to the edge of gated space at Damp. Even there, it seemed, they were passive and on the defense. If Katie could beat the Grrumm Expeditionary Fleet, there'd be no succor for its survivors short of Damp. And her allies also reported she'd beaten the Grrumm to Rho Cygni. They were still on their way here.

But good news was the least of what they'd brought Katie. They'd also supplied a half dozen additional fireships. A huge sacrifice on their parts as the clans and other small groups the Frontier peoples were divided into often saved for generations to purchase a single ship, which would then continue to be used for many more generations. Each ship was a one-off project constructed wholly or partly from hulls bought in gated space in small ad hoc shipyards. The largely lawless state of the Frontier made larger, more permanent facilities into vulnerable targets. So Katie was genuinely grateful and appreciative of the sacrifice. The coming battle was still a huge gamble, but the additional fireships improved their odds significantly.

Rho Cygni, like Epsilon Cygni, was a large orange giant. Which meant it had a large, flat gravitational field. Made it an easy target for long jumps, but also meant it took some time to transit. It was ideal for the trick Katie meant to use, which would allow her to get in among the large Grrumm ships while not losing too many ships on the way there.

In Epsilon Cygni, she'd verified the fact that in-system micro-jumps were possible even for her larger ships. She'd even managed to squeeze in some fleet level practice runs.

It was still a huge gamble, but Katie, fingers crossed, was convinced victory was possible.

She smiled, and head dipped, looking around the *Bonnie's* flight deck at her gathered alien allies, "I assure you your investment will pay off. We will win here, though you understand I cannot reveal the details of my plan yet, and having achieved victory, we will rebuild. Rebuild at Assherraskill and Earth both, and once our shipyards are operating again new ships, bigger and better than those you have sacrificed here, will be first in line to be built. You will be fully compensated and more. You have my personal gratitude. You have the gratitude of my government and my people. We will not forget."

Much stomping of feet and dipping of heads greeted that from the Galactics. The humans cheered and hollered.

It warmed Katie's heart.

She hoped they were as happy when the upcoming battle was done.

You could lay odds on the outcome of any battle, but they were rarely completely predictable.

The enemy always got a vote.

That there'd probably be a horrible cost was the only safe bet.

* * *

"Ma'am," Comms announced, "Task Force Three reports it's in place and ready."

"Thank you, Comms," Katie answered. It wouldn't be long now if their intelligence was correct. Katie had no real doubt it was. Katie looked around her Flag Command Center and wondered if this was the last time they'd be doing this. Their last battle. That'd be nice. Assuming they survived it. There was a slight tension in the room. Given what was about to happen and the stakes involved, that was only natural.

Hood was at her side, as usual. She glanced his way. He gave a reassuring little nod back.

She turned her gaze to the giant tactical display taking up the forward wall of the Flag Command Center. It showed an augmented natural view. Even out beyond the jump point from down-arm, Rho Cygni burned brightly in its center. Thin super-imposed lines terminated by blocky bits of lettering showed the jump points' locations, the projected path of the Grrumm fleet between them, and that of her own forces. They also showed the place where Katie expected to jump to and where she expected to most closely engage them.

Given the tight execution she knew the fleet was capable of, they should arrive close in to the enemy all at once. The Grrumm shouldn't have the time to take out any number of fireships before those ships immolated themselves and their Grrumm targets.

All was ready.

They were only waiting for the Grrumm to arrive on stage for the show to begin.

It shouldn't be long.

To the Bone

Katie's gut twisted. Mini-jumps were even harder than the normal system to system ones. Less stable, less predictable, and more gut-wrenching.

"Ma'am," came her Comms officer's voice over the intercom built into Katie's combat pod, "jump successful. *Bonaventure* and crew are fully functional. Command Group ships all intact. Formation is good. Only eighty-seven milli-light-seconds short of our target location."

"Thank you, Comms. Sensors! Our Task Forces? The enemy?"

"Coming up on the main tactical display now, ma'am," her Sensors officer, LTSG Miki Kawasaki, replied. Her voice was dead even and professional. This wasn't their first rodeo. "All our units appear intact. They're still in the process of reporting exact status. Task Force One is right on target and its formation is good. Task Force Two over-jumped by point two light-seconds and is slightly dispersed." She paused before continuing. "Task Force Three appears to be dispersed for a half light-second along its jump axis and to be slightly ahead of its target point. Leading units are within missile range of the enemy. The enemy is exactly where predicted. They have retained their formation of three disks perpendicular to their axis of advance. The battleships are all in the middle disk, ma'am."

Nobody could see her in her combat pod, so Katie allowed herself the luxury of a sigh. "Thank you, Sensors," she said over the command net. It was very good news indeed that the fleet had survived the mini-jump without losses, mostly in good formation, and not too far from where they should be. Not perfect and maybe that'd be a problem. Still, it was a good start.

She inspected her tactical display to verify that. Rho Cygni A was showing as a visible disk off to one side. She'd not have dared the trick she'd just pulled off in a system with a smaller primary. But it had worked. The Grrumm weren't going to be able to avoid them, they were likely just now overcoming their surprise and closing up to combat stations, and, most of all, they weren't going to have long to pick off Katie's ships, particularly her kamikaze fireships, before the humans were in amongst them at point blank range.

Katie checked the relative velocities of her force groups to the enemy fleet. It'd been one of the hardest things to work out when making their plan. The mini-jump had introduced issues. Higher velocity made for a more stable jump but a less precise one that ended with a higher velocity on exit. Lower velocity made each ship's jump less predictable, but potentially more accurate, and meant a lower velocity on exit. Exactly what velocity on exit was desirable was a trade-off with no perfect answer. Higher velocity meant closing with the enemy quicker and taking fewer losses in the process. A lower velocity meant a greater chance of each of her fireships managing an intercept with an enemy, and it meant that the two fleets would remain within fighting range longer.

In her earlier battles, Katie's goal had been to get in quick, do what damage she could, and get out quick before her losses became too great. Not this time. This time she was aiming at the annihilation of the Grrumm fleet. If it meant losing her entire force, so be it.

Every time Katie thought of this, a cold lump formed in her

belly. But the cold strategic equations of the situation were clear, and the fact Katie didn't like them was irrelevant.

Somewhat more relevant was the fact that they'd reached the conclusion that taking out the Grrumm ships in the face of their shield technology required that the energy directed at them be concentrated in time. Energy dispersed over time appeared to allow the enemy shields to regenerate and, therefore, was relatively ineffective. Which argued for a fast closing with the enemy with tight formations. Already her main attack force's formation was less tight than she'd have liked. What about their relative velocity to the Grrumm? Katie keyed a private channel. "Hood, what's your take on Susan's relative velocity to the enemy?"

Katie couldn't see Hood's face, but his voice told her he wasn't happy. "Too slow. If she wants to engage so as to concentrate her attack, it's going to delay her even further."

"Thank you," Katie replied, out of habit. Katie's gut told her to pile in willy-nilly with as much as possible, as fast as possible. Their plan said take longer and hit all at once. That that would have the best chance of overloading the Grrumm shields. In any case, Susan was closer to the scene and a good tactician. Katie would refrain from interfering.

"Ma'am," Sensors announced calmly, "we've just lost the *Indus*, DD 036. Task Force Three's leading ships have entered enemy maximum beam range."

"Ma,am," Comms reported, "Commodore Fritzsen has just ordered General Chase for Task Force Three. She clarifies. All of Task Force Three's ships are to close to point blank range zero velocity rendezvous with the enemy battleships in their individual minimum times. Evasion Scheme Gamma."

Katie frowned. Gamma was the minimum of evasive maneuvers. It was one step removed from boring straight in and being a sitting duck for enemy beam attacks. "Thank you, Comms," she managed to grind out.

She'd deliberately jumped her forces as close in to the enemy as she dared so as to deprive them of reaction time. In the process, she'd also severely limited her own reaction time. She needed to decide what to do quickly. Did she countermand Susan's orders, or double down on what her old friend had initiated?

"Ma'am," Sensors bit out, "Commodore Haralson has echoed Commodore Fritzsen's orders to Task Force Three to Task Force Two. Task Force Two has been ordered to close with the enemy at their best possible velocities with minimal evasive maneuvers."

"Comms," Katie declared. "Order Task Force One to conform with Task Force Three and Two's maneuvers."

Before her Comms officer could comply, Sensors broke in, "Ma'am, Task Force One appears to have gone to Evasive Scheme Gamma."

"Confirm that, ma'am," Comms reported. "Commander Campbell has ordered Task Force One to Evasion Scheme Gamma and to close as quickly as possible with the enemy."

"Thank you, Sensors, Comms," Katie answered. "Comms, belay last."

"Yes, ma'am."

They all knew events had overtaken Katie's attempt to control them. Well, she couldn't fault her subordinates for lack of initiative. And they were sticking to the spirit of their plan. It was hardly their fault that the plan in question had an inherent tension between the goal of closing with the Grrumm ships as fast as possible, but doing so in a co-ordinated and concentrated in time fashion.

"Ma'am," Sensors reported, "We just lost two more destroyers, the *Parthia* and *Lusitania* from Task Force One."

And that's what minimal evasive action gets you, Katie thought. Aloud she said, "Thank you, Sensors. Just report type and numbers from now on. We don't need to know their names. We'll save that for the after-action reports." Hope that didn't seem too harsh, but this was definitely a do or die proposition. She had to go all in.

"Comms, message to CAG. Launch all the torpedo bombers. Plan Omega. Remind your pilots it's critical to co-ordinate with the fireship strike and try to concentrate our attack to the greatest degree possible. Kincaid out."

"Roger, ma'am. Torpedo bombers to attack. Plan Omega," Comms replied. Mere seconds later she added, "Commander Air Group acknowledges order to launch torpedo bomber strike using Plan Omega."

"Thank you, Comms. Message for Lieutenant Commander Ste. Marie on the *Normandy*. You are hereby detached from the Command Group. You are to take command of the corvettes *Daisy, Bluebell, Pansy, Begonia* and all the supply ships in the train. You will remain out of the battle. You will only attempt rescue operations in the event of enemy annihilation or surrender. Kincaid out."

After Ste. Marie acknowledged her orders, Katie continued, "Message to Command Group. Flank speed towards the enemy. Evasive plan beta once within weapons range, but our priority goal is to co-ordinate our attack timing with Task Force Three. Kincaid out."

There they were all in: she'd committed everything but a frigate, their corvettes and their supply ships, none of which could have done much more than have been targets for a brief time.

Her tactical display continued to flash the red of ongoing losses.

The thump-shudder of bomber launches vibrated through the *Bonnie*'s frame, seeming to underline them.

"Ma'am, we just lost one of Task Force Three's DD sized fireships," her Sensors officer said. Bad news. If enough fireships didn't get through, everybody else's sacrifice would be wasted.

As planned, it was all happening very quickly and yet, it seemed to be taking an eternity.

"Ma'am," Kooperman, her Ops officer, announced, "Task Force Two is now in weapons range from the enemy and beginning to engage."

Good, Katie thought. It ought to take some of the strain off of the main attack by Susan's Task Force Three. "Thank you, Ops," she said.

And indeed, the distraction provided by Thor Haralson's Task Force Two did seem to help. At a cost. Overall, losses had slowed, but Task Force Two was paying a price.

"Ma'am," Sensors, Lieutenant Kawasaki, reported. There was an edge to her voice. "The *Implacable* is heavily damaged." Damn, that was Thor's flagship. A brief pause. "She just exploded, ma'am," Kawasaki added quietly.

"Thank you, Sensors," Katie said out of habit. She sounded perfectly normal, as far as she could tell. Likely the Space Force's finest tactician, and an old friend, gone just like that. It reminded her that Susan had refused to move her flag off of the *Triumph*, their only other remaining carrier and, as such, surely a priority target for the enemy. She did hope Susan managed to beat the odds.

She listened distantly as her sensors officer confirmed the mounting losses her tactical display and her own eyes showed her. So far they still seemed to have enough, barely enough, fireships still in one piece, even if they were less tightly co-ordinated than she'd have liked. Pretty soon, they'd know if it'd all been worth it.

"Task Force One is now within weapons range of the enemy and is engaging," Sensors reported.

Good. "Thank you, Sensors."

Shortly after an erratic jerking about reached Katie, even in her combat pod and despite the inertial compensators. The *Bonnie*'s evasive maneuvers were that violent.

"Ma'am, we're within enemy weapons range now," the Ops officer reported.

No kidding.

"Enemy battleship destroyed by a fireship," Sensors announced, unable to keep a note of glee out of her voice.

It was about time. "Thank you, Sensors," Katie said. Too bad Task Force One and the Command Group were lagging, but Katie didn't say that aloud.

The decisive phase of the battle had begun.

The yellow stars of fireships ramming enemy ships were interspersed with the red of further human losses.

Sensors was hard put to keep up. "Third enemy battleship gone. They're down to a dozen cruisers. Several seem damaged. Half of Task Force One is gone. We've lost another couple of fireships. Fireship from Task Force Two just took out another enemy cruiser. They seem to be ignoring our bombers."

And so it went.

Finally Sensor's reported. "We've lost or expended all our

fireships, ma'am. Bombers are still attacking."

Katie could see the enemy hadn't been eliminated yet. She asked for confirmation. "The enemy?"

"They're down to eight cruisers, half damaged. Five battleships, three showing visible signs of damage, ma'am."

So, they'd hit the enemy hard, but not finished them off. Unfortunately, they didn't have much relative velocity and there wasn't much chance the remaining human ships could disengage before the Grrumm exacted their revenge. Maybe the bombers would manage to finish off some of the damaged ships. A forlorn hope, but a glimmer of one for all that.

Strangely, the enemy fire seemed to slacken. They'd previously suspected that both the enemy shields and their beam weapons drew from the same energy sources. Maybe they suffered from having to make a trade-off between defense and attack. Did that make sense? Katie contemplated issuing a general retreat, but the bombers had yet to push their attacks home. She'd hold off until they'd done what they could.

"Bombers now launching torpedoes," Sensors announced.

"Thank you, Sensors," Katie automatically replied.

Somehow, the next few tens of seconds passed with almost no losses among the torpedoes or the bombers that had launched them. There were no further losses at all among the larger ships. Miraculously both her carriers, the *Triumph* and the *Bonaventure*, remained intact. The bombers might have a home to return to. The *Bonnie* had been a bit late to the party, but how the *Triumph* still survived Katie didn't know. Didn't mind, but didn't know.

"Multiple torpedo hits on all enemy ships, ma'am," Sensors reported.

Katie's tactical display flared yellow.

"Ma'am," Kawasaki on sensors said in a tone of disbelieving awe, "Half of them are gone. Sorry, ma'am. Three enemy cruisers left, and all appear damaged. Three enemy battleships left. One very heavily damaged, outgassing and appears to have lost power. The other two remaining also showing signs of heavy damage."

Katie blinked. That was a surprise. A very good one. "Ops, make sure the CAG rearms the bombers for a second strike as quickly as possible."

"Ma'am," Comms spoke up, "I have a communication from the enemy."

"Put it on the main display, Comms," Katie ordered. And for only the second time, Katie saw the visage of the enemy commander. He spoke in Galactic. "I offer surrender. I will order my crews to power down and then abandon ship in their life pods on your acceptance."

Katie didn't understand what had just happened.

But she wasn't going to look a gift horse in the mouth. "I accept your surrender," she answered.

***

Katie supposed maybe she ought to be elated. Against the odds, she'd beat the Grrumm and saved her species from subjugation. Or maybe grief-stricken because of the thousands of her people, including many old friends, that had died to make that victory possible. Or, maybe both, even. But she didn't feel either. She didn't feel anything but very tired.

She looked around her cabin. She'd done what she could in the immediate aftermath of the Battle of Rho Cygni, as she was sure the history books would call it. She'd taken the surviving Grrumm prisoner. Put prize crews on their ships. Rescued all the survivors she could of whatever species. Done a preliminary tallying of losses. She could now get some physical rest, at least.

Doubtless, she'd feel better for some sleep. She didn't expect it'd resolve her malaise. She'd set herself a goal back when she was still on the brink of adulthood. She'd been a talented, clever, and, indeed, prescient child. But she'd still been a child. Her entire adult life she'd spent working towards the goal she'd just achieved. And now she was done.

In truth, there was more. She'd made promises she needed to see were kept. She still had duties. The politicians back home could still mess up the legacy she was leaving them. As much as she hated political machinations, she guessed she ought to keep an eye out for that. Fact was she'd never really thought much about it. In truth, she'd never really believed she'd make it this far. It'd been an all but impossible journey.

The hard part was done. The finish line crossed. She just

wanted to pat herself on the back and retire.
She was tired. Hadn't she done enough?
Hadn't she given enough?
Maybe it'd look different after a long rest.
She didn't think so.
She tidy up after herself. She always had.
But Katie figured she'd done enough for any one woman.

* * *

Now that he was not so busy, and he had time for such indulgences, Rrolff found his primary feeling was one of profound relief. Not despair. Not anger. Not horror. Just relief.

He was happy to be alone. The humans, after taking him prisoner and after he'd elected not to be repatriated, had given him a small cabin on the *Imperial Dominance*. She was a sister ship to his former flag. Gutted of her weapons and repaired sufficiently to be space worthy, she was taking the Grrumm prisoners, who'd not chosen to be paroled and returned to the Empire, back to the human home world instead. What awaited him there he didn't know and didn't much care. It had to be better than the disgrace and humiliation that he'd find back in the Empire.

He was happy to be alive and to no longer be responsible for a disaster in progress that he still couldn't see any way he could have prevented. He looked around his little cabin. It was cozy and perfectly acceptable, given his minimal needs. Most of all, he appreciated that it allowed him to be alone and to not have to hide his feelings.

He'd led most of the Grrumm under him, noble officers and non-noble spacers and soldiers both, to their deaths. That was nothing to be happy about. And those that had survived would never get the respect for their sacrifices that they deserved. Rrolff would bear most of the responsibility and accompanying shame and humiliation for their disastrous defeat, but back in the Empire it'd be a shadow over the social standing of all who'd been involved.

Neither was fair. Generations dead and the schemers back in the core worlds deserved more of the blame, but they'd not receive it. Rrolff could see being bitterly angry about it. But he wasn't. It was the way of the world. He'd been unfairly privileged before. Now he was unfairly condemned for something not of his doing. He was going to lose his titles and the estates generations before him had handed down in trust. His family was going to be better off and happier if he didn't return to be an ongoing embarrassment to them.

Still, it made no sense to succumb to emotions that would only corrode him from within because of it.

He did wish there was something he could do to ameliorate the situation. The Empire had lost its FTL-capable expeditionary fleet. None of the many ships it had that depended on the gate system to move between stars would be the least use to it beyond the Frontier.

He was no scientist or economist, so it was unclear to him how long it would take the Empire to rebuild that fleet of FTL-capable and shielded ships that had allowed it to dominate the barbarians at will. Given the shield technology's apparent dependence on hand crafted crystals produced by a single family business now defunct, he wasn't even sure it could.

The humans seem convinced that knowing of the technology, it was possible to reproduce it. And the humans now knew of it and had captured samples of it.

Worse, some Grrumm technicians had been happy to defect to the barbarians and share their knowledge rather than returning home to disgrace. Even if rather mild disgrace compared to what Rrolff faced.

If the Empire did manage to rebuild its Expeditionary Force, Rrolff had little doubt it'd find itself facing human ships with the same shield technology as it had. The Empire had lost its advantage.

And so the Lord Earl Sweets-Swiper's life was also over.

Rrolff, the former Imperial noble, now a disgraced nobody, might continue his existence, but the Lord Earl was done.

Life was a gift Rrolff was willing to accept, but what he could expect from it now was a mystery to him.

When the barbarian leader had interviewed him, she'd been brusque but not hostile. She'd suggested human cubs and scholars might both find him an interesting curiosity and that he might earn some compensation entertaining them.

That might be a way of earning his meals.

An honest one, even.

Who knew?

He'd see soon enough.

* * *

Yet another party on Far Seat. They were having a lot of those recently. Shadowguide didn't begrudge beings finding a little joy in their lives, but he wouldn't mind it when life returned to being a bit boring and routine, either.

Indeed, he was thinking of perhaps going into semi-retirement. One thing about regularly being one of the first in the know; you got to front-run all sorts of quite profitable investments. And Shadowguide's needs were minimal. His one great source of amusement was watching what other people were up to. Generally not only free, but something you could get paid for.

Life was good.

Shadowguide didn't wish to succumb to complacency. The Grrumm had recently supplied a lesson in where that could lead, but he couldn't help but share in some of the happiness of the other folks here in his favorite Varkoid owned and operated dive.

Yes, Shadowguide looked into his drink and had to admit he was feeling both smug and happy. It'd all turned out far better than anyone had a right to hope for. And he'd had his hand in that, supplying a little nudge here and there to events. It was good.

Indeed, an expectation that things would turn out exactly as one wanted was something worthy of only very young and sheltered children, but on rare occasions one beat the odds and had improbably good luck. There was nothing wrong with enjoying one's good fortune for a short period.

The Grrumm Empire had been fragile, true, but an Empire has a lot of ruin in it. It could have lingered on for further generations, inflicting a great deal of discomfort in its death throes. It hadn't. Worth drinking to.

The human success could have been overwhelming and have left them over-powerful and full of arrogant hubris. It hadn't been. And they weren't. Their fleet remained the strongest in local space, but they'd lost a lot and would need the help of their neighbors to rebuild. Their people and leadership were well aware of that, and of how close run the whole thing had been. That was good. And also worth drinking to.

The details were unclear, but the rough outline of the future of this part of the galaxy was apparent.

The Grrumm would growl, but leave the Frontier folk in peace.

The humans would keep pirates and worse predators in check, but were too weak and uncertain of themselves to be much of a problem.

It was good.

And Called It Peace

Rob Hood put the finishing touches on the report, checked it over briefly, and hit the send button. That done, he sighed, and sat up, stretching and working his shoulder muscles. He looked around his dimly lit cabin, exercising neck muscles that'd tightened up while he was physically hunched over in one place, his mind elsewhere. The place was empty of anything personal. It had only the Space Force issued necessities. He was alone. He'd sent Tanya Wootton off to bed hours ago when they'd finished the first draft of the report.

Rob was very tired and needed sleep badly, but he'd been that way for hours, and he'd been pushing back against it all that time. Right now, he needed a little time to relax and get reoriented. Also to think a little less about what they'd learned from the recent battle at Rho Cygni and what it meant for the galaxy, and Admiral Kincaid, and a little more narrowly about Rob Hood's future.

Rob's parents had raised him on a small farm on Mars. They'd been middle class and small business people, and that was the world he felt happiest in. It'd all come crashing down with their deaths when the farm's dome had collapsed. Rather literally. He'd clawed his way out of that misfortune via the Space Force, retired and started an electrical contracting business on Earth. Once again middle class and a small businessman. Then the current crisis had intervened, and he'd somehow ended up a commissioned xenologist working for Katie Kincaid.

Somehow, his life kept being knocked off its rails. He'd like to get it back on them. Back to what it ought to be. He couldn't see himself as a peacetime Space Force officer. He'd never quite fit in. Wrong social background. Never been to the Academy. He couldn't see himself as an academic, either. It wasn't that the field wasn't interesting; it was the thought of having to deal with other academics that did it. The thought of years of petty squabbling over dry theories in the pursuit of some sort of reputation left him cold. Duty might have reconciled him to either career choice, but the fact was that Tanya Wootton knew everything he did and was better suited to both career paths. She wouldn't even feel it as a sacrifice of any sort.

Fact was, the only thing he'd miss about his current job was the people. He'd grown fond of both Wootton and Kincaid. He'd miss them both, but only exceptional circumstances had ever thrown them together and those circumstances had changed.

The crisis had been resolved.

The world would be returning to normal.

Rob hadn't really given it much thought before. Hadn't seemed worth the effort. He felt lucky to have survived. He figured humanity in general had been pretty lucky. He could only hope the politicians back home didn't muck it up. But that was above his pay grade. He'd worked out the kinks in his thinking.

He could rest now.

***

Thorn-Paw stood at the back of the *Celestial Dominance*'s bridge, the fleet commander's position, and surveyed the scene before him. They'd just jumped out of the Clear Ponds system. They were halfway home, and it looked like they'd make it all the way there.

It was more than Thorn-Paw would have dared hope for several paws of days ago when he'd stood on this bridge and listened to the reports of their fleet being destroyed ship by ship. He'd thought that his life was over then, and, worse, that the Empire he'd served the whole of that life had taken a possibly fatal blow.

Watching the bridge watch before him going about their duties calmly and properly in tune with the long-developed traditions for such things, it was easy to forget the catastrophe that had befallen them.

The fact was that their ship had been gutted of its weapons and the shield technology that had rendered it so fearsome to the Empire's foes. And it was a flagship without a fleet. The humans had kept what was left of that, save this one vessel to return those whom they'd paroled, and wished it, to civilized space and the Empire.

The returning survivors were only a fraction of the Grrumm who'd set out on their ill-fated expedition. They were only half of those who'd survived. Many of the Grrumm survivors had elected not to return home. They'd defected.

None of the survivors could be sure of the reception they'd get back in the Empire. It'd be something less than a joyous celebration, that much was certain. Condemnation and disdain were distinct possibilities.

Thorn-Paw wished he didn't understand why the Grrumm that had defected to the humans had chosen to do so. But he did. They had little hope of resuming a normal happy life back in the Empire. They feared not unreasonably that they'd be sources of shame and embarrassment to what family and friends they might have there. Better to have been lost somewhat honorably than to return alive from the debacle.

Thorn-Paw and the others on the *Celestial Dominance* were returning to the Empire out of a sense of duty more than anything else. In some cases, maybe it was a simple lack of imagination. In any case, whether the schemers who ruled from the core planets recognized it or not, they were going to need the expedition's survivors in the coming seasons.

Thorn-Paw didn't expect them to acknowledge that

publicly. But he couldn't imagine any of them would be eager to go to the Frontier and remove themselves from the seat of power. Moreover, none of them were as competent or as experienced as Thorn-Paw was.

He'd be dressed down and then graciously allowed to resume command of the Frontier fleet where he'd be responsible for keeping the barbarians from bothering civilized space.

It'd be a thankless job, but it was one Thorn-Paw had long accepted as his lot.

He had hoped to retire to be with family in their ancestral homeland, but that had probably been optimistic even before.

It wasn't going to happen now.

He'd have to be happy knowing he was doing his duty.

Somebody had to hold the line.

* * *

Tanya almost wished she like drinking and partying in general. It'd been wild since they'd got back to Earth. No Space Force member, and certainly nobody that had served under Kincaid, could buy themselves a drink anywhere. People insisted on buying their heroes drinks, meals too, sometimes they opened their homes. Younger men and women threw themselves at spacers they'd convinced themselves were seven feet tall and could do no wrong.

Tanya hoped it hadn't gone to too many heads. She knew her history. There was bound to be some backlash. But right now, no member of the Space Force could do any wrong. They were all heroes. The population was determined to fete them and show their thanks in any way they could.

Here on Goddard Station, where a large part of the population was Space Force itself, it wasn't too bad. Tanya had gone out for supper with a number of her on-call colleagues in the intelligence branch to a place called the "Ye Olde Pub and Grubhouse". They hadn't been overly bothered by people wanting to express their thanks. It'd been rather nice.

Still, when Tanya had finished eating, after stuffing herself full of complimentary dessert in fact - it'd have been impolite to refuse - and decided she was tired of the noise, and made her excuses, no one had objected too much. Odd fact was

Tanya was technically, as Hood's second-in-command, their boss.

Even if she'd been more of a people person, it made it hard to completely relax around her.

So Tanya was back in her cabin, alone with her thoughts again. Something that suited her fine. And there was a lot to think about.

She'd got to see a lot of the local galaxy as part of recent events. It was changing in fascinating ways. She hoped her bosses wouldn't object to her publishing some papers about it.

Hood she wasn't worried about. He tried to act tough, but she could wrap him around her little finger without much effort.

Kincaid was a different story. On the other hand, as prone to tunnel vision and focusing on short-range objectives as the woman was, she wasn't stupid, and she was pragmatic.

Kincaid understood as well as Tanya did herself that defeating the Grrumm, keeping them from subjugating humanity and destroying their influence on this part of the galaxy was all well and fine, but it didn't mean humanity could expect to get its own way in everything. Things were not going to go back to the way they were before contact. There were a lot of different actors in this part of the galaxy and Kincaid had made a lot of implicit and a few explicit promises to them.

It was important that Earth's leaders avoid hubris. Arrogant overreach would backfire badly. Kincaid knew this and Tanya didn't doubt she wanted everyone else to realize it too. So she'd probably support Tanya in making that clear to everyone.

That made Tanya happy.

The fact that it meant her work would no doubt be of continuing interest to the gods of funding also made her happy.

It looked like interesting times ahead.

* * *

Neither the sunshine nor the bright blue sky were quite what Rrolff was used to. No two planets are exactly the same.

Nevertheless, the sunshine was warm and the blue

pleasant. The air was still and warm, too. It was quiet with the only sound that of the insects the humans called bees. Bees were makers of a nectar the humans called honey. Rrolff quite liked it.

He also liked the fact he could call this place his own. The surrounding woods, the little meadow he was in, and the cabin in its middle were all his. He'd purchased them with part of the proceeds from a book deal. He didn't know what astounded him more, that the humans would make such a deal or that they were so willing to sell off parts of their home planet.

On the Grrumm worlds, every little piece of land was someone's legacy and rarely bought or sold. When it was, it was always because of some distress befalling the owning family and a tinge of disgrace clung to seller and buyer both. The seller for failing to hold on to their patrimony, the buyer for taking advantage.

That didn't appear to be the case here. The transaction by which Rrolff procured his new home had been through an agent, but that disturbingly upbeat individual had told Rrolff that the previous owners had held the place as a vacation retreat. They'd bought it scant years before but then decided to move off-planet and therefore no longer needed it. No Grrumm was so cavalier about owning anything, let alone land. The humans were obviously very different. Rrolff felt guilty about taking advantage of them, but not so much that he was willing to pass up the opportunity. He'd already begun falling in love with his new home.

After all, it wasn't like he could return to his old one. He hadn't heard that he'd been stripped of his estates yet, but he had no doubt it was coming. It wasn't too likely he'd be tried for treason and given a death sentence for his failure, but not impossible, and deep abiding disgrace and ostracism were guaranteed.

He still had family and friends, true. But his disgrace would cling to them too. The more loyal they were, the more it'd cling. He was doing them a favor by not returning. If he returned, he'd be nothing but a lingering embarrassment to them. Better make a clean break and allow them to start anew faster and easier. Not forcing them to endure his public trial and then to make excuses for him was the greatest gift he could give them. Having been abandoned, his wife could find a new mate and his children a new father. Any up-and-coming merchant would welcome his wife's social skills and knowledge. His children were well brought up and had had the best education. They'd be solid assets.

It wouldn't be easy for them, but they'd manage better without Rrolff than with him. So not all was right with the world, but life went on.

He'd miss his estates. He'd miss his family and friends. However, he did like his new home. It was enough for him alone. He'd be kept busy. The humans had talked about more books and some had suggested teaching a course or two on Galactic politics at a nearby university. Maybe doing an online version. That was good. And the humans, in their pride, thought it no disgrace to lose to their Admiral Kincaid.

So there was that.

Life went on and could be pleasant and interesting both. Only he'd not be making any more life and death decisions. Which suited Rrolff just fine.

* * *

Katie was sure she'd seen something like this victory ceremony in a video. Made sense really, the organizers must have got their inspiration from somewhere.

She wondered if they were fully cognizant of their sources. Movies weren't a great source of information for the realities of war, and some of the technically greatest celebrations of military power from the early days of movie making in the early industrial age of the twentieth century were culturally and morally tainted. They'd in fact celebrated the ascendancy of genocidal nut jobs who'd failed their people quite disastrously. Just how disastrously had taken generations to be revealed. Katie didn't want to rain on anyone's parade. But celebrations of military power had bad historical connotations for her and she really hoped the body politic here on Earth wasn't falling prey to arrogant hubris.

They were certainly doing this on a grand scale. They'd found the largest venue possible within commuting distance of the capital. It was a concert venue with a huge field featuring a large permanent stage on one side and additional infrastructure in the form of wide paved walkways, light standards, concession kiosks, parking, and transit access. Right now, the entire open area was festooned with banners and filled with people. Upbeat military tunes played over the sound system. Another detail that grated on Katie's nerves. She'd never been that fond of marching.

But she had one more march left in her. There was a wide path from the back of the field straight up to the stage. The crowds on either side were being kept back by red uniformed guards from the local polity. Very resplendent guards, though Katie would prefer a marine in dented space armor any day.

Anyhow, Katie was going to get to march up that aisle followed by other so-called heroes. After that, she'd get to stand around and listen to embarrassing praise before being decorated with some pretty bits of metal and ribbon. It wouldn't bring anybody back to life. She had her doubts it ensured anything positive for the future.

But she didn't want to rain on anybody's parade.

And, yes, folks did have reason to be glad it had all turned out as well as it had.

She didn't think many of them realized how much it had depended on having good allies or how much they needed the continued goodwill of those alien allies. She really hoped this whole thing didn't indicate an unfounded optimism about the future. She really regretted Amy and Colleen and so many others weren't here for it. She really hoped she wasn't seeing the beginnings of arrogant overreach.

Hopefully, it wouldn't be her problem. She'd collect her medals today. Say nice nothings to everyone. Do some interviews saying more nice nothings and she'd retire. Study history and write her memoirs. Take long walks on the estate she'd inherited from her grandmother.

With any luck, she'd not need the political machine she'd also inherited from the woman.

The war for humanity's survival was done.

Katie had done her bit, she figured. She hoped that'd be enough.

She hated politics.

She'd do her duty,
though. She always had.

If you enjoyed this novel, please leave a review.

To be notified of future releases visit my website at http://www.napoleonsims.com/publishing

Appendix A:
Order of Battle for Original Human Fleet

Overall Fleet Command: RADM Katherine Anne Kincaid
Chief of Staff: CDRE Wolf Hoffman
Intelligence Section Head: LCMD Robert "Rob" Hood
Flag Captain (Bonaventure): CMDR Timothy McLeod
Commander Fleet Marines: BGEN Heinrich von Luck

Command Group:

Commanded by: CDRE Thor Haralson

Flag:
Bonaventure	CV 003	(CMDR Timothy McLeod)

Escorts:
Majestic	CV 002	(CMDR Stephen Lee)
Freedom	CL 001	(CMDR Dave Caldwell)
America	DD 005	(LCMD Andrei Ghukov)
Normandy	FF 006	(LCMD Jeanne Ste.Marie)
Daisy	K 111	(LTSG Kasi Date)
Bluebell	K 104	(LTSG Sasha Klutrova)

Support Group:

Commanded by: CMDR Henry Vane

Flag:
Magnificent	CV 004	(CMDR Marilyn Seabright)

Scout Group (LCMD Brian Broomfield)

Escorts:
Determination	CL 005	(CMDR Isai Manda)
Resolution	CL 004	(CMDR Danior Dady)
Britannia	DD 009	(LCMD Jorge Pereira)
Mon Pays	DD 015	(LCMD Azur Talaqani)
Italia	DD 010	(LCMD Markov Rumiantsev)

Eire	DD 012	(LCMD Kyrk Dolby)
Pansy	K 117	(LTSG Thomas Rompkey)
Begonia	K 103	(LTSG Jela Franco)

Train:
Provider	AOR 201	(LCMD Rolando Eger)
Provisioner	AOR 202	(LCMD Aldonza Serna)
Supply	AOE 301	(LCMD Lavra Dulka)
Mercy	AH 901	(LCMD Rajani Patla)
Workshop	AR 401	(LCMD Cari Turk)
Quiver	AFS 501	(LCMD Mischa Marov)
Haversack	AFS 502	(LCMD Rocio Peres)

Reserve Task Force 004:

Commanded by: CDRE Amy Sarkis

Flag:
Glory	CV 004	(CMDR Takeo Menda)

Scout Group (LCMD Tamera Wentzell)

Escorts:
Hercules	CV 005	(CMDR Oleg Melankov)
Endeavor	CL 003	(CMDR Michael Milligan)
Independence	CL 002	(LCMD Michel Decamp)
Intrepid	CL 014	(LCMD Max Rana)
Furious	CL 015	(LCMD Arthur Ghazali)
Deutschland	DD 006	(LCMD Jamie Wong)
Rossiya	DD 007	(LCMD David Sagan)
Canada	DD 016	(LCMD Maxim Hvorostovsky)
India	DD 017	(LCMD Erica Kujath)
Anatolia	DD 023	(LCMD Poul Felsing)
Batavia	DD 024	(LCMD Tasha Isyanov)
Scythia	DD 033	(LCMD Maiya Kawashima)
Ruthenia	DD 034	(LCMD Willem Mikle)
Bactria	DD 037	(LCMD Nicky Howell)
Australia	DD 038	(LCMD Mirza Demirel)

Devonshire	FF 004	(LCMD Marina Natal)
Alberta	FF 009	(LCMD Anita Milbrath)
Ohio	FF 010	(LCMD Robert Maddox)
Saxony	FF 013	(LCMD Joao Rosa)
Belogrod	FF 014	(LCMD John Little)
Tyrol	FF 021	(LCMD Vina Golas)
Tipperary	FF 023	(LCMD Catrina Peres)
Shandong	FF 034	(LCMD Jorden Peters)
Texas	FF 036	(LCMD Lintang Bintang)
Aster	K 101	(LTSG Eva Taras)
Trillium	K 112	(LTSG Christy Kardas)
Buttercup	K 106	(LTSG Henry Abrahams)
Dahlia	K 108	(LTSG Manfred Moller)
Magnolia	K 114	(LTSG Blanca Centeno)
Hickory	K 121	(LTSG Peter van Alebeck)

Train:

Vittles	AOE 302	(LCMD(R) Sara Benga)

Right Task Force 001:

Commanded by: CDRE Lawrence "Larry" Wong

Flag:
Terrible   CV 006   (CMDR William Cartwright)

Scout Group (CMDR Abegail Brown)

Escorts:
Powerful   CV 008   (CMDR James Jarvis)

Enterprise   CL 016   (CMDR Cara Campbell)
Innovation   CL 009   (LCMD Richer Dent)
Generosity   CL 012   (LCMD Kenneth Hunter)
Irresistible   CL 020   (LCMD Chiko Shintani)

Zhongguo   DD 008   (LCMD Asmund Rosenkranz)
South Africa   DD 018   (LCMD Jeanette Callen)
Hellas   DD 022   (LCMD Gian Saletta)
Caledonia   DD 026   (LCMD Lap Lam)
Gallia   DD 028   (LCMD Kristanna Carson)
Sinae   DD 032   (LCMD Hamir Gokhale)
Norway   DD 040   (LCMD Vasyklo Kost)
Sudan   DD 042   (LCMD Jayden Stuart)
Thailand   DD 044   (LCMD Willard Leib)
Columbia   DD 046   (LCMD Lyn Brooks)
New York   FF 003   (LCMD Jennifer Kline)
Kerala   FF 008   (LCMD Gil Watkins)
Catalonia   FF 015   (LCMD Curt Menges)
Bavaria   FF 019   (LCMD Jan Tarnowski)
Brandenburg   FF 024   (LCMD Johan Pulkkinen)
Kursk   FF 027   (LCMD Lee Wong)
Rostov   FF 029   (LCMD Margaret Wiggins)
Carinthia   FF 031   (LCMD Ehren Roma)
Norfolk   FF 032   (LCMD Desideria Ozuna)

Spruce   K 120   (LTSG Paul Wise)
Acacia   K 103   (LTSG Gustave Jobin)
Iris   K 111   (LTSG Gavrel Stolin)
Lilac   K 113   (LTSG Rolly Gue)

Yew	K 119	(LTSG Juan Sing)
Wisteria	K 116	(LTSG Matthew Barker)

Train:
Ammo   AOE 303   (LCMD(R) Samuel Hearst)

Vanguard Task Force 002:

Commanded by: CDRE John Smith

Flag:
Leviathan   CV 007   (CDRE Colleen McGinnis)

Scout Group (CMDR Ravi Shankar)

Escorts:
Warrior   CV 010   (CMDR Thomas Moakler)

Liberty   CL 007   (CMDR Arlene Gibel)
Dedication   CL 010   (LCMD Ariadne Papas)
Implacable   CL 019   (LCMD Terri Hicks)
Indefatigable CL 022   (LCMD Karie Steenberg)

Hibernia   DD 011   (LCMD Chul Tan)
Eygpt   DD 019   (LCMD Ata Moana)
Bithynia   DD 023   (LCMD Thomas Richardson)
Libya   DD 031   (LCMD Jamie Mclaughlin)
New Zealand   DD 039   (LCMD Kranti Kothari)
Congo   DD 041   (LCMD James MacDonald)
Ethiopia   DD 043   (LCMD Jaymee McFarlan)
Nippon   DD 045   (LCMD Waluyo Sukarno)
Argentina   DD 047   (LCMD Giulo Zottola)
Brazil   DD 048   (LCMD Chiamaka Huboka)

Ontario   FF 005   (LCMD Nadja von Heine-Geldern)
Tuscany   FF 016   (LCMD Alexander Reeves)
Chaco   FF 020   (LCMD Sanket Rout)
Yunnan   FF 025   (LCMD Fai Gau)
San Juan   FF 030   (LCMD Charles Middleton)
California   FF 033   (LCMD Cathenna Niktas)
Yorkshire   FF 037   (LCMD Julee Rogier)
Victoria   FF 038   (LCMD Anna Riggs)
Quebec   FF 039   (LCMD Luke Norton)

Daffodil   K 109   (LTSG Sean O'Conner)
Azalea   K 107   (LTSG Royce Couturier)
Pine   K 118   LTSG Xiu Lo)
Maple   K 123   (LTSG Stephen Moore)

Oak   K 125   (LTSG Ayla Manheim)
Cedar   K 128   (LTSG Sandie Nanos)

Train:
Biscuit   AOE 304   (LCMD(R) Ann O'Malley)

Left Task Force 003:

Commanded by: CDRE Susan Fritzsen

Flag:
Triumph	CV 009	(CMDR Paul Rodgers)

Scout Group (LCMD Iris Gregorian)

Escorts:
Ark Royal	CV 011	(CMDR Anne Elizabeth Novak)
Ferocity	CL 006	(CMDR Michael Landry)
Constitution	CL 008	(LCMD Krishan Rama)
Adventurous	CL 013	(LCMD Can Ngo)
Audacious	CL 018	(LCMD Jussi Ranta)
Ostland	DD 014	(LCMD Dong Hur)
Hispania	DD 020	(LCMD Istar Pahlavi)
Lusitania	DD 021	(LCMD Arthur Crawford)
Helvetia	DD 029	(LCMD Waylon Karl)
Mauretania	DD 030	(LCMD Madelene Kotkin)
Parthia	DD 035	(LCMD Andrew Thompson)
Indus	DD 036	(LCMD Caterina Tome)
Bohemia	DD 025	(LCMD Andreo Rojas)
Nordland	DD 013	(LCMD Padric McCoy)
Arabia	DD 027	(LCMD Andre Giraud)
Queensland	FF 007	(LCMD Jason Seif)
New Jersey	FF 011	(LCMD Susan Caldwell)
Wessex	FF 012	(LCMD Mikkel Junge)
Hunan	FF 017	(LCMD Ilyse Lansburgh)
Victoria	FF 018	(LCMD Neva Kursinska)
Grodno	FF 022	(LCMD Alexander Keith)
Alabama	FF 026	(LCMD Paul St.Laurent)
Brittany	FF 028	(LCMD Duron Omer)
Manitoba	FF 035	(LCMD James Ready)
Gladiolus	K 102	(LTSG Ishan Garg)
Belladonna	K 105	(LTSG Samuel Adams)
Hyacinth	K 109	(LTSG Zenda Muqimi)

Poppy	K 115	(LTSG Filcia Large)
Birch	K 122	(LTSG Ho Lau)
Poplar	K 127	(LTSG Timothea Palamara)

Train:
Drink	AOE 305	(LCMD(R) Andrew Tarasov)

Appendix B:
Order of Battle for Human Fleet at Rho Cygni

Overall Fleet Command: RADM Katherine Anne Kincaid
Chief of Staff: CDRE Wolf Hoffman
Intelligence Section Head: LCMD Robert "Rob" Hood
Flag Captain (Bonaventure): CMDR Timothy McLeod
Commander Fleet Marines: BGEN Heinrich von Luck

Command Group and Train:

Commanded by: Under direct command of Admiral Kincaid

Flag:
Bonaventure   CV 003   (CMDR Timothy McLeod)

Scout Group (LCMD Brian Broomfield)

Escorts:
Normandy   FF 006   (LCMD Jeanne Ste.Marie)

Daisy   K 111   (LTSG Kasi Date)
Bluebell   K 104   (LTSG Sasha Klutrova)
Pansy   K 117   (LTSG Thomas Rompkey)
Begonia   K 103   (LTSG Jela Franco)

Train:
Provider   AOR 201   (LCMD Rolando Eger)
Supply   AOE 301   (LCMD Lavra Dulka)
Mercy   AH 901   (LCMD Rajani Patla)
Workshop   AR 401   (LCMD Cari Turk)
Haversack   AFS 502   (LCMD Rocio Peres)
Ammo   AOE 303   (LCMD(R) Samuel Hearst)

*Fireships: None.

Task Force 001:

Commanded by: CMDR Cara Campbell

Flag:
Enterprise	CL 016	(LCMD George Rodney)

Escorts:
Irresistible	CL 020	(LCMD Chiko Shintani)
Zhongguo	DD 008	(LCMD Asmund Rosenkranz)
South Africa	DD 018	(LCMD Jeanette Callen)
Hellas	DD 022	(LCMD Gian Saletta)
Caledonia	DD 026	(LCMD Lap Lam)
Sudan	DD 042	(LCMD Jayden Stuart)
Thailand	DD 044	(LCMD Willard Leib)
Columbia	DD 046	(LCMD Lyn Brooks)
Kursk	FF 027	(LCMD Lee Wong)
Norfolk	FF 032	(LCMD Desideria Ozuna)
Carinthia	FF 031	(LCMD Ehren Roma)

*Fireships:
  1 CL fireship
  3 DD fireship
  1 Allied fireship

Task Force 002:

Commanded by: CDRE Thor Haralson

Flag:
Implacable	CL 019	(LCMD Terri Hicks)

Escorts:
Hibernia	DD 011	(LCMD Chul Tan)
Bithynia	DD 023	(LCMD Thomas Richardson)
Libya	DD 031	(LCMD Jamie Mclaughlin)
New Zealand	DD 039	(LCMD Kranti Kothari)
Congo	DD 041	(LCMD James MacDonald)
Nippon	DD 045	(LCMD Waluyo Sukarno)

Argentina	DD 047	(LCMD Giulo Zottola)
Ontario	FF 005	(LCMD Nadja von Heine-Geldern)
Tuscany	FF 016	(LCMD Alexander Reeves)
San Juan	FF 030	(LCMD Charles Middleton)
Quebec	FF 039	(LCMD Luke Norton)

*Fireships:

1 CL fireship
3 DD fireship
1 Allied fireship

Task Force 003:

Commanded by: CDRE Susan Fritzsen

Flag:
Triumph   CV 009   (CMDR Paul Rodgers)

Scout Group (LCMD Iris Gregorian)

Escorts:
Constitution   CL 008   (LCMD Krishan Rama)
Freedom   CL 001   (CMDR Dave Caldwell)
Ardent   CL 025   (CMDR Isaac Goldberg)
Resolution   CL 004   (CMDR Danior Dady)

Hispania   DD 020   (LCMD Istar Pahlavi)
Lusitania   DD 021   (LCMD Arthur Crawford)
Bohemia   DD 025   (LCMD Andreo Rojas)
Indus   DD 036   (LCMD Caterina Tome)
Nordland   DD 013   (LCMD Padric McCoy)
Britannia   DD 009   (LCMD Jorge Pereira)
Mon Pays   DD 015   (LCMD Azur Talaqani)
Italia   DD 010   (LCMD Markov Rumiantsev)
Eire   DD 012   (LCMD Kyrk Dolby)

New Jersey   FF 011   (LCMD Susan Caldwell)
Grodno   FF 022   (LCMD Alexander Keith)
Alabama   FF 026   (LCMD Paul St.Laurent)
Manitoba   FF 035   (LCMD James Ready)

*Fireships:
    5 CL fireships
    9 DD fireships
    3 FF fireships
    3 Transport fireships
    4 Allied fireships

(*) "Fireships" named after the incendiary laden wooden hulks used in the days of wooden sailing ships, most famously used against the Spanish Armada of 1588, are patched up wrecks or ships stripped of most weapons and other useful gear and filled with various explosive devices, nuclear warheads, rigged fusion drives and power units, and even some anti-matter devices. Given some extra armor for their propulsion and maneuvering units, and special auto pilot programs, they are intended to make suicide runs on enemy ships, ramming them if possible, but exploding as close as practical if not. They have skeleton crews and improved fast deploying life pods. During the final leg of their attack their crews are supposed to abandon them just before they go to a final attack run involving higher Gees than living beings can withstand.

Appendix C:
A Short Dictionary of Species in the Damp Frontier Region
by Scribbles-For-A-Living of Clear Ponds Trade Hub

Introduction:

The price those of us who live in Frontier space beyond the gated systems pay for our relative freedom is often isolation and a lack of safety. If you're from a small colony cut off from regular contact with the wider galaxy, you may not have been taught much about the other species found there. This pamphlet is for you.

Of course, any one species or civilization is worth a whole lifetime and many books worth of study, but this humble, little work will serve as a good start. It may save you from making life altering and unfortunate errors.

Enjoy!

A Precis on Civilized Species of Interest:

Gossspin:
(Nick or Common names: Spiders, Many-legged Ones, Web-spinners, Spinners)

Keepers of the gates.

Physically the Gossspin have big roundish body on eight long legs. Two eyes on short stalks. Bodies are covered in black chitin with only a few coarse hairs. Central body is about four GiByts wide and three GiByts tall, but their very long (about 8 GiByts) legs hold their bodies up between three and four GiByts off the ground for a total height of six to seven GiBytes. They mass between 80 and 120 Gits.

Socially the Spinners seem to have some internal organization and it seems to have a harshly hierarchical nature to it, but nothing solid is known about it.

They like low light, low gravity, and confined environments but beyond what can be inferred from this is nothing is known of the environment they originated in.

Internal Spinner politics are a complete mystery. Externally all their dealings are through the Gate corporation.

You will have to deal with the Spinners if you move anywhere in gated, so-called "civilized" space. They control the gates. Pay their fees and don't complain. It is not advised that you do any unnecessary business with them. They are secretive and always have an angle. At all costs, avoid offending them in any way.

Squee:
(Nick or Common names: Elder Tentacles)

Elder race. Inscrutable, powerful, possessed of technology that can seem like magic to the rest of us.

Aquatic with in the form of a rough cone with a mouth in the base and long thick tentacles grouped around it. Two of the six of them are longer and finer at the ends and have a very high dexterity. They have smooth greenish yellow skin that has been observed to change color on occasion. Their bodies are five GiByts in length, their shorter tentacles eight GiByts, and the two longer ones ten GiBytes. Give or take a GiByt each is not clear if size difference results from age or not. They mass between 700 and 1100 GiByts. You're not likely to encounter one in the flesh.

We don't know if the Squee have a society as we understand it.

They are deep sea dwellers, but can survive in swallow depths and even open air for a considerable time. Very little else is known about them.

Internal Squee politics are a mystery, though the existence of the "Faithful Squee" suggests some religious element.

Inscrutable like all the elder race. Not malicious or easily provoked. Just as well because they'll crush you like a bug if you annoy them.

Chit-Chit:
(Nick or Common names: Many-armed Elders)

Elder race. Therefore inscrutable and powerful beyond belief.

The Chit-Chit have large central bodies with eight long arms. Bi-ocular with a mouth on the bottom of the central body. They are a hairless aquatic species with a color that seems to adapt with mood and background. They appear to have some conscious control of this. The central body is about two by four GiByts and the arms about six GiByts, giving them an arm span of about fourteen GiByts in all.

Social: They are loners except at mating time or pursuing some interest. How they manage to have a technologically advanced civilization is unknown.

They originated in shallow warm waters on a medium-low gravity planet to all appearances. But are physically very adaptable though they like to stay moist. They don't like intense light or radiation.

Politically the Chit-Chit can be be great schemers as individuals, but they are not prone to forming large coercive organizations. Their organizations are more like other species social clubs. They are organized voluntarily around mutual interests and activities.

Curious and often affable and friendly for an elder race, but be careful. Their purposes are hard to determine and like all the elder races if you cross them it will not go well with you.

Haarumph:
(Nick or Common names: Imposing Ones)

Elder race. Enough said.

Physically large with six limbs, and a long nose, huge ears and beady eyes. Despite the appearance of their eyes their eyesight is very good both in resolving detail and under multiple light levels. They don't miss much. They rest and move about on just four limbs usually, and use their noses and two front limbs to manipulate objects and food. They have a tough almost hairless light bluish-gray hide. They are eight GiByts in height and ten GiBytes long and mass between a thousand and two thousand Gits. This varies a great deal and it is believed to be by age, but the Imposing ones have not permitted lesser species to study them.

Socially the Haarumph are organized into large families of about a six to twelve individuals. Larger organizations are run by something close to direct democracy with councils with a representative from each component family making policy and major decisions and temporarily appointed officials assigned to carry them out.

Like many intelligent species the Haarumph seemed to have evolved in a grassland-forest transition area. In their case they seem to descended from herbivores who transitioned to be omnivorous predators. They are tolerant of a wide variety of environmental conditions without need of artificial aids. It seems like their home world probably had a heavier than usual gravity.

Politically the Haarumph rule through something resembling a consensus of family heads. This is achieved through periodic meetings of all family heads in a particular group. They mediate the very large groups through technological means but even these large virtual meetings tend to be rare and to very long times to reach just a few decisions. Once a decision has been reached on any manner the Imposing ones tend to be implacable in carrying it out.

The Imposing Ones are above you and unlikely to take notice of your existence. Thank whatever gods you have for this.

Yuful:
(Nick or Common names: Grays, Big Heads)

Elder race.

In general a very old core elder race. Powerful and inscrutable even by those standards.

Physically upright, bipedal, and hairless. With dry gray, skin they are skinny and fragile. They have large heads and eyes, but good tolerance for bright light as well as being able to see well in low light conditions. The range from three to four GiByts in height. They mass between twenty and forty Gits.

The only Gray social group there is solid evidence for is the research group.

Whatever environment the Grays originated in they appear to evolved beyond it. They are very old and very far from their roots. They appear to live in completely artificial surroundings without other living things, plants or pets present. They seem to tolerate a wide variety lighting conditions. They appear to like dry conditions and low to medium gravity. They are not fond of physical activity but have exceedingly good digital dexterity.

Nothing is known of their internal politics. They seem mostly unconcerned with other races. They have a few basic rules that are mostly common sense. For the Grays these appear to be guidelines they ignore when they wish. Everybody else needs to toe the line.

The Grays are curious but largely indifferent to the concerns of lesser species. Try not to attract their attention.

Grrumm:
(Nick or Common names: Furry Ones, Furballs)

Edge Imperials

Large upright, bipedal, and heavily furred. Their paws may look clumsy but they're in fact capable of using their claw tips in a very dexterous manner. They range in height from six to seven GiByts, and from a hundred to a hundred and fifty Gits.

Grrumm society is a feudal one tempered by both a strong Imperial bureaucracy and extensive business interests from small family ones to some very large industrial corporations. Neither the Aristocracy nor the Imperial bureaucracy allows their power to be challenged by mere merchants or craftsmen but they do take their interests into account. The naked struggle for power is considerably softened by the Grrumm preference for reasonable consensus and respect for tradition. Families are important. Usually they consist of a single male and female, but a well off male will sometimes have two or more wives. It is not unusual for adult children, cousins, aunts, uncles, and other less immediate relatives to live under the same roof. The honor, "the legacy", of the extended family is of paramount concern to all Grrumm

The Grrumm are forest dwellers and even in space like to have trees around.

Politically the Grrumm Empire is ruled by a monarch heavily restrained by tradition, his nobility, his bureaucracy and various business interests. There is a lot of court intrigue.

The Grrumm control Damp and the rest of gated space adjacent to our local region. The Grrumm can be amazingly pleasant as individuals. They are inflexibly dedicated to their Empire and traditions in general however. Break one of their rules or otherwise offend them and they are implacable. They will force you to conform. Better not to go there.

*** WARNING ***

Possession of unauthorized histories or reference materials in Grrumm controlled space is illegal. This, sadly, includes this pamphlet. If caught with such material you will get a fair traditional trial, be convicted, and sentenced to a long time in a labor camp where you will be given the opportunity to make a positive contribution to wider society. ***It is highly recommended you dispose of all physical copies of any unauthorized pamphlets and books, and purge your electronic archives before entering Grrumm controlled space.***

Note: *Our fees for replacement pamphlets, both physical and electronic, are minimal, so don't be cheap and risk it! Also if you register for our newsletter (full of useful tidbits of absolutely free information and notices about the releases of our latest works) we will replace electronic copies* ***absolutely free!***

Karook:
(Nick or Common names: Pond Lovers, Slimy Ones, Marsh Dwellers)

Edge Imperials

Physically they have four limbs; two large rear ones and two smaller, more dexterous ones. They can move by jumping or using all four limbs. Their tongues are also very useful in manipulating objects. They are amphibians with a hairless, slim colored mottled green skin.

Socially the Pond Lovers are very territorial. Each is king of his small family in his own small pond. When not competing for, or defending territory they are very reasonable and willing to co-operate. They look to the whole to defend each part's territory.

The Pond Lovers home world has extensive seaside marshes. It also has climate, seasons, and tides. The Pond Lovers sit in their part of these marshes and wait for resources to come to them. They also carefully cultivate their productivity. They don't like to be far from the water. They sit on the boundaries and wait for their unwary prey to pass by. The Karook do well in confined spaces for prolonged periods so have no problem with living in spaceships or stations. However, the moist environments they need and the pools of water they love impose high maintenance costs. They are tolerant of high gravity.

Politically the Pond Lovers are organized in a broad strict feudal hierarchy. Loyalties are by territory and not individual, a particular individual is just who currently controls a particular territory. Loyalties therefore do not overlap as they sometimes will in feudal systems dependent on loyalties between individuals.

The Pond Lovers have relatively few rules. They can be very patient and lenient in how they enforce them. Do not take advantage of this. They watch quietly but carefully if they feel you've crossed a line or become a problem they'll suddenly and without warning eliminate you. Completely and throughly.

Craah:
(Nick or Common names: Winged Ones, Raucous Ones, Peckers)

Edge Imperials

They rule their portion of space. Not generally malicious, but unpredictable, and dangerous.

Physically they are bipedal and winged. Their wingtips are capable of simple manipulations, and they can often stand on one foot and manage precise stabs with the talons of their feet, however most fine work they perform with their tough supple tongues, and their beaks. They are feathered. Their feathers are large and very black. They have a limited ability to fly or glide in short hops. They are superb pilots. They are usually around four GiByts in height but more importantly have wingspans of six to eight GiBytes. They mass thirty to sixty Gits with a tendency to put on weight with age.

Socially they co-operate very well at need but are otherwise highly individualistic.

Environmentally they like varied, irregular terrain like open forests. Their home planet has a high axial tilt and they like distinct seasons.

Politically it's almost impossible to figure the Peckers out. They seem to be completely disorganized, but to often come together to achieve their purposes despite this.

The Peckers are anarchists right up to the point you become a threat to their joint rule. In which case they'll swarm you and peck you to death. They have a lot of curiosity and are easily bored. Don't become an object of interest to any of them. It's not profitable to get involved in their squabbles. Be glad you'll probably never have to deal with them. The Grrumm are at least predictable.

Trade Hub Species:

Varkoids:
(Nick or Common names: Big Ones, Bigs, Sniffers, Large Ones)

Mainly station bound businessmen. Also mercenaries. Very trustworthy.

Physically upright, bipedal, and hairless. They have tough, wrinkly, dark gray hides. They are big, strong, and very tough. They range from six to seven GiByts in height. They mass from eighty to one hundred and ten Gits.

Socially will join and be useful members of groups organized by other species the Trade Union being a prime example. Left to their own devices they tend to be independent and self-sufficient and seen as single individuals or in small groups not related by blood. The sole exception are Varkoid families with children which tend not to deal with outsiders much. The Varkoids make agreements with other individuals which they are religious about keeping. They expect similar loyalty in return. They tend not to trust large organizations or abstract principles, though they are not ideologically fanatical about this distrust.

Environmentally the Varkoids seem to have originated in savannah like conditions on a dry heavy gravity planet. They like open dry conditions.

Varkoids are largely apolitical. They believe in agreements reached between individuals. They seem to be less opposed to larger scale organization as blind to its existence.

To sum up, good business people but not excessively enterprising. Self-sufficient. Can be depended on to keep their agreements and business deals with them are almost certain to work out, but don't tend to be extraordinarily profitable.

Limmers:
(Nick or Common names: Climbers)

Build, own, and operate most Trade Hubs as well as sometimes other stations.

Physically upright, bipedal, and furred. Their fur is longish, thin, and orange. Descended from tree dwellers they have long arms and excellent grasping hands. They are natural climbers. They range from five to six GiBytes in height. They mass fifty to eighty Gits.

Socially they tend to hierarchical organizations with rank dependent on seniority and family connections. Typically the corporation is the premier Climber organization. They form the necessary backbone of the Trade Union.

Environmentally the Climbers historically lived in the canopy of thick forests, but have long adapted to large communal dwellings. They are a station building, owning, and living species above all, but their stations all have some open concourses with trees in them. They like medium to heavy gravity environments.

Politically Climbers try to be neutral and have a strong inclination to favoring peaceful order.

The Climbers are solid, constructive citizens. They are not enterprising or very independent. They can be sharp business people.

Swish:
(Nick or Common names: Swimmers)

Traders and spacers in general, ship-owners and ship captains. Many are independent.

Physically upright, bipedal, and furred. Their fur is sleek and exceptionally thick. They range from five to five and a half GiByts in height. Slender. They mass forty-five to sixty Gits.

Socially they're organized in a wide variety of different sized groups, but tend to be independent minded and to prefer small groups. Somewhat xenophilic they often facilitate associations of diverse species. The typical Swimmer is a small business person often the owner-operator of a small trading ship.

Politically they tend to ally with whoever permits them the most independence and aim to create and maintain peaceful conditions conducive to business.

Environmentally they're basically terrestrial but at home in small bodies of fresh water. They are excellent swimmers. They prefer shaded woodland environments.

The Swimmers are good business people, fair-minded, and friendly. They value not creating unnecessary problems and try not to tweak the sensibilities of others. They call this practice "*not making ripples*". They are sometimes called *slippery* for this by individuals belonging to other species.

Raw-Kas:
(Nick or Common names: Grass Lovers, Grass Weasels, Prairie Dogs)

Business people. Clannish. Also many in independent usually hidden colonies.

Physically upright, bipedal, and furred. Between four and half and five GiByts in height on average. Forty to fifty Gits in mass.

Their large extended clans are everything to the Raw-Kas.

They originated in large open grasslands where they lived in extensive underground borrows. They like cool, low light conditions but can tolerate heat and harsh lighting for extended periods. They like medium to low gravity. In service to their clans they may spend most of their lives on stations where they will try to re-create their natural conditions, but they strongly prefer to both have families in and to retire when older to planetary surface colonies.

Politically forming and keeping their planetary surface colonies safe is the entire focus of Ras-Kas politics. They can be adaptable and patient in attempting to reach these goals. Internally there seems to be a strict hierarchy based on seniority within each colony. Colonies are sovereign but frequently co-operate. They rarely if ever come into conflict. There maybe some competition.

The Ras-Kas are the primary manufacturers of non-gated space and as such you may find it necessary to trade with them. They are sharp business people but not very flexible. Their loyalties are above all to their clan. No agreement with a Ras-Kas individual will supersede orders from a senior clan member.

Established Independents:

Kannawik:
(Nick or Common names: Builders or Star Rats)

Builders of deep space colonies. Send out large slower than light colony vessels. Keep to themselves.

Physically upright, bipedal, and furred. A little less than six GiByts in height on average. Eighty to one hundred Gits in mass.

Socially present in large, well organized colonies. Willing to trade but tend to keep to themselves. They do not often, if ever venture out, as individuals or small groups. Distinct cultural preference for slower than light travel over FTL.

Seem to have evolved in a woodland riverine environment similar to that the Swimmers originated in. It can be tempting to see them as chubby, engineering oriented versions of Swimmers. Avoid this. They are much more clannish and religious both. They are not inclined to independent action although capable of it in

Politically they avoid entanglements. Internally they are organized in to large sovereign colonies on a system by system basis. Each colony consists of several large competing clans. This competition does not lend itself to exploitation by outsiders.

The Builders are affable enough when you encounter them and can be a useful source of resources and some manufactures. In general, however, they avoid association with other species to the maximum extend possible.

Meerow:
(Nick or Common names: Roamers)

Space going. Opportunists but trust-worthy. Organized in small clans. As a group major competitors to Trade Union.

Physically they are bipedal, upright, finely furred felines. They are usually about six GiByts in height and average from about fifty to eighty Gits in mass.

Socially organized in many small sovereign clans. Each clan tends to own at least one ship, usually several with one designated as the mother ship.

They seem to have originated with a species adapted to multiple environmental niches. Primarily grasslands, savanna, and open woodlands in a range of climatic conditions. Highly adaptable stalking predators. Not currently prone to aggressive violence. They seem to sublimated their instincts into a taste for sharp active trading.

Internally they're completely obedient to clan mothers. Effectively a matriarchal elective or adoptive monarchy. At all times a clan mother will have a designated successor not necessarily more closely related than any other clan member. The designated successor may change from time to time. Externally the clans focus maintaining their independence of all outside control. They love to make deals and are very sharp. They are careful to stick to letter of their deals and are in that sense very trustworthy. Also they do not trade information about their associates to others. Because of this they are the primary trading contact of all colonies that wish to remain hidden from the wider galactic community. This privacy does not come cheap, but the Meerow hold it sacrosanct.

In summary you can trust them to keep the deals they make and not to sell out. Count the digits on your appendages after making such a deal.

Faithful Squee:
(Nick or Common names: Tentacles)

A religious offshoot from the Elder race. They form deep space colonies and like to keep to themselves.

Physically they're Squee. (See above)

Socially they're Squee which means that besides evidently sharing some sort of religion they don't appear to have any society as the rest of us understand it.

Environmentally again they're Squee and live in the Ocean depths though they can tolerate other environments for periods of time.

Politically they seem to have religious differences with the Elder Squee and they seek to form isolated independent colonies in non-gated space. That is about all we know.

The Faithful Squee have been known to treat with others for things they need. The humans remarkably sold off the Ocean depths of their watery home world in exchange for technology from the Faithful Squee. It's not clear how this was arranged, but the chances you'll ever have dealings with one of these people are very slim.

Sambur:
(Nick or Common names: Digger weasels, Diggers, Borrowers)

Found wherever there are rocks to be mined for minerals. They're generally organized in small rather poor groups and mostly depend on others for trade and interstellar travel.

Physically they're similar to skinny rather wiry Swimmers. That is they are bipedal, upright, and sleekly furred. Big eyes and prominent whiskers mean they're well adapted to small dark spaces. They're four to five GiByts in height and mass from thirty to fifty Gits.

Socially the Diggers are very gregarious and social. They love spending time with friends and family. They are essentially organized in groups of related and friendly families. They will send out small expeditions, trading or prospecting generally, composed of a small number of males or even single individuals from time to time.

Environmentally it's tough to tell where the Sambur originated. They lost their home a long time ago in the mist of history, but it appears to have been a low to medium gravity planet that was fairly wet in places. They seem to have begun as a species that dug burrows in river banks or near-by hills. Where ever they started they're now found almost exclusively living in artificial environments around and in asteroids. They deal well with low light, low gravity, and highly confined spaces. They handle both dry and wet conditions well, and tolerate poor air well also. They are tough, industrious and the species responsible for most of the mineral production in our section of the galaxy and elsewhere.

Digger politics are small scale and simple. They try to get along with everyone. They make themselves useful by doing difficult work in isolated and harsh environments. In turn they get partners to trade with and transport when it becomes necessary to move a community to a new set of mineral deposits.

The Diggers are useful but not very powerful or very good traders. They've got a solid niche as miners that they dominate. They like to avoid conflict and taxes both to the greatest degree possible.

Zneet:
(Nick or Common names: Snouts, Ratfinks)

Even more opportunistic than the Roamers the Snouts are as exactly as trustworthy as it in their self-interest to be. They form the bulk of smugglers and pirates to be found. Also found engaged in small business everywhere. Organization varies but is usually formed around families or groups of them.

Physically the Zneet are bipedal, upright, and covered with very short, fine fur. They are thin, tall, and dark grayish-blue in color. They have long pointed snouts with long twitchy whiskers. The Sneet are five and half to six and a half GiByts in height. They mass fifty to eighty Git.

Socially the Snouts are organized in large clans by preference. They can frequently be found as individuals or in small groups often related though. The Snouts are skeptical of all principles besides that of enlightened self-interest. They are not trustworthy. They will ignore what rules they can, and do their best to bend those they can't.

It is difficult to be sure what sort of environment the Zneet originated in. It was probably dry and medium gravity. They manage in both low light and harsh lighting conditions and don't seem to mind confined spaces or to suffer from agoraphobia. When given the opportunity they seem to prefer open brightly lit spaces with low greenery and many flowering species. It can be surmised they originated in some temperate bushland. They don't seem to like swimming or moist environments.

Politically the Snouts are totally self-interested but tend to organize in small families composed into large clans. After all numbers confer strength.

To sum up the Snouts are survivors. They can be useful and they don't hold grudges, but they can't be depended on except to what is clearly in their own self interest. That said they are extremely adaptable. They can always be traded with though extreme caution is recommended.

Arquks:
(Nick or Common names: Bug Eaters, Moles)

Widely found but retiring traders. They don't mix. Found in space and on dry cold planets in small colonies also.

Physically the Bug Eaters are small, bipedal, and upright. They have a medium length coarse fur. They are from three to four GiBytes in height. They mass from twenty to forty Gits.

Socially Arquks are found in very large extended families which can number from just a few to hundreds of individuals. They're not tightly organized but But Eaters dislike long term association with anyone not part of their family which means by extension anyone not of their species.

Environmentally the Bug Easters like dim lighting, confined spaces and medium to low gravity. They're tolerant of poor air and can get by on little to no water. They do not like moist or wet environments. They don't swim. As their name suggests they eat bugs, and can live almost anywhere a lot of bugs can. They're not bad at either construction or manufacturing and when families are large enough will do some of both.

Politically the Bug Eaters are very primitive, their families are only loosely organized and entirely sovereign as they seem constitutionally unable to organize to into larger groups because they refuse to fully trust any non-family person.

The Bug Eaters aren't generally dangerous or malicious, but they're not friendly either. You can do business with them, and as the larger families often produce useful handicrafts and manufactures it's often worth doing so. However, business is entirely transactional and deal by deal with them. Longer term more profound relations simply aren't something they do.

Newly Discovered Species:

Assherraskillas:
(Nick or Common names: Scaly Ones, Lizards)

Very aggressive but highly rational barbarians. Dangerous. ***It is not safe to enter Scaly One space.***

Physically the Scaly Ones are just that; scaly. Furless. They're also bipedal and upright. They have large tails that balance them when sprinting and massive jaws with large teeth. They have two, forward looking eyes that provide them excellent eyesight. They are five to six GiByts in height. They mass seventy to one hundred Gits.

Socially the Scaly Ones are organized in a hierarchy of clans, and traditionally each clan raises the clan's young communally. Sibling rivalry among young Scaly Ones is intense and often fatal. Leadership is exercised by tripartite councils. They have a large scribal class that is important but kept strictly in check. Warriors or hunters, they use the term interchangeably, are traditionally the most respected class. Scribes and merchants are distinctly less well regarded. Interestingly enough the Scaly Ones don't seem to have personal names just job titles that they are known by.

Environmentally the Scaly Ones are the apex predators of the extensive dry grasslands of their home planet Assherraskill where they hunt large dangerous herbivores.

Politically a hierarchy of clans. Practically speaking it was the military dictatorship of a triumvirate until recently. Currently it appears to be the dictatorship, albeit politely disguised for the benefit of Scaly One traditionalists and any concerned humans, of a single female individual.

A dangerous set of aggressive and predatory barbarians undergoing rapid social. The humans did us all a favor cutting their rampage short.

Humans:
(Nick or Common names: Hairless Ones, Furless Ones, Tree-dwellers, Monkeys)

The newest barbarians. Very unpredictable, but generally friendly and willing to trade. Seemingly disorganized, they've proven to be very dangerous if they perceive a threat. Largely still confined to their home planet and system though expanding rapidly. Be very careful dealing with them.

Physically they're bipedal, upright and hairless except for some large tufts on the top of their heads and in the junction of limb joins. They have thin fragile skins that come in a variety of color hues, combinations of pale pink, beige, and brown. Their forelimbs are quite dexterous, but generally they aren't very strong. They easily tolerate both wet and dry conditions but aren't great swimmers. They prefer moderate gravity. They range from a little over five GiByts to a little over six GiByts. They mass from around fifty to one hundred and twenty Gits. They generally gain weight throughout adulthood. Their females on average are on the shorter and lighter part of the range.

Socially the humans are all over the place. They are still divided into many tribes having only recently become anything resembling civilized. They seem to have a preference for small families of a mated pair and children. They have a plethora of religions and various sized organizations dedicated to all sorts of purposes. They seem to form organizations whenever they want to do something but then to never dissolve them. Individuals often belong to many different organizations and the confusion and conflicts of loyalty this creates seems to be a primary theme in their culture.

Environmentally the humans are evolved from tree-dwellers who learned to hunt in open grasslands. They were pack hunters who co- operated in chasing down large game. Recently their home planet seems to have suffered a rapid series of climatic changes and to survive they have become very adaptable. Some of this has been artificial hence their extraordinarily intensive use of clothing, skins, woven plant material, and recently artificial fabrics to adapt their rather fragile bodies to a very wide range of environments. Hence the selective hairlessness that is their most obvious feature. Given a choice they seem to like the shade of trees set among grasslands.

They are, however, tolerant of both confined spaces and low gravity and so make excellent spacers.

Politically the humans are even more all over the place than they are socially. They have even more political structures than social ones. Every special cause gets a special organization and of course each individual human can belong to many different ones. Practically speaking for peacetime purposes they seem to have something called "representative democracy" where sub-groups of a sovereign area all vote to select a representative who then sits on a large council that decides laws and policies. They have separate groups for fighting they call "militaries". The main such group of interest to others is their Space Force which as the name suggests fights for them in space. Very effectively under the command of the well known Admiral Kincaid. They claim this Admiral Kincaid answers to the leaders of one of their representative councils. It's all very confusing. One has to suspect this is not entirely accident.

To sum up the humans are a very diverse and confusing group. They are a species the whole region must no take account of and profitable business is possible with them. However, one must never make assumptions in such dealings and carefully ascertain the truth of each situation. The humans are nothing if not unpredictable.

Manufactured by Amazon.ca
Acheson, AB